GREYBORN RISING

BY DERRY SANDY

First Edition

ISBN: 978-1-7338299-2-2 (paperback)

978-1-7338299-3-9 (hard cover)

Acknowedgements

For Annmarie Bruno-Sandy who taught us the love of the written word.

For Nnenne C. Okorafor without whose support this book would not have been completed.

For Lisa C. Cyrus (keep reading it will come to you).

For Amanda Dabydeen, Alicia Omans and Theodora Joseph the first readers.

And for the ancestors, yours and mine, who lived the stories which we re-tell

Contents

Chapter 1

(1805)

I know what is out there. They slither through the cane fields and the noise of their passage is like the sighing of tall grass. They hide in the shadows biding their time. They make their lairs in all the old, dark, forgotten places where humanity's passage no longer disturbs and where humanity's wickedness has left its stain. They prey upon the unwary, the naïve and those who recklessly disbelieve their existence. They are not human. Pity is not within their comprehension. Be not mistaken, if you fall within their clutches, they will not be merciful, and prayer shall not avail.

(fourth day of June 1801)
– Excerpt from Kariega's Diary

In 1805 William Claudius Maloney owned what was then Maloney sugar estate and is today Maloney Gardens, a government housing project in east Trinidad.

Maloney, who spent more time drunk than sober, was awoken earlier than usual one morning by the domestic slave that managed his household and informed that his attention was needed in the cow pen. He reluctantly dressed and descended to the pen where he found three of his best milkers lying in the cowshed apparently drained of blood. A fourth cow was pinned to the tin ceiling of the shed with a pickaxe and a pitchfork. The remaining cows were understandably in no mood to share non-bovine company and cowered together in a corner. Maloney squeezed his eyes shut as if to clear the apparition, but when he reopened his eyes the three cows were still dead, and their less fortunate sister was still crucified to the ceiling.

There were two important lessons that any white man who owned slaves in a country where there were more enslaved people than freedmen had to learn quickly. The first was to take every word that came out of a

1

Negro's mouth with a grain of salt. The Negro would kill you with his tongue. With a grin he would send a white man down the wrong path and into a mire of quicksand then play deaf to the man's cries for help.

The second lesson was to find one slave who you could trust, one that could translate slave-speak and could break down their pagan beliefs into portions an anglicized mind could digest. This was a tall order. For this task an owner with an interest in survival ruled out female slaves entirely. This was not because it would appear improper, many white men kept Negro mistresses particularly in a colony so far from the monarchy's disapproving gaze. The fact was, that female slaves were far more devious and cunning, and thus far more dangerous than the men. The men would come at you with a cutlass while you took a shit in the latrine. Death on the latrine was straight forward, even a little humorous. The women however, would put a drop of arsenic in your tea every morning for a year and then spit on you when you finally keeled over. There was nothing humorous about arsenic. Maloney preferred the cutlass while he took his morning shit to a slow painful death and so he kept the slave women at arm's length.

Maloney's trusted man was a tall, dark, and sober Ibo slave whose African name had been Kariega Kimani Achen. Kariega had been formerly owned by a French planter Michael Le Clerc and bore the surname of his former master. Kariega had earned Maloney's trust because he had saved Maloney from malarial death, a feat the Ibo had been unable to replicate for Maloney's wife, son, and daughter.

In West Africa, Kariega had been a powerful witch doctor and had fallen afoul of his tribal king. The details of the fall from grace were sketchy but the general theme was that Kariega spared the life the king's fourth and youngest wife. The king had commanded Kariega to execute the young wife because she had been with child five times and five times she had miscarried. Instead of carrying out the king's directive, Kariega gave her supplies and sent her off to a distant village. He had then reported to the king that he had dispatched the reproductively unfortunate wife. It was therefore to the king's surprise and anger when the same woman he had sentenced to death was spotted at an intra-village wrestling match months later, very much unexecuted and holding a child conceived with a new husband.

The king, even in his anger, feared to put a powerful witch doctor to death. Instead he had Kariega arrested and sold to the slave traders. The night the slave ship carrying Kariega sailed away from the Gold Coast port of Ponni at the mouth of the Ningo, a pride of twelve massive lions slipped past the village guard and entered the compound housing the king, his three wives and his eight children.

Each lion seized one sleeping individual and dragged them into the courtyard of packed dirt where the entire royal family was mauled to death in an orgy of roars and screams. The lions then scattered and vanished into the night untouched by the hail of stones, spears, and arrows launched by the tribesmen.

Maloney asked Kariega what he thought about the cows. Kariega answered, in a very matter of fact manner, that the dead cows were the work of soucouyant. Maloney squinted and held his arms out in a gesture that indicated that he needed clarification. Kariega explained that soucouyant were men and women who were bound to Bazil, a creature of the Vodun Loa. Men and women bound to Bazil become vampires.

The first soucouyant were of French planter stock created by Bazil in Haiti. This first generation subsequently sired their own gets and passed the taint amongst slaves and whites alike.

Maloney considered himself a proper Catholic, he believed in Mary and her Son. He had never put much stock in Kariega's ramblings about the world being divided into three realms, the Grey where the creatures of legend lived, the Ether—the realm of Heaven and Hell, and the Absolute where humans made their home. But he humored the man and instructed him to make sure that no more of the cows were taken. Despite his skepticism about the spiritual isms and schisms of the Negros, he had seen enough weirdness on the island to know that not everything was black and white and heaven and hell.

Kariega in turn requested letters for himself and four others that would allow them to patrol the roads at night. This group became the first soucouyant hunters in Trinidad. Kariega dubbed them The Order.

***

The first hunt for the soucouyant that had killed the cows was something of a success. The five did not catch a soucouyant but they did find the next best thing, the skin of a soucouyant. Soucouyant can fly, but to do so they must shed their skin and hide it in a safe place. While out of their skin the soucouyant appears to be wreathed in a low, dull flame that produces no heat.

A soucouyant's skin is its only connection to the Absolute. It is not so much a skin in the biological sense as it is a corporeal glamour that covers their whole body. After a prolonged period outside the skin, a soucouyant's connection to the Absolute steadily weakens. Too long outside the skin and the soucouyant's tainted soul is swept into hell to suffer forever, thus a soucouyant separated from its skin becomes very frantic and very dangerous.

The night after the Order took the skin, Maloney awoke to the sound of breaking glass coming from the small room where he kept his liquor. He grabbed his rifle and ran into the room to confront what he believed was a slave stealing a drink. To his shock he came upon what appeared to be a naked woman wreathed in yellow flames leaning into his liquor closet and tossing fine bottles of scotch over her shoulder and onto the floor. Maloney knew she was a soucouyant. Her appearance was exactly as Kariega had described. Maloney brought the rifle up and took aim.

The soucouyant whirled. Maloney managed to get off one shot which flew wide and blew a hole in a Victorian window. The soucouyant closed the distance between them with blinding speed, grabbed Maloney by the front of his nightshirt, drew him towards her, bit into his neck, and began to drink deeply.

The hapless Maloney struggled feebly and futilely against the iron grip of the woman. Just at that moment Kariega ran into the Great House through a side door that opened directly onto the otherworldly scene. In his hand he held the soucouyant skin.

"I dreamt that you would come. I have what you seek." Kariega spoke in a commanding voice to the woman. "If you want your skin back I invite you to sit and talk."

Her head whipped around at the sound of Kariega's voice. "Your dreams told you I would come? Or is it the fact that you stole something very precious to me?" she sneered. She let Maloney fall to the floor where he lay still, eyes wide open but unseeing.

She approached Kariega with a face like a thundercloud, the image of a white flame dancing in her eyes. Kariega held the skin close to the flaming torch he held in his left hand. The soucouyant halted her approach. No man had ever had the audacity to even meet her gaze let alone threaten to burn her precious skin.

"Now, firefly of Bazil, do you wish to be swept into the warm embrace of the Loa, or do you wish to serve a greater purpose?"

"You've got some very big balls, slave," she said, genuinely surprised by the man's boldness. "But I'm sure you can see that we are at a stalemate. If you destroy my skin, I will kill you slowly and painfully and then I will kill the other men who were with you when you stole it."

"Firefly of Bazil...." Kariega began again but she cut him off with an upraised hand.

"My name is Katharine. We can stop this firefly of Bazil rubbish immediately. I have never met Bazil and I do not serve him. How do you slaves come up with these names?" She moved towards Kariega again. Kariega held the skin closer to the flame of the torch.

"Katharine. I do not wish to kill you, or to bind you to anything as Bazil has bound you to blood. I only wish to free you."

"Slave. You are strong. I feel the power rolling through you and I can taste vitality in your scent. But no one can sever the tie to Bazil. There is no cure for what we have. Besides, some consider this a gift. My mother was one of Bazil's first gets. My father was a French nobleman who fell in love with my mother before he knew what she was. He insisted on being present at my birth and, when he held me to his chest, I bit him and fed from his neck. So you see, I was born a soucouyant but though I never sought Bazil, perhaps I wish to keep his gift." Kat paused and took stock of the man standing across from her. "I would also wager that I could flay you, don your skin, and eventually it would be as good as my own. Please spare me the inconvenience of breaking your skin in."

"First, my name is Kariega Le Clerc, not *slave*, and second, I make no idle boast. I can break your tie with Bazil without diminishing your considerable gifts. Please sit and we can talk about it and perhaps you will see that there is need neither for me to be flayed nor for you to be inconvenienced."

She was angry, but also intrigued by the man's boldness. As it often did, curiosity got the better of her. "Fine I guess there is no harm in hearing you out. Give me the skin and pour me some of this dead fool's scotch," she said gesturing briefly to the dead Maloney. "And let us talk."

Kariega replied, "How about we pour some scotch and I hold on to the skin until we reach a conclusion and you have promised not to take the skin off my back."

Kariega and Katharine sat across from each other in the smoking room of the great house to discuss their mutual fate. The pair talked through the night exchanging stories and by morning they were communicating like old friends. As dawn approached Katharine stood. "Kariega you make me forget myself. I cannot be caught in the sunlight without my skin. We have talked the night away and you have not proposed a damn thing."

Kariega cut her off with a wave of his hand. "No need to worry." He gestured toward her. "I warded you while we spoke."

She glanced down at her body gasping in surprise. She was no longer clothed in flames, in fact, back in her human form, she was not clothed in anything.

"Nice trick, Kariega," she said making a half-hearted attempt to cover herself with her slender hands. Although over a century old she, like all her kind, had aged to her prime and then no more. She was small, shorter than average, but well-proportioned. Her body was slim and firm and bore not a scrap of excess fat. Her breasts were full and her legs shapely. Her milky copper complexion revealed her mixed ancestry and her curly hair framed a beautiful face. When she smiled her teeth were straight and white. Only her slightly pointed canines hinted that she was more than a lovely maiden.

She fixed Kariega with her almond shaped, olive-colored eyes, and gave him a smile which emphasized the mole above her lip. "But I agreed to no bargain, did I say I wanted this?" she asked, a hard note entered her tone as she weighed the slave's audacity.

"Have a seat and I will explain how this works, then you will tell me if you wish to continue in your current state." Kariega seemed to recognize he was treading on dangerous ground and spoke in a calm tone.

Katharine, having swiftly overcome the original shock of her nakedness, sat and poured another glass of scotch.

Kariega, reaching into his pocket, withdrew a small finely woven silver crucifix on a thin silver chain. Tossing it to her he said, "Wear this, it will strengthen your bond to this world and hide you from your coven. Also, you will not need this again," he continued, gesturing to the skin he still held. He motioned with his hands and the skin burst into fine, gray ash which floated away like mist.

Katharine gasped mostly due to the flippancy with which Kariega had dispensed with a thing that had so recently been vital to her. As for her coven, she had joined with the two other soucouyant after fleeing the upheavals in Haiti, they were not of Bazil's line and far more blood-thirsty than she was. She would not miss them.

Kariega continued, "What I have done has removed your thirst for blood, but you can no longer float. Your new skin is just like a human skin and cannot be shed. In time you will find that you will develop control over flames, pyromancy, if you may."

"And what do you expect in return for your...gifts?"

"In return, you must agree to help me in any way you can to protect the Absolute from creatures of the Grey, or I will remove my spell and we will be back where we started. You have lost some powers in exchange for others, but I think this new Katharine is better than the old one."

"Help in any way I can?" Kathrine knew she was sneering. "Do I look like a servant or a lapdog? Do you intend to make a familiar out of me, a pet soucouyant? Are you fast enough to cast a spell before I can tear your head off, slave?" Her voice conveyed that she was serious about her threat.

Kariega sighed. "Only a fool would try to turn a lioness into a lap dog, and I assure you I'm no fool. As you may know when the Spanish first came to this part of the world they treated the native people so poorly that those people resorted to unfamiliar witchcraft. They used power they did not completely understand and tore a very big hole between the Grey and the Absolute, beginning the period we call the Recompense. During this time Bazil escaped into this region from the Grey. The hole the Amerindians created let a host of new pureborn into the absolute, powerful creatures like Bazil who created soucouyant like your mother, who in turn gave birth to soucouyant like you." Kariega paused as if in deep thought. "Beings like you are already in the Absolute, what I would like is to ensure that no more pure greyborn cross over."

Katharine said nothing expecting Kariega to continue. "The Absolute is rightfully man's realm. I want to learn about your kind and defend mankind from those of you who would abuse their strength."

A hint of a smile broke Katharine's stony expression, she glanced sheepishly at the cold stiff body of William Maloney, "Does that count as abuse?" she asked, gesturing at the corpse of the slain planter.

"That was the old Katharine. The new Katharine would never drain a man dry like that. The new Katharine knows to drink in sips and not to drink from the same victim too often."

Katharine nodded somberly.

"One last thing before we seal our pact. You will outlive me by centuries. After I die, the spell will wane and the crucifix will be the only thing that staves off the lust and hides you from the Loa and your coven. If you willingly remove the crucifix the spell will be broken. Make it as precious as your old skin and wear it all the time. It cannot be replaced."

"You said you had dreams of me?"

"Yes, the dreams did not have details, just a sense that you will one day be very important to mankind, to the Order and to me.

"Did your dreams lead you to me specifically, or did they just tell you to pick the first soucouyant whose skin you could steal?"

Kariega's face held a small smile. "I dreamt of you."

"Well you are lucky to have had such a striking beauty grace your dreams." Katharine laughed.

Kariega replied, "You skinny mulatto women have little effect on Kariega Le Clerc, I miss the heavy backsides and bosoms and the dark skin of my tribeswomen. Now that is what a woman should look like. Where did you learn to laugh like that?"

"My laughter is a trick my mother taught me, I can make you into one of us and then you can learn it," she said sweetly. "And as for the heavy backsides of your tribeswomen. Imagine one of them trying to help you hunt down some underworld creature, her damned bosoms knocking things over, creating an unholy raucous. You'd never sneak up on anyone."

"You might have a point." Kariega conceded. "Do we have a pact?" Kariega said as he rose and held out a hand to the woman.

"Make me breakfast, Kariega and I will think on it. The quality of your food shall be the deciding factor."

This was the beginning of a strange friendship that Kariega dreamed would save the Absolute.

Chapter 2

(Present Day)

The sun was shining, the northeast trade winds were blowing and somewhere in the distance a radio bleated out a reggae tune. The song urged Kingston's ghetto youth to rise against the class oppression of urban Jamaica.

By all appearances it was a generic Trinidadian Sunday afternoon just like so many other Sunday afternoons that had passed since the beginning of time.

Rohan Le Clerc lifted his head and peered through his mirrored sunglasses at the coffins containing the bodies of his grandfather Isa and his cousin Dorian. A warm breeze ruffled his dreadlocks. His girlfriend Kamara's hand tightened on his arm in a reassuring squeeze. His grandfather had liked Kamara. He had said she had the makings of a seer, but at twenty-three she was too old to be tested.

Rohan fought to swallow the bolus of emotions that threatened either to choke him or to escape his lips in the form of a plaintive wail. The presence of the two coffins was difficult enough to handle, but even worse was the knowledge that the body of a third Orderman, Kimani, was lost altogether. That body lay where it had fallen in the Paria forest and would lie there until it turned to dust because as much as he loved his brother-in-arms, Rohan, certainly wasn't going back to retrieve the corpse. Not after he himself had only narrowly escaped death.

Everything had gone wrong on their last hunt. What had begun as a mission to eliminate a single lagahoo in the Paria forest, had become a prolonged midnight battle against a pack numbering in the dozens. Dozens! It had been years since anyone had seen a pack of the werewolf-like creatures that large. Before that night, the Order had come to accept as fact, that the taint of the original greyborn was diminishing. Every year fewer people were infected by lycanthropy or vampirism. Of late The Order had had precious little to do. The events of that night were cause for belief that the relative peace of the last few decades was at an end.

***

Rohan Le Clerc and his kin were not ordinary men. They had superior senses, speed, strength and stamina. While in the womb Rohan had been blessed by four mayalmen, knowledgeable herbalists, healers, and practitioners of limited sorcery and necromancy. Shortly after he was born he was marked with a lion's head on the flesh above his heart; eagle's wings around his feet, and down his back along his spine, vertebrae bones with a sheen like metal. The ink of the tattoos was a mixture of shapeshifter blood and the ash from the funeral pyre of a mayalman. Each tattoo was a small gateway to the Grey, channeling that realm's mystical power and bestowing on the wearer attributes represented by the tattoos. In Rohan's case he had gained courage, speed, and durability.

His gifts were considerable, but he had been badly wounded in the initial round of the fight, as badly as he could remember ever having been wounded. His arm was partially torn out of the shoulder joint and there was a deep bite in his thigh. These were the most serious injuries among a thousand other claw marks and scratches. That he could still run, although not very fast and certainly not indefinitely, was testament to his gifts. His grandfather and his cousins had all been hobbled by similar wounds.

The monsters pursuing them had been immensely powerful. They looked like massive Irish Wolfhounds that ran upright. They had huge shaggy dog's heads with long jaws that opened to more than ninety degrees and bit down with the force of a sprung tiger trap. Their arms of dense muscle covered in thick hides and coarse hair could uproot saplings. But what Rohan hated most about them was their speed. They ran about six times faster than the fastest man and thus about two or three times faster than Rohan could manage on his best day, and today was not his best day.

Rohan and his kin had fled through the forest as dappled moonlight and dark shadows took turns revealing then obscuring the horrors around them. Though he knew that their pursuers had once been human, Rohan would do anything for more silver shot. The pack could have and should have overtaken them, but for some reason the beasts had seemed happy to simply chase them, like overzealous dogs pursuing a car with shiny hubcaps.

The pack's goal was revealed when the forest ended abruptly in a clearing. The clearing, even more abruptly, ended in a two-hundred-foot drop to a rocky, rough sea. Standing on the edge, Rohan felt the sea mist every time the angry waves assaulted the cliff face. The four men had been corralled, brought to bay like deer before hounds. They turned to meet the blazing eyes of the dog-men all around them and found in their gaze no humanity. They were hemmed in with the cliff behind them and the pack closing in on all other sides.

There was a brief pause, a moment of utter stillness and then the night exploded in violence. Three lagahoo launched themselves at Rohan. Their movement was almost faster than his brain could process. Their snapping fangs and wicked claws were everywhere. Rohan had no time to think, only to react. He dodged to one side. The most zealous of the three flew past him and sailed in a neat arc over the edge of the cliff.

One appeared to his right. He didn't consciously go for the knife at the small of his back, in the heat of battle he operated on sheer muscle memory. His knife materialized in his hand. He flicked his wrist and the knife buried itself, blade-first, into the forehead of the dog faced beast. The entire sequence was over in the span of half a wink. To varying degrees, greyborn were allergic to silver, and lagahoo were particularly vulnerable. Silver caused painful flesh wounds and death if a vital organ was struck. This one was dead before it hit the ground. Rohan glimpsed his grandfather out of the corner of his eye. With his ancient short sword, Gladius, in hand, Isa Le Clerc danced among the dog men. Limbs and heads flew about as if expelled from a fountain. The razor-sharp silver blade cauterized where it cut, and the air was filled with the smell of burnt blood and fur and the howls of the maimed and dying.

Kimani and Dorian were also engaged in pitched battles for their lives. Dorian held a hatchet in each of his fists. Where he lacked Isa's grace and finesse he compensated for with massive power, splitting the lagahoo with powerful blows that dismembered most assailants.

Kimani moved with fluid and animalistic grace, a true student of his grandfather's methods, but his skill would count for nothing. They were outnumbered and outflanked. Rohan had no more knives. He punched the closest lagahoo in the chest and heard its sternum crack, but he broke two fingers in the effort. The creature's legs crumpled. As Rohan turned to face another foe, a lagahoo came up behind him, clamped its toothy maw over his shoulder, and bore down. Searing pain ripped through his entire upper body. The creature kept a crushing grip on Rohan's shoulder while shaking him like a terrier would shake a rabbit.

Through a thick haze of pain, he had heard himself call out for help. Another lagahoo, seeing that Rohan was immobilized, rushed in to finish him. Rohan kicked out as hard as he could, catching the onrushing beast square in the throat. With a gurgled mouthful of blood, the lagahoo went down, but the blow was not fatal and Rohan could see the crushed throat reconstruct itself under the fallen creature's skin. Without silver, the dog-men were simply too difficult to kill.

Suddenly the fight halted. The lagahoo stopped attacking at the precise moment that they could have pressed their advantage and killed the four cornered men. The creatures stood still as if in a trance. Dorian took this opportunity to hack down two of the closest creatures. They made no attempt to defend themselves and Isa signaled for Rohan and his cousins to start moving away.

Before the Ordermen could retreat, the beasts let out a chilling howl. Into the clearing strode a creature of legend. Rohan recognized it immediately. He had heard many stories told by the elders of the Order about master lagahoo, pureborn of the Grey, allowed into the world of men by the events of the Recompense. The master lagahoo was nine-feet tall and massively muscled, half again as tall and twice the mass of its once-human ancestors. Its long arms, which ended well below the knees, were tipped with razor-sharp black claws. Its eyes burned with a mixture of rabid ferocity and intelligence and it appeared to have psychic control over the pack. Rohan was deeply disturbed by its appearance. Not a single pureborn had been seen in the Absolute in centuries. Its presence meant one of two things, either someone had opened a new gateway, or this guy had been sharpening his horticultural skills in the Paria forest for two hundred years.

The beast stood for a beat as if evaluating the four men. Then it moved. One instant it was at the edge of the clearing, the next its mouth was clamped over Kimani's head, manifesting in their midst as if it had teleported. The other lagahoo looked on, making a bloodcurdling noise like hyenas at a kill.

The bite killed Kimani instantly and Rohan felt a deep, stabbing loss. Isa made a sound that was part sob, part shout. The master released the dead Orderman's lifeless corpse and the body fell to the earth. All three of the remaining warriors rushed the master as one.

The massive lagahoo moved. It back fisted Dorian in the face providing no opportunity for the stocky man to react. The power of the blow snapped Dorian's head all the way around so that his fading eyes met Rohan's who was standing behind him. The master moved again with baffling speed. It grabbed Rohan around the throat and before he could raise an offensive response, cut off his air supply with a crushing grip.

Rohan heard the telltale whistle of a blade and a wet sound as a weapon bit through flesh. The creature roared, dropped Rohan and turned toward Isa who was in the act of lifting his sword for a second strike. Rohan rolled to the side and wrenched a hatchet out of Dorian's death grip. He rushed back into the fray. The huge creature turned to face the attacking Isa, apparently considering Rohan as the lesser threat. It slashed at Isa who dodged just outside the reach of the telescopic arm and wicked claws. Rohan hurled the axe at the beast with all the force he could muster.

His throw was on target but the master's head swiveled at the last instant as if it heard the missile's approach. It caught the axe by the handle inches from its face. Isa used the momentary distraction to attack again slashing upward. The short-sword grated against bone as it entered the creature's gut and exited at the shoulder in a spray of blood, the cut however was not deep enough to be effective. With a roar the master whipped out an arm and caught Isa. Its claws and fingers pierced deeply into the lower part of the elder's neck. Rohan made two running steps forward and launched himself into the air intending to kick in the creature's throat or at least get it to drop his grandfather. In response the beast hurled the limp elder at the airborne Rohan as if the man weighed no more than a pebble.

Rohan could do nothing to brace for the blow. Isa and Rohan slammed together in midair with the force of a car collision. Rohan expected pain, but he felt nothing. He and Isa fell to the ground in a tangled heap, ten feet from where the lagahoo stood. Rohan could do nothing but lay where he fell. There was an odd sensation in his back. When Rohan attempted to rise his legs refused to comply. He was now at the mercy of the creature. The master slowly approached the fallen pair, wearing a grim parody of what Rohan thought could be a smile.

The lesser lagahoo howled a blood chilling cacophony announcing their master's triumph to the night. The master still held the axe Rohan had thrown. It reached Isa first, and grabbing a handful of the elder's locks, lifted him off the forest floor, sliced the elder's throat with Dorian's axe, then discarded the body over the cliff edge. The creature's smile seemed to widen as it continued its approach to where Rohan lay. Rohan tried to retreat, to stand, to move. Not a single body part complied with the frantic messages supplied by his brain. Even in that moment he did not panic. Every Orderman knew that his life would probably end violently. He closed his eyes and, in his mind, he traveled to a dark place, almost completely black except from a billion pinpoints of starlight far above. He still could not move, but in the darkness, he sensed someone was with him. He could not see her face, or even a silhouette but he knew it was a woman.

"I've got something here for you," she said, and a thick rope of blindingly white light sprang from her chest and snaked towards him. Even with this new illumination Rohan still could not see her face. When the snake of light touched him, it felt as if he was hit by lightning.

His eyes opened and he was back on the forest floor. His body began to repair itself. He felt a snap in his back as the bones righted themselves. He rolled over and onto his knees as the heat and the pain of healing took over. The flesh on his shoulder crawled as it re-knitted without leaving a scar. The wound on his leg closed as if it had never been inflicted. His body was whole in a matter of seconds, and there was still strength left over for fighting.

Rohan could not suppress the onrush of new power, and there was no doubt what he would use it for. He rose from his knees and on to his feet in one smooth motion. His body felt supple and his senses were even more powerful than before. He could see the individual hairs on the body of the master lagahoo even in the dark. He could hear its heartbeat and he could smell the blood on its claws and on its breath. The blood was Isa's, Dorian's, and Kimani's. He rushed the beast where it stood, seemingly perplexed by his prey's sudden convalescence.

The master hurled Dorian's axe at Rohan's head but to Rohan the flying axe appeared to move in slow motion as if the air was cold honey. In fact, everything around him moved more slowly than he did. He tapped the axe aside just before it struck him, diverting it into the bush towards one of the lesser lagahoo.

The master came at him in a rush of violent intent but he might as well have been strolling. The beast swung a talented fist and Rohan moved just out of its reach then flowed back to land a crushing fist to the creature's mid-section, a chop to the throat, and a round house kick to the head all in the space of half a second. The master tried to fend off the flood of bone breaking blows, but its efforts were futile. Rohan's fists and feet found every opening in the master's guard.

That night he had beaten the master back towards the cliff edge. And just before he drove it off the precipice, Rohan seized it by the throat and drew its face downward so he could meet its eyes. It tried to pry Rohan's hands from its neck but could not make them budge. Pure hatred blazed in the greyborn's eyes. Rohan knew his own eyes burned with a similar loathing. He discerned an odor under the lagahoo's stink, an acrid scent which by some dark instinct he knew was the smell of fear. He tore its throat out and was bathed in a spray of hot blood. The dead master fell backward over the edge of the cliff and down to the black sea and its impaling rocks.

With the object of his immediate interest gone, Rohan felt as if he was going insane. His newly acquired force threatened to draw him to a place from which he did not think he could return unless he could find a way to unleash it. He turned to the other lagahoo and pounced on the closest one. The creature made a futile attempt to escape and Rohan punched the back of its head so hard that his fist went right through its skull, through the warm brain, and out the front of its face. He was swept up on a tide of a gleeful rage, determined to slay them all. They scattered, fleeing in all directions, and he cackled hysterically as he pursued them.

He glided through the forest as easily as if the thick branches and undergrowth made room for his passage. The lagahoo were no match for his speed and strength. He was crazed, he only wanted to kill.

The morning sun climbed over the mountain tops as Rohan sprang into a clearing pursuing a fleeing lagahoo, savoring the smell of its terror. The white sunlight seared Rohan's eyes and he fell to his knees in pain. The wound in his shoulder re-opened. His tongue felt swollen and parched as if he had swallowed mouthfuls of hot sand. Sweat poured from his body in rivulets and the new strength flooded out of him leaving behind agony and, as he succumbed to unconsciousness, an intense disappointment that he had not been able to kill all the fleeing, monsters.

***

As Rohan stood at the graveside of his fallen grandfather and cousin, he puzzled over how the Order had rescued him and recovered the bodies that lay in the coffins. He also wondered about the mysterious woman who had given him the power to heal, survive, and to kill so many lagahoo by himself. He promised himself to meet with the Watchers' Council as soon as possible where he hoped that the circumstances surrounding these occurrences would be illuminated.

He held Kamara's hand as they walked along the gravel track that led out of the Arima Public Cemetery. Another breeze ruffled Kamara's curly hair and wafted the smell of her shampoo towards him. Her reassuring grasp tightened around his upper arm and he shifted her hand higher on his sleeve. He was wearing a shoulder holster under his jacket, and if he needed to go for the gun he didn't want Kamara's hand in the way. For the time being Rohan Le Clerc was the last living member of the Stone Chapter, and he intended to survive to see Stone's ranks replenished.

Chapter 3

Jean and Dinah, Rosita and Clementina
On the corner posin'
Bet yuh life is something they sellin'
And if yuh ketch dem broken
You can get it all for nuttin'

— The Mighty Sparrow

Clarence 'Caramel' Jeremy stood on the corner of Abercrombie and Knox streets which formed the northwest apex of Woodford Square. It was after sundown, all the honest men had left, and the square was now the domain of transients, vagrants, pickpockets and whores.

Clarence's face was heavily powdered. His long red wig and his tight yellow dress were at odds with his day-glo pink nail polish and lipstick but matched his platform club shoes perfectly. He was tall and thin, a thinness exacerbated by the terminal disease that was not so slowly killing him. A diet of cigarettes, soda, and cocaine did little to improve his gauntness.

Clarence did not feel so well that night, but the show had to go on. At fifteen he had been banished from his family home, when his father finally conceded that his romantic interest in other boys and his penchant for women's clothing was not just a passing folly. Since then he had made a living the best manner he knew how, whoring.

A long black car pulled parallel to the curb in front of Clarence in a hush of displaced air. The rear window rolled down and Clarence sashayed over to the car. The passenger lounging in the back seat was partially caught in a triangle of sulfur colored light cast by the street lamps. His face remained obscured in the shadows, but Clarence could tell that the man was tall. The chauffeur was clearly illuminated and proved to be a small black man of indeterminate age. The driver held the steering wheel precisely at the prescribed ten and two o'clock positions and studied the distance beyond the windscreen as if he did not wish to partake in the sins of his benefactor.

"How are you doing?" The passenger spoke to Clarence in an unaccented and cultured voice.

"Me? I'm pretty good. Are you looking for a good time?" Clarence had seamlessly donned his street persona Caramel, who was flirtatious and fun and whose speech was a collection of the clichéd phrases of whoredom.

In response to his question the rear door of the car opened soundlessly. Ever since the time he was picked up by one man and taken to a house where five other men were waiting, Clarence had become very wary of getting in to strange cars. That ordeal had almost killed him, but he had learned a very important lesson. Now he usually arranged to meet his clients at a run-down guest house near Queen's Park Savannah and he would have been there tonight, but the expenses of his addictions were driving him to work longer hours in less familiar places.

Clarence was about to arrange to have the stranger accompany him back to his room when a familiar voice spoke to him from the cavernous maw of the back seat. "Clarry, my son, won't you come sit next to your dad…I'm sorry for the way things are between us." His father's voice choked back a sob. "I'm so sorry, son. So very sorry."

On some level Clarence was certain beyond a doubt that his dead father was not speaking to him from the shadow-drenched backseat of the chauffeured car. But his mind was suddenly clouded. He heard his own voice respond as if a ventriloquist's hand was up his behind puppeteering his lips. "Dad, all I ever wanted was for you to love me, accept me for who I am, that's all."

"I realize that now, Clarence. Please, come in. Let's talk. Everything will be better. We will fix everything."

His father's voice spoke words that Clarence had not realized he had been yearning to hear. Clarence had no recollection of getting into the car, but he came to himself when the door closed with a hydraulic susurration followed by a thump that rattled his bones like the first clods of soil on his coffin.

The enchantment cleared and was replaced by unmitigated, naked terror. He frantically searched for a door handle, but the interior of the car was seamless. The stranger and his driver said nothing while Clarence searched for an escape. As the car pulled away from the curb, a mewling, plaintive noise escaped Clarence's throat. Clarence slammed his hands against the glass, but greasy scuff marks were the only impact he made. Realizing the futility of attempting to escape, Clarence reached into his clutch for the icepick he kept there.

Holding the weapon in front of his face, Clarence put as much room between himself and the stranger as the car would allow.

"Clarence, my friend." The man's warm voice filled the backseat. The overhead streetlights created an alternating succession of light and dark but the speaker's face somehow remained cloaked in shadows regardless of how bright the back of the car got. "Clarence, I've been watching you. You are the lowest of the low, a reject amongst rejects. If a mangy dog could scrape together your fare you would allow it to have you."

"Please just let me out." Clarence barely recognized the voice that came from his mouth, so thick was it with fear. "Let me out and I will forget this happened. I won't go to the police." Clarence spoke and hoped that the stranger was unaware that the local police did not give half a broken fuck about what happened to a male prostitute like him.

"Let you out, Caramel?" The man's voice continued to carry a warm friendly tone, at complete odds with the desperation Clarence felt. "Let you out for what? So you can continue clinging to your leprous existence?"

Clarence had heard enough. He knew he could not negotiate his way out of this situation. He stabbed at the stranger. The man caught Clarence's hand at the wrist and twisted it, snapping the bones as easily as if they were rotted kindling. Clarence started to cry out, but a fist slammed into his face, and again and again. The stranger maintained an iron grip around his broken wrist while beating Clarence mercilessly. Teetering on the edge of consciousness Clarence slumped down into the narrow floorspace between the back seat and the front. The stranger angled his body and kicked and stomped him. Clarence's mouth filled with blood and he began to choke and gag at the taste.

"Don't die now, Clarence. You have been called to a higher purpose. You will be given the chance to atone for the last twenty-four years of your life." With that the man leaned over and punched Clarence viciously in the temple. A warm darkness closed around him like a familiar and welcome blanket.

The black car sped through the streets of Port-of-Spain. The Trinidadian night continued and didn't miss Caramel the whore.

***

Clarence came to in the dark, suspended from the ceiling by his wrists, one of which was broken. It was difficult to breathe through the ruin of his nose and his lips were swollen, crushed, and encrusted with a film of dried blood, snot, and spit.

His pain was distant and incorporeal, a dull, omnipresent, holistic throb on the outskirts of his perception. He had lost one of his high heeled pumps and the front of his dress was damp with urine. The memory of what had happened came to him in fragments as he hung suspended in silence.

A soft groan made him aware that he was not alone. It took him three attempts before he could get words past his broken lips.

"Is someone there?" His voice was brittle with fear and thirst. There was silence. Clarence spoke again. "If someone is there, please talk to me." Again the only reply was silence and Clarence wondered if he had imagined the sound.

Then a woman's voice responded. "Please, please let me go, I didn't see your face, I swear I won't tell anyone, just please, please let me go."

Clarence felt immense relief that he was not alone. "I'm sorry lady, but I'm in the same situation. How did you get here?"

"A car pulled up and a man spoke to me. Last thing I remember is the car door closing. Then I woke up here."

"How long have you been here?"

"I don't know. Hours? Days? I don't know." The woman's voice broke with despair.

A shaft of light pierced the room as a door opened behind the suspended pair. The light was followed by an even deeper darkness when the door shut again. The newcomer lit a candle and set it on a table also behind them. On the far wall Clarence watched the shadow cast by the newcomer approach the shadow of the woman suspended next to him. Without warning, the quiet in the room was pierced with screams. Clarence longed to block his ears as the newcomer inflicted some horrible torture on the woman.

Wet sounds from the horror the stranger was inflicting punctuated the brief pauses between her screams when she gathered enough air to scream again. Hers was an unending serenade to agony. Clarence's bladder voided itself in a hot, pungent stream down his legs and he began to cry. When the woman finally fell silent, the smell of blood, piss, and excrement filled the void left by her quieted cries. The still unseen stranger exited, extinguishing the candle on the way out leaving Clarence alone in the dark with the dead woman.

Clarence did not know how long he hung there in the blackness, but eventually a voice spoke from the same position that the woman's voice had come previously. This however, was a rough and sibilant voice devoid of humanity or fear. "Clarence when he comes back he will make you into one like us and then we shall be set loose to feed."

The final shreds of Clarence's frayed and tested sanity fell to bits like a moth-eaten sail in a typhoon. The room was now filled with laughter, a high-pitched feverish laughter from Clarence and the gravelly and coarse laughter of whatever the woman had become.

Chapter 4

The morning after the funeral found Rohan on an eight-mile run which covered a loop of forested trail in the acres surrounding Stone House.

His wounds were healing well. A mayalman attached to the Order had visited and had given him vile things to swallow to speed his rehabilitation. The speed of his current recovery was nothing compared to the swiftness with which he had healed in the forest but between his innate healing powers and the mayalman's magic, the wounds he had sustained in the forest were well on their way to being painful memories. He wondered if the mayalman had something that would heal the pain in his heart caused by the deaths of his family members.

He was on his fifth mile and someone had been tailing him since mile two. The person was skilled at staying out of sight and, had Rohan not possessed heightened senses bestowed by his Order marks, he may never have noticed he was being followed. As it was, Rohan heard the footfalls and breathing of the mystery individual more than half mile behind him as they struggled follow while remaining unseen.

A massive tree stump marked mile six, where the trail swung into a blind turn which initiated the loop back toward Stone House. The left side of the turn bordered an embankment and the right side of the trail fell off into a steep but shallow drop down to a small stream, a perfect spot for an ambush. Rohan sprinted up the track to the spot where he would lay in wait.

He wore his usual running gear; black shorts and sneakers with no shirt. But considering recent incidents he also carried a small loaded gun and a knife. He still felt woefully under armed and unprepared.

Hidden by the blind corner and the embankment, he flattened himself in the leaf litter and waited for his pursuer to catch up. The individual shadowing him would round the bend and would not see him until the trap was sprung. A few minutes elapsed then he heard footfalls. A male voice muttered something unintelligible. Rohan waited until the man had passed him on the path then rose silently, took two soundless steps and placed his gun against the back of the man's head.

"Why are you following me?" Rohan said in a voice that was calmer than he felt.

The man replied in a deep drone, "Is that how Stone House greets strangers?"

With that the man spun around with the speed of a Lycan, knocking the pistol from Rohan's grip and sending it sailing into the bush. Rohan realized that the person in front of him was not an ordinary human being. He had a second to wonder why he had not sensed the man's inhuman nature but recovered when the man reached under his jacket. Rohan leapt back simultaneously reaching for and throwing the knife at his ankle. The man dodged to his left and the flaying knife cut a neat slash in the upper sleeve of the well-tailored suit jacket.

Rohan landed in a fighting crouch facing the man-creature. The individual lay on his side in the leaf litter where he had fallen when he dodged the knife. He propped his head up on his hand as if he were relaxing. He looked up at Rohan with a quizzically angry look.

"Calm down Le Clerc. I'm not an assassin." Then he saw the hole in the jacket sleeve. "For Christ's sake, this suit is practically brand new." He spoke in a deep monotone that had a European luster. He continued muttering, "I told them I did not want to do this shit, but the Watchers always feel they know best."

The man was of Indo-Caribbean heritage. Good looking in a rough-hewn way, he looked to be in his late twenties. He was tall, had deep brown skin, straight black hair pulled into a man-bun. His arms tested the seams of a well-cut lightweight gray suit, a suit ruined by sweat stains. His nose was hawk-like and slightly off-center as if it had once been broken. A strong jaw and thin lips completed the face that stared up at Rohan. Rohan decided the well-dressed stranger lying in the leaf litter was unlikely to be an assassin and walked forward to offer him a hand back to his feet.

"Is there a reason you are following me?" Rohan repeated. "This trail does not lead to a men's fine clothing store."

The man seemed amused. "My name is Voss Prakash, the Watchers sent me to serve as your bodyguard until further notice." Voss reached into his jacket pocket again causing Rohan to tense. Voss either didn't notice or pretended that he was unaware of Rohan's disquietude. From the pocket he withdrew a long, envelope, made of thick cream-colored paper that had somehow survived Voss' fall without crumpling. He tossed it to Rohan and continued talking. "This is proof of my assignment."

Rohan turned over the envelope, which was sealed in wax and embossed with the sigil of the Watchers' Guild. The deep gold sealing wax was impressed with the relief of a great silk cotton tree and under the tree sat a gnarled old man seated cross legged with a short, knotty walking staff across his lap.

"You know," Rohan said, "I don't think that any Orderman has ever been assigned a bodyguard. We are regularly dispatching greyborn. Don't you think that, at the very least, qualifies us to protect ourselves?"

"With your House elder and your chaptermen dead or missing, Stone House has dwindled to a membership of one. The Watchers will raise new initiates for Stone but you know selection and training takes time. In the interest of maintaining Stone's continuity, the Watchers want to ensure that you stay alive." As Voss spoke, he attempted to rub the grass stains from his knees.

Rohan regarded the letter. He was about to use his thumbnail to break the wax seal. *Who the hell still used seals?* he thought, when the little wax man embossed on the seal stood slowly and shook his short wax walking staff. The leaves on the silk cotton tree trembled as if moved by some invisible breeze, and the golden seal transformed into a huge yellow butterfly which rose off the envelope and flew into the tree tops. Rohan's breath caught in his throat. The Watchers' had enchanted the letter with a protection spell to ensure that he alone opened the letter. No doubt had someone else touched the wax seal with the intent of opening the letter, the seal would have morphed into something much less pleasant than a big golden butterfly. Shuddering slightly Rohan unfolded the letter. Typical of the Guild, the letter was curt and to the point.

Greetings,

The Council at the Watchers Guild requires a meeting to confirm the deaths of Isa Le Clerc and Dorian Le Clerc of Stone House Chapter of the Order, and to discuss the whereabouts of Kimani Le Clerc also of Stone House chapter. Evil stirs ever, but the House of Three has had the foresight of a greater evil. Make haste to appear before the Council. Voss Prakash, bearer of this letter, is to stay at your side until the meeting. We await your appearance. The future of Stone hangs in the balance.
The Council at the Watchers Guild.

Always so formal, Rohan thought as he refolded the letter. The future of Stone hangs in the balance? He almost laughed.

The Council at the Watcher's Guild assisted the Order in dealing with the various miscreants that occasionally leapt out of folklore. However, they never got their hands bloody. They were psychics and seers, responsible for intelligence gathering of the supernatural sort.

Their functions also included media suppression. They worked tirelessly to ensure that the wider public kept on believing that monsters were the stuff of myth. The Watchers planted false stories, bribed witnesses, and were not above the employment of magic, hypnosis or intimidation to keep stories from making mainstream news. One more important function Watchers performed was confirming the deaths of members of the Order. Something in the letter struck Rohan…discuss the whereabouts of Kimani Le Clerc. Kimani's body was in the forest, rotting. There was nothing to 'discuss.'

Rohan turned to Voss, "How soon do I have to be there?"

"You know the Guild, they expect you to be there today. Now," he replied.

Rohan turned around on the path and started to run back to Stone House, leaving Voss to keep up.

Chapter 5

The grey sedan meandered through the upscale Woodbrook neighborhood with Voss at the wheel and Rohan and Kamara, who they had picked up at the house, seated in the back. They drove in somber silence, each preoccupied by their own musings. The windows were rolled up and the sounds of the outside world were muted.

The car was a cocoon of melancholy. Rohan's grief over Isa inevitably led to thoughts about his parents. His mother, Isa's daughter Renate had been committed to leading a normal life. When Rohan was six, both Renate and Martin, his father, fell sick. The doctors said it was a severe bacterial infection, but Isa believed it was obeah, the fulfillment of a vendetta against him by one of the many enemies he had made as elder of the Order. Neither of his parents recovered. Isa had seen to it that Rohan had been tested and marked and had raised him as his son. Isa and the Order had become the family he knew. When he lost his parents at six, Rohan knew something tragic had happened, but he was young enough to recover quickly. He was no longer six, however, and the grief he felt at Isa's loss would not fade easily. It waxed and lingered and threatened to consume him.

Voss brought the vehicle to a stop announcing that they had arrived. They got out and stood on the sidewalk in front of a large house. The house was built in the turn of the century Victorian architectural style that was unique to Trinidad. Though very old, it had been meticulously preserved. Its steep sided roof of green corrugated sheet metal contrasted with the wooden lace-like lattice work of the gable trim.

The wide wooden windows had hand carved frames and displayed a patina which reflected countless years of being varnished and revarnished. The porch tiles were a deep ocean green that matched the roofing. The house itself was painted peach with white accents. A thick bougainvillea hedge encircled the grounds, its blooms a riot of peach, violet, and white. Mature palm and fruit trees dotted the lush, manicured lawn.

Voss pressed the doorbell button that was recessed in the short square concrete gatepost. Above the bell button was a marble inlay with golden lettering advertising that the location housed the office of Dr. Premkumar Luchman, as well as the law offices of Glazer, Williamson, and Stewart.

A female voice answered the intercom. Voss identified himself and the gate swung open. The trio followed a winding white gravel path that was bordered by an Ixora hedge in full bloom. The mahogany double doors were open and they stepped into the clean, cool air of a large and well-appointed waiting room. The off-white walls were covered with paintings by Caribbean artists. Waterfalls, forests, and birds were the primary inspirations.

Behind a heavy wooden desk, a petite, pretty, dark-skinned woman in a well-tailored skirt-suit, stood, extended a manicured hand, and smiled in greeting, shaking each hand in turn. The brass nameplate on the desk introduced her as Lisa Cyrus and she directed them to take a seat, assuring them that they would be called upon shortly.

Rohan sat and allowed himself to be mesmerized by the lazy spinning of a ceiling fan with blades that mimicked banana fronds. There was a time when the Order's three houses; Stone, River, and Wood had been filled with initiates but as the numbers of greyborn dwindled so had the membership of the houses. Fewer children were born who could survive the rituals that conferred the powers Rohan used to track, fight, and kill.

Attempting to tattoo an unproven child could result in infection or worse, death. Potentials therefore had to be tested. There was a time maybe a century ago when more children passed the test that there was room to accept. Now, finding a suitable recruit was rare.

The scarcity of new initiates had not worried the men of the Order because those who bore the tattoos lived a very long time. Additionally, since the diminishing numbers of recruits seemed to dovetail with the diminishing number of greyborn, some members of The Order felt this reduction of recruits was the Absolute's way of setting the balance. But the three deaths at Stone underscored how easy it was for an entire house to be wiped out.

Lisa Cyrus rose and asked Rohan to accompany her. Voss and Kamara stood to follow.

"They only need Rohan for now," Lisa said, motioning that Voss and Kamara should retake their seats.

The small woman walked ahead of him, her back straight. Her tall red heels clicked rhythmically on the hardwood flooring. The two ascended a spiral staircase, went down a wide hall, and stopped in front of a tall black door covered with carvings, the most prominent of which was a wrinkled old man sitting below a silk cotton tree, the Watchers' seal.

Lisa knocked once and entered without waiting for a response. Inside, the room was bathed in warm sunlight entering from its picture windows. Three men and two women sat around a large table the surface of which was polished to a mirror finish. Rohan knew most of the faces but only some of the names of the people seated around the table. "Please sit, Le Clerc." The man who spoke sat at the head of the table. Rohan noticed with interest that although he was the blackest man he had ever seen, his eyes were bluer than a clear sky. His voice was deep and gravelly as if he did not use it often.

Rohan did as he was asked. Lisa turned to leave. "Lisa, stay, you may have a seat as well."

Rohan objected, "The receptionist stays while Kamara is left downstairs like a stranger?"

"Rohan, we understand that this is an awful time for you. You have lost friends and family. Christopher and I also mourn." These words were spoken by the elder of the two women. Her straight steel gray hair was pulled back revealing a face that was more handsome than pretty. Rohan thought he remembered her name to be Miriam or was it Martha or something else pious and mundane. She motioned towards the dark-skinned man who nodded in solemn agreement as the woman continued. "Isa was a good friend and a great man. But we ask you to be patient and listen. There is a lot you do not know."

"The Order depends on you lot for psychic intelligence gathering," Rohan responded. "You are also supposed to find potential recruits. A potential has not been tested in twenty years, not since I was raised. You were also the ones who informed us that there was a single rogue lagahoo in Stone House's jurisdiction. You left us to blunder into a massive ambush led by a master. How did you fail to see the psychic ripple always created by anything moving between the Grey and the Absolute? If you had seen it, done your job, my chaptermen would be alive."

There was a momentary silence before Christopher spoke again.

"Rohan, we will address your concerns, but first a matter of equal importance. The life candles of Isa and Dorian have been extinguished. Their bodies are dead, their essence has moved on, and we mourn their loss. The candle for Kimani Le Clerc, went out on the night of the battle but burns again. A life candle that has gone cold, has never in our history come back to flame. We do not know what to make of this."

"That is not possible." Rohan exclaimed. "If Kimani was alive he would have returned to Stone."

The older woman responded. "This is unbroken ground for all of us. We simply have no idea how this should be interpreted. All the other candles burn with a yellow light but since Kimani's candle reignited it has burned blue. We have tried to find him; our eyes have been extended throughout the Absolute and into the Grey but we are blind to his presence. As you know we cannot see into the Ether. Those of the Absolute who go there neither return nor have candles that burn."

Rohan stared at the mirrored table top, trying to make sense of what he had heard. Life candles were the Order and the Guild's method of determining whether an Orderman was still alive and thus worth searching for or if he was dead. A candle was lit for each Orderman on the day he was raised, and it burned until the day he died. Anger filled him as he thought of Isa and Dorian's extinguished candles.

"If he is alive then use your talents and find him. Isn't that your job? Based on what I have seen we need every seasoned man." He knew he was being unreasonable, but their calm inaction was infuriating. He paused again to consider his other unanswered questions. "How were the bodies of Isa and Dorian returned? How was I found?"

Christopher responded. "We found their bodies washed and wrapped in shrouds. One of the seers had a dream that led us to their location. We found you nearby. You were unconscious, but your wounds were cleaned and dressed. We believe the forest people, either the Duens or Papa Bois, are responsible for your return.

The younger woman spoke for the first time. She wore a navy business suit as if she had come to this meeting after working at a regular job. "In the dream, the seer was led by the hand by a forest child to the exact spot where you were found. The Duen have mild psychic abilities, a group of them working together could muster the power needed to plant a dream."

Rohan shook his head. He could not believe that the faceless forest children known for their mischievous ways would have been this helpful. "Duen do not behave in the manner you have described. What makes you think they retrieved the bodies? Why do you think they wanted me found? They are usually aligned more with the creatures of the Grey than with the men of the Order," he responded.

The table was silent until Christopher spoke. "I think they know that there is a greater danger." He paused for a meaningful breath. "The reason most of us did not see the master enter the Absolute is because someone very powerful opened the gate and hid the master's presence until it was too late. When it finally leapt from the Grey, the suddenness and violence of its psychic signature blinded the third eye of two seers and gave another some sort of metaphysical stroke. Since the Guild was established nothing has ever been able to cross into the Absolute from one of the other realities unseen."

"You said most of you were blind to it? Did someone actually see it enter?"

"Yes. Lisa saw it." Christopher gestured to the receptionist.

Rohan spun. "She's not a receptionist?" he stammered. Lisa grinned at him, with a wide but lovely smile.

"Well, of late I'm an apprentice seer, but I'm also an impoverished university student and I need to pay tuition somehow, so receptionist it is," she responded continuing to grin.

Rohan's anger returned. "And I am supposed to be happy that the only person from the entire House of Three that saw the lagahoo master come into the Absolute, was an apprentice, part-time receptionist, university undergrad? And why was an alarm not raised. We should have been warned."

Lisa's smile faded and her eyes narrowed with what Rohan thought was annoyance.

"Well to clarify, I'm a full-time receptionist who does evening classes. Secondly, I didn't ask to be included in this occult nonsense. Two weeks ago I was just a regular person and an actual receptionist for Dr. Luchman, who I now know is also a witch doctor. By the way, I feel like you people need to put those facts in the job ads, but I digress. Just after I began working here, I started having these dreams, dreams like I never have had before, vividly real, dark dreams, and I started being able to guess the winning numbers of Play Whe with frightening accuracy. Then I started having the dreams even while I was wide awake. An entire hour could go by and I would not remember what happened except for the visions. I was zoning out during classes, parties, my favorite sitcoms, it was annoying. I spoke to Dr. Luchman. He called in Christopher and Miriam," she gestured to the dark-skinned man and the gray-haired woman. "They made me drink some bitter dishwater tasting swill then they poked at me and told me I was Seeing."

Miriam spoke, "At twenty-seven she is a bit old to be coming into her power. We think the fact that she is such a powerful clairvoyant coupled with the fact that she was unwittingly surrounded by sorcerers and seers opened her third eye. She is a late bloomer, but so far very impressive."

"What did you see on the night of the attack?" Rohan asked.

"At first not much, initially the vision was…slippery. I was sitting at my desk when it came to me. I reached out with my third eye and it was like trying to grab an eel while wearing silk gloves. It came in flashes. I saw the four of you fighting and running. I saw your chaptermen dying. But the more I focused on it the harder it was to see. So, I stopped trying to reach for the vision and allowed it to come to me." Lisa swallowed visibly and fussed with one of her freshwater pearl earrings. "Then I saw glimpses of the man who was holding open the gate to let the master into the Absolute."

Christopher interjected, "The man she saw was shrouding the magic needed to open a gate to the Grey. All of us were blind to it. We believe that it was this person's intention to open the portal longer allowing more masters into the Absolute."

"So why didn't he do it then and there. It seems to me that someone powerful enough to blind the entire Guild, save the receptionist, would be powerful enough to open the gate for as long as they wanted."

"That is not necessarily the case. It takes a lot of power and very specific knowledge to open a large hole. We think he is not completely ready and this was a test to see if he could even achieve an opening. Maybe he does not have all the elements in place yet. But there is more, let Lisa finish her story," Christopher said.

Lisa took a breath, "When I stopped actively trying to see the vision, it all came to me; I knew what the person was attempting. I saw more monsters waiting to squeeze through the small gate he had opened. So, I hit him. He must have lost concentration. His obeah dissolved, and he vanished."

Rohan was confused. "You hit him? How? I always thought the visions were like images on a video feed."

Miriam spoke before Lisa could respond. "The only explanation we can make is that Lisa traveled in the astral plane between the realms to the place where the obeah man was casting his spells and she hit him as if she was physically there, but it was her essence. What she did was extremely dangerous" Miriam glanced at Lisa. "A thousand times more so because she did it inadvertently. Death in the astral plane means death to both the physical and spiritual self, it means nothingness, no reincarnation, no heaven not even hell." Miriam paused then continued, "The skill required to simultaneously hold open a portal to the Grey while working another spell to blind every psychic to what you are doing is considerable."

"How do we know he doesn't have all the elements for a bigger hole?" Rohan asked.

"Because he was trying different things over and over, arranging the spells differently, like he was experimenting," Lisa said.

Christopher continued, "Since that night nothing further has happened, and we fear we will be unable to locate him until he again draws on as much power as he did on the night of the attacks. He was interrupted the last time, but we know he will try again. He must be found and killed before then."

Rohan scoffed, "Found and killed?" he said, mimicking Christopher's gravelly tone. "How and by whom? I'm the only one left at Stone and I survived by some magical fluke. River house has five men and Wood has seven. This obeah man could not have chosen a better time to try his hand."

"Your survival was not a fluke. It was Lisa who saved you," Miriam said. "Tell him Lisa."

"After I struck him he dropped something, a thing of magic that is invisible in the physical world. I knew instinctively it was the key he was using to channel power to open the gate. I picked it up. By that time the master had already crossed into the Absolute and called the lesser lagahoo to harry you. Dorian and Isa were dead, and you lay there with a broken back. I tried to strike the master with power drawn through the key but I couldn't do that from where I was, so I brought your essence to the plane and used some of the power to help you."

"Help me? Wait, what?! That was you? You pulled my soul into the astral plane, pumped me full of some mysterious power that you stole from an obeah man then returned me to my body?"

"That's a pretty good way of putting it. I wasn't exactly sure what I was doing. It was all very intuitive," Lisa said as she fussed with her necklace.

Rohan stammered in shock, but finally managed to get control of his tongue. "You seem to know a lot about obeah for someone who was 'normal' two short weeks ago."

"She has an amazing intuition for the craft." Miriam chimed in.

"And the key, do you still have it? Seems like something he would want back?"

"No, I didn't know how to keep ahold of it when I returned to my body."

Rohan sighed. "Did you see Kimani in one of your dreams do you have any idea where he could be?" Rohan asked.

"I have not seen him since after he fell off the cliff…" Suddenly Lisa paused. "Did anyone else see that?" She stared intently at the smooth mirror-like finish of the wooden table top.

"See what?" Christopher asked.

"I thought I saw something move in the table?"

"You mean on the table?" This came from another of the three men, a balding bespectacled gentleman; *Leon? Lennox?* Rohan felt like he really should make it a point to learn the names of the members of the Watcher's Guild.

"No, I mean in…there it is, over there." She pointed to the area of the table under Miriam's elbows.

Rohan squinted and was about to dismiss Lisa's suspicions as the result of an over active imagination, but then he saw it too. A small shadow moving sinuously like a snake in water. Miriam stood so suddenly she knocked over her chair.

"What is that?" she cried, backing away.

The shadow began growing like the silhouette of an aquatic creature rising from a murky pool. Everyone around the table was standing, making sure that no part of their person touched the table. The shadow continued to rise within the table, as if the surface of the table was the surface of a slimy lagoon. The air became thick and humid, like the air of a primeval swamp. The room reeked with the organic stink of mildew, decay, and rot. The shadow had taken on a shape however, the silhouetted creature was so massive that only parts of it could be viewed in the table at a time. Rohan thought it looked vaguely crocodilian with a long snout and a ridged tail, but with longer arms. The creature would swim out of sight beyond the borders of the table's edge and swim back into view, as if the table was the window of an aquarium. Everyone was staring spellbound when, without warning, the shadowy creature thrashed its massive tail from within the surface of the table, like an alligator would from beneath the surface of the water. The table top buckled upward, splintering and sending chips of wood everywhere, and with that the phenomenon ended, leaving a shattered table and a shaken group of people.

Rohan was the first to break the silence. "What just happened."

"I think we just had a glimpse into the Grey, which suggests that the barriers between the realities are thinning." Christopher sounded a lot less confident than he had before, but Rohan surmised that an otherworldly crocodile swimming in your office furniture would shake anyone's confidence.

"That thing is called a Leviathan. It patrols the swamps of the Grey. I don't know how I know, but I know." Lisa stood as far away from the table as she could without leaving the room. Rohan gave her credit for staying.

Miriam seemed to have composed herself. "Whenever someone opens a hole between the realities, the barriers grow thin everywhere. The barriers are naturally thinner in some places than in others, in places where holes have been opened before, and in places where sorcery and obeah are frequently worked, like here for example."

"So, in summary, we have to find and capture or eliminate this man before he can open a permanent gate." Christopher was also collecting himself.

"Do we even know his name or know what he looks like?" Rohan asked.

"Sorry I only saw his essence, a suggestion of a man, no actual features," Lisa said.

"Lisa will stay with you until further notice. The men of the other houses will, of course, also give aid."

Both Lisa and Rohan were taken aback. "She can't stay with me, she doesn't know anything about the greyborn or about obeah, she's going to get herself or all of us killed."

Lisa echoed his objections, but Christopher was adamant. "She knew enough to save you from certain death, to strike an obeah man on the Astral Plane, and to disarm him of the key to his power source. The rest of the Guild cannot find him, so unless you have an alternative, Lisa is your best bet. She has the most familiarity with the man we are seeking. Besides she's a very quick study."

Rohan suddenly remembered Voss and Kamara downstairs. What if the Leviathan's appearance had not been limited to the table? He left the room without a word and bolted down the stairs.

The waiting room was a disaster; the entire floor was a ruin of broken wood. Voss and Kamara were nowhere to be found. Rohan rushed outside and found Voss restraining Kamara telling her that it was safer outside. Kamara was fighting to return to the house arguing that Voss was Rohan's bodyguard and not hers. When she saw Rohan, her relief was palpable.

"There was an image of something swimming up from within the floor, Rohan. I couldn't let her stay inside."

"You did the right thing, Voss."

Kamara was not pleased. "He's your bodyguard, why didn't he drag you out of the building?"

Lisa cleared her throat and Rohan took the opportunity to avoid an argument with Kamara by explaining how Lisa's role had changed in the last half hour. Miriam appeared in the yard to share some final words of warning. "With an obeah man this strong, things are apt to get very strange and very dangerous."

Lisa said, "Wait, my dog, I need to get my dog."

"A dog?" Rohan asked. "You take a dog to work?"

"Well, yes. He doesn't like to be left in the house alone."

Lisa hustled off to the back yard and returned with a large black dog.

"German Shepherd?" Kamara inquired.

"I'm not sure what he is. He showed up on my doorstep two days ago."

"You adopted that monster as an adult?" Voss sounded impressed. "What's his name? Aren't you afraid of him?"

"He's Agrippa, Caesar's right-hand man, and no, he's a gentleman."

They got back into the grey car. Rohan entered the front passenger seat. Lisa and Kamara sat in the back with Agrippa between them.

As Voss drove east toward Stone House, Rohan thought of Kimani and the shocking news that he might still be alive.

Chapter 6

Why Voss chose to return through Port-of-Spain rather than around the city, Rohan could not quite fathom. Why he chose to drive down Charlotte Street in particular, was less mysterious than it was sadistic.

Charlotte Street is an old thoroughfare through the heart of a city designed with the horse and not the automobile in mind. The street allowed for a single lane of southbound traffic.

The sidewalks were lined with hawkers, mongers and peddlers of all manner of goods. Their stalls and tables spilled from the sidewalks, straddled choked drains and narrowed the street in some places to the point where the side mirrors of cars barely squeezed past. Pedestrians stepped off the sidewalks and into the thoroughfare without warning. Vagrants acting as porters for the vendors labored slowly up and down the street pushing heavily laden carts or bearing boxes of fruit or buckets of fish on their heads. Street disc jockeys also plied the route with carts armed with speakers blaring an arsenal of reggae and soca. The midday traffic crawled.

"I need some fresh air, can we crack the windows?" Lisa asked.

Fresh air on Charlotte Street? Rohan thought, even as Voss obliged and lowered the rear windows.

The midday sun bore down with brutal, consistent, and proximate brilliance. A commotion up ahead brought traffic to a stop. Rohan leaned forward and saw two women standing in the center of the narrow street. They were arguing loudly and vulgarly over some perceived slight. Onlookers heckled and egged them on as they stood toe to toe, their greasy necks straining in anger, their heaving, heavy bosoms almost touching.

The small boy, who snatched Kamara's necklace through the open back window, did so with the lightning quick ease of a well-practiced cutpurse. His arm flicked in through the window, his hand closed around the thin gold chain and he fled, vanishing into the crowd. Bedlam erupted in the back seat. Kamara yelled in surprise and Agrippa leapt through the window and onto the sidewalk in pursuit of the boy, almost hauling Lisa through the window as she clung to its collar in a vain attempt to restrain the beast.

Rohan exited the car in pursuit of dog and boy. He could not see his quarry, but the sight of the large ferocious-looking animal barreling down the sidewalk left a trail of squeals and shouts that was easy enough to follow. Rohan caught a brief glimpse of the dog as it veered across the street, leapt over a table covered with blue crabs and vanished down a urine-drenched alley.

Rohan wondered why he was even chasing the dog. The necklace could be replaced and the dog had been adopted a mere two days ago. But something about the way Agrippa instantly leapt into action impressed Rohan. Perhaps the Order needed a mascot. He crossed the street and sprinted down the alley.

The path was narrow and strewn with garbage. The walls were so close that sunlight never penetrated all the way to ground level. A cool, stale, dusty gloom clung around Rohan's legs below the knees. He hurdled over bags of garbage, slipped on the corpse of dead rat the size of a Pomeranian, and splashed through a puddle he sincerely hoped was water. The dog cut left down another alley. Rohan got to the junction just in time to see the animal take another corner. He doubled his efforts. The waif had to be flying to have eluded both him and the dog for so long. Rohan got to another junction but there was no sight of the animal. He realized he had to find the dog now as he wasn't sure he could make it out of the labyrinth without its help.

Relying on intuition, Rohan picked an alley and sped down it. It seemed that the alleys doubled back on each other, because about fifty feet into his pursuit the boy barreled into Rohan from the left, while glancing back over his shoulder at the pursuing Agrippa.

Rohan managed to keep his balance, but the force of the collision knocked the boy on to his rear end. Winded and trapped between Rohan and a growling Agrippa the child conceded defeat. Rohan looked at him closely for the first time. He was perhaps ten or eleven years old, wiry and sun browned. He had a narrow face with bright eyes and a mouth that wore a sheepish smile as he reached into his pocket, brought out a broken necklace and offered it to Rohan.

"The necklace you stole did not have a broken clasp. I'd like to have that one back."

The boy had no answer.

"Get up," Rohan said, extending a hand to the sitting child. "I probably can't find my way back to the street without you."

The boy accepted the extended hand and Rohan yanked him to his feet. Something on the boy's wrist caught Rohan's eye and his heart rate accelerated sharply. He raised the hand for closer inspection.

"Where did you get this?" Rohan snapped. Agrippa snarled, mirroring Rohan's mood.

"What you talking about? Yuh breaking my hand."

Rohan held the boy's wrist up to his face and pointed to the tattoos of ravens in flight that ringed the boy's wrist, each raven about the size of a child's fingernail. The tattoos had the familiar black-silver sheen of the Order's marks and Rohan intuitively knew they were real. The ink was fatally and agonizingly poisonous to all but a select few, but the boy seemed no worse for wear. If he was a member of one of the Order's Houses, he would not be a pickpocket on the streets of Port-of-Spain. Who but the Order tattoos children?

"I don't know," the boy responded, wriggling under Rohan's grasp. "I've always had them."

"Do you have any others?" Rohan asked spinning the boy around inspecting him.

"I have a couple others, but there is no way I'm taking off my shirt for some weird man and his dog in an alley."

"Where do you live? Take me to your parents."

"I don't have no parents, I live with…what does it matter. Just take me to the station." The boy had decided that police custody was better than his current circumstances and he redoubled his efforts to escape.

"Ok, ok look, sorry I scared you," Rohan said, releasing the boy. He took half a step backward with his palms upraised attempting to appear less threatening. "These tattoos say something about what you are…who you are…what you can be. I would like to see where you live and after I would like to take you to some people."

"Take me to some people? I don't like how that part sounding but…" The boy looked thoughtful. "If I take you where I live, what's in it for me?"

Rohan laughed, "So we have a little opportunist eh? Ok here's the deal, take me to your home and I'll buy you dinner."

"Can I keep the gold chain?"

"We can speak to Kamara about that one, but most likely she'll let you keep it. What's your name, small man?"

"Tarik. Tarik Abban."

"My name is Rohan Le Clerc and my large toothy buddy over there is called Agrippa. I only met him today so I can't really vouch for his character. So far he's been pretty useful for capturing pickpockets though."

The boy grinned sheepishly.

When Rohan, the dog, and the boy emerged from the dank maze of alleys and back into the sunlight, Rohan phoned Kamara. Voss had parked outside the Unit Trust Corporation building on Independence Square and they were all waiting in the shade of some tamarind trees on the adjacent promenade. When Rohan, Tarik, and Agrippa approached they found the ladies engaged in a lively chat, apparently having become fast friends. Voss sat on a nearby bench feeding some blackbirds and pigeons with the flaky crumbs of a beef patty.

Rohan explained that he needed to ask the boy's guardian some questions and then take the boy to the Guild if allowed. The six of them were one too many for the sedan but Rohan was reluctant to leave Lisa and Kamara alone, given the strange events of the day. They squeezed in, Lisa and Tarik sharing the front seat, while Agrippa, Rohan and Kamara sat in the back.

Voss started the engine.

"Where are we headed, boy?" he asked.

The directions the boy gave led to a slum on the outskirts of the capital called Sea Lots, an area fairly or unfairly, known for its crime and poverty. Rohan subconsciously fingered the butt of the gun in his shoulder holster.

Chapter 7

"We were of the mistaken belief that the witch doctor's thralls could only be unleashed after sunset. Imagine our terror when we were set upon during broad daylight. It is almost laughable that I use the phrase "imagine our terror" as if a murderous animated corpse can be made any more terrifying than is de facto the case. But surely, there is something more obscene, more irreverent, and yes, more terrifying about a shambling corpse disemboweling the faithful while the Lord's sun sits high in the sky. We are leaving Haiti on the next ship that calls at Port au Prince. This is the devil's land and he may take them all" —Excerpt from the diary of Siobhan Jenner, Catholic Missionary to Haiti, written December 25, 1901*

The swollen red sun sat low on the horizon when they entered the sprawling neighborhood of squatter's shacks and industrial properties called Sea Lots, so named because the government of the time had made lots of land available to impoverished citizens. These lots of land were bordered by the Churchill Roosevelt highway, an extensive mangrove swamp, and the Caribbean Sea from which the area drew the other part of its name. Some honest people made their home there, but the area was also a refuge for criminals, fugitives, drug traffickers, and gun runners. Four well-dressed people in a nice car would quickly attract the wrong kind of attention.

Rohan drew the desert eagle out of his shoulder holster, checked to see that a round was in the chamber and then re-holstered the weapon. Kamara performed a similar inspection on the small pistol she carried in her clutch. Rohan knew from their initial encounter that Voss kept his gun at the small of his back in a Mexican carry and wondered how the bodyguard could sit comfortably with the weapon holstered in that spot.

Voss took another pistol out of the glove compartment offered it to Lisa. She declined the offer.

"You guys do realize that we live in Trinidad where guns are illegal right? Do you all have permits? Anyway, I have never handled a gun before. If this turns into a shootout I'm more likely to put a hole in my pedicure than into a bad guy."

Tarik directed Voss through the narrow streets, apparently unfazed by the amount of ammunition carried by the people with whom he now kept company. Paved surface eventually gave way to dirt as the road veered toward the mangroves. Tarik pointed out a hut so close to the edge of the swamp that the back of the hut stood on stilts in the water.

Voss parked in the shade of a large mango *vert* tree as far along the overgrown path as the car could travel and they all disembarked. The sun had almost retired for the day. Shadows were long and the twilight gloom played tricks on Rohan's eyes. Every now and then something would splash in the water, conjuring a disconcerting memory of the leviathan that had appeared in the table at the Watchers' Council.

The shack was constructed from a patchwork of sheet metal and odds and ends of boarding. A picture of an oversized smile and half the image of a Colgate toothpaste tube dominated part of the outer wall, that panel having been appropriated from some billboard. A short but steep flight of termite-afflicted stairs led to the front door. The roof of the shack was carpeted with the flowering vines of a Mexican creeper plant, the violet blooms were an unexpected splash of beauty in the otherwise glum yard. A small raft was moored to the stilts in the back.

"How many people live here?" Rohan asked the boy.

"Just me and my grandmother. She's blind but always knows when I'm coming home."

"Ok. Go in and tell her some friends would like to speak to her."

"Cool, but she probably already knows you are here. She always knows."

While Tarik made his way to the hut the four adults decided that Rohan and Kamara would be the ones to enter the house. Voss, Lisa, and Agrippa would keep watch in the yard. Before the boy reached the door, however, a voice from within the hut called out, "No needs to continue milling about. Come in here and let Kat have a look at you."

Rohan was briefly taken aback, but he and Kamara made their way to the hut after sharing a glance. A burlap sack with the words 'Tableland sweet potatoes' hung in front of the doorway. Rohan drew it aside and entered with Kamara swift on his heels.

His eyes adjusted rapidly to the dimness and he scanned the room for threats, knowing it would take Kamara's eyes a few additional seconds to acclimate. The inside of the shack was cluttered, but clean. Makeshift shelves lined all four walls to the ceiling. The shelves were crammed with jars holding all manner of things including herbs, mushrooms, dried flowers, powders, a bird's skeleton, a pickled lizard, and a living snake. An entire section of the wall was devoted to insects and arachnids; assassin bugs, moths, scorpions, and a massive harlequin beetle were just a few of the creatures in the strange menagerie of miniatures. From the ceiling hung herbs and bones.

An earthy scent, a mixture of incense, candle wax, mud, and rain-water filled the room. Below the stronger scents Rohan could discern the faint metallic sharpness of blood. He had been in places like these before and could always tell if the proprietor was a genuine practitioner of obeah or a quack. He concluded that Tarik's grandmother knew what she was about and that knowledge made him apprehensive.

A voice spoke from a dark corner. "Tarik, light a candle for our guests."

Tarik lit a candle and set it on small, rickety table. The flickering light illuminated a woman that Rohan could only describe as ancient, however, she exuded vitality. Her pale leathery skin was deeply lined. Her hair was white but thick and full and fell in a single braid to her lap in where it coiled several times like a sleeping cobra.

She sat on a mat on the floor, her legs extended and crossed at the ankle, her back straight. She wore a simple gray cotton dress. When she smiled at them, she revealed a mouth of small even white teeth. Rohan noted that her canines were oddly pointed and that her eyes were a milky green color and appeared to have neither irises nor pupils. He found them disconcerting.

"Please sit. I've been expecting you."

Rohan and Kamara shared a look but sat on the floor in front of the woman.

"My name is Kat," she said, fingering a small, finely crafted crucifix on a thin silvery chain about her neck. Her voice was strong which was odd, considering her age. "Did my grandson steal something from you?"

"He did, but that is not why we are here. We are interested in his tattoos."

"Ahh, you want to have similar work done?"

"I think we both know that's not what I mean. His tattoos are special."

"Yes, they are special. But, Rohan Le Clerc it is not your job to find potential recruits. That is the Guild's work."

Rohan started but managed to keep his composure. "How do you know my name and about the Guild."

"Does it matter how?" She was silent for a moment. "I'm blind, but some things I can see better than those with sight can. Of late the things I see disturb me."

"What do you see?" Kamara asked the woman.

"Bloody rivers, choked with the bloated bodies of many dead." The silence hung heavily in the room once more. The only movement was that of shadows dancing on the walls, their sinuous forms quickened by the draft-blown candle flame.

"But you aren't here to learn about the dreams of an old crone, right? Tarik, come here and show the man your marks."

The boy stepped out of the shadows from a corner of the hut. The candle light cast his small face in a disturbing shade of orange. Pinpoints of light reflected in his eyes. He removed his threadbare t-shirt and turned to show his back. Kamara gasped quietly and Rohan stared at the boy's back for a full minute, rising and leaning in for a closer inspection.

The boy's entire back was covered in a detailed mural depicting three men in roman centurion armor doing battle with a legion of lagahoo, soucouyant, ghouls, and jumbies. Despite the apparently insurmountable odds the men prevailed. Above the entire scene blazed a stylized sun the rays of which were spears that pierced many of the host below. It was a stunning work, with every detail rendered with painstaking care. All of it was done in the silvery black ink of an Orderman's ceremonial marks.

"I have never seen anything like that."

"Well, I do have an artistic streak." The old woman smiled.

"You did it?"

"All but the blackbirds on his wrist. He came to me with those."

"You said he came to you? Your son or daughter placed him in your care?" Kamara asked.

"The boy is my grandson only because he is young and I'm old. One night there was a storm, the ocean swell threatened to wash away my little hovel, but it did not. Others were not so fortunate. In the morning I heard a babe squalling on the shore and I found him, in a wooden crate amongst the storm debris. No matter what you do, the smell of shape-shifter blood cannot be completely cleansed away. I knew he bore the marks and thus I knew he could bear more."

"But, why would you mark him at all? How do you know what the marks mean? How do you know my name?"

The woman laughed. "One question at a time, Le Clerc. I have been around for a long time and I made a promise to someone that I intend to see through to the end. The person I made this promise to taught me about the marks and his dreams told him that you would come to me here. Kat paused as if she was weighing her next words. "Rohan, someone is working to kill us all and time is short. Stone House has chosen an inopportune time to dwindle to one warrior, his consort, a bodyguard, a part-time secretary turned seer, and a dog."

"Technically the dog et cetera are not part of the Chapter," Rohan muttered. "And how do you know about what is happening at Stone."

"I hear some things and I see others." Kat said, raising an index finger to one blind eye.

"What can you tell us about our enemy?" Kamara asked, elbowing Rohan.

"Unfortunately, not much. He wishes to open the Grey and we all know what that means; greyborn will come again and spread their taint to man. If the hole is big enough and is open long enough, man will be forced to fight for their survival as a species. Humanity is not ready for what the Grey has to offer. I have attempted to find him in the astral plane, but my only reward has been pain and terror. There is a wall of black evil surrounding him through which the third-eye cannot see."

"Our part-time secretary-turned-seer may be able to penetrate that wall," Kamara said with a wry smile.

"I'm impressed but she must tread with caution. What troubles me about our quarry is that I cannot determine his motives. If he wishes to tear the curtain between the Grey and the Absolute, he either has a means of controlling whatever comes through or he is just doing evil for its own sake. If the latter is true, he is reckless and even more dangerous."

"What should we do?" Rohan asked.

"Kill him. Lisa bought you some time, but he will eventually find or make another key."

"Yeah, we kinda understand that we need to kill him, but how?"

"Well, you had a meeting with the Watchers today, what did you glean from them."

"How do you know...never mind you seem to know it all."

"Rohan Le Clerc, sometimes what seems to be mystical is actually fairly mundane. I had the boy follow you, spy on the meeting, and report back to me. Then he stole the necklace as a means of making an introduction."

"Tarik, you sneaky little rat," Rohan said in mock indignation. "He really sold being reluctant to comply with my requests to come back here. As for the meeting, it was not particularly informative and it ended abruptly."

Just then Lisa barged into the house with Agrippa at her heels. "We have a problem. Some of the local residents want to speak to the old woman."

"Call me Kat, please, the old woman nonsense can stop right now," Kat said with exaggerated gruffness.

"Sorry ma'am, their words not mine," Lisa said apologetically.

"Now, what could they possibly want with an old woman at this hour?" Kat said smiling.

"They are saying you are a witch and they want you gone from here," Lisa replied.

"Witches and lagahoo and soucouyant? In this day and age who believes that nonsense anymore?" Kat spoke with a sarcastic smile and a wink of one blind eye.

The five of them went outside, Tarik leading Kat by the elbow. The moon had risen and the path leading to Kat's house was bathed in silver. Kat leaned towards Tarik, adopting a feeble hunched posture and a mild demeanor that reflected every year of her advanced age. A group of about fifty people stood in the moonlit yard engaged in a silent face-off with Voss. To the uninitiated Voss appeared to be absentmindedly chewing a long grass stalk, but Rohan knew he was ready to commit violence should the need arise. Rohan approached the group, but he and Kamara stopped short of Voss. He could not put a finger on it but something about the crowd triggered an uneasy feeling in his stomach.

With hands raised and a broad grin he spoke. "Ladies and gentlemen, what do we have here? No one told me the star-gazing convention was meeting tonight." Sarcasm and humor were how he addressed tense situations. Kamara on the other hand felt that his way often made tense situations worse, so he was not surprised when she inconspicuously elbowed him in the ribs and spoke to the crowd in a more mollifying tone. "We're just visiting our grandmother. Hopefully we are not bothering you?"

She was met with blank, ossified faces until a woman dressed in ceremonial Shouta Baptist white robes and a red head wrap came forward. "We know what does go on here and it must stop. The soucouyant mus' leave." She punctuated every word of her last sentence with violent jabs of her index finger toward Kat. The crowd behind her muttered their support.

"Ma'am, the legend of the soucouyant is an old wives' tale born out of the old-fashioned gender oppression of unmarried women of a certain age. It is unacceptable in modern society. This is my poor blind grandmother and to be quite honest, you're scaring her," Kamara replied, placing an arm of support around Kat's shoulders as she donned her cloak of university-conditioned indignation. Rohan nodded.

"So because we from Sea Lots you think we foolish? You came in that nice car, with your expensive clothes, but your 'poor blind granny' lives in

48

a hut that ready to fall into the swamp? We not chupid. We know what she is and we want her gone."

"Kamara, what is a So-koo-yarn, anyway? he asked, loud enough for the woman to hear him.

The leader was growing angry. "You eh go confuse me with yuh University English and yuh tricks, let me speak to the old woman." She stepped forward but Voss moved to block her way, meeting her eyes with a fixed stare.

"Let her come forward," Kat said, her voice quavering with age.

Rohan instantly knew where Tarik had learned the ability to role play so well. The woman who had confronted them in the hut was gone. Nothing about Kat's demeanor or appearance suggested that she was anything but a poor old woman eking out an existence at the edge of a swampy, mosquito-ridden slum.

Voss stepped aside and the large, bosomy woman strode up to them heralded by the swish of her voluminous skirts. A wooden, rosary bounced on her ample chest. Rohan noticed that she was barefooted. He made way and she stopped right in front of Kat, looming over the older woman who stood supported by the short knobby piece of mangrove root that she used as a cane.

"I have ah question to ask you, grandmother," the woman sneered. "By your ties to the Loa, and to Bazil the demon from which you draw power, speak the only truth you are bound to speak. Are you a soucouyant?"

Rohan was taken aback by the direct question. The woman was obviously familiar with how the tie to Bazil functioned. According to lore, soucouyants, if asked directly about their true nature must answer truthfully unless they are inside their lair when the question is posed.

Kat's head was bowed and her blind gaze downcast, and for the first time Rohan wondered if the woman's accusations could be true. Kat stood like that for a moment before lifting her head to meet the woman's glare. The moonlight reflected off her pupil-less eyes so they looked like twin pools of quicksilver. When she spoke, it was in the voice with which she had addressed them in the hut a voice that resonated with authority and mettle. The charade of the feeble old woman fell away entirely.

"I met a man, a very, very long time ago. He had a thing for big-boned women with heavy chests. I think he would have fancied you. That same man broke my bonds with the Loa so I'm no longer bound to answer your question." Kat grinned and Rohan thought those pointy canines looked all the pointier. "However, because you took time out of your busy schedule and came all the way out to the mangrove forest to see me, I will answer you truthfully. I am a soucouyant, one of the last ones living. I am old and I am strong. And now that we have cleared the air, I have a question for you." Kat said as she squinted her sightless eyes as though evaluating the woman with a sixth sense. "Did you really come here tits-a-bouncing, skirts-a-swishing to my front door, interrupting my family reunion, just to evict Katharine from her home of a hundred years or is there something more sinister that you hope to accomplish tonight?"

Rohan was in shock and he suspected his companions were as well, except for Tarik who looked like he had heard this story ten times before, and Agrippa who was currently very interested in the scent of something in the grass. Kat took a step forward and the woman took a step back. Kat raised her head and sniffed the air, as if testing for something beyond the ability of her guests to discern. "I have another question for you. Who lent you the power to puppet these fifty corpses?" Kat gestured to the would-be lynch mob.

Puppet…corpses…what? Rohan was about to voice his questions when the large woman produced a long dagger from beneath her white robes. As they watched, she drew the blade across her own palm leaving a gash that oozed black crimson in the moonlight. The woman shrieked a word and flailed her injured hand at them spraying bloody droplets on all the members of Rohan's party.

"My blouse," Lisa shrieked. "This bitch…"

Lisa's tirade was cut short as the situation instantly descended into chaos. At the word the woman had wailed the crowd's appearance changed. The eyes of each mob member became desiccated and yellowed; their skin grayed and their jaws slackened.

Jumbies, jumbies, Rohan thought in a panic.

"Lisa and Tarik back to the hut," he commanded.

The mob swarmed forward, their now empty eyes bereft of emotion. Rohan glanced back in time to see Lisa kick off her heels, hike up her skirt, grab Tarik by the wrist and sprint back to the hovel with surprising speed. Ahead of him, Voss had already been pinned by the weight and massive strength of a jumbie which was vigorously attempting to bite his face off.

Voss, with level-headed ruthlessness, put five shots into the creature's neck then tore its head off when the muscle and skin had become sufficiently perforated. The decapitated head however continued to snap at him from the ground where it had fallen.

The crowd swarmed past Voss and approached Rohan and Kamara at a dead run. Rohan drew his gun.

"Shoot them in the legs," he shouted to Kamara and Voss. "They are just puppets. No nervous control, no brain. We have to try to slow them down."

He shot the nearest corpse in the knee. The injured corpse, having lost the use of its legs crawled towards him on its stomach. Kamara stood at his side in a shooter's stance, picking her shots, aiming at their eyes rather than their knees. Agrippa leapt into the fray with a roar.

Kat shouted something Rohan already knew, "They aren't zombies. Gunshots will slow them down a bit and dismemberment will render them a useless pile of squirming parts but nothing will really stop them until the puppet master is stopped."

"Where did she go?" Rohan asked between gunshots.

"She opened a doorway and stepped through, but she has not gone far. I will find her shortly." Kat stood motionless. She looked as if she was concentrating intensely.

The mob continued to charge at Rohan and Kamara, gnashing their jaws, but for reasons unknown to Rohan the jumbies ignored Kat. Expert marksmanship kept the mob at bay but Rohan and Kamara were being pushed back towards the swamp.

"Ahh I have you now," Kat muttered. She made a gesture and vanished. Rohan tried to contain his surprise. He was used to seeing strange things, but the last couple days of his life were repeatedly raising the bar for weirdness. He scanned the scene. Agrippa and Voss were obscured by the mob and Rohan had heard no more gunshots, but he heard curses and sometimes one, sometimes two sets of snarls.

"Shit. I'm out of bullets," Kamara half-whispered.

"Run back to the house. I can hold them," Rohan shouted.

Kamara shook her head. "Give me your gun and you fight them by hand. I can still help."

Rohan didn't have time to argue. He handed her the weapon and walked out to meet the first jumbie. *Dismemberment…I can do dismemberment,* he thought. A jumbie rushed up to him, its foul mouth agape. Rohan took the invitation. Flattening his palm he thrust his hand into the gnashing mouth, speared his fingers through the back of the creature's throat and tore out a section of its spine. The thing collapsed in a boneless heap, though it remained 'alive' from the neck up. A second and a third rushed him and he dispatched them in similar fashion. Kamara fired repeatedly, picking her shots calmly. Then Rohan heard a scream from the hut, he turned around and saw a group of jumbies attempting to enter. One was tearing a hole through the roof. Rohan knew the hut wouldn't provide shelter for very long.

"I've got the ones at the house." A gravelly voice spoke to him. Rohan turned around and barley recognized Voss. The man's hands had transformed to claws and his forearms were covered in gore up to the elbows. His eyes glowed like an animal's and his teeth had extended to fangs.

Agrippa was at his side, a jumbie's lower arm in his jaws. Both Voss and the dog sped toward the house. With Voss and Agrippa no longer running interference behind the jumbie ranks, the remaining creatures swarmed Rohan and Kamara. Rohan heard Kamara's gun click empty again, but he was busy with five of the creatures. Out of the corner of his eye he saw her grasp the gun by the barrel and hammer one of the creatures repeatedly between the eyes. He shouted for her to run. She was an ordinary human being, very brave, but she made of regular flesh and bone. She had no place in a fight with fifty jumbies.

A jumbie grabbed a handful of her hair from behind, Rohan screamed something wordless and leapt towards the creature. The beast pulled her close, bit into her where her neck met shoulder.

Kamara screamed. Blood ran down the front of her shirt. Rohan struggled to get to her but one of the creatures grabbed his hand and bit into it. A crippled jumbie ensnared his legs from below bringing him to his knees and began chewing on his ankle. He realized with horror that he was being eaten alive. A third and fourth jumbie piled on him. They were immensely strong, operating at the absolute limit of the structural integrity of the human bodies they had owned in their former life.

Kamara reached over her back and crushed the eyes of her assailant with her thumbs, but the jumbie would not release her. Rohan roared in anger and frustration, the pain inflicted by his multiple attackers approaching the realm of the unbearable.

Two more of the creatures approached Kamara. He called for Voss, but the bodyguard and the dog were in a pitched battle of their own. Tears of pain rolled down Kamara's face and blood soaked the entire front of her body. One of the creatures grabbed her throat in both of its hands and started squeezing. Rohan struggled to free himself, but it was like trying to swim while rolled in a carpet. The monster was choking the life out of Kamara, and he was going to have to watch her die, just like he had watched the deaths of Dorian, Isa, and Kimani.

Then with shocking abruptness the jumbies collapsed like puppets whose strings had been sliced. Rohan supposed that is exactly what had happened, their ties to the puppeteer had been cut.

Kamara fell to her knees, bleeding and wheezing. Rohan struggled from under the pile of dead weight and limped to her side. She was bleeding badly and a nasty hand shaped bruise had already formed around her throat. What would her law school classmates think? Rohan could see muscles twitching inside the wound on her shoulder and the front of her blood-soaked shirt clung to her body. She looked up to Rohan with bloodshot eyes and began laughing.

"Is this what you do every night, Ro?" Her laughter broke off with a wince and a cough.

"Oh this?" he said, gesturing to the piles of bodies. "This is a slow night for me, I usually fight greyborn, fresh from the Grey." He took off his shirt, balled it up and applied pressure to her wound.

She made a hissing noise through her teeth. "This shit hurts like hell. Am I going to become one of them now?"

A voice from behind spoke. "No, they are jumbies not zombies. Zombification is caused by a virus. These *mendo* are the work of obeah or voodoo." Rohan turned. A petite, beautiful woman walked up the path with a larger woman slung over her shoulder in a fireman's carry. Rohan recognized the larger woman as the mob leader who disappeared. But he did not immediately know who the younger woman was. Then he noticed the crucifix around her neck, fine silver in a woven pattern, Kat's crucifix.

"Kat…are you? Who…what are you?"

"Rohan Le Clerc, your great-great grandfather Kariega would say that you are as blind as an intestinal worm in the ass of an ox. You didn't think I was an ordinary old woman did you?"

Rohan recovered from his shock. "No of course not, but I also didn't think they offered such excellent anti-aging solutions in the mangrove swamps."

"I'm a soucouyant, Kariega knew that you would need my help someday and that day has come, so here I am, helping." She shifted the weight of the woman on her shoulder.

"Umm so you can just change your appearance."

"A little obeah goes a long way. After Kariega died, I had to wait for you at this specific location. I had no idea when you would come, only that you would come eventually and that it would be at sunset, so I had to be here every day, at least at sunset. At first I lived somewhere else…somewhere nicer and I came here every day at sunset. But then it was easier to simply buy the land and assume an identity. When you are ageless time doesn't really mean that much anymore and I couldn't very well sit here for the last hundred plus years looking like a young woman. People get suspicious and jealous when their neighbors do not age. Even in a slum like this."

"Wait for us? Didn't you send the boy to bring us here?"

"The boy has been following you off and on for five years, Rohan, ever since I pieced together what Kariega's visions meant. I had to wait until I could get all of you here at the same time even the damned dog."

"You could have just let me know in advance to come when I had assembled the appropriate team."

"Kariega's instructions were clear, neither me nor my agents could speak to you unless you initiated contact. I disobeyed him once. The results were... undesirable."

"But didn't Tarik initiate contact?" Rohan knew he was being difficult but he needed to make sense of at least some of the madness that had overtaken his life, and Kat seemed to be the one with answers.

"The boy grabbed your girlfriend's necklace and you initiated contact by chasing him."

"Seems like a really technical argument to me," Rohan replied dryly.

"Is she alive?" Kamara asked pointing with her chin to the woman slung over Kat's shoulder.

"Yes, she's alive, unconscious but alive. Rendering her unconscious severs the tie to the mendo. This one was using borrowed power. No practitioner of necromancy has been able to steer more than five jumbies simultaneously since Papa Niser and five was a stretch even for him. We need to know who her benefactor is." Kat patted the unconscious woman's broad rump. "But first we must attend to the wounded."

Rohan picked Kamara up like a child and held her against his chest. Kat led the way back to the hut, toting the large unconscious woman as easily as if she were a sack of down. Lisa was at the door her arms wrapped around Voss's right arm as if he was the trunk of a tree she had climbed to escape a pack of wolves below. She was shuddering but her lips were set in a hard line of resolve. In the small yard Tarik played fetch with Agrippa. The 'stick' was a jumbie's forearm.

Chapter 8

(1810)

Canst thou draw out leviathan with a hook? Or his tongue with a cord which thou lettest down? Canst thou put a hook into his nose? Or bore his jaw through with a thorn? Will he make many supplications unto thee? Will he speak soft words unto thee? Will he make a covenant with thee? Wilt thou take him for a servant forever? Canst thou fill his skin with barbed irons? Or his head with fish spears? Out of his nostrils goeth smoke, as out of a seething pot or cauldron. His breath kindleth coals, and a flame goeth out of his mouth. Lay thine hand upon him, remember the battle, do no more. – Excerpt from Job 41 King James Version.

Kariega Le Clerc awoke, ejected from sleep by the same nightmare that had driven him awake many nights before. Now that he was awake the countless small sensations of being alive slowly coalesced and reintroduced him to reality; the sheets beneath him, the whine of a mosquito close to his ear, his own rapid breathing, all mundane and reassuring.

He peered into the darkness next to him. Katharine's eyes stared back at him, unblinking and glowing faintly blue in the black of the room. She never stayed asleep through his nightmares. Kariega suspected that perhaps she never actually slept at all, at least not in the human sense. He was all but positive that she simply lay in his bed with her eyes shut, more to set him at ease than anything else.

It had been five years since the night they met. At first their relationship had been limited to her teaching him and the other members of the Order about soucouyant and everything she knew about creatures from the Grey. She shared a treasure trove of information, and, an avid student, Kariega documented it all in writing. When the Order hunted rogue greyborn this extra knowledge was worth its weight in unspilt blood.

Kariega was not quite sure how their relationship had evolved from what it started as to what it now was. Katharine represented everything that a man of his circumstances and cultural background eschewed in a companion. She was disquietingly opinionated, incorrigibly headstrong, blasphemously irreverent, and disobedient. She was also frettingly slender. Her skin color and speech pattern marked her as planter class and above it all, she was a soucouyant and not even a made soucouyant, she had been born this way and had never been human. From day one Katharine however, had proven her worth beyond that of a mere teacher.

A plantation without a master could not be kept secret. If it could, Kariega would simply have continued running the place as he had been doing for so many years while Maloney had perpetually vacillated between dysfunctionally inebriated and regretfully hung-over.

Maloney's death upon Katharine's fangs could only be concealed for so long. The plantation's few white employees, the drivers, and the journeymen who visited for seasonal repairs, could never be co-opted into a cover-up.

Kariega and the other founding members of the Order flirted with the idea of slaughtering every white man who came to the plantation but creating a pattern of vanishing Caucasians would be the surest way to squander this fortuitous turn of events. It was a boon that Maloney had been killed on a Saturday. The drivers would not return to work until Monday morning, giving Kariega and Katharine a full day to prepare an explanation that corroborated with the circumstances.

The slave drivers were a punctual bunch. On Monday morning the six of them arrived at the plantation well before sunrise, the last arriving within ten minutes of the first. They were surprised when Katharine met them at the outer gate dressed in the black of mourning. She introduced herself as William Maloney's estranged daughter who had sailed from France to visit her father only to find that he had died over the weekend. That the man had died in a fall down the stairs was plausible enough, drunkards often fell and occasionally such falls were fatal. However, the knitted brows of the six drivers conveyed that they were suspicious of the fact that Maloney had never mentioned having a bastard daughter in France and that Katharine's arrival coincided so closely with the planter's death. Nonetheless it was precisely this coincidence that allayed their apprehensions. No daughter who planned to murder a father would do so on the very weekend of her arrival.

Katharine assumed the administrative duties of the plantation and had announced that, in respect of the dead, there would be no work that day. The drivers returned to their homes and the slaves to the slave row.

Maloney's death still had to be reported to the local authorities, and they always investigated the deaths of planters whether they appeared to be accidental or not. Around noon a lone, bony, gnarled white man dressed in wrinkled, sweat stained khakis arrived. The white man's tough hide was so tanned that he almost appeared black. He dismounted his mule, adjusted his wide leather belt, and unholstered a long gun from its place in the saddle. Shouldering it he advanced toward the great house in a bow-legged saunter.

Katharine met the scowling sheriff with Kariega a silent presence at her elbow. She invited the man into the drawing room where Kariega served tea and Katharine served the story of a grieving daughter. The man listened then demanded to see the body. Katharine obliged and led him out to a shed where William Maloney was packed in salt and rapidly melting ice. It was a small blessing that Katharine had not killed the man in a more physically ruinous manner. Katharine had been able to cover the bite marks on his neck with makeup and the body's state of decomposition served to further conceal the small puncture wounds. They had however, to resort to snapping the man's neck so that it supported the story of a fatal fall.

The sheriff conducted a perfunctory evaluation of the body, all the while covering his nose with a handkerchief and muttering under his breath about pampered planters and their lethal drunkenness. He then asked if the man had left a will.

"His documents are all in a safety deposit box in London," she informed the official with an air of scorn that gave no doubt of what she thought of the idea that such an important document would be secure on the plantation. "I will present the documents in a month or two once they are delivered."

When the man left after commanding them to see to the burial rights immediately, Kariega and Katharine both breathed a sigh of relief. Within a few weeks they had very convincing forgeries of the ownership documents fabricated and presented to the local constabulary. Per the forgeries, ownership of the plantation fell to Maloney's daughter Katharine and Kariega was to share management of the plantation as a freed-man. Maloney's family had preceded him in death so there was no one to challenge the legitimacy of Katharine's inheritance.

In the beginning their relationship had been courteous and amicable. When they spoke, it was with politeness borne out of mutual need. Katharine was free from her bond to the Loa and Kariega needed Katharine to back up the tale of Maloney's death and to function as the European face of the plantation. Slowly however they realized that they were alone in the world save for each other. Kariega was a witch doctor, sold into servitude by order of his king. Even the other men with whom he had formed the Order never really understood him and eventually the other men chose to leave the plantation. Despite the advantages Katharine had provided, their discomfort over her true nature led them to follow the mandates of the Order in the way they saw fit.

Katharine was a reformed vampire who could never actually join the world of human beings but to whom the world of her own coven was closed. They were both caught in social limbo. Each evening discussion became successively more personal. Everyday each shared more about themselves. Many times, they conversed through the night, their discussions running the gamut from philosophical topics, to the technical aspects of plantation management, to the downright silly.

A deep, but unspoken bond developed and one evening Kariega was surprised to realize that he had become attracted to her, that perhaps she was not as unflatteringly slim and pale as he once thought and that her obstinate, irreverent qualities made for better conversation.

A hurricane was raging the first night she came to his quarters. The winds howled in a ferocious attempt to enter the great house through any crevice. Rain assaulted the slate roof with a sound like muffled drums. In the fields the tall stalks of sugarcane whipped the low night sky, their frenzied lashings occasionally silhouetted against the undulating horizon by violent flashes of lightning.

Kariega had been asleep when her presence woke him. Even in the pitch darkness and with his back to the door he knew it was Katharine. Maybe it was the faint smell unique to her or maybe his subconscious mind recognized the sound of her breathing. He turned over and all he could see was the dim blue glow her eyes emitted, visible only in pitch darkness.

She stood at the door waiting, for what he did not know. He wondered how long she had been there. He asked her what she wanted, she responded with silence. He got out of bed and went to her. He stood in front of her and still she said nothing.

"Are you afraid of the storm?" he had asked simply to break the silence. He knew the woman to be fearless.

"Two hundred-year-old soucouyant are afraid of nothing," she responded.

They stood facing each other in the darkness, each reluctant to be the first to cross a boundary that could not be uncrossed. Kariega took her by the hand, and she stepped forward, pressing herself against him. She was naked, which was not out of the ordinary. Kariega had seen her unclothed many times before. For the first time however, his body reacted to her nakedness.

He took hold of her slender waist in both hands and kissed her. Her body was warm. She returned his kisses hungrily. They never made it back to the bed. The storm barely drowned out the sounds of their passion.

In the morning she was not beside him having left before he awoke. They did not speak of what had happened, and went about their daily routines, running the plantation. That night however, she returned and every night after that but always she left before he awoke.

After about a month of this pattern, Kariega confronted her.

"Why is it that you never stay the night? Do I snore?"

She thought for a moment then responded. "You snore like a sawmill, but that is not why I do not stay. Before this," She said, fingering the crucifix. "I always returned to the coven's lair after a night drinking blood. I think leaving is just instinct."

He replied, "Well, you do not drink blood anymore. I am your coven and this room is your lair."

Now when his nightmares woke him to a world silent but for the sound of crickets chirping, she was there.

That night he felt her get out of bed. She stoked an oil lamp, left the room and returned with a warm pot of chamomile tea. She poured two cups and sweetened them with honey.

"Same dream?" she asked tying a white silk robe about her body in a rare concession to sartorial proprieties.

"Yes," he responded. Kariega's smooth muscular torso gleamed in the lamp light with a thin sheen of sweat. "The black weight bearing down on us—you me, this house—impossibly massive impossibly heavy, malevolent and omnipresent."

"What do you make of it?"

"I don't know. A warning, perhaps? A foretelling of evils to come?"

"Do you fear it?"

"It does not inspire fear so much as despair. In the dream we are powerless before it."

"Is there any hope?"

"If there is any hope it lies in a man who has suffered a great loss, a woman who is his companion, a child and you. Sometimes there are others, an animal, some sort of wolf or dog maybe. Another woman and another man are sometimes in the dreams. But the first four are the vital components. Without them all is lost."

"When will the darkness come?"

"I do not know, could be a day, it could be many years from now."

This exchange had been repeated many times before. The nightmare would wake Kariega abruptly. Once awake he would find that Katharine was already awake and the conversation that followed was always the same. The repetition was their way of controlling something that was otherwise mystical and outside their control.

"Maybe it is just an ordinary nightmare," she said, attempting to assuage his discomforts, and to this Kariega smiled. Katharine extinguished the oil lamp and they both lay awake in bed, Katharine's head on Kariega's chest, his arms around her shoulders.

"Kariega," Katharine began. "There is something I must tell you."

"There is something I must tell you too," Kariega said. There was a pause as each waited for the other to speak first. Kariega broke the silence. "I have to travel back to Africa to consult someone who may understand the dreams."

Katharine said nothing, but Kariega felt her body grow warm then hot. Then her flesh became so hot that it was too painful to allow her to continue lying against him. He pushed her away.

"What's the matter, Katharine?"

"What is the matter? What is the matter? Do you really have to ask Kariega Le Clerc?" She spoke in an angry hush, and a white flame, a vestige of her heritage leapt alive in her eyes. "You are going to travel back to your village, back to the place from whence you were banished? You would abandon everything we have built here? And for what, a dream that may or may not come to fruition for decades, centuries even? You yourself said so." Katharine paused briefly before relaunching her tirade. "And how do you propose to travel to Africa? In the hold of a slave ship? Have you forgotten that you are African? Can you even find your damned village?" She allowed her voice to often. "We are happy here. Whatever evil the dream portents we can face the threat together."

Kariega felt waves of heat radiating from her. His own sweat began dampening the sheets below him.

"Katharine be still, the dream is of dire importance, I know that much. I need a better understanding of its meaning and the only person who will know is my teacher in the village. I will be back eventually."

His latest words only enraged her further. "Kariega, the sail to Africa is, in the best of times, three months long and fraught with danger. Your tribe was nomadic, it may take months or even years to track down your teacher and that is assuming he is even still alive. Your magic saved me but it also made me alone, one of a kind, a soucouyant without a coven, unknown to any of her kind. Then you befriended me, accepted me for what I am. I will not lose my only friend to some flight of folly."

"Katharine, this is something I have to do. The fate of man may rest with understanding the threat that is coming."

The bed suddenly erupted into flames and the curtains followed. Kariega rolled off the bed frantically beating at his now-ignited trouser legs. Katharine sat in the center of the bed, her silk robe burning but her flesh remaining untouched.

"Would you abandon me Kariega? Would you abandon your seed that grows within me?" With that Katharine tore the crucifix from about her neck and hurled it at Kariega. Her body now a ball of flame, she leapt off the bed and flew out the window. The flames extinguished completely upon her exit.

Kariega was at once shocked and mortified. *Katharine was pregnant?* And now she had flown off without her ward. Her coven would become instantly aware of her presence in the world they would also know that she had been hidden from them, that she had abandoned them. Such was the nature of the bond between soucouyant of the same coven. They would come for her, to punish and perhaps worse.

Kariega fled the house in pursuit of the woman he loved. On his way out he grabbed a cutlass and looped the lanyard cross-ways over his shoulder so that the scabbard fell at his side. He dashed headlong to the stable and leapt upon his horse without taking the time to saddle Shepherd, his tall black stallion. Into the night he plunged. Kariega knew where she would go, an old haunt, one of the places where she used to hide her skin when she had been a soucouyant. He hoped to convince her to don the ward before the coven found her.

The horse galloped through the night with Kariega crouched low over its withers, fistfuls of mane in his sweat slicked palms. Branches stung his chest, tall grasses whipped against his calves and bare ankles. The horse began to lather beneath him, but he did not ease the pace. When he got to the derelict great house, he leapt from Shepherd's back before the horse had come to a complete stop.

Drawing his machete, he sprinted across the overgrown yard and up the steps. The doors were boarded shut with planks of sun-bleached wood which he swiftly split with the blade. Shouldering the door, he entered.

Inside, the house was dark and silent as a tomb. The floorboards groaned beneath his bare feet and with every step he left footprints in a previously undisturbed layer of ancient dust. He strained his ears for sounds but heard nothing. *Perhaps she had not come here,* he thought.

Slowly Kariega made his way down the long dark hallway. The hallway eventually opened to a large, high ceilinged circular room. At the base of the double staircase foyer, he found Katharine. Bound tightly atop a large table, she was unconscious and bleeding from bite marks all over her body. The tatters of her burned nightgown were bloody. Kariega approached cautiously; scanning the ceiling and the upper floors and began slicing through the ropes. When she was freed he tied the crucifix around her throat and threw her over his shoulder.

Turning around to make his way back down the hall and out of the house he found his way blocked by three women. They stood silent, gaunt, and pale in the moonlight that entered through holes in the high ceiling. It was obvious who they were, Katharine's coven. Their lower jaws were smeared with her blood.

"Let me pass. You have drunk her nearly dead. She has been sufficiently punished," Kariega said.

"Magician, do you dare instruct us on how to administer the matters of our coven?" said the woman on the right. "We will be the final arbiters of the sufficiency of her correction. Now set her down and we may allow you to crawl out of this place."

Kariega set Katharine down gently and stood before the women, who now floated a foot above the rotted floorboards, the flames of their soucouyant birthright a dim mesmerizing halo around their bodies. They began circling Kariega and Katharine, taunting him.

"The child in her belly is an insult to us. We will see that it is scraped out of her," one of the women shrieked.

Kariega cringed. He marshaled his power and whispered, "Shepherd, my guardian, come."

None of the three women saw the massive lion enter the room behind them. The creature that used to be Kariega's horse sprang onto the back of the nearest woman and bit into her skull with a crunch. Kariega used the moment of surprise to cut into the face of the second woman with his machete.

Shepherd sprang at the third soucouyant. The woman moved like lightning. She tore a section of rotted stair rail and hurled it at the airborne cat. The make-shift spear entered the creature's chest with a wet sound and the immense cat bellowed in agony. The wound was mortal but the lion fought still, falling on and pinning the woman to the ground with its bulk. Kariega was engaged in a pitched battle with the soucouyant he had cut. He was already bleeding in several places where her sharp talons had slashed him. Shallow cuts crisscrossed his arms and chest.

It required the full extent of his skill and strength to fend her off. Kariega heard a noise from behind and half turned just in time to see the other living soucouyant yank the section of railing out of the dying lion and hurl it toward him. There was nothing he could do, she was too fast. Pain like fire bloomed in his body as the banister pierced his back and erupted through his chest.

Kariega crumpled to the floor and knew he was about to die. But perhaps there was a chance that he could secure the life of his love and the offspring she carried. He crawled towards the unconscious Katharine. The two remaining soucouyant mocked him as he inched toward her, leaving a trail of blood as he went.

He grabbed hold of Katharine's foot and hauled himself forward so that he could press his lips to the limb, it was cold and clammy, but he needed to be in contact with her bare skin for this to work. Kariega could feel his strength bleeding out of him through the hole in his chest. He whispered against the pale skin of the sole of Katharine's foot.

"A final gift, to you from me,

The Strength to bind,

The Eye to see

To you a gift do I bestow,

A spear to pierce…

...Our foes below
I gift the strength, which once was mine
My power wielded
Is now thine."

Kariega's eyes closed slowly. Katharine's eyes shot open and with her awakening came knowing. She understood Kariega intimately, his fears, his joys, his love for her. It was an extreme sort of empathy, as if the man had lived his entire life inside her head.

She inherited his memories, his knowledge of the arcane, and his strength in witchcraft. She knew what he had done and she knew he was dead. She knew everything. Sorrow welled up in her chest. She knew it was her temper that had led to the death of her only friend and lover, the father of her unborn offspring.

The two remaining soucouyant stood above her, oblivious to the conference of power that had occurred. Katharine envisioned them bursting into flames and they obliged by exploding into twin pillars of white fire which, unlike their own soucouyant fires, burned their flesh.

They screamed and begged for mercy. Katharine gave them none. Though the fires burned fiercely it took more than an hour for the women to go silent. Katharine watched, sitting on the floor, with her hand on Kariega's chest. When the women had been burned to ash she broke up floorboards with her bare hands and erected a pyre for Kariega right in the center of the room. She then climbed up to the roof and opened large hole in the ceiling above the pyre so that the heavens might bear witness to the passage of a great man.

When the preparations were done she laid Kariega and his lion next to each other on the pyre and called forth fire. Flames rose from the center of the pyre and quickly consumed the entire thing. Katharine stood watch, soot stained tears rolling down her face. She stayed until the fire burned out and the embers cooled. It was hard to leave the place, but eventually she had to go. She left the body of the soucouyant Shepherd had killed to rot where it fell, but she took the stake that had pierced Kariega's body.

Four months later Katharine was in the African bush searching for Kariega's mentor and teacher. It took her another six months to track the man down and when she finally found him, she stayed an additional year with the ancient little witchdoctor, learning from him and sharing her own knowledge. While there she slowed her gestation as soucouyant can, protecting her child in her belly until she returned from her journey

When she returned to Trinidad, she brought with her Kariega's thirteen-year-old son, Onyeka, a son Kariega had fathered a mere month before his exile and whom he had not known had existed. The boy had been harshly treated. As a result of his father's exile and the subsequent death of the entire royal family, Onyeka and his mother had been forced to dwell on the fringes of village society, eking out a living. Eventually his mother had died, broken under the weight of cumulative hardships.

Katharine's return was celebrated by the entire plantation and Kariega's first son was introduced to the Order The four original Ordermen disdained interacting with Katherine, but they recognized that the boy, unlike Kariega, could be groomed in their image as the Order's first initiate. Two years later Katharine gave birth to a boy. The child was born with a birthmark that looked like a ring of ravens in flight around his left wrist. Katharine named the child Tarik and from the very beginning the boy was special, the son of a reformed soucouyant and a dead obeah man.

Chapter 9

'78 was the year of the woman…
they give the whole of 79' to the children
but brother man Black Stalin say beware
'81 in Trinidad is Vampire year
          —Excerpt from Vampire Year a Calypso by Stalin

Kamara lay semi-upright in a hammock clad only in her bra and her skirt. Her torn and bloody blouse was beyond salvage and had been discarded.

Kat had tended to her wounds with the deftness of a surgeon, cleaning the bites then pouring on a thick white liquid that smelled like camphor and burned like molten gold. After that she had soaked a clean cloth in a red scentless liquid and commanded Kamara to hold the cloth to the wound. The pain of the first treatment subsided as soon as the cloth touched her shoulder. Within moments Kamara felt vastly better. She peeked under the cloth and saw that the ragged bite marks were already half their original size.

Kamara followed Kat around the room with her eyes. When the soucouyant had seen to all the wounded she went to the section of the hut's wall dedicated to insects and selected a jar filled with squirming larvae. One of the dead jumbies lay with the upper half of its body across the threshold of the doorway, its desiccated eyes frozen in a surly, sightless glare. Kat walked up to the body, turned it on to its back, and poured some of the larvae from the bottle into the mouth of the cadaver.

Everyone in the hut gasped when the corpse deflated like a balloon as the voracious larvae went to work. The creatures ate their way from the inside out, devouring everything. Within ten minutes all that was left were twenty fat pupae cocooned in hard brown casings lying on the porch. Kat scooped these up into a separate jar which she then set on her insect wall.

"What the hell are those things?" Voss said breaking the silence and gesturing to the jar full of larvae.

"Larvae from scarab beetles found in the Grey," Kat replied. Voss nodded as if he understood completely. Kat then called to Tarik, handed him the jar of larvae, and told him to see to the rest of the corpses in the yard and collect the pupae when they were done feeding.

Kamara observed the boy as he left the house with Agrippa at his heels. The child was fearless, observant, and never hesitated to obey Kat's instructions. Kamara mused that his life must be quite odd for him to maintain such gravitas under the current circumstances.

Rohan approached her and laid a hand on the nape of her neck. "Are you all right?" he asked in a low voice, concern creasing his forehead.

"I liked that blouse, now it's covered with mendo spit," Kamara replied, imitating Rohan's customary flippancy and grinning. Rohan however would not rise to the bait.

"You can't continue coming along on these excursions" he replied gravely.

"Firstly, you were the one who insisted that we all come rather than splitting up, and secondly, why would I want to miss all this excitement? Besides no one twisted your arm and made you tell me all the company secrets, Rohan." She smiled and he smiled back.

Company secrets. Kamara thought back to when she had met Rohan two years earlier. At the time she was a first-year law student at the University of the West Indies Hugh Wooding School. After a late night of studying she was heading toward the car park when a large shape erupted from the shadows around the paved walkway, tackled her, and pinned her to the ground.

Her first thought was that it was a large dog but even in the darkness she could tell that it wore clothes. She struggled hard, screaming for help, but its grip was like a metal vise. Its maw descended toward her face as she strained backward to delay the inevitable. Then, just when all seemed lost, someone pulled the creature off her. Both the beast and her rescuer tumbled into a dense Crown of Thorns hedge. She could not see the scuffle, but from what she could hear it was intense and violent. Then there was quiet and a dreadlocked young man picked his way out of the thorny shrubbery.

He wore a wry smile when he said, "Those stray dogs are really becoming a problem on campus."

A lawyer in training, Kamara prided herself on her ability to spot a lie. "That was not a dog," she replied.

"It was a dog." The stranger responded dismissively, but Kamara would not be put off.

"It held me down as if it had hands. I would believe that it was an ape of some sort before I believe it was a dog. Tell me what it was."

"Fine, it was an escaped baboon. Why do you think I know any better than you do? It is very dark in that hedge. Besides whatever it was it's gone now. I can walk you to your car to make sure no more baboons or dogs attack you."

On the walk back to the car Kamara saw that the man's arms were covered in scratches from the thorny bush. Then she noticed that he was dripping a trail of blood from a gash along his ribs.

"The baboon-dog bit you and it looks bad, let me see it." Kamara said with genuine concern. The stranger glanced at the tear in his shirt and flesh as if he had not felt the wound before.

"I'll be fine, I have been bitten by many dogs. Once I see you to your car I'll take care of myself."

Kamara intuitively knew something was different about the man, and curiosity about the truth of the encounter ate at her, but she decided not to press him further. When they got to the car, she asked for his name, he hesitated a moment before responding. "Rohan Le Clerc," he said.

Then she ventured hers without waiting for him to ask. As they were about to part ways, she invited him to lunch as a way of saying thanks and he declined politely. She insisted and he accepted her invitation after the fifth repetition. She got into her car, drove around the block, parked, got out, and took another route on foot back to the scene of the attack. From a bush she watched as Rohan and four other men dismembered and buried the corpse of a man-sized wolfish creature clad in the ragged remains of trousers and a shirt that looked like no animal she had ever seen. Kamara's heart pounded. When she met Rohan at lunch few days later, she cut to the chase.

"Your baboon-dog was wearing trousers?"

Rohan grinned. "You're not very good at sneaking, Kamara. We knew you were hiding in the bushes."

"You're not afraid that I will tell someone what I saw?"

"Tell someone what exactly? Do you know what you saw?"

"I think it was a lagahoo," she replied matter-of-factly using the name of a creature from stories her grandmother used to tell her. She studied his face for a reaction. Rohan had schooled his expression quickly, but the brief and slight widening of his eyes told her all she needed to know. He laughed off her suggestion.

"A law student should know better. Lagahoo are old wives' tale. It was nothing but a stray dog, dressed up maybe, as a prank."

"You took great pains to cut it up and bury it, Rohan. Just tell me the truth." Kamara had been raised single handedly by her mother, a stern, hard-working woman who had taught her to take no bullshit, particularly from men.

Rohan looked into her eyes for a moment, "Truth is a cold, dark, lonely mountaintop. The valley of lies is comforting, verdant, and warm."

"Where is that quote from?" she asked.

"My grandfather," he replied.

Kamara felt like she was on the edge of a precipice. The reality she believed in would not survive a leap off the edge. The pit of her stomach felt empty and queasy. She could turn back now and return to the warm comforting valley, or she could press onward, the reward for which might be knowledge of a frightening and alien world fundamentally and danger-ously different from the one she knew. "I want to know the truth," she replied.

Rohan studied her for a moment and then he told her everything. He told her about the Grey the Absolute and the Ether, about lagahoo and soucouyant and the Watchers Guild and the three houses. He told her about blood magic and about astral travel, his words quickening and his enthusiasm rising as if the telling was a catharsis. When he was done, he asked her if she believed. Strangely enough she found that she did believe what he had told her.

"I have never told a valley dweller the truth, and I'm not quite sure why I shared these ancient secrets with you. By any rate you will probably be placed on psychiatric evaluation if you ever told anyone else, and now you'll probably jump at every other shadow." She knew he was right.

"Not all of the creatures are out to get you. They are like men, some are good, some are bad. The main difference is, instead of guns and knives the bad ones use fangs, claws, and magic. The majority walk around among us passing for human to all but the best-trained eyes. A couple of your girlfriends might be soucouyant." He grinned and she shuddered.

They began to see each other on a regular basis. Eventually she brought him home to meet her mother and he brought her to Stone House to meet Isa, Kimani, and Dorian. Now two years later, he was standing there with a concerned look on his face, probably regretting inviting her up to the summit of Mount Truth.

***

By now all the wounded had been tended to and attentions gradually refocused on the obeah woman who still lay unconscious on the floor. Kat selected a small figurine from her wall of shelves, a carving of an elephant seated on its haunches. The carving was fashioned from a creamy brown material that could only be very old ivory. It was small, and would easily fit atop the cap of a soda bottle. The features of the carving were worn smooth as if it had been handled for generations.

Kat held the figure to her lips and whispered something inaudible. Then she placed the elephant carving upon the chest of the prostrate woman, right between her mountainous breasts. Kat then knelt close to the woman and spoke some words into her ear. The woman's eyes shot open and she screamed as she attempted to sit upright. The tiny elephant carving however, had apparently taken on some of the weight of its living counterpart because the woman could not budge.

She gasped for breath and attempted to move the carving from her chest. It was impossible, she pried at it with both hands yet it did not move an inch. The candle light of the room was reflected in a thousand beads of sweat that formed on the woman's face. Her breath escaped in gasps and gooseflesh pimpled her arms and neck. Kamara was unsettled by the sight of the woman, struggling beneath what should have been an insignificant weight.

Kat sat cross legged on the floor next to the woman and allowed the woman to squirm and writhe beneath the burden until she gave up.

"A lifetime ago someone told me a story about a hermit witch-doctor whose best friend was a wild bull elephant known as 'The Mountain that walks.' The witch doctor had met this elephant while gathering herbs for his medicines. The elephant had fallen into a hunter's forgotten pit snare and had been pierced through with bamboo stakes. The doctor removed the stakes from the beast's body then, using his potions, nursed and fed the elephant back to health. The elephant regained its strength but was still trapped at the bottom of the hole. The hermit then slowly filled the pit with sand thus raising the bottom of the pit so that the elephant could eventually walk out. From that day on the elephant and the hermit were inseparable. When the hermit died, the elephant could not be consoled. The creature sat vigil by his master's grave until it too died.

"After the elephant died, another witch doctor carved the massive tusks into several items and sold them. In the end he was left with one oddly shaped piece of ivory that he carved into a small elephant. It is said that if you whispered the name of the Mountain to the carving, the spirit of the Mountain gradually fills the carving making it heavier and heavier by degrees as the essence of the mighty creature returns to sit vigil at his master's grave. I have never tested the truth of this but so far it looks like the myth might hold water." Kat spoke like a tenured history professor who did not really care if her students passed or failed the course.

The trapped woman took a laborious rattling breath. Her gaze darted wildly around the room. Kamara focused on the tiny carving looking for signs that an elephant's ghost might be returning to live in it, but the carving looked as innocuous as ever even as the woman's breathing grew ever more strained. Kat continued speaking. "I want the name of the obeah man who lent you the power to raise the jumbies."

"I...I...I can't give his name." The woman spoke in a voice that was somewhere between a wail and a shriek.

"Well then you will be crushed to death. Slowly," Kat said matter-of-factly.

"Please...don't...let...." The woman's voice trailed off in a wheeze. Kamara saw the woman's eyes roll back into her head as she fell unconscious. Kat spoke again, "Mountain, your master is not here."

Kamara imagined she heard the faint trumpet of an elephant. The prone woman gasped awake and immediately swatted the elephant carving off her chest. She rolled over onto all fours and, not willing to squander the time it would take to rise to her feet, began crawling frantically toward the doorway. Kat's arm shot out in a motion that Kamara's eyes could not follow and caught the woman's retreating ankle. The woman continued attempting to claw her way forward in raw fear.

"Voss, bind her."

Voss stepped forward and pulled the woman's arms behind her back, binding her with a bit of cord he found somewhere. He then did the same to her ankles. His movements were so deft that Kamara wondered how often he tied up struggling people. When the woman was bound he deposited her next to Kat who remained sitting cross-legged on the floor.

"This little hovel is filled with many things like the elephant, things that hold nasty surprises. Some of them I have tested, others I would not try because no test subject deserved the potential results. I am, however, in an experimental mood tonight. Your stubbornness makes me feel like dipping into a bag of tricks, the contents of which make even me shiver."

Kamara had no doubt Kat meant what she said. The woman spoke in an unemotional, detached tone that lacked compassion. During her first year as a law student, Kamara's class had a chance to sit on a live interview with a convicted serial killer, a psychopath who had butchered more than twelve people. He had spoken about his crime with a similar detachment that convinced listeners that his confession was true and that if he had to do it all over he wouldn't change a thing. It appeared that the woman was also convinced by Kat's words as she started sobbing.

"I-I-really can't." She heaved between wails.

Kat pondered a moment then spoke. "Tarik, bring me the jar of red powder on the top shelf, be careful not to drop it."

Tarik brought the large jar forward and Kat undid the metal lid. It popped and hissed as if it had been vacuum-sealed. Kat immediately screwed the lid back on the jar but the contents had already congealed into an amorphous black mass like a living pool of oil flecked with iridescent streaks of grey. The globular creature began thrashing against the sides of the glass, desperate to get out. The sight filled Kamara with revulsion. In her peripheral vision she saw Lisa make the sign of the cross. Voss cursed under his breath.

"I want his name or I will pour the contents of this jar into your ear and make a note of what happens."

The woman's eyes were wide with fright, but she held her tongue.

"Voss, hold her in place," Kat said. Kamara noted that Voss hesitated for a moment before stepping forward and she wondered if he was beginning to feel sorry for their captive just as she was. Nonetheless, he knelt next to the woman and pressed her shoulders to the floor. Kat moved forward with the jar. Kamara felt the increasing tension in the room. Rohan was silent, but his lips were pressed in a tight line. Lisa's eyes were squeezed shut and her face turned away. Agrippa looked on, points of light reflected in his eyes.

"Cassan Davilmar," the woman blurted. "I got the power from Cassan Davilmar, but he is a middle man, not the source and I do not know who the source is."

"You are speaking the truth," Kat said with certainty. "Tell me what you know about this Cassan."

The woman's eyes flicked to the jar, with its malevolent, unnamed contents and she shuddered. "I woke up one morning and there was a letter for me, telling me that I was to go meet Cassan."

"And you always follow the instructions of mysterious letters?" Kat asked with exaggerated incredulity.

"The letter was written on a piece of leather." the woman said, pausing as if that was all the explanation that was necessary.

"And you always follow the instructions of mysterious letters that are written on leather?" The sarcasm in Kat's tone was more biting than before. Something about the nature of the letter had changed her mood for the worse.

"Soucouyant, you know what sort of letter it was. Don't pretend," the woman said.

"If you truly want me to extrapolate meanings from your hints, then perhaps I can come to my own conclusions, in which case you will be useless and we can just have you drink this jar of malice," Kat said with a grin but with a look in her eyes that mirrored the rage of the bubbling contents of the jar, thrashing around in search of an exit.

"The letter that came to me was writ on a man's skin, and to answer your next question, I know it was a man's skin because it was the skin off the face of some poor soul, complete with ears and eye holes."

"Written in a glyph?" Kat said.

"Yes, the Unspoken language," the woman replied.

"I'm surprised that anyone in this generation of weekend wiccans even knows what it is, let alone can translate the black magic of the Unspoken's glyphs," Kat said with a thoughtful look on her face.

"I was taught the required magiks by my grandmother."

"The nature of this communication did not unnerve you?"

"To a necromancer, there is no message more urgent or important than one written on dead human flesh in the Unspoken tongue."

There was a pause, then Kat said, "The note instructed you to meet with Cassan Davilmar?"

"When I performed the required magic, the face spoke the instructions that were written upon it."

"Well…?"

"The face told me to go to the Kings and Commoners night club. Cassan met me there. The face also told me that I should eliminate you once I had seen Cassan."

Kamara knew about the Kings and Commoners. It was an exclusive nightclub in Cascade, the lines to get in usually stretched around the block. Though it was one building, Kings and Commoners was two clubs in one.

There was a main floor usually flanked by people in lines waiting to get in. The second area was for private members or invited guests.

"We should pay this Cassan a visit," Voss growled.

"You can try, but we met in the Kings section of the Kings and Commoners. It is impossible to enter unless accompanied by a member."

Kat chuckled, "We will figure something out. Did Cassan mention anything else, a name, did he let anything slip?"

To Kamara's surprise the woman looked thoughtful, as if she was genuinely searching her memory of the night for the answer.

"One of the bodyguards muttered something while I was there, a name... he said...he said..."

Kamara exhaled sharply in surprise as a freezing cold descended on the hut. The woman paused mid-sentence. Her breath crystallized into a visible mist and gooseflesh pimpled her exposed skin. The others in the room were also exhaling puffs of mist as if winter had suddenly come to the Caribbean. The woman on the floor whimpered, "Ah talk too much, he find me."

"It appears that he has," Kat said.

Everyone in the hut slowly backed away from the woman in anticipation of the strangeness that must follow the sudden, arctic cold. They did not have to wait long. The only light in the room was the candle and the shadows cast by the candle flickered and danced in response to the movements of the flame. The woman's shadow however, displayed far more initiative as it assumed a life beyond the will of the candle-light, rose up, and attacked her.

The shadow wrapped sooty black hands around the bound woman's throat and began to throttle her. Kamara, Rohan, and the others in the room stared in frozen shock as the woman's eyes bulged and she began to gag. To the woman's credit, she raised a valiant effort, at least as valiant as she could whilst being bound hand and foot. Her heels drummed against the floor, her thick body twisted and heaved.

Rohan was the first to react. He snatched the wooden bucket Voss had used to wash himself and hurled it at the shadow. The bucket passed right through the specter and clattered against the wall on the opposite side of the room.

Voss moved toward the murderous shadow as if to grab it.

"Are you insane?" Kat and Lisa hissed simultaneously. The intensity of their cries halted his progress towards the bizarre scene.

Kat continued, "It is a manifestation of the power she borrowed. A booby trap meant to tie up a loose end. Its focus will be exclusive to her if no one interferes."

"So we're just going to let it kill her?" Lisa asked, as the woman's breathing petered out to a gurgle.

"No," Kat responded, and with that she uncorked the jar containing the angry, oily nightmare soup and flung the entire thing at the shadow.

Unlike the bucket, the jar shattered on contact with the Shadow's head. The broken pieces of the jar continued through the shadow, but the amorphous black mass clung on, expanded, and enveloped the shadow's face like a snake attempting to swallow a meal that might in time prove to be too large.

A violent struggle erupted. The shadow released the obeah woman and used its hands to pry the thing from the jar off its head. The thing in turn adhered to the shadow's face so fiercely that Kamara suspected it was indeed quite hungry and considered living shadows a particularly rare delicacy.

An eerie, keening wail erupted and Kamara did not know whether it was a wail of agony or triumph nor did she know which of the struggling anomalies was sounding it. The shadow fell to the floor with the Jar thing still clinging to its face. The matte black of the Shadow's head was visible inside the stormy, translucence of the thing's body, enveloped like a hapless shrimp inside the bell of a jellyfish. The Shadow continued to try to pry its attacker off, but it was a fruitless struggle and soon the Shadow's arms went limp and the wailing stopped.

Something even more disturbing began to happen. The shadow, once the silhouette of the bosomy obeah woman, began to emaciate, growing thinner and thinner until it looked as if it had been cast by a desiccated ca-daver. The blob then detached itself, and lay on the floor, its once stormy surface now looking like a dark lake, reflecting clouds passing slowly in a night sky above. It did not appear any larger as a result of its feast, but Kamara interpreted a decidedly satiated aura from the way it lay peacefully.

"Pick it up, Kamara," Kat commanded.

Kamara jumped. "You're kidding," she responded in concert with Rohan, who took two steps toward Kat.

"Trust me Kamara," Kat said, ignoring Rohan's angst.

Kamara walked over to the fallen bucket and took it up. She intended to toe the shadow-eating mass into the bucket to spare herself from handling it directly.

"No," Kat said. "Pick it up with your bare hands."

"Are you insane?" Rohan said between clenched teeth glaring at Kat.

"Have a little faith, Le Clerc."

Kamara's breath caught in her chest, but she moved slowly toward the resting blob. She was forced to step over both the unconscious woman and the dead Shadow. As she stepped over the shadow the slight breeze of her passage caused it to dissolve into a pile of brittle black ash like that from a stack of burnt newspaper. Voss had a firm grip on Rohan's arm. She sensed everyone in the room was holding their breath as she advanced.

She bent over and picked up the jar's contents. The thing was warm and pulsed at intervals as if it was breathing. She looked at Kat. "What is…."

Before she could finish her question, the thing enveloped her hand suddenly just like it had done to the shadow's head. Kamara shouted in surprise. A hot pain shot up her arm. She was barely aware of anything else in the room except the pain, but she saw Rohan break free of Voss' grasp and charge toward her. Kat grabbed him by the back of his collar as he bounded past her.

"Get it off me," Kamara shouted.

"What the hell is this, Kat," Rohan bellowed as he struggled in the iron grip of the soucouyant who now held him in a bear hug to prevent him from going to Kamara's aid.

"Trust me," Kat said.

The sudden, sharp pain subsided gradually and was again replaced by a sensation as if she had stuck her hand in a vat of warm gelatin.

"Hold your hand over the bucket," Kat instructed.

Kamara did as she was told. The black mass slid off and fell into the wooden bucket with a slosh. Kamara inspected her hand expecting to see burnt flesh. Instead, thirteen small elephants, each the size of a Trinidadian ten-cent coin marched a serpentine path from her middle knuckle to just above her wrist joint. Each elephant grasped the tail of the one ahead of it with its trunk. The images had a silvery black sheen, somewhat like the surface of the thing that had made the marks, and just like Rohan's tattoos. She realized with shock that the elephants were Orderman's markings.

"You marked me for the Order?" Kamara asked.

"You fight jumbies, don't you" Kat stated as if that was a full answer.

"You could have warned us first," Rohan said as Kat released him and he rushed over to inspect Kamara's markings. "The process could have killed her, and I have never seen anyone marked in that manner, by a… whatever that thing is."

"Sorry, I have been a hermit for too long and I forget my manners from time to time. Besides I had a gut feeling she would survive the process." Kat smiled broadly. "Also, there are many things you have not seen in your short life Rohan Le Clerc, it does not mean they are necessarily bad."

"A gut feeling? You exposed her to a potentially fatal process based on a gut feeling?" Rohan was incredulous.

"I have a very accurate gut." The soucouyant smiled and shrugged.

Kamara noticed she could now see the others in the hut a little more clearly. She could also hear better, as if her ears had been partially stopped up all her life and the stoppage had suddenly been cleared. She suddenly felt exhausted.

"What are we going to do with those?" Lisa yawned, collectively motioning to the pile of ash left by the shadow and the still unconscious obeah woman who the group was still reluctant to approach.

"I have a couple ideas. But she will not pose a problem," Kat replied. "It is 2 a.m. My advice to you all is to go back to Stone and get some rest. I will come to you after sunset and we will decide how to proceed."

"Are you going to explain to us what just happened?" Lisa asked with another yawn.

"Later perhaps," Kat replied.

On the way back to the car Kamara leaned heavily on Rohan, who would have carried her save the fact that he too was exhausted. Voss took the wheel and they all piled in. Kamara inspected her new tattoos. Rohan had told her that different marks conferred different gifts, and she wondered what powers hers would impart. She would ask Rohan what he thought later, or maybe Kat would explain when she came by. Kamara closed her eyes. She felt happy to be alive, but she was not sure she could cope with many more nights like this.

Chapter 10

He had died and gone to hell. This is what Clarence concluded after what seemed like an eternity suspended in the cold, dank, foul room. Pain danced through his body every time he took a breath. His only companion was the woman, except that now she was something more, some sort of monster or demon. She spoke to him, sometimes in the voice of the woman, shrill, breathless and scared, but more often in sibilant gravelly tones. That she was now a demon made sense as they were in hell.

Clarence had no way of tracking the passage of time. No natural light entered the room. No sentry came to feed him or to give him water. Water, that was it, he had to have been down here less than three days or he would have died of dehydration, unless of course this was hell, then he would be able to hang here indefinitely, with his thirst increasing forever but never reaching the crescendo that would usher in his death.

In time the pain, the thirst, and the terror nullified each other, and he passed into a fitful sleep. He awoke with a jerk when light entered the room briefly as a door groaned open. Clarence was suspended with his back to the door, so he could not see who had entered. The door closed again allowing the blackness to reclaim its dominion and impose itself twice as strongly as before.

Someone struck a match then lit a candle. Clarence began to tremble involuntarily. This series of events was similar to those that preceded the cell mate's transformation. She let out a gravelly chuckle and spoke in a voice that sounded as if she had swallowed broken glass. "It's your turn, Clarence. Time to join us."

Clarence wanted to scream but his parched, abused throat would not lend itself to anything stronger than a breathy hiss. Though his voice was inadequate, his terror was absolute. Clarence heard the low shrieks of rusty gears being pressed into service and felt his body rotate counterclockwise slowly.

He was thankful that he was not rotated in the other direction, this way he was spared the view of what the woman hanging on his right had become.

He could now see that there were two men in the room. A short man, who Clarence recognized as the chauffeur, worked a large manual crank on the wall. The man was short and lean almost to the point of malnourishment and so the effort of turning the crank required both of his hands. The second man held a candle. Even in the light of the candle, a gloom bathed the man's face, rendering the details of his features indiscernible.

Clarence was sure he was the passenger from the car, the man who had beat him. He was well over six feet tall, broad through the shoulders with excellent posture. His black leather wingtips reflected the candle light. He wore a crisp shirt that may have been white or light blue tucked into well-tailored gray slacks. The sleeves of his shirt were rolled up to reveal strong forearms. He exuded confidence.

When Clarence had rotated 180 degrees, the man handling the crank stopped working and took the candle from the taller man. The gloom around the man's face deepened in the absence of the direct candle light.

The tall man walked forward deliberately. The creature, now on Clarence's left chortled in delight. When the man was within arm's length of Clarence, he produced a bottle of water from behind his back. This close Clarence could make out a few features of the man's face; a strong chin, an aquiline nose.

"Clarence Jeremy, or do you prefer Caramel? You have been here for roughly two days and you must be dying of thirst."

Clarence nodded that he was thirsty, suppressing a suspicion that the contents of the bottle might not be water. The man lifted the bottle to Clarence's lips and fed him a controlled stream of liquid. The first sip burned his throat like acid and Clarence thought the man had fed him some sort of poison, but then he realized that it burned because his throat was ragged and dry. He drank until the bottle was empty. The man tossed the bottle off to one side and produced another. Clarence drank again. He almost cried in relief. When he was done drinking the man also tossed that bottle away.

"Since you know my name, it's only courteous that you tell me yours, and why am I here?" Clarence was surprised at how confident he sounded.

"I have had many names, but if a name makes you feel more comfortable you can call me Lucien. Why you are here is an infinitely more interesting question. I need you to bring me someone, Clarence."

Clarence cleared his throat and tested his voice again. "I don't understand why you would need me. You picked me up pretty easily, why can't you just get this person too?" A voice in the back of Clarence's mind was shouting that he should be silent, but he reasoned that he was probably going to die here, so he would at least die having his curiosity satisfied to the full.

"She will see me coming if I go for her personally."

"See you coming?" Clarence was genuinely confused. "In that case why can't you send the lady-thing hanging next to me."

"Rebecca?" The man gestured to where the woman hung just outside of Clarence's peripheral vision. "Rebecca and those of her kind are also part of the reason you are here. Rebecca's is not completely within my control. She is murderous and always hungry. If I send her to do my bidding, she may very well eat the target and I need the person brought back alive. I want you to become like her, but I want you to control her and those like her."

"You kidnap innocent people, perform some sort of experiment on them and you expect me to be your willing guinea pig?" Clarence almost burst out laughing at how ridiculous this conversation was.

"None of my subjects is innocent. Rebecca here is a child murderer." The man gestured to Clarence's left as he spoke. "To everyone else she was Nurse Rebecca, an accomplished midwife, but I know that in any given year she kills about two babies born in her hospital. Thrusts a needle between the uncalcified joints of their skulls sending them into a coma. The deaths are passed off as a sudden infant death syndrome, crib death. The wound is almost impossible to detect. She has been doing this for about fifteen years, so by a conservative estimate she has killed thirty babies, although I suspect that she has killed many more. She fights the urge to kill so valiantly, but the evil is within her. It's like a stain on her soul that she cannot get out. All I have done is free her of her last inhibitions."

Clarence said nothing. The man continued speaking. "I have made a couple dozen of like her, and none are innocent. They are the worst that humanity has to offer, molesters, rapists, and murderers of the most deviant sort. They walked around passing themselves off as normal but in truth they are happier now that they have been freed to be their true selves."

"But I'm not a murderer or a molester," Clarence stated.

"That is exactly why I need you. The obeah I used to make Rebecca and her ilk is very old, and parts of the procedure have been lost. As their creator, I can compel them to do my bidding, but I can only control one of them at a time and even so it requires my full focus. Any lapse in concentration and they break free of my will, and if they are outside of my control things get very messy. However, they are all joined by a psychic link that will allow the strongest amongst them to control the others in a more complete manner than I could. I can make you the strongest and you will control them to do my bidding."

"Why do you think that I would be less likely to break free of your control than the others?"

"You already know why. You can be controlled because you are nothing, Clarence. A dying and abused whore. Your entire life you have submitted to the will of others. You have no will of your own. None of the others that I have turned is as servile as you. That is the difference between you and them. Join me and I will give you strength, strength that you have never had and you will serve only me, instead of the hundreds of others who have used you night after night, year after year."

"But what if I just want to go back to my life?"

The stranger chuckled. "Clarence, if you truly wish to go, I won't let you return to that shell of a life you had. I will heal your disease, I will give you a change of clothing, I will give you money and I will set you free. I will allow you a two-day head start. Then I will send Rebecca after you. It will be difficult to control her, to keep her on target, but I may manage. If you survive Rebecca, I will send Anthony and Marcus, controlling two of them simultaneously is a stretch but if I really focus, I might just manage it. If you survive them, I will send Juma, Nathan, and Antoinette. It is impossible to keep three of them controlled, they will stick to the basic plan, finding you, but they will slaughter many, many people before they caught up to you. You see where this is going. One of the beasts will eventually catch you, and when they do they will slowly eat you alive the only aspect you can control is how many other people die because of your selfishness."

Clarence considered his odds. How far could he run in the two days before Rebecca was sent on his trail? How hard would she be to kill, how hard would Anthony and Marcus, Juma, Nathan and Antoinette be to kill? How many more of them were there, the man had mentioned that he had dozens. Could he just go to the police? As quickly as he thought them up he dismissed these possibilities. He had never been a fighter. His talent lay in succumbing, submitting, bending like the reed in the storm and surviving. This man had displayed power from hell, had spoken to him in the voice of his dead father, had obscured his face with permanent shadows and had turned kidnapped serial killers into…whatever the hell he turned them into. However, if he was going to be Lucien's errand boy there was one more thing that he had to do.

"Let me look at her."

"Rebecca? Are you sure?"

"Yes."

Lucien nodded at the chauffeur, who set the candle on the floor and went back to the wall to the gear crank. The room filled with the grinding creak of rusty gears and Clarence spun slowly to his left. His heart pounded as he turned then the grinding sound stopped.

His vision was completely black for a moment until he realized that his eyes were squeezed tightly shut. He opened them. Rebecca was stripped naked and was suspended by her wrists from ceiling chains just like Clarence. Apart from her suspension she seemed to be in no worse shape than he was. She appeared to be unconscious or asleep, or simply ignoring them. Her head hung between her shoulders. Her damp stringy hair obscured her face.

Rebecca looked to be in her mid-thirties but apparently kept herself fit. Her stomach was flat and her body was toned but not overly muscular. She was neither short nor tall. Clarence could not believe that this woman had been a child killer and was now something more.

"She looks normal," Clarence said.

"The changes can be seen by some if the light is right," Lucien replied cryptically. "So, you will do this? Unlike the others, you must invite it willingly."

Clarence had already made up his mind. There was no escaping Lucien or this dungeon. And even if he somehow escaped, his old life was worthless anyway. "Yeah, I guess I'm your guy," Clarence replied, and as soon as he said the words he felt relieved.

Lucien did not hesitate. He touched both his hands to his face and some of the shadowy gloom transferred to his hands when he took them away. As soon as he did this, the woman bolted awake. "No, Clarence do not accept it, every word he says is a lie," she shouted. But then the creature took over and Rebecca let out a nasty, gravelly moan of delight. "Yes, Clarence, join us."

Clarence was about to shout that he had changed his mind, but Lucien thrust the shadowed hands into his abdomen. Lucien's hands went through his clothing and into his body as easily as a white-hot ice pick would pierce lard. There was no blood but the pain was so intense, so all encompassing, so complete that Clarence could perceive nothing else. There was no dark room, no Rebecca, no weird Igor-like chauffeur-assistant. There was just Caramel the whore and his pain.

Every nerve in his body was exposed and torn by mad dogs made of flame. Every tissue and fiber, every muscle was being speared with lances of iron and ice. He was simultaneously being scalded and lashed; scourged and crucified; burned and branded; and frozen, mauled, blinded, eviscerated, and flayed. In his suffering he bit through his tongue and the sensation was a cold candle against the backdrop of a thousand suns of agony. He suffered at a cellular level. Fat beads of blood sprouted on his forehead and crawled down his face like sweat.

Clarence would have gladly repeated every painful, humiliating moment in his life if only this horrific agony would cease. The pain would not let him go unconscious. Pain this exquisite demanded that he remained awake to savor it. His heart pounded faster and faster, Clarence knew that his mind and body could not stand much more. His body was giving out, succumbing to the agony. Finally, a cool, velvety black descended over his mind and he died from the pain. In the end Clarence had the last laugh, Lucien had lost his man.

Chapter 11

"Them want them pocket full with blue, blue silk,
Them want them statue drinking full cream milk."
- Madman's Rant by David Rudder

When Clarence awoke, he did not know how long he had been dead. The room was silent. He was no longer chained, but lay on his back on the cool, stone floor staring up at the stone ceiling. The room was weakly illuminated by a thin shaft of light entering through the gap left by the ajar door. He was naked and Rebecca was gone, or perhaps he had been moved.

Sensation slowly leaked back into his body and Clarence realized he felt better than he had in years, perhaps better than he had ever felt in his whole life. For the first time in a very long while he felt truly alive. He stood, flexing his toes, stretching his back. He felt strong…more than strong. Then he realized he was not alone; the room was empty but he could feel others. He was intimately aware of them; Rebecca, Anthony and Marcus, Juma, Nathan and Antoinette along with dozens more. Some were in this building in adjacent cells, others were further away, but if he wanted to he could point the way to each one of them accurately.

These were Lucien's soldiers and they were his to command, he could tune into their thoughts and could see their memories. In short order he knew about all the people they had murdered or raped or mutilated. The group was collectively responsible for several hundred killings. Their cumulative wickedness was staggering. Together they operated as a unified consciousness, like a hive of insects.

Can anyone hear me? He spoke to them through their shared mental channel. None of them responded. He knew they were testing his mettle. They were aware of him, just as he was of them. They were wary, exuding a predatory malice, poised to strike like the vipers they were. His inclination was to reason with them, to try to persuade them. But he reasoned

89

that when he was on the street the strongest people did not persuade, those people gave orders and punished those who did not obey. He was the hub, he was their commander, he would command, but first he would punish them for resisting him. He focused on an image of blinding light combined with searing heat and he unleashed it on all members of the hive.

They groaned at the psychic onslaught. Speak to me, identify yourselves by name, one by one. He did not need this information, he already knew them all, but this was an exercise in compliance and for the first time in his life Clarence relished being dominant. This time they responded. One by one they identified themselves. In all fifty-six souls named themselves. But there was another, number Fifty-seven, who had not responded to his command.

Number Fifty-seven lingered on the outskirts of his perception. Clarence applied more force to his inquiry. SPEAK, his psychic voice echoed off the walls of a telepathic well. Still there was no response from number Fifty-seven. Clarence focused and could see her more clearly in his mind's eye. She was a small skinny girl in a torn dress, chained in a room, just like he had been. He tried one more time, but this time the girl slammed some sort of metaphysical wall between them. He lost the mental image. She fell completely out of his extrasensory perception.

Clarence was intrigued. Lucien had said that everyone who was chosen was guilty in some respect, monsters masquerading as men while they waited for someone like Lucien to authorize their worse inclinations. But this girl could not be more than nine or ten years old. Surely, she did not fit Lucien's criteria. And why was she chained when the others were free to roam their cells?

Lucien's voice filled Clarence's head, severing his connection with the others, and demanding his undivided attention. Clarence tried but realized that he could not determine Lucien's location like he could for the rest of the hive.

Welcome back. How does it feel to be powerful? Lucien did not wait for an answer. *Remember though, you are mine, Clarence, just as they are yours. Have a sample of what will happen if you disobey me.*

The pain returned, surging up from some internal reservoir and striking him like a hammer between his shoulder blades. It was just a sliver of what he had experienced before, but it was enough to flatten him completely. When the agony dissipated and his vision cleared, he managed to get to his knees. He coughed and spat up a rusty clot of blood. Lucien continued to speak into his mind.

The others are yours to command, use them to complete the tasks that I will set for you. Leave this room and go upstairs. Someone is waiting. They will give you something to wear and further instructions.

Clarence hastened to comply, not willing to risk another dose of pain. He rose to his feet, went to the thick wooden door, and pushed it the rest of the way open. Outside the stone room was a long hall with a low ceiling. The hall was lined with many other doors that led to rooms he knew housed some of the others. The air was stale and smelled faintly of mold and more faintly still of decaying flesh. Overhead a string of naked electric bulbs flickered on and off and swayed on vagrant drafts. The inconstant lights cast multiple dancing shadows in various shades of black and gray, an effect that was altogether disorienting.

Clarence hastened down the hall eventually coming to a staircase that led upwards. The moment his foot touched the bottom step all the lights in the hall simultaneously dimmed and then died. The darkness was so complete that Clarence felt as if he had been dropped headfirst into a barrel of crude oil.

He found however that he was unafraid. There were soldiers at his command who would heed his will even unto their own destruction. Besides, with every breath his own strength increased, he could feel power infuse his bones and muscles. He ascended slowly, arms outstretched ahead of him until he touched a wooded surface that he assumed was a door. He banged on it with a fist and waited knowing that if he had to he could probably tear through it himself. There was no need. He heard the unmistakable clinking of a bunch of keys. The door opened and blinding light entered riding a wave of cool fresh air.

A small hand grabbed his wrist and pulled him out of the doorway. The door slammed shut behind him. His eyes slowly adjusted to the light.

He was in the hallway of a house. The door through which he had come, now closed, looked like part of the wall. There was not even a seam to indicate that a door might be there.

There was a girl. She was a year or two older than Fifty-seven yet thin in the pre-pubescent way of Caribbean children. She was Indian and quite pretty. Her long dark hair lay in a Cascadu braid over one shoulder. Her narrow face was brown, sun-kissed to copper. She had large dark eyes that slanted upward slightly at the outer corners and were bordered by eyelashes that were long, dark and lacy. She was well on her way to becoming a striking woman. She wore a crimson sari trimmed in gold draped in the Nivi style. She and Clarence stared at each other for a moment. The girl seemed unfazed by his nudity.

"What's your name?" Clarence asked.

"My name is Ghita. Follow me." She turned and left without waiting for him to respond. Her sari followed in her wake, fluttering like a gold and red butterfly. The house was simply yet richly furnished in the architectural and decorative style of the east. Each item of the decor appeared to have been selected with an eye for quality and detail. Clarence followed Ghita across a room with a floor that was tiled a deep glossy amber and seemed to glow from within. The walls were painted in coral yellow. Along the hallway were alcoves housing pedestals upon which stood statuettes of various deities from the Hindu pantheon. Clarence recognized Kali dancing with her necklace of skulls, Ganesh with his elephant's head, Narasimha the lion-man the fifth avatar of Vishnu, Hanuman bearing a mountain aloft. An ivory statuette of Lakshmi caught Clarence's eye. The eyes of the many limbed goddess seemed to follow him as he passed by, shaming him for his nakedness, judging him for his choice.

"Where are we, Ghita?"

"We are where we need to be," the girl responded without turning around.

The pair exited the room and continued across an outdoor bridge connecting the upper floors of the house and spanning a garden below. A waist high wall ran along both sides of the bridge and at regular intervals there were arches the inner edges of which were masoned to look like the silhouettes of lotus flowers in bloom.

Clarence inhaled deeply. This was the first time he had been outside since the night he was kidnapped. The setting sun cast long shadows and the air was perfumed heavily with incense and the exotic scent of frangipani flowers. Below them lay in a lush green lawn and flowers of all kinds were blooming. Bougainvillea climbed the walls like ivy but bore a riot of purple, peach and white blooms, white Bermuda lily stood next to the orange peach of the Barbados lily. The borders of the lawn were hedged in Alamanda bushes with their waxy green leaves and trumpeted yellow blossoms.

Crickets chirped to herald the coming night and, in the distance, a crapaud croaked. Clarence followed Ghita in silence. They entered the section of the house to which the bridge led and continued a short way down a hall until they came to a dark wooden door. Ghita held the door open and Clarence peered inside.

"Go in," she said, and Clarence obliged. The door closed quietly behind him and in a brief panic he fumbled for the handle but found that it had not been locked. He re-opened the door but Ghita had vanished. He closed the door, opened it, and closed it again, a neurotic repetition to ease his doubts about being trapped.

The room was spotless but, unlike the rest of the house, utilitarian. There was a full-length mirror and Clarence inspected himself. He found that he looked remarkably different. The dark circles under his eyes were gone. His cheeks had filled in and his body was now lean rather than gaunt, his hair thick and healthy. The bones that had been broken in Lucien's assault had healed and he was sure if he was administered a blood test that he would pass with flying colors.

He looked at himself for a long time, eventually breaking into a smile, at which point he noticed his teeth were clean and his gums were healthy and pink. He was a lovely man. In a closet he found clothes, slim black jeans and a black tee shirt, both fit as if they had been tailored for him. Under the bed was a pair of desert boots. In a drawer he found a gun and a wad of blue hundred-dollar bills held together with a silver money clip.

He slipped the money into his back pocket but left the gun where it was. He then lay on the bed and stared at the wooden ceiling wondering what would be the next step in this new life. Eventually he dozed off. Lucien's voice in his head jolted him awake.

Clarence, I trust that you are enjoying your return to the land of the living.

Yes. Who is the girl?

Ghita? She's just a girl.

I'm not talking about Ghita, although I doubt that Ghita is just a girl. Who is the other girl, number Fifty-seven? The one in chains.

Clarence was surprised at how quickly he had grown used to conducting mental conversations.

She is yours to command just like the rest.

She is different.

She is what I say she is, Clarence.

Lucien spoke those last words with a finality that brokered no further discussion.

Answer the door, Clarence.

There was a soft knock. Clarence opened the door. It was Ghita of the red and gold sari. In her hand she held a manila envelope which she offered to Clarence. He took it and wondered why they had not just put it in the room before he had arrived.

He looked up from the envelope meaning to ask Ghita, but she was gone, no footsteps no rustle of fabric. She's just a girl, right. Clarence went back to the room and closed the door again. He sat on the bed and opened the envelope with a fingernail. Inside were four pictures of the same woman, obviously taken without her knowledge. She was small in a womanly way, petite, well-dressed, Caribbean girl-next-door pretty. She looked like a business woman perhaps, or a lawyer's secretary. There were no descriptions or dates included with the images. In one picture she was smiling, the display of even white teeth and dimples making her even lovelier.

Her name is Lisa Cyrus. She has taken something from me and I need it back. Your first task is to bring her to me alive.

Clarence wondered how Lisa had managed to steal something from Lucien and his ugly chauffeur-Igor-lackey. He was relieved that he only had to snatch her and not to kill her, though he suspected being kidnapped by Lucien was only mildly less pleasant than being killed. Clarence had no talent for kidnapping, but he knew exactly who the accomplished kidnappers among his group of Myrmidon were.

I will need Nathan and Damian, they are in cells, free them. Send Rebecca too, my former cell-mate.

Done.

I will also want number Fifty-seven.

No.

She will make an excellent decoy, besides, I'm the one executing, and I'm requesting her.

If you need a decoy use Ghita.

Ghita weirds the shit out of me. I want Fifty-seven.

Your stubbornness is already becoming taxing Clarence. Why do you persist in calling her Fifty-seven? Don't you know her name?

Clarence knew Lucien was mocking him. Surely the man knew he was unable to extract anything from the girl.

No, she refused to tell me.

She refused your compulsion and you still want her along? Fine, Fifty-seven is yours to use on this mission. But let me warn you, if the target is killed, broken, or despoiled you will suffer far more than you have already suffered. Ghita will give you further instructions. With those words Lucien's presence winked out of his consciousness again.

Clarence was not eager to interact with the strange Indian girl again but he made his way back to the garden bridge to look for her. Night had fallen and hundreds of fireflies drifted over the lawn and among the flowers and plants. Above it all a harvest moon rose, fat, low, and yellow.

The intra-floor bridge was about two stories above the yard, but Clarence felt that he could jump down without harm. He vaulted the wall, landed lightly without incident and continued searching for Ghita. In the distance he heard soft singing and he followed the sound.

Behind the house was a hill, and atop the hill a group of people surrounded a funeral pyre. They were observing Antyesti, the Hindu funeral rights. A male mourner walked around the pyre sprinkling water. Atop the pyre lay a small person, their feet pointing southward so they could walk into the land of the dead. From that distance at the base of the hill Clarence could not make out the features of their face but the person lying atop the pyre was clad in crimson and gold. Ghita?

"Clarence." A voice behind him spoke his name. He spun around and Ghita stood there. He glanced back over his shoulder in time to catch a last glimpse of the body on the pyre just before flames leapt to consume the crimson and gold sari of the person laying there.

"Is that you on the pyre, Ghita?"

"There is a white panel van at the front of the house. Pick up the people you requested then kidnap the woman. She is not to be harmed. Once you have her, you will be given further instructions." Ghita ignored his question.

Clarence stole another glance at the hilltop. The pyre was now completely engulfed in flames. He could feel the heat all the way down at the bottom of the hill he turned back to Ghita but she was gone.

He walked to the front of the large house. The panel van was there as Ghita had promised. He opened the door to the van and got in. The keys were in the ignition and a sheet of paper taped to the steering wheel. Written on the sheet was an address.

Clarence started the van and pulled into the roadway. He headed to pick up Rebecca, Nathan, Damian, and number Fifty-seven, all of whom Lucien had set free from their cells. He needed no directions because he could tell where they were through the psychic connection they shared.

As he drove away, a realization settled in his gut like sack of dead grave worms. He remembered that when he and Ghita were walking across the house-bridge, the setting sun had cast long black shadows off the decorative concrete blocks that made up the low safety wall and even off the leaf-cutter ants that scurried along the top of the wall. Ghita however, had cast no shadow.

She is just a girl. Yes, a girl hanging around to witness her own funeral, Clarence thought. Antyesti was meant to allow a Hindu's soul to enter the land of rest. Clarence suspected that Ghita would find no rest as long as she was within Lucien's clutches.

Chapter 12

Rohan had never been as happy to return to Stone House as he had been that morning when they finally pulled into the driveway. The meeting with Kat, the jumbie fight, the interrogation of the woman, the shadowy assassin, the glob Kat had thrown to slay the shadow, and Kamara's marking, all of it had made for a very long and exhausting night.

The sun was already setting when he finally woke. He and Kamara lay in the same position in which they had fallen asleep that morning. He disentangled himself from her web of arms, legs and hair, pausing briefly to inspect the elephants marching up the back of her palm and wrist, before slipping out of the room to stretch his legs and clear his mind.

He walked past the adjacent bedroom. The door was ajar and a partially-undressed Lisa lay diagonally across the bed as if she had fallen asleep in the process of disrobing. He pulled the door closed.

The original Stone House was large and had been very old, until about three years before when a soucouyant had attacked inside the house triggering a fire that had razed old Stone to the ground. After the fire Stone house had been rebuilt in a modern style. The men of Stone had solicited designs then voted on the submissions. The Order's wealth was old and substantial and the new building was one of the most beautiful homes in Trinidad.

As Rohan walked along the corridors he recalled the voices of his grandfather and fellow Ordermen that had filled the halls all too recently. He stopped when he came to the large airy room that housed the martial arts sparring and practice areas. The sparring mat was a safe place to release some of the stress that had built and was continuing to build over the past few days. The mat was also where he and his chaptermen had spent countless hours. He felt close to them here. Physical exercise will help clear my mind.

He was not in the least surprised to see Voss in the room practicing a form with a katana. *An odd weapon for someone in the Caribbean*, Rohan thought. The razor-sharp blade cut through the air with precision as Voss gracefully and powerfully executed an elaborate sequence of slashes and parries against an imaginary foe.

The sword itself was a work of art with an ornately engraved blade and red tsuka-maki that contrasted with the ebony of its handle. Rohan did not recognize the sword and he knew every sword, knife, gun, and dagger in the armory, the only room that survived the soucouyant fire. That room was the size of a modest house, boasting a double wall of cinder block laminating a solid half inch thick plate of steel, and a fireproof door. It housed their arms and ammunition, as well as ancient handwritten documents and irreplaceable texts.

Rohan waited until Voss had finished his routine before entering the room.

"Did you sleep at all?" Rohan asked as Voss lovingly slid the blade into the red lacquered scabbard until it locked with a click.

"I napped," Voss responded. "Nice place you guys have here. The butler gave me a tour, but he refused to let me into the armory, faithful servant that he is."

Rohan knew that the butler Voss was referring to was Jonah. Jonah was the housekeeper, repairman, chauffeur, grounds' man, emergency medical technician, repository of sage advice, and general all-round Man-Friday. Jonah had been with the Order for as long as Rohan could remember and knew all the company secrets. He would cringe at being referred to as the 'butler' or 'servant.'.

The other member of the Stone house staff was Imelda who was Jonah's wife who also functioned as their cook. She was a tower of a woman. Built like a tank, she stood a full foot taller than Jonah. Where Jonah was mild and easygoing, Imelda was fiery and mercurial. She was their brood-mother and was taking the deaths of Rohan's comrades very poorly.

Stone House belonged to Imelda and Jonah more than it belonged to Rohan. The elderly couple spent far more time there than he did and they ensured that the house ran smoothly. They paid the bills, tended the gardens and grounds, ensured that the fridges were stocked and the cars had gas. Without Jonah and Imelda, Stone would probably slowly starve.

"He's not a butler per se," Rohan responded, declining to explain the full extent of Jonah's functions. "Nice sword. Didn't know you practiced."

Voss looked slightly offended. "Nice? Practice? I have forgotten more sword techniques than most masters will ever know and this sword is a priceless treasure."

"Aren't you a portrait of humility," Rohan said sarcastically, "In that case you would not mind a friendly match. We can use *bokken*," Rohan said, motioning to a rack of the wooden practice swords affixed to the wall. The hardwood swords were carved to resemble and perform like katana.

"Bokken? Why not *shinai*?" Voss responded glancing at the rack of bamboo practice swords that were far safer than the hardwood bokken.

"Are you worried Voss? You were doing pretty well against that invisible samurai just now."

Voss looked mildly amused, "It's you I'm worried about, Le Clerc."

"Good, it's settled then, go pick one out, and I'll change into my ass-kicking clothes."

Moments later Voss and Rohan faced each other across the practice mat. Rohan adopted a stance from *Musō Shinden-ryū* a *battojitsu* style of fighting where the sword starts in the scabbard unlike other techniques where the fighter draws the sword to begin. Rohan's preferred bladed weapon was a machete. He was competent wielding two as done in *Escrima* or one in the *Tire Machete* Haitian fencing style. But he missed practicing Japanese sword techniques against competent partners.

Voss adopted a stance Rohan did not recognize. The man held the sword overhead in a two-handed grip, his right foot ahead of the left, the muscles of his torso straining in anticipation of the violence to come. They stared at each other searching for some opening that could be exploited. The room was cool, but Rohan felt a single bead of sweat roll down his back. A mosquito buzzed past his ear and he thought about how often Isa had expressed the wish that all mosquitoes would spontaneously self-combust.

Voss seized Rohan's momentary lapse in focus and was upon him in an instant. The man moved like lightning. He took one step forward, closing the distance between them and bringing the bokken down with the full power of both arms. Rohan stepped to the side allowing Voss's sword to cleave the air where he had just been standing and executed a blindingly fast *batto-jitsu* cutting draw. He had moved so fast that Voss's sword was still travelling downward while his was travelling toward the back of Voss's head. He was already coming up with some sarcastic comment to use after he knocked Voss on his backside. Voss however had other plans.

The man ducked Rohan's wooden blade shifted his weight and struck at Rohan's gut with the pommel of the bokken. Rohan managed to position his other arm between the butt of Voss' blade and his stomach but the blow was powerful enough to knock him back a step. With that move Voss proved himself a worthy opponent. Rohan pressed the attack more technically, stepping forward and slashing three times in rapid succession. Voss danced backward so gracefully it was almost like he floated away, his feet barely touching the ground as he dodged each of Rohan's three strikes.

Rohan executed a quick shuffle and struck a fourth time, faster and harder than the previous three slashes. Voss ducked under the attack and came up inside Rohan's guard. Rohan felt a moment of panic. Voss struck and Rohan parried, the hardwood blades slamming into each other. Voss' blade struck so powerfully that Rohan almost lost his grip. Instead of striking again Voss moved his full weight behind the sword by placing one palm behind the blade and pressing forward with all his strength. Rohan slid backwards as Voss ploughed forward, the bare soles of his feet getting friction burns from the sparring mat. Rohan was eventually crushed against the bamboo wall of the room with Voss' maniacal grin inches away from his nose.

"Yield," Voss commanded through clenched teeth as he applied more of his considerable strength behind the painful sword press. Rohan would choose unconsciousness before he yielded to Voss, and if he could have drawn a breath he would have expressed this. With superhuman effort Rohan brought his knee up into Voss' solar plexus. The man grunted and loosened the pressure on Rohan's neck slightly. Rohan pivoted and swept

Voss' feet from under him with his instep. Voss' body was completely horizontal in midair and Rohan brought the bokken down in a two-handed grip as Voss fell.

Nowhere for you to escape this time, Rohan thought.

But Rohan had once again underestimated his opponent. Voss flexed his spine like a falling cat's and, changing direction in midair he moved just outside the reach Rohan's descending blade. Rohan's bokken struck the padded mat with a dull thud and Voss landed in an ungraceful heap an inch outside of the danger zone.

The two men stared at each other. They were completely out of breath. Rohan broke the silence first, "I'm willing to call it a draw if you are."

Voss used the sword like a crutch and got to his feet. "I must be a bit rusty," he responded grudgingly. "I guess we could call it a tie, except for that part where you almost went unconscious."

"Hey, I call that the rope-a-dope, I was lulling you into a false sense of security," Rohan said between gasps.

"Yes, yes of course. Another round then?"

"Best of three?" Rohan asked. That phrase, which he and his Order-men brothers had often used to settle sparring disputes triggered grief that he was not yet ready to address fully. His grandfather had always advised them to mentally address matters that were emotionally distressing, and Rohan was sufficiently self-aware to recognize that he was willfully suppressing his sadness.

"Deal. This first one doesn't count though," Voss replied, interrupting Rohan's thoughts.

"Your funeral, buddy." Rohan assumed a *Kogan-ryu* pose. His arms were already tired, but there was no way he would admit exhaustion to his bodyguard. Voss faced him with another unfamiliar stance and they began once more.

***

Kamara woke slowly. Sleep was like an ocean and she was a diver clawing her way back to the surface from an unassisted dive to an extraterrestrial depth. The darkness and the cold of the unfathomable hemmed her in on all sides. A thousand bloodthirsty behemoths pursued her to the surface.

Her heart pounded, her lungs were either about to collapse for want of air or she would suck down a mouthful of cold brine. But suddenly, she was fully awake and the nightmare dissipated like old gossamer before a brisk wind, forgotten even in the act of opening her eyes. *Who am I? I am Kamara.*

She certainly did not feel like herself. She felt wired, animated, as if she was plugged directly into the source of whatever powered life itself. She experienced no sleepy transition into wakefulness, she was already running full throttle. The world around seemed sharp, the edges of the table looked as if they could cut her finger, and she could make out the individual weaves in the fabric of the sheets. She smelled the faint scent of man that Rohan had left. On the windowsill a Siamese fighting fish swam in a five-gallon tank and Kamara felt that she could count every scale on its scarlet body from where she sat on the bed. She looked at the tattoos. *Is this their effect?* she wondered.

She got out of bed and stretched. Barbs of electricity danced down her spine. Then she heard it, a faint clatter like staves being bashed together. Someone was sparring, and from the sound, they were using bokken rather than the safer hollow bamboo swords. Now that she was tuned in she could tell that, whoever they were, they fought at a frenetic pace. At some points the parries came so quickly that it sounded like staccato fire from an automatic pistol. That could only mean that it was Voss and Rohan letting their testosterone and competitiveness get the better of them. She put on shorts and left the room, bound for the practice mats. The door to the room where Lisa had slept was open. The blankets were folded, the bed had been meticulously made, and the woman was nowhere to be seen.

When Kamara arrived at the practice area the competing men had an audience. Lisa sat on a prostrate punching bag eating a bowl of what appeared to be plain shredded wheat, the breakfast she had skipped that morning in her exhaustion. Agrippa and Tarik sat next to each other on the padded border of the sparring area and Jonah and Imelda stood off to one side.

The spectators were so focused on the two men in the center that none noticed her arrival. Rohan and Voss were dressed in baggy *hakama* sparring pants, Rohan wore traditional black and Voss wore red. Their bare, unprotected torsos were covered in sweat, welts, and bruises. The pair engaged each other with such speed, ferocity, and grace that the effort looked choreographed. She knew however that it was serious. Back and forth they went, neither gaining an advantage, then each simultaneously spotting some weakness in the other and attacking it with equal viciousness. The match ended in a draw.

"Another tie, fellas," Jonah said. "What is that? Five in a row?"

Voss wore a bemused look. "I really must be out of practice, let's do one more."

"If you like being battered with a stick then who am I to deny you that joy?" Rohan retorted, twirling the bokken so that it blurred, never one to decline a challenge. Kamara knew Rohan would fight until he collapsed or until Voss conceded, whichever came first. His stubbornness was simultaneously admirable and frustrating.

She felt a surge of adventurousness that seemed to be a continuation of the new vitality she had felt upon waking. She stepped forward. "I want to try."

Everyone turned to look, noticing her presence for the first time.

"Jonah, you can referee the match," she continued.

Rohan spoke up. "Do you feel well, love? Why are you suddenly interested in sparring? You never liked my lessons before." He came forward and theatrically placed the back of his palm against her forehead as if checking for a fever. She shoved him away playfully then wiped his sweat from her hands on the seat of her shorts.

"I feel just fine and seeing as you taught me all that I know I would like to try against Voss."

Rohan grew serious. "That may not be such a good idea, Voss is a sadist." He held up a hand to display a pair of dislocated fingers.

"She'll be fine," Voss said. "I like her a lot more than I like you Rohan. Grab her a *men*, a pair of *kote*, and a *shinai*," Voss continued, asking for the helmet, gloves, and the bamboo sword designed for sparring safety, gear he and Rohan had not used.

"Bokken not shinai, and I won't be needing any of the other equipment. One match don't hold back," Kamara said, a little shocked at her own confidence.

"Kam, you really must be ill. At least take the helmet," Rohan coaxed, beginning to look concerned.

"It's just one match, Ro. How bad could it be?" Kamara responded. Rohan spent the next few minutes attempting to convince her to abandon the idea of facing Voss without the padded gear, but Kamara remained firm and eventually he gave up in the face of her stubbornness.

Rohan walked over to Voss and they shared a quick word. Voss nodded solemnly and Rohan clapped him on the shoulder, then walked back to Kamara, handing her the dented bokken he had been using. Mildly annoyed by the cautionary exchange he had obviously had with Voss, she accepted Rohan's bokken but walked over to the wall rack. She set down the oak bokken he had been given her and selected a pale one made of ash.

"Picky, picky," Rohan teased.

Voss kept the wooden blade he had been using in his matches against Rohan and adopted the stance he had used against Rohan in their first match. Kamara mirrored Rohan's semi-crouching batto-jitsu stance, the wooden sword sheathed in her waistband in lieu of a scabbard. Her hand was poised over the bokken's handle midway up its length. Voss moved, pressing the attack. Kamara did not move fast enough to step out of the way of the descending blade, but instead of trying to sidestep and draw like Rohan had, Kamara just drew.

She felt as if she was having an out of body experience. She had never practiced what she was about to do, yet her body seemed to know what technique to apply to the situation. Her draw was fast but it was a feint, meant to give the illusion that she was slightly out of range. Mid swing she adjusted her grip and allowed her hand to slide down the handle of the sword so that she barely grasped the last inch or so of handle as it sped through the air.

The modified grip brought Voss well within the cutting arc of the rapidly travelling business end of the bokken. Kamara saw a brief look of shock cross Voss' face. He changed the direction of his own downward swing and placed his sword where it would parry Kamara's blow. Kamara's ash blade struck the side of Voss' sword with a crack like shattering bone. Her bokken broke right through and continued onward to strike Voss across the temple. Voss stumbled backward clutching the broken handle of his sword. Unable to keep his balance he fell onto the mat, blood already seeping from a gash in his forehead. There was absolute silence. Kamara dropped her sword in shock.

"Where did you learn that?" Voss groaned, clutching his head, blood welling between his fingers.

"I'm so sorry, Voss," Kamara said as she rushed over to check on her fallen opponent. "I made that up on the fly. I didn't think I would hit you with it."

"Nah, it's not your fault. Obviously I'm tired from a long day, and this bokken has obviously been weakened by the previous matches. Obviously..." Voss slowly attempted to regain his feet but ended up deciding to remain seated.

"You want to go best of three, Voss?" Rohan said, attempting to lighten the mood. Voss snarled something unintelligible in response. He had finally managed to get back to his feet with Kamara's assistance. Jonah examined the wound, but Voss was already well on his way to being fully healed.

Kamara faced Rohan. "What is going on?" she asked.

Rohan replied in a thoughtful semi-whisper, "As you know every Orderman's mark has a different purpose. Even the same marks on two different people may manifest differently. I'm not familiar with the marks that Kat's creature gave you. Maybe we can find some information in the archives. But even if your marks are described in the archives, the exact effect on you will only be determinable through observation. So far it looks like strength and speed are part of your package. Also, one day after you have practiced more you will understand the significance of what you just did. Breaking a bokken and almost beheading Voss with one hand with a transition from batto-jitsu into *nagare-boshi* is genius-level swordsmanship. We will have to monitor you closely as the marks take hold."

Kamara turned towards the door of the training room. "I think she's here," she said in a half whisper.

"Who's here?" Rohan asked, just as Katharine sauntered into the room. *How did Kamara know? Was this an additional aspect of her marks?*

The soucouyant looked stunning in black skinny jeans, a black silky blouse with the top three pearl buttons undone, and a pair of white crocodile skin stilettos with heels that looked like stainless steel. Her outfit was cinched at the waist with a slim crocodile skin belt that matched the shoes. Rohan wondered if she had killed the crocodile herself.

"How did you get in," Rohan asked.

Kat did not respond directly. "I promised I would be here after sunset and here I am. We have much to discuss. Additionally, it's a fine night for the ladies to go clubbing, specifically at the Kings and Commoners." Rohan and Voss shared a look.

Jonah, sensing the building tension in the room spoke up. "Imelda and I will prepare some refreshments. You folks get clean. We can all circle-up in about fifteen minutes in the second floor living room."

"Sounds good." Kat beamed, her even white teeth framed by lips made blood-red by lipstick.

"Fifteen minutes it is then. Thank you, Jonah," Rohan said. "Voss, you can take two extra minutes." Rohan was enjoying needling the man. Voss growled a response again.

Kamara sidled up next to him and took his arm. "I'm really sorry about Voss, I didn't mean to." She really felt guilty about hurting the bodyguard.

"You're fine and he'll be fine. It's mostly his pride that's bruised," Rohan replied. "We'll have to determine exactly what effect the marks will have on you, in the meantime just be very careful. I certainly won't be sparring with you," he finished playfully.

They all filed out of the room. Rohan wondered what the soucouyant had up her couture sleeves.

Chapter 13

"Is it not a horrible travesty that man does not remember the experiences of his past incarnations? This state dooms him to repeat his mistakes life after life, turn after turn. Because of this, mankind's progress to nirvana is incrementally slow."

— An Immortal's Musings by an unidentified soucouyant

The hobo's world is a whimsically cruel place. Samdeo remembered the night he had been drawn into a no-holds-barred brawl with a toothless vagabond over the rights to a discarded box containing mostly chicken bones. (Why a toothless man would fight over bones was a question that still baffled Sam.)

While they wrestled with each other in a rancid embrace of sweat and grime, a stray dog had made good the opportunity to slink off into the night with the prize. Samdeo caught a glimpse of the dog's narrow, leathery backside as it loped off with the morsels over which he was fighting, cruel indeed.

That Samdeo was insane was a question that had been answered clinically. Every evaluating doctor at St. Ann's agreed that something was mentally amiss. The real challenge was in diagnosing exactly what was amiss. A hundred theories were advanced and discarded; Schizophrenia perhaps? Split Personality Disorder maybe? No one was quite sure.

His psychological problems had a single source—the memories. Well, at least what he considered to be memories and what the doctors considered to be illusions manufactured by his, yet to be identified, mental disorder.

The memories had started six years prior, when he was about twelve. At the time Sam was an academically gifted student who teachers described as a 'pleasure to educate.' On the specific day in question he was on a class field trip to the Port-of-Spain museum. His group was chaperoned by a museum assistant who led them from exhibit to exhibit, delivering pre-programmed commentary about the artifacts on display.

Sam was deeply interested in Caribbean history and he already knew most of what the guide was saying. He was thus only subconsciously aware of the guide's prepared drone. The group paused in front a painting of some Spanish conquistadors landing on a jungle beach, triumphant in shining armor. The painting also depicted native Amerindians in various subservient poses paying homage at the feet of white men with beatific faces. The tour guide confirmed the accuracy of the depicted scene in his monotonous buzz.

"This, boys and girls, is an oil painting showing the very first landing of the Spanish conquistadors on Trinidad's shores," he said and Sam was suddenly fully engrossed. A small voice in the back of his mind prompted Sam to speak, although at the time, he thought that the desire to speak was his own.

"That's not what happened," Sam said.

"What do you mean?" the guide replied, unenthusiastic about being contradicted.

"They were starving and weak when they got off their stinking boats, their armor was rusted, not gleaming like in the painting." The words came out of Sam in a rush.

"That's very interesting young man," the guide responded dismissively and continued with his spiel. The tour group moved on, but Sam hung back, staring at the painting and growing more and more agitated the longer he stared. The painting was a bold-faced lie. Something had to be done. Something would be done.

Sam ducked under the velvet rope that was put in place to ensure that small boys did not get within arm's length of the irreplaceable artifacts. He examined the painting up close. *All lies,* he thought. Suddenly his mind was filled with memories. Not just voices but sounds, smells, and sights, a complete immersion.

He remembered the first conquistadors vividly because he had been there. They had been lice ridden, afflicted with scurvy and dysentery. The stink of death and brokenness followed them in a putrid fog. His nose wrinkled at the alien stench.

The men had launched their worm-eaten longboat from their battered ship. It had taken the weakened lot close to six hours to row the two miles from where their large ship was anchored in the deeper waters of the bay heaving with the tide, its timbers and ropes groaning like some stricken behemoth. When the longboat beached, it was all the seventeen men could do to crawl off and lie prostrate in the sand. His people should have killed them then, cut their throats or drowned them or simply just left them to die on their own. But that was not his people's way.

They had nursed the men, tended their blisters and their pus-filled sores, and fed them from the brink of starvation. Twelve of the original seventeen survived. When the men were strong enough his people gave them sufficient provisions to return to their distant home, a journey that his people all deemed impossible in their mildewed and rotted ship. But the white men had apparently made it back because they eventually returned to his people's island with more men and still more men and with their rats and their swine and their goats, with their swords and their muskets, and with their diseases the deadliest of which was greed. This time their armor gleamed.

The memory faded and Sam found himself clutching shreds of canvas. The ground around him was littered with the broken glass of the display and spattered droplets of blood from a three-inch gash across the knuckle of the hand he had apparently used to smash the pane. His tampering had also triggered a silent alarm. The security guards caught Sam in the middle of his defacing act.

Sam knew instinctively that he had to hide the truth about what happened, but his parents persisted in asking him why he did it. His adolescent mind could not manufacture a satisfactory lie and so he eventually told his mother exactly what happened. She did not believe him. She and his father chalked up the incident as 'a cry for attention' and slotted the episode away in that mental file cabinet labeled Offspring Indiscretions that all parents keep.

But then Sam ate Simone and his life took a turn for the cesspit. Simone was the family's pet parrot. He had been playing with her one evening when once again he was possessed by the memories of an old life. Again he lost all sense of self and he was consumed by the experience. The person whose life he was experiencing apparently thought that parrot made a fine meal. His mother discovered him roasting Simone in the backyard over a small pit fire. To say she freaked out, would have been putting it mildly. Her screams had broken the spell of the memory and he spent the next twenty minutes simultaneously crying over his dead pet and retching up bits of roasted macaw.

After he gained a sliver of composure, he again explained to his father and mother what had happened and they in turn launched the parental full court press.

Sam spent the next six months enduring a battery of tests, scans, evaluations and examinations. The doctors could find nothing wrong with him physically, no lumps no tumors no chemical or hormonal imbalances. Apart from the two dissociative lapses Sam's psychological evaluations raised no points for alarm. He was given a clean bill of health and his life returned to normal for the next four years until his sixteenth birthday. One-minute Sam was having a birthday dinner with his parents, and the next, he was secured to a bed with padded manacles, in a room painted buttercup yellow.

The only other occupant of the room was a lady dressed in a nurse's outfit. Sam asked her what had happened and why he was here. The woman did not respond but left the room and returned with an older Indian man in a white coat embroidered with the name Dr. Roshan. Dr. Roshan proceeded to tell him that he had had a dissociative incident that had lasted three weeks. He had fled from the dinner table where they were celebrating his birthday and vanished. The police had found him on the streets a week later and he had been committed to the hospital.

Being hospitalized had not improved his state. He had ranted about sacrifices and closing a gate to another world. The doctor said sometimes he spoke broken English and other times he spoke in a language no one could understand. In summary, he flipped his wig. When his parents visited, his mother cried the entire time.

The first night they released him from his manacles he fled the hospital through a window that someone had left open (who leaves the windows open in an asylum?) Since then he had lived on the streets, fighting vagrants for scraps, scrounging and begging.

The memories had now taken on a personality, an otherness. For weeks the Other had wrestled for control of Sam's body, trying to take him on another dissociative jaunt. But Sam had learned to read the signs and symptoms of its attempts to gain control and he suppressed them.

Did he dare speak to the other consciousness that shared his mind? Wasn't it a sure sign of his own lunacy that he even considered reaching out to the artifact-destroying, parrot-munching psychic hitchhiker?

Sam wished that he could go home to his mother, but he could not return until he got himself sorted out. The sidewalks and alleys of Port-of-Spain weren't so bad, so long as you got over the rats. *The conquistadors' rats,* a voice said and Sam was unsure where that thought came from.

The harvest moon hung jaundiced and gibbous in a cloudless, inky sky. Its eerie light forced the stars to settle for mere supporting roles.

A shaft of silver light penetrated a slit in the cardboard roof and shone across his face. The light split his visage into halves, one illuminated in silver, the other concealed in darkness. It appeared that even the moon recognized the struggle that Sam was having with the other consciousness that inhabited his mind. The Other was here tonight, not trying to wrest control of his body, but talking to him, an incessant voice in the back of his head, nattering on and on about old things, ancient things, things that crawled in the night, things that did more than just crawl.

Tonight, the topic of discussion was the moon and the creatures that came out when the moon was as ripe as it was tonight. The Other was very concerned that Sam was sleeping out in the open. The Other thought he should know better.

Hide yourself, Sam. Get out of the moonlight.

The witching hour was approaching and this area of Port-of-Spain was cloaked in eeriness. The quiet was broken only by the howl of the occasional dog, or the grunts of two homeless people each finding some momentary solace in the warmth of the other's crotch.

"Shut up you." Sam hissed. "It's your fault we are where we are, out here in the night." Sam was dismayed that he had used the word we, a Freudian acknowledgment of the Other's legitimacy.

They are coming. They like to hunt by the moonlight. Get out of the light, Sam.

"I'm not moving. This is a good, dry spot. Go away and stop bothering me."

They will eat us alive, the maboya. You must get us out of the silver light, anywhere but in the light. Move…move…run…moverunmoverunmovemovemove…MOVE!!!

"SHUT UP!" Sam clapped his hands over his ears even though the voice was internal.

Too slow, Sam. Too late. They are here.

Then Sam heard other voices in the park, two males and a female.

"Lucien set that man-whore above us, such a weakling," one of the male voices said.

"Hey at least we are free for the moment until Clarence picks us up, free to have a little fun. I'm fucking starving. Let's eat. Captain Clarence is coming I can feel him getting closer," the female voice replied.

"We can all feel him and you're always hungry, Rebecca."

"You too, Nathan," Rebecca shot back.

"Shut up, you two. I'm going to gorge myself tonight before Clarence picks us up to go hunt this Lisa chick."

"Clarence thinks he got all the information when he joined the hive. He thinks he can control us with pain. By the time he finally figures out that his control is not as complete as he believes, it will be too late. We'll teach the little whore a lesson," Rebecca ranted.

Sam lay very still in his cardboard tent. He had no idea what the trio were talking about, but their voices resonated with evil. Why would they come to Tamarind Square if they were hungry? Surely his vagrant neighbors did not have enough food to spare.

It is not too late Sam, they have not seen you yet. Crawl out of your tent and hide in the shadow of the Columbus statue.

The voice was back and was hissing at him. To his surprise Sam found himself complying. He crawled out from under the cardboard lean-to and hid in the shadow of the first conquistador.

Now look at them Sam, see with your own eyes.

Sam looked. The trio walked down the pathway in the center of the square, three dark silhouettes of ordinary stature, but when the dappled moonlight shone on them they became monstrous. The effect reminded Sam of the invisible ink pens that came with a spy kit his mother had gotten him for his twelfth birthday. Words written in the ink were only visible under a black light.

When the moon shone on the trio, they doubled in height; their bony, reptilian bodies were covered in scabs and weeping sores. Their mouths were wide lipless slashes in their bloodless faces. They had neither nostrils nor eyes, but this did not seem to hamper them at all, and what they lacked in facial features they made up for in teeth, rows of hooked, pointed teeth like a pythons. Rebecca's breasts were pendulous and shriveled, the men's sexual organs dangled to their knees. But for all their beastly hideousness, they moved with predatory grace. The hideous shapes were like mirages superimposed on their human bodies, translucent costumes only visible in the moonlight.

See, Sam.

Sam thought that this was an inappropriate time for an 'I told you so' from his mental hitchhiker. The three creatures walked into the shadows. The monstrous mirages vanished and they now looked like three ordinary people again. They stopped next to a makeshift tent of rags and newspapers erected by some resourceful vagabond. The tent was bathed in moonlight. Sam inhaled with the intention of raising a word of caution.

Don't you dare, Sam, the Other blurted in a near panic.

"Meal number one," said Rebecca as she reached into the tent and hauled out a disheveled and grimy individual by the ankles. All homeless men are light sleepers. Robbery, rape, and worse are the price of a good night's rest on the pavements of Port-of-Spain. The homeless man came out swinging, armed with a broken bottle. He caught Rebecca flush across the face and Sam saw gouts of black blood well out of the wound and drip onto the grass. Rebecca twisted the homeless man's ankle violently, snapping bones both at the ankle and at the knee joints. The man inhaled sharply to scream but one of the men stomped violently onto his throat silencing him swiftly.

The three knelt around the corpse and began ripping handfuls of warm, dripping meat from the body, stuffing their mouths, and swallowing the gory chunks whole. When that method of feeding became insufficiently rapid they bit directly into the man like a pack of wolves. Soon their entire heads were covered in blood and thicker things. Sam sat frozen in terror as they ate the entire man; bones, guts, clothing and all. The nightmarish event was over in less than ten minutes. The two men rose up to move on, but Rebecca stayed, licking the last remnants of blood off the pavement.

One of the men hauled her up by the collar, "Get a-hold of yourself Rebecca, there are many more to choose from." Rebecca complied grudgingly. "I wish we could wash them before we ate them," she said as she stood.

They walked past several other dark shapes of people asleep in the shadows but the next person sufficiently ill-fated to attract their attention was a man asleep in the moonlight, out in the open. Sam could not watch another episode like the first and he began to creep away. But the voice of the Other returned.

Wait for the cloud shadow, Sam. Then run.

The sky is clear. There will be no cloud shadow, Sam replied in his head.

Then call the clouds, Sam.

"What?" Sam whispered. "What do you mean call the clouds?"

Well then hide and be silent before you get us eaten, Sam.

"What are they," he whispered.

Rogue Amerindian spirits raised and pressed to do someone's bidding. Now stop talking before we get eaten.

The three were devouring their second victim with similar haste. Suddenly they froze.

"He is here," Rebecca said. "He is calling to us."

114

"We can hear him, Rebecca. You do realize we all hear him simultaneously," one of the men replied with thinly-concealed scorn.

"I'm not going to him," the other man said. "I refuse to be controlled by that whore."

"You are not strong enough to resist him, Nathan. You must come, or it will be bad for you," Rebecca coaxed.

"No, this foolishness ends now," Nathan said and he began walking towards another moonlit, sleeping vagabond. Mid-step Nathan doubled over and began vomiting a thick stream of red. He fell to his knees and began choking on the grotesque river. His meal poured out of his mouth and nose, he could not breathe. Somehow he managed to turn around and crawl back the way he came. Only then did the projectile vomiting cease.

"Clarence is getting creative," Rebecca said, a hint of admiration entering her voice.

"Fuck him," Nathan spat, "He will pay for that."

"You look awfully tough on your knees in a pool of your own vomit, Nathan dear." Rebecca grinned. Nathan snarled something in response.

Sam saw a white panel van pull up to the corner. He could not make out the driver, but the three abandoned the half-eaten corpse and walked towards the van. Sam took this as his cue to leave. He rose and started a stooped run towards the inner city and away from the van. Just as he began his escape run he bumped right into a skinny girl. She stood in the moonlight, wreathed in the hideous translucence of the maboya's manifestation. Sam, who had been knocked onto his rear by the collision, began to scoot backward away from her. His horror precluded words.

What are you doing? You're going to get seen by the others. The Other was practically shouting between his ears.

"I've already been seen by this one," Sam shot back as he continued his crab-like retreat.

"You're going to get seen by the others," the girl-monster said.

At this point, Sam was ready to re-commit himself to St. Ann's psychiatric hospital. He was willing to undergo any number of invasive tests, ready to be strapped to a bed, in a pastel yellow room, clad in a backless gown. He was ready to receive his daily dose of mind-numbing drugs, anything to save him from this weird world.

"Please don't eat me," Sam begged.

"Be silent, when the cloud shadow comes, leave here and never come back. I will know if you do, I will remember your scent."

"But there are no clouds tonight," Sam whimpered.

"There are now," the monster-girl said, pointing upward where the wind now chased fat rain clouds across the inkiness of the night sky. "See?"

"Are you going to eat me?" Sam asked.

"Maybe I'm already full or maybe I like to chase my dinner or maybe you look like you will taste bad."

Sam scooted back a few inches.

"Here come the clouds. Time for us both to go," the girl said as she stepped around him and headed toward the panel van.

The clouds obscured the moon and a clap of thunder heralded a violent shower. Sam ran northward on Nelson Street towards the inner city as the voice in his head chanted praises and thanks to some ancient god.

Chapter 14

A heady medley of fragrances—shampoo, body lotion, nail polish, and small dabs of expensive perfume—acted as a vanguard for the three women as they descended the double foyer staircase of Stone. But underlying the scent of beauty products was the smell of woman-a mixture of rain, passion, and pheromones discernible to those with noses sharp enough to catch the bouquet of smells. It was intoxicating and enticing, almost edible.

The three women were no less beguiling. Kat had taken it upon herself to buy Lisa and Kamara new clothes for their visit to the Kings and Commoners. The soucouyant had said that she hadn't shopped in decades and couldn't resist the urge. Rohan doubted her excuse. He suspected that the woman had, long ago, gained control over her every impulse and whim.

Kat remained in the black and ivory clothing in which she had arrived at the house. Lisa wore a small white club dress and tall red heels while Kamara sported skin-tight black leather pants with a thin silver chain at her waist, and a white blouse. Her shoes were metallic silver. Rohan was not familiar with designer brands of women's clothing, but he knew quality when he saw it. The women were wearing several thousand dollars' worth of clothing, but none of them had seen it fit to pack a gun.

The brief meeting in the drawing room had proceeded as Rohan had expected. Kat reported on a few additional tidbits she had gleaned from the captured obeah woman after they had left. The gist was that Cassan Davilmar was the man with more information and he ran his operations from an office in the Kings and Commoners. When asked what she had done with the obeah woman, Kat had employed her skill of changing the topic of discussion and deflecting the attention onto someone else. Rohan knew the soucouyant well enough by now to know that she would not be goaded into revealing anything before she was good and ready to do so.

This time she had refocused attention on Kamara by explaining that the marks she had been given were called the Nights of Need. They conferred on their wearer any of the powers represented by the other marks when the need arose. Kat stressed the important distinction between want and need. Kat then went on to explain that the marks would change appearance from time to time so Kamara shouldn't be shocked if they transformed.

Rohan glanced surreptitiously the hand in question, but Kamara had covered the marks with makeup. The discussion had become most animated when Kat had repeated that the women would be the ones to visit the Kings and Commoners to speak with Cassan.

"Explain to me why you need Lisa and Kamara?" Rohan asked.

"I expect to have a conversation not a fight, so it will be safe," Kat rebutted. "Also, neither you nor Voss has the necessary finesse."

"Finesse?!" Rohan responded, mildly insulted.

"Why don't we simply kidnap and interrogate him?" Voss chimed in.

Kat responded by holding both hands toward Voss as if he had perfectly illustrated her point about finesse. "Cassan appears to be, at least on paper, a legitimate businessman, we cannot simply run around torturing regular people."

At least on paper, right. Rohan knew exactly what Cassan was, and he for one had no qualms about kidnapping the man and twisting his arm a little. In the end however, the steel-willed soucouyant prevailed and Voss and Rohan stood at the bottom of the staircase as the three women descended, ready to head out to the night club.

"At least take a gun." Voss urged as they filed past the men.

"For what Voss? To start a firefight in a crowded club? Besides I haven't shot a gun in generations, Lisa hasn't shot one in her life and Kamara's pants are too tight. Where is she going to conceal it?"

Rohan had to smile at that. Kamara's pants were indeed very tight and were doing a good job emphasizing her long legs. Kat continued. "We are going to converse, not to wage a mini-war. Additionally, the Kings and Commoners has a strict no guns policy."

Voss was still in a bad mood following his loss to Kamara earlier and his response was a stormy silence.

Rohan cut in, "Ok fine, we get it. Tonight, requires a woman's touch or whatever other sexist colloquialism you are referencing to get your way on this. You were born a long time ago and you haven't realized that we men have rights too, equal suffrage and what not. If there is trouble, call us immediately. You do know how to use a cell phone right, old timer?"

The soucouyant grinned, "In a witty mood are we, Le Clerc? I have handled more trouble on my own than you will live to see, but I realize that you feel left out. If there is a problem I will call you so that you can assist in cleaning up the mess."

Kamara stepped up to him before Rohan could say anything. "We will be fine, hun, it's just a trip to the club, we will be back in a couple hours, and there is nothing to worry about." She gave him a conciliatory pat on the arm and a peck on the cheek and with that the women filed out the wide front double door.

"At least let us drive you guys there," Rohan shouted after them.

"Kat is driving," Lisa replied.

"Driving what? A horse drawn buggy? Doesn't she have cataracts by now? Arthritis in her wrists or something? She's a hazard on our nation's roadways," Rohan said, trying to get in as many barbs as he could before the door closed behind the women.

Agrippa barked in support for Rohan and ran after his owner. Lisa commanded him to stay and he whined but complied as they left.

"You really should not needle her about her age," Voss said when the door had closed. "Soucouyant don't like that, especially those who have had sad lives."

"She's bullet proof," Rohan replied, "Besides how do you know she has had a sad life?"

"She waited for us at the edge of a swamp for years, pretending to age so as not to raise suspicion. Only a tremendous sense of duty could trigger that sort of devotion in one so powerful. She owes someone a deep debt."

Rohan was thoughtful for a while. "Duly noted."

"So, are we going to sit here waiting for them to return like good househusbands or is there something else we can do?"

"I requested a list of names from the Guild, potential suspects for the man we are looking for that they have not emailed yet. I would also like them to look at Tarik. We should pay them a visit while the women club it up."

"This early?"

"Early? It is almost midnight."

"Exactly, the moon is strong tonight. Maybe we should wait for it to set before going there. You know the moon strengthens the occult."

"You don't trust your own handlers now, Voss?"

"My right hand does even trust my left hand."

"Must make it difficult for you to wash yourself," Rohan smiled. "Let's just drive by and see how the situation develops."

"I'm coming." This from Tarik who had appeared from somewhere balancing a plate heaped with food in one hand.

"Of course, you are. Let's make it a guys' night out," Rohan said. Voss muttered something about children eating too much well past their bedtimes.

The group of men dispersed with an agreement to reconvene in ten minutes for their midnight drive.

***

Lisa felt good. The clothes Kat had picked out fit perfectly and were of a style she would have selected for herself. Even the shoes fit. She wanted to ask Kat how she had made such great choices but somehow she knew she would not get a straight answer. Instead, as Kat drove, they talked about what to expect when they got to the Kings and Commoners. Kat's instructions had been that Lisa and Kamara should just follow her lead. If they saw anything strange they were not to gawk, stare, or comment. They were to act as if they belonged at the Club.

Most importantly, if she told them to run, they should run immediately. Lisa was not sure how she was supposed to run in six-inch heels, but she would try. Kat had also shown them the locations of five well-maintained weapons stashed in the SUV in various secret compartments that would withstand any level of scrutiny short of tearing the car apart completely. The weapons included a Remington 870 tactical shotgun with a pistol grip and a fully automatic HK G36C. Kamara had not seemed surprised when the woman revealed the weapons, but Lisa had believed Kat's speech about the non-necessity of guns.

"I thought we didn't need guns?" she asked.

"We can't be armed in the club," Kat replied, "but it always pays to be prepared."

Kat parked. They exited the car and went directly to the front of the long line that snaked around the corner of the multi-storied building that housed the night club. Kat whispered something to the large bouncer in a too-small shirt and they were ushered into the club. The three women were immediately enveloped in a cloud of smoke from a fog maker. Swirling, colored lights were reflected and refracted by the smoke in a dazzling display. The smell of expensive liquor mixed with the sharp scent of a plethora of perfumes and colognes, the smell of sweat, and pent up lust. The thumping bass combined with the noise of the reveling throng was disorienting. Lisa felt like she had been tossed into a tumble dryer with a box of exploding firecrackers. It took her a moment to adjust.

The bouncer led the way through the crowd to a door in the back wall guarded by two equally oversized men. Kat held up her hand and showed them the ring she wore. The bouncer allowed her to insert the ringed finger into a round hole in the door where the keyhole should have been. There was a click and the bouncer pushed the door open and held it while the three women filed in. He shut it behind them.

The noise died when the door closed. They stood in a short dark hallway which opened into a vaulted main room. Lisa guessed they were now in the Kings section of the Kings and Commoners. On one side of the richly-appointed room was a bar that occupied the entire length of the wall and was staffed by six bartenders. A rack holding drinks extended two stories tall to the ceiling, and full access to the shelves required track rolling ladders like those Lisa had seen in large libraries. She imagined they must have every type of rum, liqueur, vodka, whiskey, and tequila ever distilled. One of the bartenders opened a door in the side wall of the bar and Lisa caught a glimpse of refrigerated beverages shedding frost. She was suddenly very thirsty.

121

The rest of the room was set up like a restaurant. The walls were lined with booths that seated up to six persons. In the center of the room, a team of chefs prepared gourmet meals in a roofless glass box that reduced the kitchen noises to a hush. The wooden floor was polished to a warm sheen, and indirect lighting created a dim ambiance conducive to the birth of schemes and plots.

Attractive waiters glided silently from booth to booth ensuring that no crystal glass remained empty. Lisa heard the murmur of conversation mingled with the muted hum of vintage calypso music wafting from craftily-placed speakers.

The trio were ushered to a booth and seated. Lisa tried to mimic Kat's cool detached demeanor, although, sitting across from a soucouyant in an exclusive night club, she felt completely out of her depth. She had been born in Port-of-Spain General Hospital and had grown up and gone to school, as a child and as a teenager in Belmont, walking distance from her home. Her parents had been, and still were, very protective of her. Her most rebellious act before discovering her psychic ability had been double-piercing both ears as a secondary school student. Now, although she had never even been on an international flight, she had somehow managed to travel the Astral plane and had made snap decisions in high-staked situations. Her parents would be horrified.

They each ordered a drink which arrived almost instantaneously. Kat whispered into the waiter's ear and he nodded. They sat in silence nursing their liquor until a large man in a dark, well-tailored suit came to their table and politely asked that they follow him. The women rose, abandoning their beverages to create little pools of condensation on the teak tabletop.

They were led into a gold elevator upholstered in red leather. The man swiped a security card, pressed the button for the third floor, then exited with a nod, leaving the women in the elevator. Lisa thought, *Three women on the third floor. Maybe that was a good sign.*

On arrival at the third floor, the elevator door opened behind the women which caught everyone but Kat by surprise. Apparently the size of the guards increased proportionally with the floor they secured because the man who opened the elevator door was not only tall, but so muscular that his arms at rest could not lay flat against his body.

He led them wordlessly down a hall to a tall door. He knocked once and the door opened to reveal a room furnished in leather and wood. A massive fish tank occupied the entire back wall. Several meal-sized fish swam lazily about the tank. A large, dark desk dominated the middle of the room and behind the desk sat a middle-aged Indian man. His features were sharp and clean and his hair was slicked back. He wore a charcoal business suit with a wine-colored shirt. Although the two uppermost buttons of his shirt were undone, its French cuffed sleeves were clasped together by sterling silver and amber cufflinks monogrammed with the letters 'CD'. He sat forward, his fingers interlaced in front of him, his keen, deep-set eyes missing nothing.

There were two other occupants in the room. One, a large ebony man stood in a corner studying the women. The muscles of his chest tested the seams of his black suit-vest every time he inhaled. The other man was a tall, lean, Caucasian man with colorless eyes who sat in a leather chair off to one side, flipping through a magazine, but observing every move the women made.

Bodyguards, Lisa thought.

"Please sit." The man behind the desk gestured to a leather couch off to the right of the desk. He then rose, came around the desk, and propped himself on the front edge. "My name is Cassan Davilmar. How may I be of service?"

"We would be best served if you stopped lying. You are not Cassan," Kat said flatly. "You fit the description, but you are not him."

Lisa raised her eyebrows, initially surprised by Kat's bold accusation but then she remembered that Kat seemed to be able to discern truth from lies.

The man seemed taken aback. The pale-eyed bodyguard started to rise, but Cassan motioned him to sit back down.

"I'm Cassan. If you do not believe that well then you can leave."

"You're in his office and you are wearing his clothes," Kat said pointing to the monogrammed cuff. "But you are not him, which leads me to believe that something bad has happened to him and you are trying to get to the bottom of it. Perhaps I can offer some assistance in locating him. But if you value maintaining your ruse above finding Cassan then our business here is over." Kat rose to leave and the other women followed suit.

As the women headed for the door, Cassan's imposter and the pale-eyed bodyguard shared a hushed but animated conversation.

"Stop. Hey, hold on, stop. You are very perceptive. I'm Dr. Uriah Davilmar, Cassan's older brother, and you are right. Cassan has disappeared." Uriah dropped the contrived Trinidadian accent and now spoke with a London accent as he firmly shook each of the women's hands in turn.

"Cassan vanished and you feel safe masquerading as him?" Kamara asked when Uriah took her hand.

"Well, we look a lot alike, and impersonating him has been a good way to meet the people who come to his office. One of them may be able to give a clue to his location." Uriah returned to his seat behind the desk. "Cassan also made me promise that I would oversee the business if something was to happen to him, at least until an orderly transition could be arranged." He turned to Kat. "How did you know that I was not him?"

"Well you do look a lot like him, almost identical. But I have a talent for sniffing out lies," Kat replied. "Also, I met Cassan once some time ago, and, while our meeting was brief, the circumstances were unforgettable. He would have known who I was when I entered."

That Kat knew Cassan should not have shocked Lisa. Kat's membership at the Kings and Commoners was the reason they had made it into the office in the first place. Lisa felt silly for not having put two and two together earlier.

"Cassan's clients are not the type of people who make house calls so when you ladies showed up and asked for him I took the risk of seeing you personally. You said you might be able to assist in finding him?"

"Perhaps. You said you are a doctor?"

"Yes, a psychiatrist." The man relaxed, his shoulders rounding as he adopted his own persona. "Three days ago, Mr. Wrise calls." Uriah gestured to the Caucasian bodyguard, "and tells me that Cassan had been abducted and that I should fly here from London as soon as possible, pursuant to my promise to run the business should anything happen. So I came and since then I have been trying to find him," Uriah said.

"Why would Mr. Wrise call you instead of the police?" Lisa asked.

Uriah choked on a laugh. "Well, in the first place, the nature of Cassan's business does not lend itself to legal channels of recourse if something goes wrong. Secondly the circumstances of his disappearance are beyond strange, not the sort of thing our police force would or could deal with. Thirdly, Wrise was following Cassan's clear instructions. I just want to find my brother and return to my practice in London."

"Beyond strange disappearance?" Kat echoed, raising a well-manicured eyebrow.

"Perhaps it is best that Mr. Wrise explain as he was on scene when the Cassan was taken."

"Uriah, we do not know these women. You have already told them too much." Wrise spoke in a quiet, even tone that still managed to contain an air of threat. Lisa suspected he never raised his voice.

Uriah considered Wrise's words. "How do you know Cassan?" he asked looking at Kat.

"I needed certain rare ingredients for spell. Cassan had them." Kat replied, divulging just enough information to signal to Uriah that she was not a neophyte to the occult.

Uriah contemplated her response in silence. "Mr. Wrise, I know your loyalty is to Cassan and to the business, but these women are the best lead we have had so far. The sooner we get Cassan back, the sooner I can get out of your hair. So kindly share with these women the circumstances of my brother's disappearance."

Wrise's pale eyes narrowed then he shrugged his shoulders in acquiescence. He reached for a remote control on a small table next to his leather chair, pointed to the ceiling, and clicked a button. A large flat panel monitor descended. Wrise pressed on the remote again and a video began to play.

The video appeared to be from a warehouse security camera feed, and, while the video was in color, there was no sound. Five men stood around a wooden crate about the size of a mini-fridge. One of the men was Wrise. The other recognizable person in the video was a man who looked a lot like Uriah, but who had a younger more rakish cast to his face and a haughty look to the eye. Lisa assumed this was Cassan. Two other men were prying open the lid of the wooden crate with crowbars, while the fifth man stood a couple feet back, armed with an AK-47 rifle that he trained unwaveringly on the box.

Though the video had no sound, Lisa imagined she could hear the men's hearts pounding. Their postures radiated tension. The lid of the wooden crate was finally pried off and the four side panels of the container fell sideways to the floor to reveal a solid black cube about three-feet tall. One of the men knocked his crowbar against the black box then put his ear to it, listening. He turned and his mouth moved as he began saying something to Cassan but he never finished. A pale arm shot out through the side of the box and clawed across the man's throat. The injured man's hands clutched his neck in a vain attempt to stanch the arterial spray but a crimson pool had already started spreading on the floor.

Wrise's lips mouthed a curse and he drew a gun from a shoulder holster. By this time another arm had emerged from the box. The side of the box buckled and flexed outward as if it was made of cold molasses as the creature inside hauled itself out.

A head emerged, eyeless and nose-less with a mouth that was a wide thin slash. That mouth was armed with rows of small hooked teeth. The creature emerged from the box slowly as if the box was resisting its egress. AK-47 man opened fire and Wrise started shooting a second later. They were both good shots and most of the bullets pulverized the thing's face. The creature, however, was not perturbed by the well-placed fusillade. It hauled the rest of its body through the box and paused for a moment on all fours.

It was curiously shaped, like a bony man but with pale almost-translucent skin. Its knees bent in the wrong direction and its elbows had two joints. The macabre nature of the creature and the silence of the video made the whole scene surreal. The man with the crowbar hit it across its ruined face and in response, it disemboweled him with a claw.

AK-47 man reloaded. Wrise reloaded. Both opened fire again. The man with the machine gun walked toward the thing as he fired in bursts grouping his shots closely, the gunmanship of someone who was well-trained. The creature ate the punishment. It was still on all fours as if escaping the box had exhausted it. AK-47 man emptied his clip and was reaching for a side arm when the creature rose with the speed of a lagahoo, grabbed the man, and bit him in the face removing his lower jaw complete-ly. The man fell to the floor bleeding and clutching his face.

The creature was upright now and it approached Cassan, ignoring Wrise completely. Cassan made no move to run. Wrise however began to move between the monstrosity and his employer. Cassan held up a hand staying Wrise, then he held up a hand to the creature and his mouth began to move as if he was speaking. The creature's approach slowed and its movements became more laborious as if the atmosphere around it had congealed into something thicker than air. Cassan's mouth continued to move and the creature took a forced step back toward the box.

Then Cassan and the creature seemed to reach some sort of equilibri-um. The creature could make no forward progress, but Cassan could force it no closer to the box. Wrise brought his gun up and pulled the trigger hitting the creature in its pale bony chest. Its focus switched to its attacker and it moved toward Wrise like a train. Cassan's invisible bonds apparently only applied when he had the creature's attention. Cassan's mouth moved in a shout. The creature switched directions and was upon Cassan before he could raise a new defense. It grabbed him by the throat and dragged him towards the box. Before Wrise could move, it plunged into the vis-cous surface of the box with Cassan in tow. Wrise tried to follow them but slammed into the box, its surface having apparently become solid once more.

The video ended with an image of Wrise talking frantically into a cell phone while checking the pulses of the downed men.

"So, Satan has Cassan," Lisa said glumly after the video had ended. She felt as if she was being constantly introduced to brand new horrors.

Kamara elbowed her and Lisa sat up, marshalling her face into an expression she hoped suggested that she saw men dragged into solid boxes every day.

Kat asked, "Why do you even think he is alive?"

"I've looked at the video several times and this looks like a kidnapping. The creature only killed people who got in the way. If it wanted Cassan dead he would be dead." Uriah turned to Wrise. "Kindly elaborate on the circumstances under which this box came into our possession."

"Uriah, for the record, we do not know these birds, and I don't think we should be talking to them."

Uriah again spoke patiently as if reasoning with a recalcitrant patient. "Wrise, when we rescue Cassan, I will ensure that he knows that all the information we shared was shared based on my orders. The worst has already happened Cassan has been taken."

Wrise peered at the women, sighed, and began. "The business we do here is, in theory, pretty simple. We are facilitators. Our clients either have personal property that needs long-term protection or property that needs to be delivered to another owner or property that needs to be held temporarily. Basically, it's an escrow-storage-delivery service.

"The items that come into our possession are, of course, not the sort that you can hand to the postman or keep in any ordinary storage facility. Some of it is what you would expect, items of an ordinary but illicit nature. However, we also move, hold or transfer items of a more…magical persuasion. Clients pay fees based on an established formula weighing, among other things, the nature of the items protected as well as whether the client wishes to remain anonymous and wants the contents of his parcel or container or storage box to remain anonymous. Full anonymity, where we do not know the client or the contents is categorized as a 'Full Black' and storing a Full Black incurs an upfront fee of one hundred thousand dollars and five thousand dollars for every day it remains in our care." Wrise paused and glanced at Uriah once more before continuing. "This crate came to us as a Full Black. The fee was paid upfront in cash before we collected the box."

"So why did you open it, it being a Full Black and all?" Lisa asked.

"Sharp as a tack, aren't you," Wrise commented. "The one thing we absolutely do not do, is traffic living human beings. Cassan detests the trade. We heard a woman crying from inside the box."

"So you were going to rescue the woman?"

"No, well yes, but this was different. We received the box on a Thursday and placed it at a secure location. The crying started on the Friday night and we all heard it regardless of where we were. No matter how far away we got from the crate, we heard her. The effect was limited to those who did the initial pickup, me and the three men who died on the video. We heard it all day and all night, even in our dreams, an incessant weeping, like a voice from the bottom of a well, begging for help.

"We have had strange things happen before but this ranked pretty close to the top of the list. However, the crate was scheduled for an anonymous drop-off within a couple days and the four of us wanted to keep it quiet until the drop date came. Then hopefully it would become another person's problem."

"Which one of you caved and told Cassan about the possibility that there was a woman in the box?" Kat asked.

"Yohan, the guy on the video who hit the thing with the crowbar. He caved and told Cassan. Once the boss knew, there was no way he was delivering that box if there was even the slightest chance that there was a living person in it. We called up the other guys and went to the warehouse. The rest is on the tape."

"Who did the box come from?"

"I have no idea. Cassan gave me instructions for the pickup. I assembled the team. The crate was left essentially in the middle of nowhere. A clearing in the Moruga Forest. It took us a day to hike to the location and three days to hike out with it. It weighed a damn ton. We probably should have airlifted."

Wrise turned to Uriah. "I've done what you asked. Now what?"

"Can you help us?" Uriah asked Kat. "Do you know anything about this box and where my brother might be?"

"The box is called an Apandoradra," Kat explained. "It is a gateway that allows beings to travel from one place to another within a given realm or even to travel from one realm to another. The thing that took Cassan is a maboya." She paused. "Defining what a maboya is, is difficult, that word is used to describe a wide range of bad Amerindian spirits. Those spirits can act independently, but more often they possess a person, causing physical and mental changes. I think you are right. I think Cassan is alive somewhere. If you let us look at the box perhaps we can figure out where the last user travelled to."

"Why do you assume we kept the damn thing?" Uriah replied.

"Because you probably would not destroy a box into which your brother had disappeared. You may have moved it. Secured it in a steel vault somewhere, set guards with more guns on it, but you would not have destroyed it."

"Can other things come through?" Wrise asked, obviously with a mind toward security.

"It depends, coming through an Apandoradra, particularly one that has been used many times, is not easy. It's physically taxing even for the strongest monsters. Each box therefore has a finite number of uses. The boxes were one of the first attempts at creating gateways between the realms and within them. They are the steam engines of astral travel. As you have seen, they are a good way to send a nasty little gift.

"Why do you think it was sent for Cassan? The box was scheduled for delivery to a third party."

Kamara piped up, "Maboya are controlled by the one who releases them, I believe. The maboya would only take Cassan if its handler wished it. Right?" She looked at Kat.

"That is only a B-plus answer, Kamara," Kat commented. "They can be controlled, but only if the correct spells are used in the first place. The spells to raise maboya are very specific and they are written in Arawak, Carib or Mayan hieroglyphics the interpretations of which are imprecise at best. Perhaps this maboya was under the proper controls of his master. Or maybe it was meant for someone else, who can say for sure. The fact that no one has contacted you for delivery of the box speaks volumes. Take me to the box and I may be able to tell you where the maboya took your brother and boss. We are wasting time."

Uriah pondered a moment then rose and walked to the back of the room. "Well don't just sit there. Come with me," he commanded. The women rose to follow. Uriah walked to the back of the room to a life-sized metal sculpture of two men stick fighting. He yanked on one of the metal sticks and a trapdoor opened in the floor to reveal a narrow but well-illuminated staircase.

"I apologize for the theatrics. This is Cassan's office not mine," Uriah said with a sheepish look at the secret door.

He started down. Kat hesitated for a moment before she stepped on to the stairs. Lisa and Kamara shared a look then followed. Wrise formed the rearguard of the procession. The stairway was long and doubled back on itself at regular landings. They descended at least six floors. The stairway terminated at the start of a long high-ceilinged hallway. The hallway itself opened on to a wide well-lit chamber. Inside the chamber was a massive vault door.

The chamber was guarded by six men in black fatigues and body armor. A fifty-caliber belt-fed machine gun was mounted on a swivel that allowed it a 360-degree command of the room. The gun was manned by two more men. A ninth man sat inside a bullet-proof kiosk that appeared to house the communication equipment. All the guards bristled with weapons, semi-automatic rifles that looked sleek and venomously insectile. Lisa could smell the gun oil.

"Please don't let the guns bother you. We had to take extra precautions after the incident. In any event there would be armed guards here regardless," Uriah said. "This is one of Cassan's vaults, one location where he stores escrowed items. The security feed you saw before is from this room." Uriah led the way to the door. The silent guards evaluated every move the party made.

Uriah punched in a lengthy security code, swiped a key card, then turned the massive wheels on the vault door. Wrise repeated the procedure with his own credentials and turned the vault lever the opposite way. The door opened smoothly revealing a climate-controlled warehouse. Beyond the threshold there were rows and rows of tall, steel shelves bearing boxes, crates, tarpaulin-covered shapes, pieces of furniture, and all manner of what appeared to be mostly junk.

They entered the subterranean warehouse. The shelves created a maze, but every shelf was labeled with some sort of mapping code. Uriah seemed to know the way. The party soon arrived at a cleared area in the warehouse.

In the middle of the floor sat a cube-shaped object covered with a tarp. Uriah approached the object and gingerly removed the covering. Under the tarp was the solid cube they had seen in the video. It was so black it seemed to drink all the light that struck it and it was perfectly smooth without being glossy. Lisa thought, it looked innocuous. Doorways are not really dangerous…it's what comes through them.

Kat made no move to join Uriah next to the cube.

"Lisa luv, you're up," Kat said cheerily indicating that Lisa should get closer to the cube.

Lisa sputtered, "W…w…what do you mean I'm up?"

"Touch the box, see what it tells you."

"Me? I have no training for this."

"Sometimes beginners' luck is all the training you need. Jump right into the deep end. I know how you saved Rohan. Just relax and let the psychic energy flow. Look at Kamara. She followed my instructions back in Sea Lots and she got to keep all her fingers." Kat grinned, her bright eyes twinkling.

Lisa frowned but started towards the cube. The first few butterflies of what she suspected would become a swarm, took flight in her stomach. As fearful as she was, she understood that Cassan was their only lead to the malevolent sorcerer and so she had to push past her fear. Instinctively, she trusted Kat but the soucouyant operated in a manner that while perhaps well-thought out, because she never shared the intermediate steps in her reasoning, seemed reckless. "Should I use one hand or two?"

"Do you want to gamble the loss of both hands at once?" Kat asked still grinning.

"Now isn't the time for jokes, Kat," Kamara scolded.

"Who says that I'm joking," Kat said allowing the grin to fall from her face. Uriah observed the exchange in silence. Lisa stood in front the cube.

"Let the record show that I do not want to do this." With that she placed both hands on the light-absorbing cube. It felt as smooth as it looked but surprisingly it was warm like a living thing. The box began to hum, the vibrations in sync with the natural frequency of her very cells. A cold wind slammed into her and suddenly she was floating through the air. Up through the ceiling she went. Up through the ceiling and out into the night.

As it was before when she had traveled to assist Rohan, she felt neither fear nor discomfort. She found herself above the Kings and Commoners. She saw the white Mercedes SUV where they had left it in the parking lot. She floated high above Port-of-Spain, commanding a clear view of its unique skyline. The mountains that bordered the city's northern outskirts were dark bastions against a moonlit sky. To the west, the Gulf of Paria was a black expanse dotted with illuminated buoys and bigger brighter oil tankers. She had a moment to look toward the direction of her house in Belle Eau Road, Belmont. The hills of that area were bejeweled with the lights of many houses and the warm promise of home beckoned to her.

She moved eastward, away from the city toward Laventille. Sporadic late-night traffic was visible around Independence Square. Next, she traced a path above the Eastern Main Road following it until she was above the back road that led to Troumacaque and Pashley Street.

From there she traveled over the hills of Laventille proper. Her forward motion halted above the red steel roof of a large dilapidated house secured by a high wall. She slowly descended toward the rooftop. She thought her feet would slam into the metal surface of the roof, but she continued downward, through the galvanized sheet metal as if she was a specter.

There was no sensation to indicate her passage through the roof. She passed through as if it was as insubstantial as the air. She found herself in a room on the uppermost floor of the house. The room was bare save for a rusty metal bed with a thin mattress and a chair. There was a window that was heavily barred with wrought iron. A man paced the room. He was small, wiry, and of Indian descent. His clothes were rumpled but well-tailored. When he turned in her direction she noticed that he looked like a younger, handsomer version of Uriah. This must be Cassan.

"Cassan," Lisa whispered, but the man appeared not to hear her. She hissed louder, "Cassan." The man continued pacing. She floated over to him and clouted the back of his head. His response to the assault was to scratch the back of his head as if her blows had no more force than a mosquito's landing. She concluded that in her current state she could not be heard or seen. She decided to reconnoiter. She exited through the door without opening it. *This is lovely,* she thought. She felt light and happy and free. Perhaps she would stay like this forever.

She made note of where the room was in the house, memorizing its position relative to the other rooms on the upper floor. *Why am I memorizing this location again?* she wondered. *Oh right Kat and Uriah will want to know. But who was Uriah?* She could not seem to remember. This is so nice. She went back to the room and entered through the door again. She floated about three feet off the ground observing the man and wondering how she could communicate with him.

Suddenly, the door opened and a lovely girl in a red and gold sari entered. The girl's head jerked upward and she made direct eye contact with Lisa. *Can she see me?* Lisa wondered. The girl walked slowly over to her with her head cocked to one side and when she was within arm's reach she grabbed Lisa's ankle.

The contact was like a jolt of electricity, shocking Lisa out of her reverie and into full realization of where she was and what she had come to do. She instinctively tried to escape through the roof, but the girl was like an anchor. Panicked, Lisa kicked the girl in the face and wrested her foot free. Her return was not the pleasant journey that the first passage had been. She slammed into her physical body back in the subterranean warehouse and immediately felt weighted and sluggish. When she opened her eyes, she was staring at the ceiling, her view obscured by the barrels of four guns. Above the guns were the dispassionate faces of men, she was sure would shoot her if necessary and would not lose sleep over it. But among those faces were those of two women she thought she should recognize.

Her brain began to awaken. Her mind felt as if it were coated in fuzz and lint, but the women's names came to her.

"Kat…Kamara, what the hell happened?"

"What is your name?" Kat asked.

"My name is…my name is…I'm Lisa Cyrus and you asked me to touch the box. I have a black dog and I work at the Watcher's Guild." She blurted out as many facts as she could to establish her identity.

There was an almost palpable release of tension. The armed men took a step back and Kat and Kamara knelt at her side and helped her to sit up. The story tumbled out of her. "I was flying and I saw him and there was a girl who saw me and she grabbed me but I escaped."

"You know where Cassan is?" Uriah asked excitedly.

"Yes, I can take you to the place."

"A girl?" Kat asked.

"Yes, a girl in a sari. She came to the room. Cassan could not see me, but she could. She tried to hold me there."

"She tried to steal your body. That girl is probably a specter, she could have followed your trail here and taken your body, leaving you the ghost. You began to thrash about just before you returned and we thought a maboya had possessed you. Ergo the men with the guns."

Lisa looked thoughtful for a moment, "It's not so bad, being without a body. To be honest it is pretty nice, it is like a dream."

"For a short time it is like that, but that level of existence is fraught with its own perils. You did well, Lisa, better than you can appreciate right now."

"Why didn't you go, Kat?" Lisa asked.

Kat smiled, "If I were to go, who would pull on the tether to draw you back. Look." With that Kat pinched something invisible in the air.

"I don't see anything."

"Look closer."

And Lisa did. Then she saw it. Leading from Kat's fingers was a fine thread like a single strand of spider's silk. The thread was attached to the hem of Lisa's dress.

"The way forward is marked by the passage of the last ones to use the cube, but if you travel in spirit, it's safer if someone is there to pull you back."

On the way back up the stairs, Lisa walked in silent thought as Uriah and Kat made plans for rescuing Cassan from the house in Laventille.

"We can take it from here," Uriah said. "Just let Lisa draw us a map and I can have some of Cassan's best men assault the house."

"You send your men into that house and you will never hear from them again," Kat replied. "I have two men in mind who are better than all of yours combined."

"This is my brother. I don't know or trust your men."

"Uriah, within an hour of arriving here, we located your brother. It is also in our best interest to see him safely returned. Trust me when I tell you, my men are better."

"I want at least one of our men inside."

"Fair enough. Wrise is acceptable." Kat replied quickly as if she had already considered it.

"Mr. Wrise, I assume you are fine with this?" Uriah asked to which Wrise grunted an affirmative response.

When they finally emerged from the stairway and back into the office, it was three in the morning. "Wrise, follow our car and I will introduce you to your teammates for this adventure. We are going to have to raid the house as soon as possible before Cassan is killed or moved. This little girl might have been a lost spirit or she may be under our obeah man's control so we cannot assume that we will have the element of surprise."

When the ladies finally got back to the car and closed the door, Kamara asked, "Why Wrise?"

Kat was thoughtful for a moment. "He reeks of blood, and where Rohan and Voss are about to go will require bloody men. Wrise will not hesitate to pull the trigger if needed."

"You think it will be dangerous?" Kamara asked, worry creeping into her voice.

"Extremely," Kat replied and let her response hang without elaboration.

As they drove back to Stone, it occurred to Lisa that there was a reason only immortals did this sort of work. This lifestyle would stress any ordinary person to death in a week. She yawned. It had been another long night and the headlights of Wrise's car shining through the back window reminded her that the night would only get longer.

Chapter 15

"Yuh talk about run.
Ah nearly bus' mi head. Run.
De livin' running from the dead. Run.
A ghost say "don't run mi lad,
come leh we play a game of cards." Run.
Well is now ah runnin' in truth. Run.
Mi foot stick in a mango root. Run.
Ah fall down inside a tomb. Run.
Ah get up with a zoom.

—From "Love in the Cemetery" by Lord Kitchener

Rohan, Voss, Tarik, and Agrippa had been cruising around St. James waiting for the moon to set so they could visit the Guild, when the ladies called to say they were headed back to Stone. The soucouyant being her usual cryptic self would give no further details about what transpired during the meeting at Kings and Commoners. Instead she requested that the men cut short their outing and return to Stone immediately.

Voss turned pointed the car eastward, but before returning to the house stopped to purchase doubles along Ariapita Avenue. Tarik ate seven, Agrippa ate nine, Rohan and Voss settled with two apiece, after which they piled back into the car.

"Is it just me, or has Kat summoned us?" Rohan asked as they were driving off.

"I feel pretty summoned," Voss responded.

As they pulled away from the curb, a white panel van clipped the front of their car, causing them to stall. The van itself was derailed by the impact and ended up running into a lamp post. Voss and Rohan got out of the car.

Drunk drivers on Ariapita on a Friday night, nothing new here, Rohan thought. Voss started towards the van, but Rohan placed a hand on his shoulder. Something about the occupants of the panel van made him hesitate. Agrippa's fangs were bared and a snarl rumbled through his body.

"Hold on, something isn't right here."

"I just got this thing waxed," Voss said pointing to the broken head light and the dent on the right side of the car.

The people in the van did not get out. The driver was attempting to restart the van but it was choking. Voss' eyes narrowed. "What are they doing?"

The occupants got out of the van, three men, a woman, and a small girl. The party of five ran into the middle of the street forcing traffic to stop. Agrippa's snarls were now a thunderous roar but he stayed put. Two of the men approached the first car in the halted line of vehicles and hauled a young man out through his driver side window and dumped him on the ground. A vicious punch to the face of the shocked man ensured that he stayed floored.

The hijackers entered and sped off in the stolen car, pursued by a wake of curses and horn honking. The entire thing had happened in under a minute.

"What the f…" Rohan stemmed the curse with a glance at Tarik.

"Do you smell that, Rohan?" Voss asked.

"I do," Tarik replied, wrinkling his nose. "They smell like dead bodies."

"Shall we follow them?" Voss suggested.

"No, let's get back to Stone." Rohan replied, weighing Kat's urgent summons against the urge to pursue the people who had so brazenly stolen the car. "I will call one of the other houses and let them know what happened.".

By now a small crowd of motorists and late night limers had gathered around the unfortunate carjacking victim and a couple was helping him to his feet. Rohan couldn't help but think that the man was lucky to be alive.

Thirty minutes later when they pulled into the driveway at Stone, Rohan noted a strange car parked next to Kat's SUV. He entered the house and Jonah directed them to the conference room where the women were seated conversing with a stranger. The man observed their arrival warily. Rohan noticed that his hand inched closer to the hem of his jacket where a trained eye would note a bulge that Rohan knew was a gun. Voss stepped forward and held a hand out to the man. "Wrise, what a pleasure it is to see you again." Voss was smiling but the smile did not reach his eyes.

"You know this man?" Kat asked.

"Yes, Wrise and I go way back."

"You have not aged a day, Voss," Wrise said as he stood and took Voss' hand.

"Long walks on the beach, eight glasses of water a day, and no caffeine." Voss replied, still wearing a plastic smile. "You look pretty good yourself."

Kat made introductions and spent the next few minutes filling the men in. "We need to hit the house tonight, well this morning, before he is moved or killed," she ended. "Lisa has drawn a map and can give you additional details about security."

Rohan looked at the map and whistled. "Do you know where this is? This house is in Ward Seven territory, right in the middle. There will definitely be guards."

"Ward Seven?" Lisa asked.

"The narcotics gang that controls East Port-of-Spain."

"And that is why we have our three best boys doing the wet work," Kat responded.

"Best four. I want Richard on this too." Rohan replied referring to his close friend Richard of River House.

"I don't know Richard, but I trust your judgment, Rohan."

Rohan held a hand to his chest in mock abashment. "Well, surprise, surprise. My judgment passes the Kat test."

Kat ignored the jibe.

Voss then spoke up. "So the way I see it, we need to make this very stealthy. A quick in and out. We'll use close-quarters combat firearms, suppressed of course, try to avoid the guards, but silence them quickly if necessary. If Lisa's map is accurate, we can go over the back wall. One man can then scale the outer wall of the house to Cassan's window while the others cover. We cut the bars, extract Cassan through the window, then exit over the wall."

Wrise cleared his throat before replying, "The only issue I see here is cutting the bars. Who knows how long that may take. The guy on the wall will be cannon fodder if we are spotted. Hell, Cassan might even raise an alarm. I say we go in through the back door, put the guards down floor by floor, then exit through the same back window from inside. We might even be able to do a hard hit: flash-bang, and tear-gas grenades and be out before they know what's going on," Wrise finished.

It was Rohan's turn. "I'm with Voss on the fact that we have to be stealthy. No one hits a Ward Seven safe house not even the police. If we go in hard, it's likely they might simply shoot Cassan. Then we'll be engaged in a prolonged firefight just to get out. On the other hand, Wrise has a point. I don't want to be the man dangling from a window sill, with a potentially hostile rescue target on the other side. He was unguarded when Lisa saw him, but who knows if there is a dude in there now with a sawed-off. I say we go in quiet and put down any resistance as quickly as possible. Then either we get Cassan to recognize Wrise or gag and bag him and rope him down to the yard after cutting the bars from the relative safety of inside the room."

They went back and forth for a while, hashing out the finer details until formulating a plan that was a hybrid of Voss' and Wrise's method as suggested by Rohan. By the time Richard had arrived it was close to four am. The group decided that his job would be to cover the target house with sniper fire from a nearby abandoned apartment building. For that task he had brought two guns a L115A3 AWM which was a British gun manufactured by the revered firearms company Accuracy International. His second weapon was a Barret M85 a fifty-caliber anti-materiel rifle that he lovingly called Denise Belfon.

Chapter 16

Once they had agreed on a plan of attack they put it into effect swiftly. The men suited up in dark-colored street clothes and body armor from the Stone House armory.

Once dressed and armed they left in three vehicles at five-minute intervals with Rohan and Voss driving a beat-up old-model Land Rover, Wrise in a black Nissan Sentra B13, and Richard in an ancient Datsun 180-B. None of their vehicles would raise any suspicions travelling through Laventille. Each of the men carried a side-arm. Voss and Rohan also had compact sub-machine guns designed for the close confines of a building. Wrise had a pistol grip shotgun with a suppressor. They also took knives, rope, smoke canisters, and a few flash-bang grenades. If the situation really got sticky they were ready with four incendiary grenades. Additionally, they each pocketed several pairs of plastic restraining cuffs. For cutting the bars on the window they brought an industrial bolt cutter and Rohan also packed plastic explosive charges just in case they really had to beat a hasty retreat. Always be prepared.

"How do you know Wrise?" Rohan asked Voss as they drove off into the night.

"Wrise and I were mercenaries for competing outfits. We've worked in Afghanistan, Iraq, Vietnam, Croatia, Bosnia, Serbia, The Congo, Rhodesia before it was Zimbabwe. Basically every other hot spot you can think of."

"So I take it he is not exactly a buddy. Is he like you?"

"No, not a buddy and I honestly have no idea what Wrise is. By all appearances he is an ordinary human being, at least physically. But mentally he is an entirely different creature. He is bloodthirsty, psychotic, and a very efficient and remorseless killer. Do not turn your back on him, do not trust him and do not leave him alone with anyone you love. To be honest I'm just waiting for a good moment to put a bullet in his brain." That Voss, of the fangs and claws was referring to someone else as violently inhuman took Rohan aback.

Voss turned off the main road and drove up Pashley Street. Every rut in the tarmac was transmitted through their bodies via the stiff suspension of the old Rover, and there were many ruts. Voss drove halfway up Pashley then pulled aside just before the steep hill that led on to the extension road. He parked the van behind a dumpster piled high with refuse. Across the street there was a man-made drainage channel about ten feet across and eight feet deep. They planned to use the channel as cover for their approach to the house. Wrise would approach from another direction and Richard would let them know when he was in position.

The men were linked via inner-ear short-wave radios and throat microphones. Rohan and Voss hugged the vertical wall of the drain as they approached the house at a brisk, stooped jog.

Wrise's voice came over the intercom startling Rohan. "We have a problem. They walled up the window to Cassan's room. I'm looking at it right now and there are fresh bricks and mortar filling it."

"Something else guys." This was from Richard. "I'm scanning the upper floors with the thermal scope and there is no one in the walled-up room. There are three armed men in one room and in the adjoining room there is one person who might be Cassan."

Voss exhaled, then said in a low tone, "Okay, fine. We enter the house and hit the one-man room first. If Cassan is not there we are going to have to do a floor by floor search top to bottom. Wrise, scale the wall and find a hiding spot. We'll be with you in under a minute. Richard, monitor the movement of the guards and be prepared to provide cover fire if needed."

Rohan and Voss stoop-ran about another four hundred meters down the overgrown drainage channel. They stayed in the shadows cast by the wall in the moonlight. The bushes and wild shrubs that grew along the side walls of the storm drain provided further cover. When they reached the exit point Richard confirmed that it was clear to scale the walls. From his vantage point in the upper floors of an abandoned building about a third of a mile away he had a clear view of the target house and the surrounding walls and yard. The security wall of the house was built directly on top the wall of the drainage channel creating a twenty-five-foot climb. Rohan tossed a grappling hook up the wall and quickly scaled to the top. He scanned the yard below then dropped down to the other side gingerly avoiding the roll of wickedly sharp concertina coil that topped the wall.

Landing silently on the overgrown lawn he promptly slipped behind a clump of tall bull-grass and lay flat on his stomach. The yard was unmanicured, with waist high grass, large bushy shrubs and even small trees all of which provided ample cover but also made it difficult to move silently. Voss joined him a second later and whispered into the communications mic. "Wrise, what is the situation at the entry point?"

"Two guards and a dog. No way we are getting in with them all alive. If sniper-boy can take the dog I can hit the guards before they know I'm there."

"We must minimize collateral damage and avoid a firefight. Hold tight we're heading to your location," Voss replied, then off air to Rohan. "See? Blood thirsty."

Wrise was crouched low behind a patch of wild banana trees when Rohan and Voss found him. He had a pistol drawn and his shotgun strapped across his back with some sort of hi-tech rig. He looked very much at home hiding in the bushes waiting to kill someone.

Rohan surveyed the scene. The guards stood chatting and smoking right in front the door they planned to enter. The door itself was about fifty feet away and obliquely to the right of their position. A massive dog, some brand of athletic mastiff or bandog sat alert at one of the guard's feet. It was not on a leash and it was sniffing the wind suspiciously. Richard's perspective was ninety degrees to the left of the door so that the guards, with their backs to the door, presented their profiles to him. Voss, Rohan and Wrise were downwind of the security detail otherwise the dog would have already raised an alarm.

Rohan evaluated the situation and said, "I agree with Wrise, the dog definitely has to go, but I can get the men before they know I'm here, without killing them that is. Richard on three put the dog down, I'll handle the rest. Do not miss," he emphasized. "One..." Rohan slowly broke cover in a crouched jog. "Two..." he scooped up a smooth, fist sized rock that looked like it had been part of some, now defunct landscaping project and broke into a dead run at the guardsmen.

The men were still chatting, but the dog's large head swiveled towards Rohan. For a moment the dog looked at him quizzically as if it thought he was completely insane. It sounded no warning bark or growl as it charged him. The men's heads turned to trace the dog's trajectory. "Three..." Rohan launched the stone and it took the first man in the temple with a sickening thud. The unlucky guard fell in a heap.

Rohan leapt into the air and the massive brindle-coated dog leapt too. The second guard was overcoming his shock and moving his AK 47 into firing position. Richard's bullet took the dog in its right side while it was in mid-air. The high velocity round struck the dog just behind the shoulder joint, knocking it off its collision course with Rohan. It was dead before it hit the ground. Rohan's boot heel slammed into the face of the second guard an instant later, before the man could fire a shot.

The injured man staggered backward but gamely clung to consciousness attempting to bring his gun up again. Rohan punched him, hard. This time he went down and stayed down. Rohan began gagging and bagging the two downed guards securing their wrists and ankles with the plastic ratcheting cuffs. He never heard the second dog that slammed into him from behind. He did however hear a buzz then a snap, which was a small sonic boom of a bullet travelling faster than the speed of sound, as a round zipped past his head and struck the attacking dog in the face.

"You're welcome Ro." Richard said into the intercom.

"We could have just shot them," Wrise said grudgingly as he and Voss jogged up to Rohan.

Voss unscrewed the single naked bulb overhanging the door so that they were again enveloped by the moonlit dimness. One guard had a bunch of keys which Rohan took. Wrise dragged the still-unconscious guards back to the banana patch and left them there. The keys unlocked the back door. Richard confirmed that there was no one on the other side of the door at least as far as his thermal scope was concerned.

The men entered cautiously. The house was old and its layout muddled as if one set of people had started its construction and subsequent builders added to the building without paying heed to the previous builder's architectural goals.

They had entered a living area with three doors, one that led to a bedroom, one that opened into a hall, and the one through which they had passed. In one corner it appeared that someone had started the construction of a walk-in closet and had abandoned the idea. The area now housed a pile of boards.

Voss led the single file advance down the hall. Richard periodically relayed thermal intelligence to the three invaders. Thus far the only room with any sign of inhabitants was that single room on the third floor. A nagging thought occurred to Rohan. *The house seemed rather poorly guarded for a safe house.*

They found a set of concrete stairs that led to the upper floors. They ascended directly to the third floor and into a long empty hallway that led to the target room. Rohan felt completely exposed. If any of the guards in the room next to the target room decided to exit, the men would be spotted easily and a fire fight would ensue. As they snuck past the door to the guard room, Rohan heard muffled laughter on the other side. His uneasiness at the effortlessness of their entrance increased. When they came to the target door, where Richard had seen the seated person in the thermal scope, they positioned themselves around the door for a tactical entry.

Wrise fished out a set of lock picks from his pocket but before he could go to work Rohan interrupted him. "The door. Try the knob. It looks unlocked."

Wrise placed his hand on the handle and turned, the door was indeed unlocked. That niggling feeling hardened in the pit of Rohan's stomach.

"Something is off here, guys," Rohan rasped into the intercom. "I feel baited."

"And I feel really exposed in this hallway," Wrise hissed.

"There is one individual seated in the room. Back to the door," Richard whispered into the com.

Voss finger-counted down from three and Wrise turned the knob all the way and opened the door quickly. They entered rapidly but quietly.

Voss trained his gun on the seated man, who from behind appeared to be asleep. Rohan and Wrise cleared the room. Rohan closed the door quietly.

"Confirm that it's your boss," Voss said to Wrise.

Wrise approached the man with his shotgun trained on him, Voss and Rohan covered Wrise without approaching. When Wrise was close enough he clapped a hand over the man's mouth and the man turned around with a wild look in his eyes. Then the two men apparently recognized each other.

"This is Cassan Davilmar." Wrise said. "Boss, we came to get you out of here."

"It's about bloody time," the man replied in a gruff whisper, a look of relief crossing his face.

"So how do we get out of here?"

"Out this door, down the hall past the guards and out the back," Voss said matter-of-factly.

Cassan chuckled, "I tried that way before and it's no good."

"What do you mean?" Voss asked.

"Well, there's a good reason why I am not secured to this chair, why the door is not locked, and why the guys next door aren't really paying attention. This house is sentient. As long as it wants you here you're not getting out. Dammit, here I was thinking that you folks had a plan, but as you will soon see, you are just as stuck as I am."

A feeling coalesced in Rohan's stomach as if a nest of young rats had made their home in the walls of his gut. He opened the door. Where there was formerly a hallway there was now a freshly erected brick wall. The mortar between the bricks was still soft. Rohan yanked a brick free of the wet mortar. Behind that brick there was another brick and he knew that he could probably pull bricks out for millennia and there would always be another behind it.

"See." Cassan said as he settled back into the chair. "The little girl knows the way out, but she's under orders from someone else."

"What little girl?" Voss asked.

"That one, in the corner." Cassan said pointing. All the heads in the room whipped around. In a corner behind them stood a lovely Indian girl wearing a red and gold sari. She was barefooted and had the all the makings of a future beauty. Cassan's lips peeled back to reveal a sickeningly sweet smile. "Hello Ghita, how are you today, you weird child."

Rohan, Voss and Wrise stared. "How did you get in," Rohan asked recovering first.

"I'm the housekeeper, and you shouldn't be here. Lucien will not be happy." Ghita replied.

"Then let us out before Lucien finds out we are here," Voss replied.

"That is the exact opposite of my duty as the housekeeper," the girl responded as she sunk slowly into the floor as if it was quicksand and vanished.

"She does that from time to time," Cassan said airily.

"What the hell was that?" Wrise hissed.

"She's some sort of poltergeist I think, but she has a very strong presence here. She can move things, use keys, open doors. I have even touched her. She seems to exist on the cusp of being alive but not quite all the way here, or maybe she is on the cusp of being dead but not quite ready to take the hint. I get the sense that she's not here willingly. But Lucien, has her on the payroll somehow."

"Who is Lucien?"

"Lucien as it turns out is the name of the person who arranged for the pickup and delivery of the box from the warehouse." Cassan said after Wrise had quickly explain Rohan's and Voss' involvement. "I carried out a commission, facilitating the delivery of a message, you might say, to an obeah woman, but I was not supposed to find out who the sender was. I think my knowledge of that information is why I was brought here."

"Tell us about the box, your relationship with Lucien and with the obeah woman who came to you. Tell us everything," Rohan whispered to Cassan.

"Well I guess that's a fair request, seeing as we are probably going to have time to develop a lifelong friendship trapped here in this house." Cassan settled into the chair and crossed his legs at the ankles, slouching into a more relaxed pose. "I possess a talent and that talent is fearlessness. Now, this is not to be confused with recklessness, I act with the same modicum of caution toward the preservation of life and limb as any of you might, but ever since I was a child I have been fearless, I take risks.

"Uriah, my esteemed brother is terribly risk averse. He has never done anything exciting in his life and when he dies, his family will weep respectfully and his eulogy will be filled with phrases like 'he was a real standup guy'. I am not my brother. My epitaph is likely to read 'He slept with my wife and he owes me money' Uriah's uptight personality is part of the reason I am making him run the business in my absence. It brings me great pleasure to think about him sitting awkwardly in my office doing everything in his power to get back to his grey little London office." Cassan smiled as if he really was enjoying his brothers dutiful discomfit.

"Uriah and I grew up in London with our parents who had emigrated from Trinidad and Guyana. They wanted to expose us to better opportunities. In the case of my brother, this worked. He did the whole Oxford scholar thing, married a nice British girl with solid Hindu roots and has a lovely family. He did everything by the book written by Mummy and Daddy Davilmar.

"With me, the parental lessons did not take root. I dropped out of high school, got into fights, was arrested numerous times. Then I was stabbed, almost to death, spent six months in the hospital, three of which I was comatose. When I got out my mother and father packed me off back to Trinidad to live with my maternal grandmother in Caroni. That, ladies and gentlemen, was the turning point in Cassan Davilmar's life. Hold please I need to use the bathroom."

Cassan rose, walked to the door, shut it, and re-opened it. Where there had previously been a brick wall, there was now a small bathroom. Cassan went in and closed the door behind him, after a moment there was the sound of a toilet flushing and he came back out.

"Anyone thirsty?" He shut the door and opened it again and there was a vending machine from which he retrieved a bottle of water.

"What's going on here?" Voss asked his eyebrows tightly knitted.

"I honestly have no idea, whatever I want I can get it, if I focus on my desire while opening and closing the door. And to answer your burning question, no, the house does not provide hookers, believe me I've tried. It won't let me just imagine my way home either. Any attempt to escape and you either get the brick wall or a doorway to another part of the house." Cassan opened the bottle of water and drank. "Ahh, that's some good water, but I suspect it's the same water that was in the toilet. The house has a dark sense of humor, last night I wanted a steak dinner and I opened the door and there was a dead rotting cow pinned to the ceiling with a pitchfork.

"But to continue my story, I moved to Trinidad to live with granny. Granny is a bit of a dabbler, not a full-fledged obeah woman but she has been known to cast a curse or two and she can read the weather. Not just today or tomorrow's weather but years in advance, she always knows if we will have a particularly parched dry season or if the rainy season will swell the Caroni River so that we could fish for tilapia off the back porch. When Granny saw I was fearless, she asked me to help her with some things, spells, magic, stuff like that. She always lamented that the world was becoming a place where those of us who believed in Obeah were thought of as unsophisticated and backward. It had come to the point where we had to hide who we were. That is how the idea for my business came about.

"Necromancers, obeah men, mayalmen, witches, they all needed a place to store their paraphernalia anonymously and safely. They needed a security deposit box, a transfer service, a bank vault. Someone who could move their items of power around without asking questions. Someone who could stuff the ghouls back into the coffins if they escaped. Someone who could feed their Buck while they went on vacation, somewhere to store the ashes of their dead obeah-man grandfather, which by the way you do not want sitting on the mantelpiece in a regular urn. But that is another tale.

"I met those needs. Soon I became their chief facilitator and a broker. People came to me because I was good. But even putting my client service talents aside, I was the only one in the business. It has been a wild success. We were literally turning customers away. Then I received a vial of what seemed to be blood, from an anonymous sender.

"The contract was for us to act as a middle man and to simply pass it on to a certain woman who would come to my office in the Kings and

Commoners. I was to ensure that she drank the contents of the vial then and there. Now understand this, I don't pass out business cards, but neither am I in hiding. People who need to find me, can do so relatively easily. So, it wasn't strange that I allowed her to come to the office.

"The woman showed up, she drank the contents of the vial, then she went temporarily insane or maybe she was possessed, who knows, but she grew powerful. I could feel the change. She trashed my office while in the grip of her possession and had to be restrained. While under the influence of whatever was in the vial she revealed that she was supposed to raise some dead people to kill a soucouyant. That's all well and good, except that I knew this soucouyant. Her name is Katharine and she is one of the founding members of the Kings and Commoners. Though I do not count her a friend and while I believe her abrasive and aloof nature might well have driven someone to desire her death, we members of the K and C are a small group and we look out for each other as a matter of policy."

Rohan held his composure as he stored away this new bit of information about Kat. She was not just a member of Kings and Commoners, but a founding member. Although he would not admit it to her, he was increasingly impressed with the reach of the soucouyant's influence.

"My interest was piqued," Cassan continued. "I could have shot the Shouta woman in the face then and there but I had no real fear that Kat was in danger. Kat is, after all, hewn from a slab of granite. So I let the woman go and sent Kat a warning, to which she never responded which is typical of her. As for the vial, I sent that to a friend at a forensic lab to see if they could run some sort of DNA trace. Long odds, particularly in Trinidad, I know, but it was worth the effort. As it turns out the stuff in the vial was blood. Even better my forensic friend was able to get a DNA match. The blood belonged to Lucien Sardis, a wealthy businessman who was supposedly killed in a robbery years ago.

"His DNA was in the crime scene repository under cold cases. But the plot thickens. The blood itself was fresh, meaning that Lucien Sardis is walking around with power in his veins. I have no idea why an obeah man with that sort of power didn't simply think to have his record wiped.

Hubris, maybe. Whatever the case I start looking for this Lucien, and the things I uncovered gave reasons for pause.

"Mentioning his name gets doors slammed in your face. Powerful people got nervous. A woman, one of the weekend wiccans, as I call them, told me that she had heard that some obeah man was giving people power upgrades if they did tasks for him, but the people who took the deal all turned up dead. Two days later she was butchered in a home invasion. There were parts of her in almost every room of the house. The Watchers' Guild wielded their influence to suppress the goriest details, but from what I heard even her fish tank was filled with blood. The moral is, when the name Lucien is mentioned death follows. I was still digging when the black box was delivered. The rest of course you already know."

"What happened to the thing that grabbed you," Wrise asked.

"It died once it got back here. The divinium bullets messed it up."

"Divinium?" Rohan questioned.

"Silver melted down and tempered in lycan blood becomes something else altogether. Divinium they call it, a divine alloy. It is the ideal thing for killing greyborn of all varieties. It is more effective than pure silver and far more durable. How do you guys not know this?"

"The Order has not exactly been innovating these last few years, fewer lagahoo and the like."

"As I hear it, the thing on the tape ate a lot of those bullets," Voss said.

"Well, divinium is not cheap. The raw materials are not easy to come by. Silver is expensive, and we don't exactly have vats of lycan blood lying around. We usually have one divinium bullet for every five regular bullets in a clip," Cassan replied.

"Why are you still alive, Davilmar?" Rohan asked. "It seems to me that you should have been killed already if this Lucien is as nasty as the rumors suggest."

"Good question, and one to which I have no good answer. To be honest, I think he wants to ply me for information, maybe about my secret clientele, the Full Black crowd. Maybe he just wants me to sweat a bit. Maybe he had other uses for me." Cassan paused for a moment. Just as Rohan was about to ask another question Cassan interrupted him. "Oh look, she's back," Cassan said. Everyone turned and the girl in the sari was there, beautiful as a picture and hauntingly melancholy.

"What do you want? We're obviously not going anywhere," Cassan huffed.

"I want to give you a chance to leave. But to escape you must play a game. You can say no, but then I promise you, you will stay here for the rest of your lives or until Lucien decides to kill you."

"A game? What are the rules of the game?" Rohan asked.

"There is only one rule, survive. The house will try to kill you and it has many means of doing so."

"What do you get out of this Ghita?" Cassan interjected.

"I want you to deliver a message for me. Tell the soucouyant to sleep, that I wish to speak to her. Tell her what I am."

Sleep, what does she mean? Rohan thought. Aloud he said, "Sounds simple enough but what exactly are you?" Rohan said assuming that 'the soucouyant' meant Kat.

"A bottled soul. Do we have a bargain?" Ghita asked.

"Yes. We have a bargain," Rohan replied, eager to accept any opportunity to escape the house.

"What about the things in a basement? Do we have to deal with them?" Cassan asked.

"The goal is to escape. The house is infested with bad spirits. Once I let you out of this room I will be unable to protect you further. The house may employ any means to kill you including the release of the creatures in the basement." Ghita's voice was like a melody, even as she relayed the frightening news.

"Wait, what creatures?" Rohan asked.

Cassan chuckled. "People. At least they used to be people. Lucien does something to them and now they are…different. At first they look like ordinary men and women but after some time the effect of whatever Lucien does changes their physical appearance and they look like the thing that grabbed me and took me through the box."

"They are Lucien's maboya and you might have to face them," Ghita responded. "The house will decide."

"Well let's get this show on the road then." Wrise said as he checked that a round was in the chamber of his gun.

"Good. Leave through the door and remember that the only rule is survival. You do not want to die here in this house. It is not a good thing to die here." With that Ghita vanished, not through the floor this time. She just faded away slowly like the Cheshire cat from Alice in Wonderland.

"Through the door, she said." Wrise muttered as he positioned himself on the side of the door, handing Cassan his side arm. Cassan checked to see that a round was in the chamber.

Chapter 17

The men gathered along the sides of the door, Voss and Rohan on the right, Cassan and Wrise on the left. "On three...two...one." Voss pushed the door gently and it swung open, not back unto the hallway but unto the guard's room to reveal the four-man security detail Richard had identified via the thermal scope. The house had already begun trying to kill them.

The men froze in mid-laugh at some bawdy joke. Wrise wasted no time. He shot the nearest man in the chest. The suppressor muffled the percussion of the twenty-four-gauge round to a loud whisper. That act precluded any possibility of peaceful negotiation. The other three guards went for their guns and the escapees cut them down in a hail of automatic weapons fire. One of the men did not immediately die and with a last effort depressed a switch affixed to the table-top. Wrise finished him off with a headshot, but not before flashing white lights began to pulse in the room and in the hallway.

Richard's voice came over the communicator line. "Guys, hello, hello can anyone hear me?"

"Hey buddy, we hear you loud and clear."

"What the heck happened, Ro? You went silent. It's almost sunrise."

"It's a long story, but we have Cassan and we need you to keep eyes on us through the thermal scope. Can you see us now?" Rohan asked.

"Yes, you're in the guard's room. Four cooling bodies are on the floor. There are also flashing lights outside the building. Did you trigger some sort of alarm?"

"Unfortunately."

"Hold on, three large vans are coming through the front gate. About ten men in each. All armed."

"I guess we know what the alarm does. They're probably going to storm the house. I need you to cover us best you can. Also, call Kamara and Kat at Stone. Let them know that the mission has gone to shit."

155

"Will do." Over the com, Rohan heard Richard chamber a round into Denise Belfon. He pictured Richard lying in the prone firing position, perhaps on a table inside a room, aiming the fifty-caliber sniper rifle out through a window at their enemies. The thought was comforting.

This room had a window, and outside the window the blue-grey gloom of pre-dawn beckoned to Rohan. He attempted to open the window, but the moment he touched the sill, thick vines sprouted out of the wall and sealed off the portal. The vine looked like ivy but had wicked thorns.

"I guess we will have to do it by the house rules," he said to no one in particular.

"And the house always wins," Cassan chimed in glumly.

From below came the sound of stomping boots and shouted orders.

"We can't afford to get boxed in up here," Rohan said. The four men left the room as quietly as possible. The guards seemed to be doing a complete sweep of the house from the bottom up. As the four escaping men entered the hallway, Rohan felt a small pang of relief having made it even this far.

His relief was short-lived. The hall had transformed. Where there were previously only two doors, one leading to Cassan's cell and one to the guard's room, there were now six.

The four new doors flew open simultaneously and ten armed men poured into the hall and opened fire. Rohan and Cassan ducked back into the guard's room while Wrise and Voss dove into Cassan's holding room. Bullets perforated the walls and floor of the hallway. Rohan pulled the pin on a concussion grenade and tossed it into the hall.

"Wrise, Voss get flat on the floor. Richard, I need you to kill everything standing."

The concussion grenade went off with a deafening bang that left a residual high-pitched whine in Rohan's ears even thought he had covered them with his hands. Then Richard opened fire, targeting every image in the thermal scope that was standing upright. The massive .50 BMG rounds penetrated the cinderblock walls and tore the men apart. When the smoke cleared and the screaming stopped Rohan peeked out at the horror in the hall. There were grapefruit sized holes in the wall where the bullets had entered and the hallway looked like the aftermath of a paintball war in which the red team had won an overwhelming victory.

"Where to now?" Cassan asked, as he toed aside a leg still in the boot.

"Let's see where one of these new doors leads," Wrise said, as he exited the guard room. "The stairs aren't there anymore, anyway." Rohan looked at the place where the stairs used to be. There was now just a wall and he found it hard to believe that had ever been a staircase there.

Suddenly there was a moaning noise in the guard room and the sound of shambling steps. Out of the room stumbled the corpse of the man who had pressed the emergency alarm. The bullet Wrise had put into his brain had left a gaping hole in the left side of his head, but the man didn't seem to mind much. Behind him came the other four men each sporting fatal injuries. They stumbled towards Rohan's team, their legs weak like newborn calves. *This is not a fete in here, this is madness,* Rohan remembered a line from one of David Rudder's songs that seemed all too applicable.

"This keeps getting fun-er," Cassan said as he entered the nearest door. The other men followed quickly. Voss, the last man through, closed the door and bolted it. The corpses outside banged on the door, moaning and scratching like cats begging to be let in out of the rain.

The room had a window, and although it opened on to another room instead of to the outside, they all went through to put some distance between them and their pursuers. The second room was a bedroom furnished in the style of the 1900's East Port-of-Spain barrack yard. On the floor lay a battered, enameled chamber-pot stained brown by use. A rough-hewn cabinet occupied one corner, the small cabinet windows faced in chicken mesh instead of glass. A scarred rocking chair stood in another corner. Its wicker seat back had more holes that wicker and its left rocker rail was missing. A wooden box with a rooster painted on its side, had been re-purposed as a leg.

Rohan tried to raise Richard on the com, but it seemed like the house had severed contact with the outside world once more. This room had no doors or windows except for the one through which they had entered. In the first room, Rohan heard the door begin to splinter as the re-animated guards continued to hammer their fists against it.

"We may have to go back out into the hall, shoot the dead guys again and try another room," Wrise said.

"They are jumbies, they won't go down easy and we are likely to need every bullet. The door will hold them for a while, unless the house decides to let them in," Rohan replied. "Search the room for a trap-door or something."

The four men began looking, knocking on floorboards and along the wall, listening for a hollow sound that might indicate an escape route. A female voice cleared her throat behind them and the men turned around in shock, guns raised.

A woman now sat in the previously unoccupied rocking chair. She was voluptuous, dark, and wore a simply cut dress with a faded floral print. The low square neckline of the dress barely contained her ample chest. She had a broad face, attractive despite a hawk-like nose, but someone had slit her throat from ear to ear. The slash did not bleed and despite the fatal wound she tapped her small, bare feet impatiently.

"Can a lady get a light?" she asked as she proffered a hand-rolled but unlit cigarette. Cassan reacted as casually as if dead women asked him favors all the time. He reached into his suit pocket and pulled out a gold cigarette lighter. Flicking open the cover produced a green flame and he held the flame to the tip of the woman's cigarette as she inhaled deeply and blew a cloud of bluish smoke, a great deal of which exited through the slash across her throat.

"Milady may keep the lighter if she can tell us how to get out," Cassan suggested.

"You have to pay more than that for a treat from me," the woman said with a throaty chuckle and a wink. "Go into the cabinet and get me my tin of tobacco and some paper to roll another." Cassan moved to comply even though the woman had barely begun smoking the cigarette he had just lit.

"Gentlemen there is a tunnel back here!" he exclaimed. When he opened the cabinet and saw not shelves but the mouth of a square tunnel.

"That happens sometimes," the lady on the chair said. "And my price for showing you the tunnel? Tell the soucouyant that she must sleep, and that while she sleeps she must not shield her dreams. The dead need to talk to her."

Rohan wondered why so many specters needed to speak to Kat in her sleep. Cassan tossed the woman the gold lighter, she caught it, slipped it down her voluminous cleavage, and blew him a kiss, before vanishing. The men entered the low tunnel through the cabinet doors and did not spare a glance behind them as the sound of the splintering door in the adjacent room grew louder.

**

Rohan could not guess which part of the house they were in, what with the house's ever-changing blueprint and the lack of reference points he had lost all sense of direction. The men were in single file, with Voss in the lead and Rohan bringing up the rear. As they progressed, the tunnel narrowed and the ceiling sloped lower and lower, until they were forced to crawl. The only illumination came from the tactical lights mounted on the muzzle of the pistols Cassan and Voss carried. Rohan advanced in constant anticipation of the moment when a cold grip would close around his ankle.

"I think we are almost to the end of it," Cassan said in a sarcastically cheery voice.

Then, without warning, Wrise dropped out of sight. When Rohan inched forward, he saw that the man had fallen through a hole in the floor that had apparently not been there when Voss had crawled over the same spot.

The house always wins, Rohan mused.

Cassan and Voss shone their flashlights into the hole in the floor. Wrise looked up at them, from several feet below. It was a wonder that he had not broken his neck.

"Looks like a room of some sort," he said. "Best we all come down."

"I think we have to," Cassan replied, shining his light into the tunnel. Where there was previously dark space ahead, there was now a smooth wall, plastered and painted white. When Cassan touched the wall, he came away with paint on his fingertips as if the dead-end had just been erected and white-washed. "I'm beginning to wonder if we're having some sort of joint hallucination," he said as he let himself through the hole.

Rohan and Voss followed. When they were all through, they scanned the area.

"Smells like dog in here," Rohan said.

"Kennels. We're probably in the kennels," Voss whispered.

"Those cages look like they are built to hold something bigger than dogs," Rohan noted.

Along the far wall was a row of cinderblock cells with barred fronts. Each was about six feet high. The room was pitch black and the small flashlights the men held were insufficiently powerful to reveal the occupants, but they could hear heavy breathing emanating from the darkness. At first that was the only sound, but then Rohan heard a creak as the cell doors opened and out of the gloomy cages bounded three dogs of the same athletic and muscular variety as those that had secured the outer yard.

"Wait!" Cassan shouted, but he was too late. Wrise stepped forward and opened fire with the shotgun, dispatching all three dogs.

The dead dogs lay still, but only for a few seconds before their bodies began to quiver. Their flesh moved and twisted as if their hides were bags filled with angry snakes. Beneath their fur, muscles moved and bulged as the dead animals increased in size. The dogs stood, each now the size of a cow, their legs, necks, and shoulders armored in slabs of dense muscle. Their eyes blazed orange in the darkness and then they charged. Rohan instinctively knew that there would be no killing these beasts with small arms. Maybe if Richard was down here with Denise but not otherwise.

Rohan broke left, running for his life. Cassan, Wrise, and Voss also scattered. No doors. They were trapped like martyrs on the sands of a Roman colosseum. One of the goliath hounds followed Rohan. The room was about two hundred square feet in size, so there was not much space to flee. He turned left sharply and the dog, unable to match the speed of his directional change, slammed into the concrete wall, its massively muscled shoulder leaving a dent. No doors. No escape. Rohan felt like a seal being pursued by a great white shark, lacking the horsepower to escape and hoping to remain agile long enough for his pursuer to tire. The matador's game. Another of the massive hounds came at Rohan head on, slobber dripping from gleaming teeth, its deep-set eyes ablaze. With gritted teeth

Rohan gathered himself to fight. The memory of his grandfather dying at the hands of the master lagahoo flashed through his mind but then there was the sound of someone singing. The voice was sweet and mesmerizing but Rohan did not understand the words.

Dhyaayedaajaanubaaham dhritasharadhanusham baddhapadmaasanastham,

Peetam vaaso vasaanam navakamala dala spardhinetram prasannam;

Vaamaankaaroodhaseetaa mukhakamala milal lochanam neeradaabham,

Naanaalankaara deeptam dadhatamuru jataa mandalam raamachandram.

The dogs halted their chase so suddenly that one stumbled and fell forward in a roll. Then they raced toward Cassan, the source of the song. He was seated in a lotus pose on the other side of the room. Wrise and Voss stood behind him with guns drawn. The first of the dogs rolled around in front of them frolicking like an oversized puppy, its large pink tongue lolling out the side of its mouth. The other two dogs joined the first. They were hypnotized like a cobra bespelled by the music of a snake charmer's *pungi*. When the song was over Cassan stood and went to the dogs. He scratched the first behind the ear. The others sniffed him and licked his face as if he had raised them with his own hands.

"See? Good dogs."

"What was that?" Rohan panted still catching his breath from the near fatal chase.

"Meditation hymn. My grandmother taught it to me. Works on all sorts of beasties. Would have worked on the creature from the box had Wrise not shot it."

"So they are yours now? You going to take them home, take them for jogs around the Queen's Park Savannah?" Rohan motioned to the three cow sized hounds.

"Yeah, why not."

"What the hell will you feed them?"

"We have enemies enough to keep them full, I think."

Voss interrupted, "That's all well and good, but there are no doors here and no dead women to show us the way."

161

"Don't you feel that draft? There is a door in the back of one of these kennel-cages, I think," Cassan said.

The four men searched the kennels one by one. Cassan's theory proved correct. Every kennel had an iron door in its back wall, assumedly for cleaning and feeding access. The doors, however, were all either bolted or rusted shut. In the last kennel they searched, the door was ajar and a cool draft blew through the crack though no light emanated from beyond.

"Those hell hounds will not fit through this doorway," Voss observed. He was right, while the hinges looked just fine and there was nothing jamming the door, none of them could make the door budge in either direction. There was just enough room for the men to squeeze through. *House rules,* Rohan thought.

Cassan turned to his new pets. They whined, already anticipating their new master's absence.

"Don't worry, ladies. I know you can get out of here and find me."

Rohan observed that at least one of the dogs was in fact male, but he let Cassan's collective salutation slide.

"In the meantime," Cassan continued, "if anything comes through that hole in the roof, tear it apart, and when you escape, come to me."

The lead hound barked as if in response. The deep sound rattled Rohan's chest.

Voss looked confused, "They understand English?"

"They understand Cassan," Cassan replied.

The dogs bounded off and sat in a circle staring up at the hole in the ceiling through which the men had originally come. They looked eager. Rohan felt sorry for the next being that fell through.

Chapter 18

A memory nagged Clarence and, unlike the numerous concerns that were additional cause for general worry, this was something specific. He could not put a finger on exactly what that concern was however and the insubstantial memory which refused to coalesce into a cogent idea was like a line of ants crawling down his neck.

While he drove, he searched the corners of his mind trying to bring this nagging thought into focus. They had been to Lisa's home at #400 Belle Eau Road in Belmont. The little woman, however, had not been there, nor did it appear that she had been there in days. The bed was made, the shower and sinks were bone dry and a thin film of dust coated the dining table. The little pink and white house in Belmont was tidy but had already adopted that feeling of emptiness that houses acquire when their tenants have been away for a while.

The visit did produce one thing however. They had her scent. Nathan had made the obscene and unnecessary point of sniffing a pair of panties from Lisa's underwear drawer. Now they were tracking her on the wind. Clarence had no idea how they could follow the days old spoor but they could. Through the mental link the others, caged and confined in cells and dungeons all around the country, were also testing the air and helping to guide the way.

The smell was faint but it was there and traceable. His team was more pliable now that the sun was on its way up, it was easier to get into their heads. They resisted him less, except for Fifty-seven whose mind was still behind a psychic wall. As he drove, Rebecca hung her head out of the window like an excited dog, sucking the air deeply and giving directions even though they could all follow the scent. Then without warning, his brain assembled the strewn components of the nagging thought. *The men they had crashed into, Lisa's smell had been on them. They had been in her presence and recently. How coincidental?*

The men had had another interesting aroma, as if they had been in death's presence so many times the smell clung to them and had, over time, become part of their own. Two men and a boy. And there was something strange about the dog too. The men had not looked alike, one was a tall, lean, dreadlocked man and one was of Indian descent. But he knew what they were, their smell gave them away, that and the wary, cynical look in their eyes. They were merchants whose wares were death and violence. Clarence made a note to stay alert for that group. Perhaps this kidnapping would not be as easy as he thought.

They were in east Trinidad now, in an upscale neighborhood of well-designed modern houses. The ghostly pre-dawn light leeched the colors out of the land, giving everything a mystical cast.

As they drove through the neighborhood, the individual houses grew further and further apart. Each house in this part of the neighborhood occupied acres of land. Then they came to a mansion that stood about half a mile from the roadway, perched atop a rise like a hunting raptor.

"She's in there," Rebecca said, pointing to the mansion. "I smell her."

"We can all smell her Rebecca," Nathan growled. "What is the plan, oh mighty leader?"

Clarence's heart rate had increased the moment he realized that they were at the house where their target was. If he displayed any fear or hesitation in front of this crew they would eat him alive.

"Nathan, the next time you speak out of turn, I will force you to eat your own thumbs. Rebecca, I want you and Damian to go 'round the back. Secure the door so she does not escape through there. Girl, you and Nathan will go ring the bell and see if you can trick someone into letting you into the house. Tell them you have car trouble and your mobile isn't working. I will be here keeping the engine running. Get Lisa, bring her back here swiftly. Remember, she is not to be hurt."

***

Kamara was awake and alone in Rohan's room lying on the bed on her back staring at the roof. At this hour Lisa would still be asleep and so would Imelda and Jonah. Kamara knew this even as she lay in bed. Ever since being marked she could tell when the woman was near.

She slipped out of bed, uncertain why she was bothering to get out of bed at all. She was not yet hungry and it was still too early for breakfast, anyway. Yet she headed for the door. On her way down the hall, her hand brushed against the butt of the hilt of Voss' sword which he had left propped against the wall near her door.

Take it, a voice whispered inside her head. She jerked her hand away and stared at the beautiful weapon, wondering if the voice had been real. She reached down and touched the sword again but no voice spoke this time. Almost subconsciously, she wrapped her fingers around the hilt and picked up the sword. It was lighter than it should be for a katana, certainly lighter than the bokken she had used the night before.

She slid the blade out of the red lacquered scabbard. It did not gleam like polished steel but was a matte grey like gunmetal. It was a work of art, the blade so ornately engraved that she wondered if it was merely a decorative sword, She gingerly tested the edge with her thumb and even that light touch drew blood. Beyond sharp. She slid it back into the sheath and cradled the weapon against her chest like a baby as she left the room.

***

Nathan had no intention of ringing the doorbell or using any sort of trickery or guile to capture the Lisa woman. He was too powerful to employ artifice. He had decided to jump the fence, kill who needed to be killed, and take the woman. The weird girl that the fag Clarence insisted on bringing with them struggled to match his stride and he decided that the first chance he got, he would twist her neck. Nathan was shielding his thoughts so that neither Clarence nor the others could listen in on them. It was another little trick that Clarence was ignorant of and that would prove their supposed leader's undoing.

"You're not going to do what he told you to do, are you?" the girl asked. He did not respond but doubled his pace. Instead of trying to keep up, she just stopped and stood staring after his advancing back. *Stupid little bitch.*

***

Rebecca and Damian both agreed they were still hungry. They could smell other people in the house, clean people, tasty people. There was absolutely

165

no way they would hide in the bushes at the back while Nathan and Fifty-seven had all the fun. When they got to the rear wall, Rebecca kicked off her shoes and scaled straight up its vine covered face like a gecko, her palms and soles adhering to the wall in a reptilian manner.

Damian followed soon after. They were both shielding their thoughts, a skill Nathan had passed on to them in his hopes that they would help him kill the man-whore when it was time. They dropped down on the opposite side of the wall as lightly as silk cotton seeds in the breeze. On this part of the property the house was about two hundred meters from the wall, and the grounds inclined on the approach to the house. There were no trees apart from those lining the winding driveway. If anyone cared to look out the back window they would be seen instantly. Neither of them cared about being seen however, it was time to eat. Their meals would not taste quite as sumptuous as they would if they were marinated in moonlight but in their famished state the difference would be negligible. The marauding maboya started toward the house at a low jog, already beginning to forget their intended purpose and savoring the violence to come.

***

In the hallway the house lights blinked on and off five times in rapid succession paused for six seconds then repeated the sequence, indicating that the perimeter alarm had been tripped. There was no barbed wire atop Stone's walls, a decision that was both traditional and aesthetic. The founding members of the Order thought that barbed wire was an outward display of weakness and the men of the Order were anything but weak. Instead of concertina coil, the tops of the walls were protected by infrared beams that were invisible to the naked eye. If the beam was broken by anything bigger than a humming-bird, it triggered the silent alarm inside the house.

The arrangement could be annoying as sometimes a squirrel, a manicou, or even a large falling leaf would trigger the alarm. But every time the system was tripped the occupants of the house followed the same protocols. Someone had to check the camera feed then manually reset the alarm if all was clear. Kamara brought up the security videos on a desktop computer in the hallway. There were twenty different video streams each represented in individual squares on the wide screen monitor, but the system automatically highlighted the camera feeds nearest to the disturbance with a yellow border.

The security video came up just in time for her to see a woman then a man, both barefoot, leap down from the top of the twenty-foot wall and land like cats inside Stone's boundaries. Something about them nauseated Kamara. They moved with predatory urgency and exuded a vulture-like aura. They were not even attempting to hide their approach to the house.

The Nights of Need tattoo itched intensely. Kamara glanced at her hand and saw that the parade of elephants had been replaced by a leaping tigress. Another feed was highlighted on the computer monitor, showing another man scaling the front fence. Like the first two, he did not bother concealing himself as he walked up the long winding driveway. Kamara keyed in the sequence that reset the alarm. She also entered the code that would lock down the house entirely, automatically closing and locking all the outer windows and doors. With the house locked down, she could simply wait the intruders out. They could bang away at the exterior all they wanted, the glass would not shatter and the doors would not yield.

They will not be kept out by the doors.

She did not know where the idea came from but the minute it presented itself to her consciousness she knew it to be true. The three advancing strangers had come from a place where doors did not matter. She reached for her mobile and called Rohan's number but it rang without answer. *He must be on his way*, she thought hopefully. She would have to hold off the intruders on her own, or at least until Rohan and Voss returned.

She considered alerting Jonah, Imelda and Lisa, but wondered what good that would do? Lisa could not wield a gun and Jonah and his wife lived in their cottage on the grounds away from the imminent danger. Alerting them would only put the elderly couple in harm's way.

She checked the camera feeds again. Motion sensors around Stone had switched on the cameras at the back where the pair that had come over the wall was now inspecting one of the rear doors. The door was made of a solid plate of steel laminated between oak panels. Maybe the voice in her head was wrong and the door would hold them.

Another security feed lit up. The man who had come over the fence was standing stock still and staring up at one of the windows on the second storey. He seemed to be sniffing the air. Then the woman at the back door lay flat on the ground and began to squeeze under the door, through the tiny gap between the bottom of the door and the tiled floor.

Kamara blinked several times to convince herself that what she was witnessing was real. The woman's body pressed beneath the door like some spineless, boneless worm, flattening as she used her legs to advance. Her progress was slow and apparently uncomfortable but she was getting in. Her companion patiently waited his turn. Kamara sprinted for Lisa's room.

"Wake up, Lisa. Wake up. We're under attack," she shouted as she headed towards Lisa's room. *We're being invaded by some new monster*, she thought. *Lisa and I can probably escape through the underground walkway that led to Jonah's and Imelda's home.*

Chapter 19

Rohan was first through the gap in the metal door. The moment he was through, a row of torches in sconces along the wall came alive. The torches burned a smoky orange that left a trail of greasy soot on the walls above the flame.

He was in a stone hallway with windowless walls that arched up toward a low domed ceiling. At regular intervals along the wall there were doors.

More doors. Nothing good ever came out of doors in this house, Rohan thought. as the other men emerged through the gap and joined him in the hall.

"Fresh air," Cassan said, "Do you smell it? There is a window or a door open down here that leads outside."

Cassan was right. The air in the stone hall was cool and fresh and smelled of the night outside. Rohan felt a sliver of hope. He longed to escape the oppressiveness of the house.

"As we have seen before an open portal does not guarantee anything," Voss replied. "I feel like we have been herded here."

Both men spoke in a hush even though the hallway appeared empty. Rohan sensed that this area of the house felt expectantly hungry, like a glutton salivating over a shank of meat. From beyond the door erupted sounds of violence. The goliath hounds were tearing into somebody or somebodies. Staccato gunfire was drowned out by screams as the hounds prevailed.

"The storm troopers followed us down apparently. Wonder what they did with their resurrected comrades?" Cassan said as he pushed the steel door to close the gap through which they had come. The door swung closed silently and smoothly though it had previously been unyielding. Rohan knew instinctively that they would not be able to retreat through that portal and he did not bother to confirm that the door would not open again.

The only way was forward, down the hall of torches and cells. The men began advancing along the hall. Rohan and Voss hugged the left side, Wrise and Cassan the right. The hall went on and on. Rohan began to think that the house intended to walk them to death.

He heard a sound. At first he held his tongue thinking that it was a figment of his imagination, but he soon heard it again.

"Does anyone else hear that? Someone singing?"

"I thought I was imagining it," Wrise replied. "There it is again."

The voice was soft and plaintive, but heartbreakingly sweet and seemed to be coming out of the walls themselves. The hall suddenly terminated in a circular junction. The junction branched off into six different hallways all of which looked identical to the one they exited. At the center of the circle, a woman knelt. Her back was to them and she was singing.

"Deeper yet, deeper yet,
Into the crimson flood;
Deeper yet, deeper yet,
Under the precious blood."

Rohan thought he knew the song, it was some sort of hymn, but for some reason he felt that the woman's meaning was different from the sentiments of the original author.

"Hello?" Wrise hissed. "Woman."

The woman acted as if she did not hear them and she continued to sing. Cassan and Wrise approached her slowly. Wrise placed a hand on her shoulder as if to turn her around and the woman crumbled into a pile of grey ash.

"I'm tired of this crap," Wrise said as he brushed his hands vigorously against the seat of his pants. He had paled visibly. Voss held a finger to his lips signaling that they be quiet. He seemed to be straining the hear something.

"Something is coming," Voss said. "We have to go. Now."

Rohan strained his ears and he heard it too, a rapid pitter patter, the sound of many bare feet slapping the stone floor in a dead run.

"The things from the cells. They're out," Voss said as he licked a finger and held it up testing the air to find the direction of the source of the draft.

"What do you mean the things from the cells?" Cassan asked. "I didn't hear a thing coming along the halls."

"They were trying to be quiet, but I heard them. Rohan, I know you heard them too." Voss said.

Rohan had heard them, but he had felt it better not to mention it. They were already in a bad situation. But the cells had contained people or creatures of some sort. He heard their breathing, low and rasping, carefully quiet but definitely there.

"They must be maboya, like the thing that grabbed me and pulled me through the box," Cassan said.

Voss pointed down one of the halls and led the way down the tunnel in which the draft felt strongest. Wrise unlimbered his shotgun. Rohan checked his own weapon. They hustled down the cell lined, torch lit passageway at a brisk jog. They came to another junction and this time there were ten hallways from which to choose.

Voss was again testing the air when the last cell in the hallway they had just exited creaked open slowly. A beast crawled out on all fours. It wore the tattered remnants of trousers, its body was completely hairless, and blue veins pulsed under the translucent whiteness of its skin. Perhaps it had once been a person, but that was a long time ago. Its arms were overlong, insectile and terminated in wicked black claws. It had two elbows on each arm and its knee joints faced the wrong direction. It was eyeless and had no nostrils, but this did not seem to impede it. Its mouth was a thin red slash in the flesh of its face and was filled with a multitude of needle-like black teeth. It rose to its full height and sprinted towards them, its feet making a slapping noise against the stones of the floor.

Rohan took aim and fired in a burst. The rounds made a neat grouping of black puncture marks in the onrushing creature's chest but it neither bled nor slowed down. All the men opened fire and the creature was driven back by the impact of the fusillade and fell, but they continued firing, even though they knew they were wasting time and ammunition on this one. There would be many more. Voss held up a fist and the men stopped shooting.

The monstrosity lay on the floor writhing and shrieking. The bullets had all but cut it in half. In the hallway eight more cells doors opened and eight more creatures crawled out. Rohan flung an incendiary grenade into the hall of cells and the four men fled down another hallway led by Voss. The heat of the explosion and the shrieks of the creatures followed them on a pressure wave.

This time the house did not wait for them to reach a junction. Cells opened left and right as they ran. The men sprinted, shooting as they went. Rohan's sub machine gun clicked empty. He drew his sidearm and was immediately forced to empty the clip into the forehead of a maboya as it crawled out of one of the cells. It fell back. The creatures seemed to be weak when they first exited the cells but their strength increased quickly and this one rose again as Rohan ran past its cell.

Rohan drew a large kukri knife from a sheath at his back. One of the pale monstrosities rose up in front of him and he slammed the butt of the knife into the creature's face. It succumbed to the blow. Rohan looked back and realized that somewhere in the mêlée he had become separated from the others, surrounded by the maboya and fighting alone. He barely had time to panic when suddenly Cassan was at his side, he held one of the iron torches in a two-handed grip and was laying about with it viciously.

"Do you have a song for this?" Rohan shouted as he cleaved the face of one of the creatures in half.

"Too many of them, we would be overrun, before the hypnosis took hold."

Cassan and Rohan cut and clubbed their way up the halls. The maboya were persistent and growing stronger by the moment. Voss and Wrise were nowhere to be seen. Rohan saw a break in the press and he and Cassan began to run. Rohan chucked his last incendiary grenade over his shoulder and ducked around a corner to avoid the blast. That action bought them a moment's reprieve. He and Cassan were in another hallway, with more cells, already wide open. The occupants however, were absent.

There was no draft in this hallway and Rohan had no idea where he should go, so he pressed forward at random. They were approaching another junction. This one led to three different halls. He and Cassan ran towards it, but just as they were about to enter, maboya swarmed. This group was neither weak nor crawling. They came like a swarm of pale, earthbound locusts, poorly clad in the tattered remnants of garments from a forgotten life. Their black teeth gnashing in a vile hunger, their eyeless gaze seeing all.

Rohan and Cassan started to run back the way they came, but the way was blocked by another group of the creatures, many of which sported burns from Rohan's grenade.

"Into that cell," Rohan shouted. He dove into the closest one with Cassan hard on his heels and he swung the door shut. One of the creatures managed to get its arm into the doorway, preventing it from closing completely. Rohan cut it off with his machete-knife and slammed the iron door closed. The severed arm crawled toward Cassan slowly and he kicked it away. There was no way to secure the door from the inside so Rohan and Cassan leaned on the door while the creatures on the other side pushed and pressed and clawed.

"Doesn't look too good, aye?" Cassan said stating the obvious. Rohan scanned the room frantically. No doors no windows, just a levered crank set into the wall and shackles hanging from the low ceiling. There was a wooden table off to a corner. The situation was hopeless. The only thing saving them was the fact that the maboya were not acting as a team in pushing the door. Some pushed while others clawed while others hammered their fists.

"You have any more bullets?" Rohan asked.

"If I did, I wouldn't be clubbing them with a torch now would I?" Cassan replied sarcastically, gesturing with the conical metal bracket.

Then Rohan noticed a pool of white liquid running under the door, as if someone had spilled a gallon jug of milk on the opposite side of the doorway. The puddle pooled around their feet. Pale hands with black claws suddenly shot out of the puddle and grabbed Cassan's legs. The hands clawed up Cassan's thighs as he kicked frantically, the puddle rapidly coalesced into a maboya and it held Cassan in its grasp. Rohan kicked at it, as best as he could while still struggling to hold the door. The creature bit into Cassan's lower arm and held on. Cassan immediately began to vomit a stream of greasy black bile even as he struggled in the creature's grip.

The press of bodies on the other side of the door forced Rohan back, an arm squeezed in, then a leg, and then maboya swarmed into the room. Rohan began cutting and stabbing, kicking and punching frantically and viciously, the press enveloped Cassan obscuring Rohan's view of him. He was fighting for own his life now.

The big razor-sharp knife severed hands and heads but there were too many. A clawed hand raked across his face, tearing his cheek to ribbons and barely missing his eye. The wound burned like a brand. They pulled him down. He was on the ground, hands gripped his limbs like steel bands and he feared they would tear him apart.

There were so many of them around him that he could not see the ceiling beyond the crowd of bodies. The maboya were not only fighting him but were fighting amongst themselves to determine who would get the first substantial bite. A clawed hand scooped a handful of flesh off his chest. An alien mouth tried to bite his foot through the sole of his boot. Rohan fought violently but the situation was impossible, for the umpteenth time this week he was going to die.

Smoke. The air was suddenly filled with smoke. Screams. The air was filled with screams and shrieks. The sounds were coming from the hallway. Then the maboya immediately atop him began to sweat drops of liquid blue flame, like rubbing alcohol set alight.

Liquid fire trickled like tears from its eyes-space, burning a thin trail down its face. It opened its mouth to scream and blue fire belched out engulfing its body rapidly. Soucouyant fire Rohan knew it well. When old Stone had burned, the fire had been blue too. Some of the fire dripped onto him but it did not burn. All the maboya were now burning. They wailed and writhed and screamed but the fire was relentless and the room grew lethally hot.

The air filled with the acrid smoke of their torment. Rohan crawled towards the door, looking for Cassan, and avoiding the shrieking flailing demons. He found the man, unconscious. His arm had been mauled badly and was putrefying. Even as Rohan watched a blackish mossy-green cast spread out from the site of the bite and leached up his forearm.

The wound stank like snail meat gone rancid. There was no occasion for second thoughts, the bite would spread sepsis throughout Cassan's entire body in minutes. Rohan swiftly tied his belt around Cassan's bicep and tightened it. Then he held the knife over the flames of the small wooden table which had caught on fire. He stretched the man's arm out and amputated it with the glowing blade, using the floor as a chopping block. He cut at the elbow, just above the advancing putrefaction. The wound barely bled.

Rohan then hauled Cassan into the hallway where burning corpses were strewn everywhere giving off a nasty black smoke that smelled of rot. The stone walls had caught fire in places. Rohan was choking and growing light-headed. His eyes burned and he fell to his knees. Even though he was unconscious, the jarring fall caused Cassan to groan. The black poisonous smoke of the dead maboya filled his lungs. Rohan could not tell up from down, right from left. He had survived the beastly horde only to suffocate on the vile smoke from their corpses

A dog. A dog was barking. Something was tugging at his sleeve, licking his face. He opened his eyes and Agrippa's snout was inches away from his nose. Rohan shook his head and the cobwebs cleared somewhat, and while the dog swam in his vision, it did not vanish.

"Are you really there?" Rohan rasped. In response the dog tugged at his sleeve then ran a little way to the left and came back. Revived by hope, Rohan struggled to his knees, grabbed Cassan by the collar of his shirt, and began to drag him in the direction the dog had gone. Agrippa also gripped Cassan's shirt between his teeth and helped Rohan.

Smart puppy.

The hall seemed to go on forever, but then Rohan felt a draft of clean air. He saw a doorway at the end of the hall, and beyond the doorway, rolling hills covered in waist-high bull grass.

Rohan imagined that the view beyond the door must be what the first views of Valhalla looked like to a deceased heroic Viking. With every agonizing step towards the door he felt stronger. When he got to the portal he did not hesitate but walked right through and out into the light, hauling Cassan behind him and sucking down lung-fulls of Trinidad's best air.

He vomited ash, he coughed up soot, he cried charcoal stained tears then he turned around and knelt to check on Cassan. Agrippa was licking the man's face. Then Tarik appeared, walking towards them through the tall grass. He was barefoot, grinning, and carrying some of Kat's ointments and cures. A more welcome sight Rohan had never seen. Rohan asked no questions as the boy poured a heavy grey paste down Cassan's throat. The man coughed and sputtered awake then spent the next ten minutes vomiting an oily green amalgam that stank like a sack of dead toads as the medicines drew out the infection.

"Their bites and scratches are poisonous. Your marks saved you from the worst of it, Rohan, but drink this anyway." Tarik handed Rohan a calabash of the same mixture he had given to Cassan. Rohan drank it without protest. It was bitter and he felt queasy but there was none of the projectile vomiting that Cassan had exhibited. When Cassan had finished vomiting and cursing, Tarik bound what was left of his arm in a cloth soaked with the same ointments Kat had used to heal Kamara's jumbie bites.

"Where are the others?" Rohan asked. "Who set the maboya ablaze?"

"Voss is safe, Wrise is not. Richard is waiting at the bottom of the hill with a van to take us home. I could not enter the house, but I did what I could from out here. Pyromancy is one of my specialties."

Given the animosity between the two men, Rohan suspected that either Wrise or Voss would not exit the house alive. He was glad that it was Voss who had survived and he wondered if it was really the maboya who had gotten Wrise in the end. The real surprise was that Tarik and not Kat had burned the maboya.

Rohan was regaining his strength, and Cassan, though he smelled like the La Basse and was missing an arm was also doing better. He was taking the amputation like a stalwart. He leaned on Rohan heavily as they made their way down the hill. Rohan spared a glance at the doorway and was not surprised to see that it was no longer there. There were only grassy hills behind them. No hint of the subterranean hell that they had just exited.

"How far are we from the house?"

"About three miles give or take. The tunnels extend for miles in all directions around the house. We are in the hills of Morvant."

"Did Kat send you?"

"No, I followed you here, but the house kept me out, Richard has been unable to reach anyone at Stone. We assume they are asleep."

Did you cut my arm off with a red-hot knife or did I dream that?" Cassan asked drowsily.

"It's good that he cut off the arm. Once the rot spreads to your torso you are done for," Tarik said.

They made their way down the grassy hillside. Rohan relished the sun on his face and he even enjoyed the feeling of dew soaking his pant legs and the invisible spider silk breaking across his forehead. At the bottom of the hill Voss sat with his back against the wheels of one of the large vans in which the guards had arrived. As soon as Richard spied them he ran over and embraced Rohan in a rough brotherly hug.

"It's good to see you, boss," he said. "We were concerned for a while."

"What took you so long, Rohan? You getting soft?" Voss' greeting was sarcastic but Rohan thought he saw genuine relief in the softening of the lines at the corners of his eyes.

"I was just cleaning up all the freaks you failed to put down." Three huge dogs leapt out of the back of the truck and ran up to Cassan, wagging their tails and whining. They had returned to their original size, but Rohan recognized them as the goliath hounds from the kennels. Cassan did his best to greet them in his weakened state and with one hand. "My girls," he said weakly. Agrippa stood apart. He neither rushed to join the new dogs nor did he show any aggression toward them.

"The house changed around and somehow the dogs found me," Voss recapped. They were still oversized then. With their help we tore through the maboya and escaped out of some door. When the sun came up they returned to their normal size, which is still overgrown." He gestured to a sickly looking Cassan. "Does he need to go to a hospital?"

"No," Tarik replied. "The wound will soon heal and the venom has been countered. He will recover."

"But his clothes will not," Rohan said pinching his nose in mock disgust.

The men prepared to leave. When Rohan saw the chance he pulled Voss aside, "What happened to Wrise?"

"He didn't make it."

"It's pretty obvious he didn't make it, but what exactly happened to him? Did you kill him."

Voss was silent for a while. "No, I didn't kill him, but it may have been better for him if I had."

Rohan pressed no further on the matter. He hauled himself into the canvas-roofed tray of the military-style truck. There were wooden benches on either side of the truck's bed but Rohan lay flat on the floor next to Cassan with his head pillowed on Agrippa's body. The truck roared to a start and lurched forward in a diesel rumble. As he lay, tossed around as Richard navigated the pothole-ridden roads, Rohan remembered the message from Ghita and the murdered *jamette*.

The dead want to talk with you, Kat. That was his last thought before he drifted into a black sleep.

Chapter 20

Jonah was already awake when the alarm went off. He had been preparing a simple breakfast for himself and his wife. While chopping the onions he whistled his favorite calypso; Obeah Wedding by Sparrow. It was a running joke between him and his wife that she had trapped him with an obeah spell like the 'Melda in the song had failed to do with Sparrow.

Jonah and Imelda lived in a small wooden cottage on the grounds of Stone that had been converted from an over-sized equipment shed. Over the years they had declined countless invitations to move into the main house, which, even before it had been burnt and rebuilt, was too fancy for their tastes. While the men of the Order said that Stone was as much theirs as it was the Order's, the small wooden cottage sitting in seclusion amongst a grove of teak trees on Stone's grounds was truly his and Imelda's sanctuary.

Secluded as it was the small house was however connected to the main house's security systems and the single light bulb illuminating the small kitchen blinked on and off when the infrared beam was tripped. There was also a desktop monitor from which he could confirm whether another wild parrot had landed on the wall and tripped the motion sensors.

A look at the monitor revealed that the offender was not a wild parrot. Jonah watched as two people came over the back wall and one brazen bloke clambered right over the front gate. They moved like fer-de-lance in high grass. He and Imelda knew what their employers did for a living. Even though they preferred not to think about it too much, they acknowledged the potential dangers commensurate with their job.

The monitor registered that someone had locked the house down. *Good job, Kamara,* he thought. Now he had two choices. These people could simply be vandals or trespassers in which case he could call the police. It was more likely however, that they were something far more dangerous. Fer-de-lance in the high grass. Jonah reasoned that he and the women could arm themselves and hold off the intruders until Rohan and Voss returned, but when the woman began to squeeze under the door, he knew there could be no waiting. He picked up the receiver of the rotary phone in the kitchen and dialed Rohan's cell number from memory. The phone rang once and a groggy voice answered.

"Jonah, what's cooking?"

"Eggs actually. Rohan, Three people came over the wall. One is squeezing herself under the door and will be inside Stone in a minute."

"Did she melt into a puddle of white liquid like milk?" Rohan's voice sounded as if he was now fully alert.

"More like a rubber chicken. It's a tight squeeze but she'll make it eventually."

"Where's Kat?"

"She left a little after you guys did, early this morning."

"Get Kamara and Lisa and get out of the house. We'll be there in about ten minutes. Do not allow the intruders to bite or scratch you."

"Sounds like a plan. See you soon, sir."

In the background Jonah heard Rohan shout something followed by the sound of a large diesel engine revving up. Jonah was confident that Rohan and his new friend Voss could deal with whatever had come over the wall, but until they arrived he was the point man.

"Imelda lover, we have ah problem."

He turned around and was not surprised to see that Imelda was already wearing a bullet-proof vest over her nightgown and a tactical helmet over the rollers in her hair. She also wore boots, gloves, and kneepads. An Ak-47 with a fat drum magazine was slung across her broad shoulders.

"I'm old not deaf honey. Suit up. We'll go through the tunnel and get the girls."

Jonah was ready in about forty-five seconds and the couple entered the underground walkway that connected Stone to their house. They normally used the passage to get to work when the weather was inclement, but it doubled as an escape-way when rubberized people came over the wall.

***

Clarence's crew believed they were blocking him out of their thoughts and he was, for the moment, satisfied with allowing them to believe that. Clarence, however, knew exactly what they were about to do. Damian and Rebecca had already lost sight of the objective. They were rabid and hungry and intended to kill and eat all the people in the house. Nathan intended to force himself on Lisa before bringing her back to the car, if there was anything left of her to bring back.

All three of them planned to kill him when their power waxed stronger on the next full moon. Their thought-shielding process was immature, and they could certainly learn a thing or two from Fifty-seven. The little girl's mind was as impenetrable as a solid steel sphere. There was not even a corner he could use to pry it open. Now that she was out of his sight he could not find her. As far as he knew for sure she could be escaping or off massacring a group of Jehovah's Witnesses, but his instinct told him she was near.

For all his knowledge of their murderous purpose Clarence would not intervene yet. He did not really care if Rebecca and Damian killed anyone else in the mansion. The house reminded him of the clients from his newly old life, beautiful and rich on the outside but inside was surely filled with secrets and skeletons. As for Nathan's designs on Lisa, he would not allow the man to have his way with her. For one, he did not trust the man not to kill her if she resisted, which she would. Secondly, he despised rapists with a fervor. But for now she was safe. Nathan was still outside trying to pinpoint her location by scent.

Clarence watched to see how this volatile situation would unfold. This was the lair of the men from the car they had crashed into. The men's predatory musk lingered in the air with the promise of bloodshed. That was the main reason he had not entered the house himself. The men were not here now and he suspected that if they were, his boarding party would already be suffering for their intrusion. But even though they were not here, entering that house was like trying to steal eggs from a giant eagle's nest. The risk of the raptor returning to roost while his hand was clasped around an egg was too great. Was he afraid of them? Hell, yes, he most certainly was. Fear was the appropriate response to the prospect of a confrontation with these men. So he sat in the car, monitored the behavior of his team and waited for something to go wrong.

***

Until the moment she decided to slip beneath the door Rebecca had no idea that she possessed that ability. It was just like scaling the wall, her body simply told her that she could do it. The sensation of squeezing beneath the door was a strange one. It did not really hurt but it was uncomfortable and disorienting. It felt as if her bones and organs had liquefied with her skin being the only thing separating her from becoming a puddle entirely.

The space under the door was so narrow that she had to become as thin as a sheet of paper. The parts of her body not under the door maintained their solidity. Her entire torso was now through and so she clawed forward with her hands while pushing with her feet and knees. Eventually she was inside the foyer.

"Can you open the door?" Damian whined from the other side.

"So you can come through the easy way? Not a chance?. I'm going to find breakfast. You better hurry."

She strode into the house.

"Is anyone here? Hello, hello, hellooo." Rebecca was in no mood for hunting. The sooner someone came out to investigate the intrusion the sooner the festivities could begin. "Come out. I can hear you breathing. I can smell you too."

In response to her taunting, a young woman stepped around a corner. She was taller than average without being too tall and very lovely. Her lean healthy body was easy to appreciate through her sleepwear. Rebecca dismissed the naked sword she held in her right hand and the blood red scabbard she held in her left. *A sword, ha.*

"I must say you look really scrumptious," Rebecca said coyly.

"And you look like you'll be dead soon," the young woman replied, making no move to retreat. Rebecca could hear the woman's heartbeat. The sound was a steady thump from within her chest. The sound of her breathing was similarly unhurried. *The pretty bitch has cajones,* she thought. The woman had to know she did not face an ordinary intruder. Rebecca was almost sorry she would have to kill her, but she was hungry. She

182

sprang forward, her hands clawed and her teeth bared. The saliva of her anticipation dampened her chin.

Rebecca knew she was fast. She was supremely confident in her ability to dispatch the other woman quickly so she was shocked when her clawed hands slashed through the empty air where the woman had been standing. Her surprise only increased when the scabbard in the woman's left hand slammed into her jaw knocking several teeth out and smashing her lips.

The clubbing blow of the scabbard was followed by a sharp, burning sensation across her chest. She took a moment to realize the woman had slashed her with the sword. The flashing blade left a deep horizontal cut across both of her breasts. She was bleeding, bleeding as if she was still human. She felt her ruined mouth begin to knit itself, but where the sword had cut was not healing at all. Out of her peripheral vision she saw the woman move.

Rebecca punched, her fist traveling towards the woman's chest with enough force to shatter her sternum and stop her heart. But the young woman was ready. She caught Rebecca's punch by presenting the blade with the tip pointing downward to the floor. Rebecca could not react fast enough to pull the punch back and her fist ran right into the razor edge, cleaving her hand between the middle knuckles almost to the wrist.

The woman violently turned the handle of the blade 180 degrees, a move that twisted Rebecca's impaled hand and broke it at the wrist. Rebecca shouted in pain and the woman hit her with the scabbard again, in exactly the same spot as before, then push-kicked her in the gut so she fell free of the sword. A once familiar but recently forgotten feeling settled in her chest. It was the feeling of fear. This woman was not going to be satisfied with just killing her, she was going to punish her.

***

Kamara was punishing the woman-creature. This was not how Rohan had taught her to fight. Rohan's purpose in a fight was always swift dispatch of the adversary. However, the tigress of the Nights of Need roared on her hand. It guided her choice of tactics and would not be satisfied with simply killing the intruder. The woman punched at her and the bladed edge of the sword caught the fist. Kamara yanked the sword's handle around

183

while the creature's hand was impaled on the blade then kicked the woman backward, but not before smashing her in the mouth with the hard scabbard yet again. The woman fell backward but braced the impact with her good hand.

"Is that the best you have, Soon-To-Die?" Kamara spoke in a voice she herself did not recognize. The woman rose from the floor, her cracked teeth and torn lips healing from the wounds of the scabbard's blows even as Kamara looked on. The wounds from the sword, however, were an entirely different matter. The hand, split in half down the center, and the cut across the woman's chest bled freely and profusely, yet the woman made no move to flee. Kamara decided that the game had gone on long enough. The next time she came close Kamara would cut her head off.

***

Kamara's shouting awoke Lisa, and now that she was awake she realized that there was something or someone in the room with her. She faced away from the window and whatever it was cast a cold shadow across her body. The being was just standing there, saying nothing, breathing and smelling very faintly of old death.

She could feel its eyes staring at her back. She lay on her left side and she slipped her right hand under the pillow to clasp the rubberized grip of the big Desert Eagle pistol Voss had given her. It was not 'a little person's gun.' Voss had warned her that the recoil was like the kick of a mule. But she could not shoot accurately anyway so Voss had given it to her, more for its intimidation potential than in any expectation that she would shoot someone with it.

It's heavy as hell, she thought. Maybe I can club him with it. There was a shuffle of clothing as the person advanced toward her. She clicked off the safety, rolled around quickly, and sat up. She held the gun in a two-handed grip and pointed it squarely at the intruder's chest, finger off the trigger, obeying all Voss' summarily imparted best practices. The gun was indeed very heavy and it required genuine effort to keep it trained on the target.

The intruder was a man, lanky and slim. He looked to be in his early thirties. The only thing striking about him was the look in his eyes. It was a look that spoke of intentions that were not benign.

"I don't know who you are or what you're doing here, but my boy-friend will be back soon. If you leave before he gets back, maybe he won't hunt you down and kill you." It was a lie of course, but as she spoke, the thought of Voss stomping on the man's wicked face was comforting. She kept the gun pointed at his chest. He stood about eight feet away and even she would find it impossible to miss at this range.

"We went to your house, Lisa. I loved your collection of lace under-wear. You smell so delicious." The man's words sent a chill down Lisa's spine and left a feeling in her stomach as if an oil-soaked rat was scurrying around in her gut. The man took a step forward.

"If you take another step I promise I will shoot you." She had never pointed a gun at anyone before, but she had always imagined that a pointed gun would have more of a discouraging effect. The man however seemed rather unimpressed by the weapon. He took another step toward her, and Lisa was forced to keep her promise.

She squeezed the trigger and the pistol barked. Voss had been right. The recoil sent a shock up her arm and almost sent the barrel into her face. The round punched a smoking hole in the man's chest through which the daylight from the window behind him became visible. The man however, bled about as much as a cardboard target.

"That really hurt Lisa." He took another step, or at least it looked like one step to her. But in that one step he completely closed the distance be-tween them. One of his clammy hands enveloped her throat while his oth-er controlled her gun hand. The man pressed her on to the bed. His eyes were wild and he licked his lips hungrily. His breath smelled like bad salami.

She was under him now, her free hand frantically sweeping the bed for anything she could use as a weapon. Her fingers closed around a nail file and she promptly drove the blade into the man's eye. He did not even wince. His response was a vicious backhand across her jaw. She almost blacked out. He hit her again. Then with one motion he tore the front of her blouse open and began unbuckling his belt.

***

Clarence looked in on Nathan through his mind's eye. Nathan was doing precisely what Clarence knew he would have done. He was atop the Lisa

185

woman, throttling her and preparing to assault her. This was an unaccept-able. Clarence readied a massive gift of pain and suffering to send to Nathan via the psychic pipeline. What he intended to deliver would feel like a roiling ball of red-hot barbed wire wrapped around every muscle of the target's body. Nathan would scream for days.

Clarence was about to deliver the psychic payload when someone shut down the connection completely, blinding him to the others as if hurricane shutters had closed over his third eye. He became as blind to all the maboya as he was to Fifty-seven. Fifty-seven, the little imp. He was so distracted by the sudden loss of his second sight that he did not hear the roar of the diesel engine coming up the road until it was too late. The large, army style truck loomed in his rearview mirror. He saw it seconds before it slammed into the back of his stolen car in an agonized cacophony of screaming metal. The impact bucked the car forward and caused him to chip a tooth against the steering wheel. He recognized two of the men who alighted, and the big black dog too. They were the men whose car he had crashed into the night before. They were armed and angry.

Clarence yanked on the door handle but the door had been jammed shut by the impact. He kicked the windshield out, clambered over the hood, leapt to the ground, and sprinted away with a speed that surprised even him. Cutting left he hurdled over the low wooden fence that bor-dered an expanse of horse-grazing pasture across the road from the house. He was sprinting across the undulating field expecting that at any time he would be cut down by bullets.

He had gained about a hundred-meter distance when he heard the words: "Get him, Agrippa." He chanced a glance over his shoulder. The big black dog led a pack of three bigger brindle-coated hounds. As the pack ran, they increased in mass until they quadrupled in size. The black dog however, maintained the lead.

Clarence's new body was fast, but the dogs rapidly closed in on him. He put every ounce of his being into his flight. He made it about fifty more meters before something hit him in the back, sending him to the ground. He knew it was the black dog. Its long white fangs snapped at the back of his head with a metallic click.

He was stronger than the animal. He shook the dog off and was rising to run again when the first of the giant hounds slammed into him with the impact of a speeding minivan. Its mouth closed over his bicep like a vise. Shortly all four of the beasts were upon him, tearing and shaking. Someone whistled and the dogs released him but kept circling, constantly snarling.

Clarence found that he could not stand, both legs had been broken in the tussle. He craned his neck and looked up. Approaching him were the two men from the car the night before. Their eyes were mercy free. The dreadlocked man scratched the ear of the black dog, praising it for its leadership. That man stood over him, his face like a thundercloud.

"Where are your friends from last night?"

Clarence coughed. "They are inside, and you better go quickly before it's too late."

The men shared a look then peeled off toward the house. The dreadlocked man called over his shoulder. "Agrippa, if he moves kill him, boy."

Agrippa's snarl was joined by the bass growl of the three goliath dogs. Clarence was going nowhere.

***

The wounded intruder transformed right before Kamara's eyes. The woman grew pale, the veins in her face grew increasingly visible like blue webbing beneath skin like porcelain. The intruder smiled at Kamara and several damaged teeth fell out. They were rapidly replaced by pointy little black ones.

Then the woman rushed forward, as she came clumps of hair fell off her head leaving perfectly bald patches. Kamara's sword moved with the speed of a viper's strike, piercing the woman's chest like a knight's lance through a jousting dummy.

Her blow missed the heart and the woman pressed forward shoving herself further onto the blade. Too late Kamara realized that she had wanted to be impaled. The mutated woman was now within arm's length. She threw her arm around the back of Kamara's neck, drew her close, then bit her in the same spot the jumbie had bitten, tearing out a chunk of red dripping flesh and blood-soaked sleep wear.

The world swam in Kamara's eyes and she felt violently nauseous. She twisted the sword and yanked it upward into the woman's chest cavity, lacerating her heart. The woman fell dragging Kamara down too. The stink of rotting flesh was coming from somewhere, and with horror she realized that it was coming from her wound. Kamara's vision was blurred. She could not think. The woman's bite was going to kill her. She managed to get to her knees but could rise no further. She vomited a stream of putrid black bile which also stank like dead flesh.

Another person approached, a man, pale like the woman had become, his grin displaying a mouthful of black spikes. The second stranger advanced, deliberately savoring her helplessness. Kamara tried to rise but could not.

"Kamara, get down." She looked over her shoulder. Jonah's voice came from inside a black balaclava. He and Imelda stood shoulder-to-shoulder, both armed with assault rifles. Imelda wore tactical gear over her pink nightgown. Kamara allowed herself to fall to the floor. As soon as she was out of the way, gunfire erupted and a horizontal hail of full metal jacket rounds ripped into the man. Both guns had barrel magazines and the fusillade continued for nearly a minute before the clips clicked empty. The man had been dismembered by the bullets. The main part of the corpse lay without a head or arms, the body did not even twitch. Imelda ran to Kamara's side while Jonah reloaded and emptied another magazine's worth of bullets into the prostrate torso.

***

Lisa struggled under the man, but he was superhumanly strong and her struggling seemed only to excite him. He tore off her underwear and struck her repeatedly. Then a child's voice spoke with the authority of an experienced headsman. "Nathan, get off of her."

Lisa and Nathan turned towards the source of the voice. A skinny girl in a dingy sundress stood in a corner of the room.

"Go away Fifty-seven, or whatever your name is. Me and Lisa are busy."

"Nathan, get off of her, or I will have you castrate yourself and eat what you tear off."

"Piss off you little…." The man's air cut off with a wheeze. Fat drops of blood welled up in the corners of his eyes and ran down his face. He seemed frozen. The girl walked up to him, then leaned in close and whispered something in his ear. The man rose from the bed, walked over to the corner of the room, and stripped his clothing off.

"Don't look at this, Lisa," the girl said, but Lisa could not tear her eyes away. The man stood in the corner, shaking like a leaf, and muttering to himself.

"Stop fighting it, Nathan. Do as I instructed," the newcomer said.

With that the man speared both hands into his abdomen. Blood poured from around his fingers where they gored his belly and ran down his legs in crimson rivulets. He kept shoving his hands deeper, cursing in the grip of agony, but the little girl's compulsion was too strong for him to resist. Then he began hauling out long ropes of blue intestine. He lifted them to his mouth and began to dine on his own innards.

After a minute which seemed like an eternity to Lisa the girl spoke again. "Nathan, tear out your heart and get this over with."

The man did as he was told and fell over dead. The still beating heart throbbing in his hand.

"Sorry you had to see that and sorry that I did not stop him sooner. It is not easy to block out Lucien and all the others at the same time. I could have just killed him, but he needed to be taught a lesson."

Lisa trembled, unable to respond. The girl continued. "You are going to have to come with me. Lucien will not stop until he has you and what you stole from him. I will keep you safe." The girl walked to the dressing table, opened a drawer, and selected a t-shirt and jeans. She brought them over to Lisa. "Put these on, please."

Lisa began to recover her faculties, "I…I…I don't know you, I'm not coming with you. You made him eat his guts. What the hell?"

The girl extended her hand.

"You're a clairvoyant yes, take my hand and know."

"I'm not touching you." Lisa began to protest, but the girl grabbed her by the wrist and the contact generated a vision. The vision was of what Lucien planned for all of them. The vision told her what she needed to know, more than she wanted to know. It left her terrified and cold. She had to go with the little girl. She knew if she stayed it would be bad for them all.

"Can I at least leave a note?"

"Be quick about it…please."

The 'please' sounded to Lisa like an afterthought but she appreciated the attempted courtesy. She scribbled a note quickly, in lipstick on the mirror.

"Where shall we go?"

"You know where. The one place he will assume we would not dare go."

"The Grey?"

"Yes."

Lisa sighed. "Ok, can I get my dog?"

"There is no time. I can only hide from Lucien for so long. Take my hand."

Lisa took the girl's hand. "What is your name?"

"In another life my name was D'mara Lockhart. Now people call me Fifty-seven."

The girl produced a small black box from a pocket in her dress. It was about the size of a Rubik's cube. She set it on the floor and it slowly grew to the size of a mini-fridge.

"You know the drill, Lisa. This time your body will travel too, not just your spirit."

"How do you know about that?" Lisa asked, the girl responded by pointing at the box. Lisa placed her free palm on the box and the girl touched the box with her other hand. Then they were gone.

***

The men stormed into Stone, guns raised. A masked gunman was kneeling next to Kamara, who was flat on her back staring up at the ceiling and looking very pale. A dead maboya lay near her, face down, with three feet of Voss' sword growing out of its back. The gunman turned out to be Imelda. Jonah stood over another of the creatures. This one had been shot so many times that it was difficult to discern if it had been male or female to begin with.

Rohan knelt next to Imelda. Kamara had been bitten and while the wound itself was festering and stinking, the putrefaction was not spreading. The Nights of Need was fighting it off, just as his marks had done for him when he had been clawed. She looked like death, though, and she was feverish.

"You are a swords-woman now? You have something against guns?" Rohan asked as he propped her head into his lap.

"It spoke to me, Rohan. The sword, it's alive, I think."

"That's just the poison talking," Rohan said, Rohan knew Kamara was not prone to flights of fancy, she was logical almost to a fault, but he was not prepared to deal with a talking sword at the moment. "Jonah, Tarik is down by the truck. Get him in here with his healing potions."

"Where is Lisa?" Voss asked. "Rohan we have to clear the rest of the house."

"She was upstairs, sleeping," Kamara croaked.

"Imelda, stay with her please, we have to make a sweep."

Rohan and Voss started with Lisa's room. There was no sign of the woman and the room was rich in reasons to suspect the worst. There was a naked man lying in the corner in a pool of blood, clutching a heart in one hand. His entrails were spread around him as if his stomach had grown dreadlocks.

One of the accursed black boxes sat in the center of the floor. Torn clothing and underwear were strewn on the bed next to Voss' Desert Eagle pistol. A single bullet casing also lay on the bed.

"Look at this," Rohan said to Voss. He pointed to a note on the mirror, scrawled in plum lipstick, and obviously written in a hurry. He read it out loud.

I went through the box to the Grey with a girl named D'mara.

Kill Lucien.

Feed my dog.

Love you guys.

Voss punched the mirror, creating a web of small cracks around his fist. "She went to the Grey, the Grey, Rohan. She didn't even take the damn gun. And who is this 'girl.' Did the girl kill our boy in the corner? Because Lisa certainly didn't."

"There was a girl with this crew last night. Maybe our guy out in the horse pasture can answer that question," Rohan replied.

This was the first time Rohan had seen Voss frayed. He put a hand on the man's shoulder. "Let's sweep the house, then we will have a sit down with dog-meat-guy and Cassan. We'll figure this out and get her back." Rohan knew his words sounded hollow. He had never been to the Grey himself, but he had seen enough lethal creatures from there to know that it was no place for amateurs.

"Where is Kat?"

"Good question buddy…good question." Where was the soucouyant.

***

Rohan and Voss swept from the uppermost floor while Richard and Jonah secured the ground level. The men checked every closet, every crevice and every hairline crack in the paint. Jonah even checked the pool filter. Rohan reviewed the security camera recording. Under the damn door, just like the one in the safe-house. But they had not gone completely liquid. Rohan wondered if their ability to fully liquefy only came when the monstrous transformation was complete.

When they were done, Rohan went downstairs to check on Kamara. Richard went to help Cassan inside and Voss and Tarik went out to fetch the man the dogs had brought down. They found him seated cross legged, in the same spot where he had fallen. His broken limbs had already healed and the four dogs lay around him, lightly dozing but obviously alert to their captive's actions. Voss walked up to the man and spoke in a tone that brokered no debate. "You are coming with us. Make one stupid move and we will kill you like we did your friends."

The man chuckled, "The one who sent me expects me to return to him soon, when I don't show up, he will assume I failed or that I ran and he will kill me."

"Good once he comes for you we can take care of that too."

"Oh, I doubt he will show up in the flesh he can get to me without being physically here" The man rose with a resigned groan and all four dogs leapt to their feet. The ground vibrated with the rumble of the goliath hounds' growls.

"Easy girls, we are taking him in," Voss said in a mollifying tone, as he patted the man down for weapons.

Tarik brought Agrippa to heel, while Voss jammed the muzzle of his assault rifle into the stranger's back to start him walking and to assure the oversized dogs that he had things well in hand.

By the time the party was back inside Stone's walls, Jonah and Rohan were tending a large bonfire on a secluded part of Stone's expansive grounds. The pair was cutting apart the bodies of the slain maboya, soaking the parts in gasoline and feeding them to the fire limb by limb, ensuring that each part burned to ash before adding another. Voss called out to Rohan from a distance and Rohan lingered long enough to butcher the last remaining body. He and Voss left Jonah and the massive dogs to guard the fire and they ushered the captive into Stone. The man was made to sit on the floor of the living room and his hands were secured with a pair of the plastic cuffs which had somehow survived the Laventille raid in Voss' pockets.

"Should we wait for Kat before we question him?" Cassan asked of no one in particular as Voss clicked the ties tight around the captive's wrists. "Her knowledge will probably make his revelations more enlightening." Cassan looked relatively sprightly for a man who had been on the verge of death not two hours earlier.

"We can always repeat his words to her." Voss did not sound as if he harbored much patience for the missing soucouyant.

"Yes, but she might have better questions. Besides we promised a ghost to pass a message to her. I feel like we should get all that out in one sitting," Cassan replied.

"Yeah, we did promise," Rohan remembered the Indian girl in the Sari.

"She's already walking up the driveway," Kamara interjected. "So we can stop debating." Kamara lay flat on the floor and like Cassan, looked a lot better as both the Order marks and Tarik's treatments worked to combat the maboya bite.

Not a minute later the soucouyant walked through the front door. She carried multiple crocus market bags. At a glance, Rohan could see fresh bread, salt-fish, ground provisions, dried coconuts and a bunch of blue crabs still alive, strung together in a coffle with nylon fishing line.

The soucouyant wore cut-off shorts and one of Kamara's old washed out tee shirts. She was all lean, tanned limbs and collegiate loveliness. With her hair pulled back in a thick, high pony-tail. The ancient soucouyant looked young.

"Where were you?" Rohan asked with a raised eyebrow. He was mildly annoyed that she had apparently taken a trip to the spa while everyone else was covered in soot and blood.

In response the woman laid the many bags to one side and knelt beside Kamara. She held the prone woman's wrist to her nose and sniffed the skin deeply. She said nothing and Rohan assumed that Kamara had passed the olfactory evaluation as she moved to Cassan and did the same to him.

"You were older and blinder the last time I saw you Kat, but I do not mind the changes one bit."

Kat ignored Cassan's flirtation. "What did you give them, Tarik?" Kat asked of the boy.

"Strong medicine for Kamara; blood-flower, poppy, cannabis, ground lagahoo bone, *alamanda cathartica* and some other ingredients I thought would work. The bites cause the flesh to rot almost instantly. Her marks did a lot of the healing work, though. As for Cassan, Rohan cut off his arm, which is probably the only reason he is alive. I still gave him the same treatment plus something to speed the healing."

"Good work, Tarik. I assume someone will tell me the whole story at some point. Rohan, to answer your question, it is Saturday, I went to the market and left Stone in the capable hands of its occupants. If you stow that bad attitude, I may even make you breakfast."

"Lisa is gone." Voss cut in before Rohan and Kat could continue their verbal sparring.

"Gone? Where to?"

"There's a note on the mirror in her room. It says she is gone to the Grey. There is also one of the black travel boxes. We have to go after her."

The soucouyant pondered for a moment. "Assuming she actually wrote the note and assuming she really went to the Grey then she is almost certainly lost. The Grey is not a place for young maidens."

"We have to go look for her." Voss was adamant. "You can track her like she tracked Cassan through the box."

"And who will hold the thread to reel my essence back? You forget that I pulled Lisa back when she travelled. Tarik has not learned that skill yet. I guess I could simply go to the Grey physically, track them by smell, but The Grey is a massive unmapped wilderness.

"It's topography also changes from time to time. A sea today can be a mountain range tomorrow. Perhaps this is because time passes differently there, days, weeks, seasons do not have the same meaning as they do here. It is a bit like a dreamscape. We don't know where she travelled or if she arrived. If she does survive the journey we do not know where she may have gone once she got there. This could also be a trap. She could be tied up somewhere in a house of horrors like Cassan was."

"One of his people accompanied her," Voss said in a quietly dangerous manner as he pointed to the seated man who had not spoken since he had been brought inside.

"Yes, there is much and more to discuss about that," Kat said meeting the sitting man's eyes until he lowered his gaze. "Was there anything else in her message? Never mind I will read it myself."

"Kat, two ghosts at the house in Laventille asked that you sleep so the dead can talk to you, whatever that means."

Kat was thoughtful again. "Ghosts you say?"

"Yes, a girl and a woman."

"Ok, we'll discuss this but there is no rush, I'm longing to cook in a real kitchen for the first time in many years."

What does she mean no rush? Rohan thought.

Voss gave voice to that opinion. "This boy here says that the man who sent him will kill him soon for failing to kidnap Lisa, and I feel like we need to make some effort to find her, as futile as it may be. She is one of us."

"Our captive will not be killed by his master because someone closed the psychic link between them. I know how the magic feels because someone closed that link between me and my coven years ago. Also, it takes two of our days to travel to the Grey, even though to the traveler it feels instantaneous. So, we have some time while she is in transit. Again, we are assuming that she is headed there. Besides, you have all had a rough morning. Let us eat and Cassan and our new friend will tell us what they know."

The man's gaze rose when Kat referred to him.

"Beware friend, I will know when you lie so you will tell us the truth, yes?" The soucouyant sauntered off after repossessing her sacks of produce. "Cassan, call your brother and let him know that you survived. He is eager to relinquish control of the business. I assume Wrise is no longer with us?" she said glancing back over her slender shoulders as she headed away.

"You assume correctly," Voss said.

The soucouyant moved gracefully toward the kitchen, almost floating along despite her many bags.

Chapter 21

The soucouyant could cook. In fact, Rohan felt like her cooking surpassed Imelda's, and that was no small feat. Within half an hour of Kat entering the kitchen, rich smells of coconut bake, saltfish bojul, and tomato choka filled Stone. She had also made cocoa tea from actual cocoa as opposed to powder and a sada roti for those who did not want bake. Within an hour a full spread was prepared.

No one else had been allowed into the kitchen while she worked. Rohan sat next to Kamara on the living room floor. She was still laying there, her head propped on some cushions. Voss paced the room but kept one eye on Clarence. Cassan lay on the leather couch, dozing lightly but occasionally rousing and staring at his stump as if coming to terms with the loss of his arm.

Imelda hovered close to the kitchen not particularly pleased at having to relinquish her fiefdom to a woman who looked like she could be her granddaughter.

Rohan's stomach had growled until the moment he had been allowed to take his share, and then he devoured six thick slices of bake stuffed with saltfish bojul and tomato choka, two muffins, a serving of eggs, and three mugs of cocoa-tea. Voss appeared too preoccupied to match Rohan's intake. But Tarik, though a wiry boy, ate as much as Rohan did. Cassan, Kamara, Jonah, and Imelda ate far less. Jonah had a reputation as a big eater and Rohan suspected he skimped as a show of solidarity with his wife.

The soucouyant's cooking was exquisite, so much so that Rohan was compelled to compliment her, talking around a stuffed mouth. He would not have thought that she had a domestic bone in her body, but apparently she enjoyed preparing the food. He did however notice that she herself did not eat. When everyone was fed, including the dogs, she took a plate over to Clarence.

197

Everyone but Voss was too stuffed to raise an objection. "So we are feeding the demons now?" the man snarled.

Kat glanced at him and in her usual way, declined to respond. She stood, towering over the sitting man. He craned his neck to meet her gaze. "Yes or no is the only answer required for now. If I untie you so that you can eat, will you cause a problem?"

"I won't, I guess that's a no."

No one protested as she cut the plastic ties binding him. He rubbed his wrists then devoured the entire plate of food like a man starved.

As soon as Clarence was done eating, the soucouyant took the center of the floor and began speaking in the steely tones she reserved for serious inquiry. Rohan had heard it before.

"I will ask you a question, you will answer truthfully. If you lie I will know. I won't bother making threats, I'm sure you can imagine what people like us can do to you." The man, *barely a man at that,* Rohan thought noting the youthful loveliness of his face, nodded in response to Kat's assertion.

"What is your name?"

"Clarence Jeremy."

"Why are you here?"

"I was sent to kidnap a woman named Lisa and bring her to a man who calls himself Lucien."

At this Cassan perked up, "Lucien Sardis is the name of the person whose blood was in the vial, that the woman drank. The woman who tried to kill you guys with the Jumbies."

"The time for your story will come, Cassan. Besides it may be a different Lucien," Kat said.

"The man did not give me a last name. He doesn't place much stock in names anyway," Clarence said.

"Why were you sent for Lisa?"

"Lucien needs her. He said she stole something from him."

These words got Rohan's attention everyone in the room perked up. Stole? Lisa had not mentioned stealing anything.

"Did he say what she stole?"

"No, he did not say, he just said that he needed her brought to him, unharmed."

"How did you meet him?"

Clarence took a deep breath and told the entire tale, from start to finish. When he got to the part about the girl in the sari, Cassan piped up again. "We know Ghita."

"Yes," Rohan interjected, "She's the one who helped us escape the house with Cassan."

Clarence continued his tale. When he was done he said, "I have no allegiance to Lucien. He snatched me off the street, beat me almost to death, then gave me a choice between death and service. But, I don't want to be sick again. I have that much to thank him for."

"Could you take us back to the house where you first met Ghita?"

Clarence thought about it. "I...I can't remember. It is as if the memory has been erased."

"Liar," Voss stated coldly.

"He speaks the truth. He really cannot remember," Kat said. "So you say there are many others, like you?"

"Well, yes and no. The others are like me, in that they have physical characteristics like mine, strength and speed. But they are unstable, mentally unstable. They are rabidly violent. Lucien has them caged. They can be controlled but maintaining control is a hands-on task, that is why he needed me."

"How many others?" Kat asked.

"Fifty-six, minus the three you killed this morning plus the one that ran off with Lisa."

"That isn't the whole truth," Rohan cut in. "We were in a dungeon this morning, there was no time to do a head count, but by my estimate there were far more than fifty-something. Did you have contact with those?"

"No...yes...I'm not sure," Clarence stammered, genuine doubt clouding his face. "I saw something in a vision, others, I could tell they were once human, but now they are monstrous."

"What did they look like, the one's you saw?" Rohan asked.

"Pale, eyeless, toothy."

"Well then Lucien lied to you, I think whatever he did to you is degenerative and when the people he has changed have devolved too far to be controlled, he warehouses them."

Everyone was silent until Kat began summing up the situation. "So we have the name Lucien, who may be the same Lucien Sardis that Cassan's investigative skills uncovered. Seeing that Cassan was kidnapped right after learning the name we can assume that Clarence's Lucien is Lucien Sardis. Lisa seems to have taken something from Lucien that he needs to complete his plan, which seems to be to open the Grey though we are not sure why. Finally, we have a member of Clarence's party missing, presumed to have gone into the Grey with our Lisa."

"That sounds about right," Kamara said from her position on the floor, "So what's the next move."

Kat answered with a question to Cassan. "Do you have an address for Lucien Sardis?"

"Yes, but after his death his home changed hands several times. Today it's an abandoned ruin, guess no one felt comfortable staying in a house where a brutal murder occurred. His wife and daughter survived but the business fell to bankruptcy."

"You said brutal murder, how brutal? I thought you said this was a robbery gone bad?" Rohan asked.

Kamara also spoke up. "And do you know where the mother and daughter live?"

"To answer the question about the murder first, several stories are floating about. The media reports on the matter read as if they were sanitized and I haven't been able to get into contact with any of the officers who were on the scene. I did manage to track down one crime scene technician who worked the location. He quit right after that job and is now a bartender. The man was reluctant to talk about that murder. Thankfully I own the bar where he works. He said that the scene was one of the worst he had ever worked. Lucien Sardis had been pulled apart. Note the use of the word pulled as opposed to torn. His bones had not been broken but had been yanked cleanly out of the joint sockets, just like a plastic doll's arms will come off. He also said the man's face was flayed off. The amount of blood at the scene indicated that Lucien had been alive for most of the ordeal." Cassan paused before continuing. "In yet another strange twist Sardis' body was apparently lost before the autopsy could be performed or positive identification could be made. The family was told that the body was accidentally cremated, but another source told me that the body simply vanished. I don't know where the mother and daughter went."

Cassan paused to itch at his stump and Kat took the opportunity to ply Clarence further.

"Clarence, is there anything you have failed to tell us?"

"I've told you what I know. I have not known Lucien that long."

"I guess that's fair enough. Now we face the question of what to do with you. You say you owe no allegiance to Lucien, but neither do you owe us anything. Perhaps gratitude for sparing your life, but that is no more or less than Lucien has done for you."

"Let us kill him and burn him like the rest." Voss' tone was low and dangerous.

"We could do that. Or perhaps Clarence will strike a bargain." Kat turned her steely gaze on the seated man. "Clarence, if you do something for me, I will kill Lucien and do my best to free you from the degenerative effect of what he has done to you."

Clarence looked up at the faces around him, their expressions ranged from Rohan's casual indifference to Kamara's weighing look to Voss' stormy anger. Kat's eyes gave away nothing. "What are the terms?"

"Follow your confederate Fifty-seven into the Grey via the box. Track Lisa by scent as you did before. If necessary rescue her from Fifty-seven and protect her, or help Fifty-seven protect her. I will give you a means to contact me, so that we can locate you and bring you back."

"You have lost your mind, vampire." Voss' voice was flat. "He was sent here to kidnap Lisa, and you are helping him continue his mission?"

"Can you read minds, Voss?" Katharine turned her attention on the man fully. "No? Well I can't either, but I can read lies. If he takes an oath and means to keep it I will know. So, Clarence, do we have your word?"

"You have my word. I will do the best I can."

"This is lunacy," Voss muttered and Rohan could not really find fault with Voss' assertion, however, they had nothing to lose. Lisa was already gone.

"Good. Come with me," Kat said to Clarence.

Only Rohan, Clarence and Jonah followed. Kamara lay where she was and Voss kept his seat, examining the bottom of his coffee mug.

"I've had enough hoodoo for one day," Cassan said as he rolled over to put his back to them.

"And I'm heading home. It's almost noon and I'm still in my night-gown," Imelda said as she shouldered her assault rifle and made for the door. "See you soon, Jonah?" The last was more a command than a question.

"Yes 'Melda."

Moments later the party of five stood in front the box. Kat wrapped her hand in a pillowcase and placed the wrapped hand onto the box. She began murmuring in a language the others could not understand. As she spoke the box gradually lightened in color, the change spreading out from where Kat's shrouded hand contacted the surface, the box turned from jet-black to midnight-blue, to navy, to gray then entirely white. Kat stopped chanting and removed her hand. The original blackness bled back into the cube once she no longer touched it.

Then she reached into her pocket and withdrew a bone whistle. "Here Clarence, take this. If you blow on it, I can hear it across the boundary. Blow on it once when you arrive, blow on it another time when you have found Lisa. Three quick blows if she faces mortal danger. I can track the sound and travel to your location. You are to stay with her in the Grey until further notice."

Clarence took the whistle. "So what now?"

"Put your hand on the box."

Clarence met Kat's eyes directly. "What are my chances?"

"The Grey is deadly, but so are you and you are more of that world than this one now. Be careful, be observant. Find Lisa, then find some-where to take shelter. We will get you out."

202

Clarence slowly reached out and touched the box but instead of a solid surface his hand went right through the side of the cube, and then he was gone, swept into the Grey.

"Can we trust him?" Rohan asked. "Voss has a point. We don't know him."

"He was speaking the truth. He means to keep his promise to protect Lisa."

"Perhaps we should have just killed him." Jonah hefted his rifle.

"Perhaps, but the Grey is a lethal place and Lisa will need as much protection as she can get. He has the best chance of tracking Lisa via scent, and if he is killed by a lagahoo or something then it makes no difference. If he finds her and blows the bone whistle then I will know exactly where they are rather than trying to track her through the vastness of the Grey."

"The plan has merit, but Voss doesn't like it," Rohan said.

"He likes Lisa, but hopefully he maintains that lethally cool head. We will need it."

Kat said two strange words and the box shrank to the size of a Rubik's cube.

"We'll get that later." Kat turned and led the way out of the room. "Rohan, I want you to tell me everything that happened in the house, in meticulous detail. I especially want to know how the woman and the girl contacted you."

Jonah excused himself and for the next sixty minutes Rohan stood in the hallway with the soucouyant and told her about the ordeal at the house in Laventille. "The girl called Ghita was acting as some sort of keeper for the house. She had tasks. She kept guard in a way, but apparently she has her own will to some extent because she let us out. The woman we encountered in the barrack yard room, on the other hand, just seemed trapped there, resigned to her haunt. They both said you need to sleep, and to open your dreams so they can reach you. That should not be too hard, right?"

Kat looked at her feet. When she finally raised her head, Rohan noted a tenseness at the corners of her mouth. "The sleep that they are referring to is not as easy as simply laying my head on a pillow and closing my eyes, but you will soon see. Lisa encountered Ghita before. The girl almost caught her when she tracked Cassan through the box. Rohan, something big and evil is afoot. I need you to be sharp. Do you trust the men of the other houses?"

"You know how we are. The relationship between the houses has always been at least mildly competitive. Every House also has its jurisdiction. We've always come to each other's aid though."

"Ok, speak to the men you trust. Tell them that Stone may call in need of aid. Stone must not fall. I will also need you and Voss to dig a grave in the back. Kamara and Tarik will assist with the ceremonies."

Rohan looked at her quizzically, "A grave? Ceremony? We already burned the maboya."

"The grave is for me Rohan. The sleep that is required to communicate with those ghosts, demands a grave."

"Kat, what do you mean?"

"You'll see. You and Voss get to digging. Send Kamara and Tarik up to me. Alone. At sunset, I go to sleep."

When Rohan turned to walk away, he thought he heard a sound like a small sob choked back. He knew Kat would appreciate it if he did not turn around to look, so he continued downstairs. Kamara had to be helped to her feet before she could join Tarik in their secret meeting with Kat. Once the meeting had begun Rohan and Voss went out to a secluded area on the grounds and began digging a grave.

Chapter 22

After digging the grave as instructed, Rohan and Voss tried to return to Stone. They found the doors and windows locked and no one answered their knocks. Mysterious preparations were underway. Kamara sent Rohan a text message confirming that they were ok, but that the men had to stay outside for a while. Voss and Rohan thus spent the remainder of the afternoon sitting on the small porch of Jonah and Imelda's home intermittently dozing and playing fetch with Cassan's dogs.

Agrippa was there too, but the big black dog simply lay in the shade of a spreading plum tree like a sleek sphinx, his sharp eyes missing nothing.

Cassan had left earlier in the day. Uriah had arrived with a convoy of armed men to pick him up. There was no room for the massive dogs so Rohan had promised to drop them off later.

Eventually Kamara called Rohan's mobile to say they were ready and that he and Voss should join them at the graveside. The sun was low when Kat exited Stone attended by Tarik and Kamara. It hung in the sky, round, fat, and red like the single eye of an enraged Cyclops, bathing the world in a citrus monochrome.

Kat was naked except for a thick garland of frangipani and hibiscus flowers about her neck. Kamara carried a length of white linen and a large silver jug filled with water and rose petals. Tarik carried a rolled leather bundle.

"What's this?" Rohan asked, averting his gaze from Kat's body.

No one replied. Kat stood by the graveside with her arms at her side. Kamara slowly poured the jug of water and rose petals over Kat's head. The fragrant water ran down her body and pooled around her bare feet. Then Kamara began wrapping the woman in the length of white linen, winding the cloth around her until only her head was free. When she was done, Kat looked like a freshly embalmed mummy.

"Rohan, Voss this is where we need your help. Lay her flat on the ground. Voss hold her shoulders down, Rohan you hold her feet," Kamara commanded.

"What's going on?" Voss asked.

"We are putting her to sleep. But she will try to kill us." Kamara replied. "Please, just do as I ask."

"What?" the men exclaimed.

"Please, we must proceed."

The men lowered Kat to the ground. The soucouyant still had not said anything. She simply stared up from the ground, her almond shaped eyes displaying no emotion. Rohan and Voss held her to the ground. Tarik came forward and knelt at her side. He carefully unfurled the leather roll. Inside was a small silver mallet and a pointy silver stake. There were also bottles containing several types of incense.

Rohan was now genuinely concerned. "Hey, you're not about to stake her with silver, are you? She will die."

"Yes, there is a chance she might die, but she has slept before and survived," Kamara replied.

"I thought she had to sleep as in sleep with a lower case 's'. I didn't know she had to Sleep. I cannot be part of this nonsense." Rohan rose.

"Rohan," Kat called up to him. "The messages that the dead ones have for me may make all the difference in stopping Lucien. Do you think I would try this if it was not important? They asked me to sleep because limbo is relatively safe from spies. Please do as Kamara asks."

Rohan sucked a deep breath but repositioned himself at the woman's feet.

Twilight had descended. Tarik removed the stake from the roll and positioned it above Kat's sternum.

"Now this is the hard part, you must hold her. If she breaks free we will all be in mortal danger. Ready on my count of three. One…two… three…"

Rohan and Voss used their considerable strength to hold the woman to the earth. Tarik hammered the head of the stake with the silver mallet driving it into Kat's chest. The sound of the mallet striking the stake was musical, like a wind chime that left a lingering ring in the air but there was nothing musical about the sound Kat made. It was a moaning scream that started low and then ripped through the air, a sound that could not be made by human lungs or throat. The woman bucked and kicked, almost throwing Rohan and Voss.

"Hold her!" Kamara shouted, but did not attempt to assist. "I can't help you in this part of the ritual. Tarik needs to hit the stake again. Hold her still."

Rohan and Voss did their utmost, but the soucouyant seemed possessed by a legion of demons. Somehow Tarik managed to hit the stake another time driving the slender pike deeper. The musical ring was barely audible over Katharine's otherworldly screams. This time the woman fought so violently that she began to tear through the multiple layers of linen that had been wrapped to bind her. "Hold her!" Kamara admonished, "One more time."

The soucouyant fought them as if she was on some sort of violent autopilot. Her pupils and irises had retreated, leaving her eyes a milky blue, just as when they had first met her in the swamp. Her body bucked and her forehead slammed Voss' chin, splitting it. She kicked out catching Rohan squarely on the nose. He fell back onto his backside heavily. With a tearing noise she ripped free of the binding wraps and then she was on her feet.

Voss leapt onto her back. Rohan tried to tackle her legs. She clawed Voss off then punched Rohan in the head. Then she grabbed a handful of his dreadlocks and kneed him in the face repeatedly until he was dazed. She was far stronger than he was, but he already knew this from when she had held him back that first night in the hut. Voss came at her again and she somehow managed to catch the man in a one-armed choke while still controlling Rohan with her other hand.

Voss struggled as ineffectually as a child in the grip of a tigress. Kat bit into Voss' neck and began to drink. Rohan knew this was bad. He tore free of her grip, leaving a few locks behind and tried to punch her. She removed her mouth from Voss' throat long enough to head-butt his fist.

"Mother." Tarik spoke softly. "You must allow us to finish the ceremony. Remember our purpose."

Rohan was shocked. *Mother?*

Tarik approached with lit sticks of incense and blew the copious smoke into Kat's face. She swayed and released Voss and he fell in a boneless heap at her feet. Kat shook her head as if trying to clear her vision. She staggered, then fell forward, and Rohan caught her and lay her down onto her back. Tarik approached and tapped the stake a third time. Kat shrieked arched her back then went still with a long sigh. Tarik and Kamara sprung into hurried action. They produced some large green leaves and began chewing them vigorously. Then they spat the emerald paste into a small mortar and Tarik frantically ground in several other ingredients with a tiny pestle.

Kamara then pulled the stake from Kat's chest and Tarik packed the wound with the greenish mixture. Kamara sliced her hand with the sharp end of the same stake and dripped blood onto the packed wound.

"We must bury her now, quickly. That means you Rohan, we cannot assist in the digging," Kamara said.

Rohan was in shock. But he picked Kat up. She seemed so tiny and slender in his arms that it was hard to believe that she had almost killed him five minutes ago. With Kat in his arms, he leapt into the grave and lay her flat on the cool damp dirt. Then he jumped back out. Voss was sitting upright but he looked to be in no condition to assist, so Rohan began shoveling dirt on to the soucouyant. The act of burying her left him with a nauseated sensation in his throat. When the grave was filled, Tarik slashed his hand with the stake and dripped blood onto the fresh mound.

"It is done," Kamara said.

"Was it supposed to go like that?" Rohan asked touching the small bald patch where three of his locks had been torn free of his scalp.

"That was actually better than the last time." Tarik said. "Last time she crippled a digger."

"She almost drained Voss," Rohan said, pointing to the man who was still seated and looking wan.

"The blood of a digger is a vital part of the ceremony. But she thought it would go smoother if you guys did not know," Kamara said. "That's why Tarik couldn't sedate her until she had drunk from one of you. Sorry."

"How can she be your mother, Tarik? How old are you?" Rohan asked.

"I'm not sure. I have been celebrating my twelfth birthday every year since before the slaves were set free. After a while we just stopped counting."

"So you're in control your appearance like Kat".

"No, I'm not. Kat can control her gestation to a degree and soucouyant children can control how fast they appear to age to a degree. But we're not sure why I am continuing to age so slowly. I'm not in control of it. While she waited at the hovel, she cast a glamor to make me less-noticeable to humans. Most people could look straight at me and not see me and for the others who could see me, they forgot that they had seen me shortly after."

Rohan tried to make sense of it all. This explained why Tarik was in many ways a child, but in many other ways he was not. His calmness while staking his own mother and seeing her buried was not childlike in the least. For that matter, it was not even human.

"Who is your father?" Rohan asked.

"Kariega Le Clerc."

"The Kariega Le Clerc, founder of The Order, my great great grandfather."

"Yes. Mother will probably speak to him now that she is in Limbo. That was the reason she crossed over the last time."

Rohan was slack jawed. Kat had borne a son for Kariega. "So we're related? Why did you guys lie about your relationship before?"

"Yes, we are related through Kariega, but you're also a descendant of Kariega's son Onyeka. Kat brought him to Trinidad from Africa after Kariega had been killed and while I was still unborn in her womb. Onyeka fathered many sons, but he died in dishonor. Kat planned to disclose the whole truth sooner or later but felt that right now disclosure would have clouded the message. You would have spent valuable time distracted by the news."

Rohan could only nod at that. His mind was spinning with the new information, trying to understand the connections. "So what's next? What will happen to her?" Rohan pointed to the grave.

"She will sleep until she wakes. You and Voss can go back inside. Kamara and I must keep vigil until she returns."

"How long will that be?" Voss asked groggily. He was slowly beginning to regain his full faculties.

"Last time she was asleep for almost a year. I kept vigil for her alone and I almost died. Time in limbo bears no significance, the dead have all the time they need. But she is better at keeping focused now and she knows she must return to save Lisa and help us handle Lucien and we devised a way to call her back. I do not expect that she will be gone a year. Also, this time we have you and Rohan and Jonah and Imelda to bring us food and water." Tarik was smiling.

"So we just wait?"

"Yes."

"And you guys have to wait here."

"Yes, we are bound to this patch of earth."

"Why both of you if you did it alone the last time?"

"One Is the minimum, two is better, three is ideal, more than three is not recommended."

"Well I'm going inside to have a shower and a nap, Voss probably also needs a shower and a nap and maybe even a trip to the E.R." Rohan helped Voss to his feet and let the man lean on him.

"Kamara, you need anything?" Rohan asked.

"A bandage for my hand, some water, a sleeping bag and an umbrella. If it really begins to rain we may need a tent. On second thought, forget the bandage." Kamara held up her hand to show that the self-inflicted slash had already closed. The Nights of Need had done their duty as Orderman's marks.

"I'm not used to healing this fast as yet."

"You'll get used to it." Rohan responded.

Rohan supported Voss inside Stone leaving Kamara and Tarik to their graveside vigil.

"Do you think she's dead? Like really dead." Voss asked as Rohan helped him to a stool and poured him a glass of orange juice.

"No, the kid knows what he is doing. Besides I do not think she is that easy to kill."

"You call that easy? She was in a trance and almost swatted the two of us."

"I guess you have a point. But I have killed soucouyant before, and that tussle with Kat was only about average difficulty by comparison. I don't expect Kat to be average anything."

"Rohan, I feel like we are losing. Not losing to Lucien. But losing in a more general sense. We've been getting our asses kicked all week. Cassan lost an arm, and even you lost some of your hair just now."

"That's just the blood loss talking. Drink the juice and get some sleep. I'll keep the first watch and wake you up in six hours."

"Another thing Rohan, could you bring me my sword. It is propped up against the door."

Rohan walked over to the door where the beautiful blade stood against the door jamb, point down, but when he tried to lift it he found that it was immovably heavy. "Is this a joke, Voss?"

"No, it's a spell. I'm the only person who is supposed to be able to be able to wield that weapon, or even pick it up. Your woman should not have been able to make it budge, let alone cut down a maboya with it."

"So what are you saying?"

"I'm saying she's getting scary. When you go out to take the things she asked for, let her know that the sword is hers. A gift."

"Hmm, ok, go get some rest.

Chapter 23

Kat awoke in pitch blackness, unable to open her eyes but she did not panic. She somehow knew that she was at the bottom of a grave, that she had been buried, that she was dead. She felt the cold weight of the dirt pressing down upon her and round about her, hemming her in, so heavy that even her eyelids were pressed shut. She heard worms and beetles tunneling through the freshly turned sod awaiting their turn to feast on her flesh. She could not breathe, but she did not really need to, she was dead after all. The taste of blood was sweet on her tongue. Voss. The name came to mind but she did not immediately remember its significance.

Juxtaposed against the sweet taste of blood was a throbbing pain in her chest. Silver. She could not remember why she was at the bottom of a grave or why she was dead, but oddly she felt very peaceful. Something called to her, though. She knew she could not stay there, could not succumb. Marshalling her preternatural strength Katharine began to claw her way upward. She fought against the press of the earth until eventually, the grave reluctantly spat her out and she hauled herself free at the surface like some overgrown grave worm.

She emerged into the dying twilight alone and on the summit of a grassy hill that sloped downward to a beach of golden sand. Behind her was grassland that sprawled endlessly toward a massive mountain range visible against the distant horizon as a monolithic blue shadow. The plain was covered in slender knee-high grasses that bloomed small white blossoms in such profusion it looked as if a light snow had fallen. A gusty updraft scattered thousands of white petals about her like snowflakes. A billion fireflies glowed above the swaying blades of grass. The fireflies signaled on and off in every color of the spectrum rather than the customary bioluminescent green. The effect was as if a net of Christmas lights had been cast over the entire plain and was so beautiful it brought tears to Kat's eyes.

She felt a marrow-deep happiness but she did not remember why she would be so happy in this place. She turned toward the beach and descended the gentle slope. She crossed the deep sand and allowed the warm foam to lap around her feet. She kept walking out until the water lifted her. Then she swam and washed herself clean of the streaks of grime left by her egress from the grave. A bait-ball of small silvery green fish nibbled at her body. A larger wave came over her head and she tasted the water, slightly sweet on her tongue instead of salty.

Kat floated until the moon rose. The water was so clear she could see every detail of the seabed through twenty feet of water, even by the silvery light. There were stars in such excess, the heavens looked like a velvet cloth upon which someone had spilled a fortune of the rarest diamonds. Finally satisfied, she turned toward the shore and swam inland with long powerful strokes. She exited the water, tore some large fronds from a windblown palm tree, and assembled a lean-to. Kat lay beneath her makeshift shelter and descended into the sweetest sleep she had had in hundreds of years.

The scent of cooking meat and the noise of a crackling fire woke her. The moon had climbed to its zenith above the calm sea, but she did not trust the moon's position to provide a reliable calculation of how long she had slept. Events in limbo were not constrained by the Absolute's rigid concepts of time. She may have been asleep for hours or for years. She was surprisingly unperturbed by the fact that someone had been able to start a fire and begin cooking a meal while she lay in oblivion. Still, she stayed put until a familiar voice called out to her, a voice that made her heart leap and made the act of dying worthwhile.

"Firefly, are you hungry?"

On the golden sand in front of the tent lounged a massive tawny lion. Beyond the lion, a man stooped on his haunches with his back to her. He was tending a fire over which an entire wild boar roasted. His dark muscular back bore the scars of a whip and another familiar puckered and ragged scar. A scar that memorialized the night he had been impaled saving her life two centuries ago.

Kariega Le Clerc rose, turned to face her and smiled. She ran into his arms with such force that they almost toppled into the fire. They embraced tightly, he savoring her warm scent and she savoring the feeling of being in his large, strong embrace. Kariega was the only person in whose company she felt she could be softer than granite and Katharine was the only person who understood who Kariega truly was. The embrace eventually grew into something more and soon they were laying on the sand kissing as if they were famished and the kiss was the only thing that would sustain them.

Then they lost themselves in each other with a savage passion. When Kat awoke again, the moon was lower over the water and Kariega was gone and the roasting boar had burned to char. The massive lion, however, remained, gazing at her with his knowing amber eyes.

"Where is he, Shepherd?" She asked of the cat. Shepherd only yawned widely, displaying an impressive set of canines.

"Katharine. It has been an age since I let my meat burn." Katharine turned to see Kariega emerging from the bushes with a freshly killed wild goat slung over one shoulder and a spear balanced on the opposite shoulder. The goat had already been gutted, but it still dripped blood.

"Well, you have not seen me for about a hundred years. I would feel insulted if you were able to mind your meal while we did our...catching up."

Kariega smiled warmly at that, but replied, "I told you that you should not come solely to see me again. The ritual is too dangerous."

"I will come to see you as often as I feel like it, Kariega. Besides this is not just a pleasure trip. There is business to do as well."

"Really? Here, skin the goat while I stoke the fire." He tossed the carcass at her and she caught it with one hand. Then he threw a knife to her as well. It had a yellowish white triangular blade about as long as a man's hand, but instead of a straight edge, the cutting surface of the blade was made of numerous small serrations. Kariega had installed a bone handle at the base.

"What is this?"

"It is a leviathan's tooth." Kariega replied as Kat held the weapon up for closer inspection.

"I know what it is, but why is it here? Leviathans are bound in the Grey and you are bound here until you decide to move and take your place with the ancestors. So how did you and it come to be in the same place?"

"A leviathan washed up, almost dead, on the shores of the Sea of Glass. I do not know how it came to be here but it is an ill portent. Limbo should be separate from the Absolute, Grey and Ether. It should be impossible for the leviathan to be here."

Kat began silently and skillfully skinning the goat with the tooth knife.

"Why are you still here, Kariega."

"You know why."

"It may be centuries before I cross and it is unfair for you to wait for me."

"It costs me nothing, Katharine. I hunt, I sleep, I ponder, I talk to the other transient souls. It is not a bad existence. When you finally cross over we shall go to meet the ancestors together, hand in hand."

"I miss you, Kariega."

"And I miss you. More than I can say. At least here in Limbo I feel closer to you. You should not come again unless it is absolutely necessary."

"My visit is necessary. Your vision is becoming reality. The darkness has come and we are hunting it."

"You were only to warn them of it, not hold their hands. The Order should be able to deal with the evil."

"The Order is fragmented. The houses have not only dwindled but have grown more competitive than collaborative. Only Richard from the other houses has even visited Stone since the deaths of Isa, Dorian and Kimani. Stone is now down to one warrior, Rohan, and while he is talented at killing, he is still a cub trying to hide the fact that he is grieving for his brothers."

"Kimani is dead? I doubt that, only Isa and Dorian crossed over to the Ether. Now is scarcely the time for bickering and cherishing of old slights. The houses must band together in this. They need to gather their strength for the storm to come."

"The other houses are weak as well. The Watchers have not tested a child in years. The Order is scarcely ready to face a significant threat. So far our defenses have only been relatively gently tested and our small force has come near to death every time. But wait. Kimani did not cross over?"

"Kimani was not with Dorian and Isa as they travelled to the Ether to be with the Ancestors," Kariega responded and Kat wondered at that for a while.

"They need my help." She returned to the more immediate issue.

"It seems that they do. How is our son?"

"Tarik will be stronger than us both."

"He is his mother's son in his strength."

"He is also his father's son."

"And my other son whose name shall not be spoken?"

"Executed by his sect as we assumed would happen the last time I visited you. He was too extreme even for them."

"The last time you came you told me they were hunting him for his crimes."

"Yes, and they caught him and executed him but only after trying to show him reason."

"The loss of a son is a horrible burden. It is my fault that I was not there to guide him into manhood and into the control of his powerful gifts."

"You were sold into slavery by your king and then killed by my coven before you could return to Africa and learn of his existence. I think the circumstances excuse you from accusations of negligent fatherhood. If anyone is to blame it would be me, for allowing him to follow the path he did."

"I did not see him cross."

"They executed him in the ritualized fashion. His soul should have been utterly destroyed, reduced to nothingness."

"A horrible fate."

"None worse."

Kat finished skinning the goat and began to season it with wild herbs that Kariega provided. Kariega fanned the coals with a large almond leaf, trying to coax the flames to return. Kat shook her head.

"Please have a seat Kariega, my cooking is better than yours by far."

Kariega put up as much resistance as was polite for a man who had not tasted another's cooking in years. Then he relinquished the task to Kat and sat with his lion. Kat called flames out of the coals instantaneously with her soucouyant pyrokinesis. She used her control over fire to dry the goat hide which she then wrapped about herself like a hairy shawl, covering her nakedness.

"Kat showing modesty? The world really must be coming to an end," Kariega said with mock incredulity. Kat busied herself preparing the goat. Instead of roasting it she cut it into many small cubes, which she then skewered with carefully split fragments of the goat's longest bones. She set the skewers to barbecue. She also roasted a whole breadfruit and chunks of a pineapple that she found growing nearby. At this point, even the aloof Shepherd was paying attention. The massive predator rose, walked over, and rubbed his head against her back like an overgrown house cat until she conceded and fed him a few cubes of goat. When the meat was cooked, Kat placed everything out on rinsed banana fronds. She motioned Kariega over and he started eating with verve, in silence for a while savoring the food.

"This is beyond amazing," he finally managed between bites.

"Cooking is the control of fire, coupled with the knowledge of herbs and minerals. I'm accomplished at both skills."

"Quite humble she is," he replied. "Will you tell me why you are here?"

"I came to see you."

"And?"

"I came to speak to the dead."

"You could have held a séance or visited the location they haunt."

"I was told to come here. I think they are afraid to contact me otherwise."

"How will you meet them?"

"I'm not sure."

"How many are there?"

"Two. A woman and a girl. So I'm told."

Kariega picked at his teeth with a splintered goat bone. "Perhaps I can help. But let us finish eating."

When they were full Kariega set aside two clean banana fronds and served two small portions of the goat meat and breadfruit.

"Shepherd bring my drum," Kariega said to the lion. The cat however, did not budge. "Please." Kariega added and the beast finally rose and sauntered off with a flick of its tasseled tail.

"He hates being sent on errands. We will need a bigger fire. Would you be so kind, Kat." Kat did nothing, mimicking Shepherd's reticence. "Please." Kariega said with inflated exasperation.

Kat focused and willed the fire to burn higher. Now fueled by the soucouyant's power instead of the firewood, the flames assumed new vigor and the tongues of fire licked upward at the bejeweled sky. Shepherd returned with a tall wooden drum, gripping the edge of the drum skin gingerly between his teeth. The lion walked over to Kariega, dumped the drum onto his lap, then stood there looking the man in the eyes as though waiting for something.

"Thank you, Shepherd," Kariega said and only then did the cat return to its spot on the sand. Kariega turned the drum over and removed the bottom which was a large cork stopper, revealing the hollow space within the drum's frame. Inside the hollow was a leather roll bound with a cord. Kariega undid the knot and gingerly unfurled the leather roll.

Within the roll Kat recognized a collection of paraphernalia. Knuckle bones from a chimpanzee, an assortment of teeth, feathers, a small petrified gecko, and a desiccated bat, its membranous wings as thin as parchment and just as brittle. There were also several cloth pouches that Kat knew contained various powders, herbs, and ground bone. The roll also contained a collection of old gold and silver coins and several vials of oil.

Kariega selected one of the vials. He flipped the drum upright and dripped a single bead of the oil on to the skin of the drum. He then smeared the drop until it covered the entire surface of the drum skin making it glisten. The oil was fragrant as myrrh. Kariega next took the dried bat, bit off a wing, crunched it up, and swallowed. He then offered her the bat.

"Surely you don't mean for me to eat that."

"Just a wing Katharine, besides this is far from the strangest ritual we have done. Have you grown soft?" Kariega smiled with mischief in his eyes. Kat knew he was right. A bat's wing, though unpleasant, was far from the most bizarre thing she would have ingested for the sake of obeah. She took the proffered bat and bit off the remaining wing. It had no taste and absorbed the moisture inside her mouth like tissue paper.

She swallowed and passed the wingless, mummified bat back to Kariega who promptly tossed the sad little body into the fire. Then he selected the pouch of ground bone and poured it into his hands. Kariega began drawing a *veve*, forming the ancient Haitian symbols by allowing a thin stream of the ground bone to drain from his hands onto the sand. Each of Kariega's hands worked independently from the other as he drew the shapes and symbols with a precision that bespoke practice. When his hands became empty he filled them again with bone dust and continued to draw. Kat recognized certain aspects of the veve. She saw the flying serpents of Damballa Weddo and the crucifix of Baron Samedi, but overall this veve was more complex than anything she had ever seen. Finally, Kariega was done.

"I do not know this one."

"The ones you have seen are to call the Loas to earth. An entirely different sort of ritual is needed to hail Absolute-bound specters to Limbo. It's like a reverse séance, where you are dead and they are living."

Kariega squatted in front his drum and began to tap out a slow deep rhythm. A lazy sensual roll uncoiled itself in Kat's belly like a well-fed python waking up. She could not resist it and she rose and began to sway with the beat, her hips matching the lethargic rise and fall of the rhythm.

"Remember, no matter how strong the urge, do not step into the veve, my love." Kat barely heard him but noted the warning. The air around her grew pregnant with power. The melody flowing from Kariega's drum fell in synch with her heartbeat or maybe she fell in synch with it. The slow roll was but a preamble. Without warning the drumming became savage and complex and Kat was washed away on a tsunami of magic. She danced the dance of Kariega's ancestors. Her body heaved as she became possessed by the beat. The stars descended to earth or maybe she rose to dance among them and her hair became entangled with strange constellations.

She glanced over to Kariega and he no longer drummed alone. Shadowy forms drummed beside him. Freed of the duty of making the music, Kariega rose and joined her, and the drumming continued absent his participation. They danced like mating eagles wheeling in the sky. They danced with the grace of winged serpents. They danced with the power of golden gods drunk on the blood of a thousand martyrs. They poured themselves into the dance, offered themselves to it. Time stretched on to infinity and they did not grow tired. The fire gave birth to a bevy of flaming forms that joined them to dance. The veve glowed white on the sand and from within the pattern, long dead people called Kat's name.

She heard her father, her mother, the multitude of unfortunate men and women whose blood she had drained before Kariega freed her from her hunger, and the voices of those she had slain in the wars before she fled to Haiti and then to Trinidad. She heard the voices of her dead coven calling to her from within the incarcerating depths of some deep hell to which they had been banished. With a final beat the drumming stopped and the magic dissipated reluctantly like the scent of an expensive perfume left by a beloved courtesan.

A cool breeze fluttered against Kat's forehead and eyelids waking her. She was not on the beach anymore, but beneath the spreading branches of a massive silk cotton tree in a rain forest. She looked down at herself and noticed that she was clothed in a white silk robe. It took her a moment to realize that this was the same robe she had been wearing the night Kariega had died or at least one identical to it, since the original had been burnt, torn, and bloody and this one was pristine. Neither Kariega nor Shepherd was present. She sat up. The spreading branches of the silk cotton tree practically blocked out all the sunlight and for a radius of several hundred feet below its shade, nothing grew, it was truly massive. Kat surmised it would take her about twenty minutes to walk around its girth and the gnarled immensity of the trunk seemed to stretch upward forever. Buttress roots the size of cars helped to anchor the behemoth and Kat felt diminutive but safe beneath this forest sentinel.

A large blue butterfly landed in her lap then flew off and landed on the ground a few steps away. Kat watched it. It repeated its actions, this time landing on her hand instead of in her lap before again fluttering off a few feet. Kat took the hint and rose to follow it.

She trailed the butterfly for the rest of the afternoon, over hills, through clear cold streams, over fallen moss-covered trunks until the sun was low. The rainforest foliage hastened the twilight and soon Kat was walking through a grey gloom. She had better vision in the dark than in the day and she could still easily follow the big blue butterfly. Then she heard voices. Kat continued walking until she entered a clearing and saw that Kariega was regaling a woman and a younger girl with some tale. They sat around a small fire, at the foot of a massive silk cotton tree that looked exactly like the one under which she had awoken this morning. *Have I walked in a circle for hours?* Kat thought.

"Is this the same tree?" Kat asked as she entered the clearing.

The three faces around the fire turned to look at her. Kariega smiled warmly and replied with lifting one eyebrow quizzically. "We have been waiting for you here all day so I'm not sure what tree you are talking about."

"Please excuse my manners," Kat said walking forward and smiling. "I am Katharine."

"Hello, my name is Ghita. We are glad you decided to come." The petite and lovely Indian girl rose and inclined her head slightly and gracefully. She remained standing and Katharine walked over and extended a hand. The girl's hand was warm and slender with a grip that was surprisingly strong. She adjusted her red sari with a shift of her shoulders and sat back down.

The other woman made no move to rise. "My name is Jenna Lockhart," she said curtly, fishing a gold lighter from between her conspicuous cleavage and lighting a hand-rolled cigarette. Kat wondered why she simply didn't use the embers from the fire to light her cigarette. When she exhaled Kat noticed that most of the smoke exited through a thin slash that split her throat horizontally almost ear to ear. Despite the unnerving mortal wound, Jenna was attractive in a womanly way. Kat thought that the word that best described her was ripe. She exuded smoldering lustiness from her husky voice to her shapely limbs. Kat felt inadequately slender in her thin white shift.

"A pleasure to meet you Jenna," Kat said, mentally acknowledging that both these strangers had died tragically and there was little pleasure in the circumstances of this meeting at all.

"So, have you all eaten?" Kat asked rhetorically.

Ghita responded graciously. "The goat you made was perfect, Katharine. Thank you."

"You are welcome," Kat replied, itching to ask Kariega how they became separated after the dance.

Kat took a seat around the fire, completing the circle of dead people. It was fully dark now and the orange flame illuminated their faces and banished the shadows to the periphery. How to start the inevitable conversation Kat wondered. Kariega also sat in silence. It seemed that Kat's arrival had added a somber note to the proceedings, perhaps reminding the women of the circumstances that brought them to this meeting.

"So why was I asked to come here?" Kat asked breaking the silence.

Ghita and Jenna made and held eye contact for a charged second. Then Jenna spoke, conceding the responsibility after their silent negotiation.

"We could not risk meeting you in the Absolute. Here we are hidden from Lucien's eyes and ears to a degree. We called you because you have an intimate relationship with death. Even when you were mortally wounded you've always bartered your way back from death's clutches."

Jenna paused and took a long drag on her cigarette while pressing the free palm across the slash on her throat so all the smoke escaped through her nostrils. "How would you feel if there was someone who was altering the rules of your familiar acquaintance death? What if the next time you slept, you could not find your way back to the Absolute? You know the ones who bury you are bound to the graveside by the ritual, unable to leave until you return. What of them?"

Kat stared into the flames recalling the only other time she had slept. That time, she had become lost in the experiences of Limbo and had forgotten that it was not her actual life. It had seemed like she had been there for mere days. Kariega too had been bespelled by their reunion. She ended up spending almost a year of real time in Limbo, a year that to her went by in the blink of an eye. As the one bound in the ceremony, Tarik was compelled to sit vigil by the grave. He had been incapable of straying more than a few feet from the mound of dirt marking the place of Kat's interment.

She had not known this would happen prior to performing the ritual. In fact they had not known very much about the procedure before that first attempt, but she had needed to speak to Kariega about the problems presented by his first son, Onyeka and matters regarding the Order.

Tarik's soucouyant physiology and his sheer will to survive prevented him from dying of mere starvation and thirst. But his body had turned on itself, cannibalizing him down to bones and skin. When she finally returned the earth around the grave had been pockmarked with thousands of holes indicating where he had dug for worms and bugs to eat.

She had found dried blood and feathers caked around his mouth, the remnants of some hapless bird that had flown by or landed within reach. It had been months before he finally regained his full strength, and even then he was never able to recall details of the last three months of her absence. The experience had been frightening and cautionary. They now knew that the soucouyant sleep required a support staff, someone to feed the watchers while they were bound to the grave. They had also learned that in limbo there was no reliable way of keeping time. *Rohan will not let Kamara and Tarik starve,* she thought, *and if something happened to Rohan there was still Voss, Imelda, and Jonah.* They had also devised a method of pulling her back if she spent too long. She could not afford to be gone for a year this time.

"Jenna, you seem to know a lot about me." Kat replied. "But you sent your message through Rohan, an Orderman. Why not have this conversation with him. The Order deals with rogue obeah men."

"There is no unity among the houses," Jenna replied.

"The Order has been compromised, we do not know who is a traitor and who is not."

Kat had considered this possibility, but she chose not to lead Jenna with her own opinions. "Tell me what you know about this obeah man," she asked.

"He is a like a soucouyant, but instead of blood he has found a way to feed on souls and ghosts. He is a strong necromancer, surpassing even Papa Niser and his control over the dead is growing stronger. He proffers philosophical arguments for opening the Grey but I think that his main reason is his thirst for new souls from people slain by greyborn. For some reason he can trap these souls easier and they give him more power. If he manages to open the Grey the resulting human deaths will give him a multitude of spirits to devour and incidentally an army of animated corpses with which he can terrify the remaining living. He will become a god."

"You two were captured by him?"

"We were both killed by greyborn. He has kept us around for many years. Me, he ignores. Ghita, he uses."

Chapter 24

The most elusive goal of necromancy is self-resurrection. Only Nagash and the Christian God have supposedly achieved it. Bringing even a small animal back from the dead requires absolute control over the magiks, and such control is obviously impossible once one's own bodily functions have ended as a result of one's own demise. Death thus makes self-resurrection a circular impossibility. But if one could teach the spirit to remember the flesh once they have been separated, then perhaps...
-Undated excerpt from one of the last surviving pages of Onyeka's five manuals on Necromancy

Kamara had never been bespelled before and the compulsion that prevented her from leaving the graveside was particularly strong. She tested its limits during the first hour that she and Tarik sat vigil. She got up and walked toward the house. She made it about twelve feet then found herself seated next to Tarik again, right where she started. She could not remember returning or sitting down. It happened in the blink of an eye.

She repeated the attempt, this time consciously willing herself toward Stone. The result was unchanged. There was no pain or any voice commanding her to return. It was like the setting that returned computers to their factory configuration. She remembered standing and walking toward Stone, but the moment she crossed some invisible boundary she was returned to the starting point, and the memory of her return was erased.

Kamara did not like it. Out of sheer curiosity she tried one more time at a dead run and again blinked and found herself sitting next to Tarik. The only difference this time was that she felt slightly nauseous. *Compulsion whiplash,* she thought.

"You can't beat it, Kamara," Tarik said with a look of amusement as he paused from flipping through the pages of a worn copy of Jack London's *Call of the Wild.* "I tried the last time and I can run much faster than you."

"What happens when I cross the boundary, I can't remember the return? Am I teleported back here?"

"No, nothing that dramatic, you simply turn around, walk back here, and sit down," Tarik replied.

Kamara resigned herself to catching up on her reading for her law classes. Reading which had been sorely neglected considering recent developments.

It was Monday afternoon and Kat had been 'dead' for two days. Rohan and Voss worked six-hour shifts guarding the grave site. It was now Voss' shift and he dozed in a hammock, cradling a long black automatic rifle. He was shirtless in the evening warmth, but an extra rifle clip was stuck in the waistband of his black shorts. Two of Cassan's hounds lay close by, massive and menacing even in repose. The third hound was with Jonah and Imelda and Agrippa remained with Rohan as he slept or exercised before it was his shift.

Voss' hammock hung outside the zone of compulsion, but close enough to allow him to respond immediately to any threat. So far it had been boring. Kamara and Tarik ate by the grave, slept next to the grave, read books in the shade of the teak trees that surrounded the grave. Tarik produced a deck of playing cards for their umpteenth game of three-hand-knock. The hours crawled by slowly and the only issue that had arisen so far was when she needed to use the toilet or take her sponge baths.

Rohan had erected a bathroom tent for them, at the outermost boundary of the circle of compulsion, where she was able to perform her ablutions. He dutifully emptied the bedpan three times a day without a complaint. This created a whole new level of intimacy between them. Tarik did not ever need to use the chamber pot. He explained that his physiology was extremely efficient at breaking down food and little was ever left undigested, and that he had last gone to the toilet about twenty years before.

Chapter 25

Kat, Jenna, Ghita, and Kariega all sat around the fire. Shepherd dozed a little way off, lying on his side, each exhale kicking up little puffs of dust. As it turned out, both Ghita and Jenna knew Lucien intimately. Kat had asked Jenna how she came to know Lucien and the woman began the story.

"When I met Lucien he went by another name and wore another face. Back then he called himself Lazarus. He discards names when he grows bored with them or when he changes bodies, but of course, I did not know that at first. The first time I saw him I was living in a tenement in East Port-of-Spain, I forget the exact year but it was some time in the late 1880's, perhaps 87 or maybe 88. At the time I was sharing the barrack-yard apartment with two other women, who, like me were unmarried and on their own. As you can imagine we made a living anyway we could. We would travel to the city and look for housekeeping, laundry, seamstress or cleaning work. If things were tight we were not above entertaining the occasional gentleman caller."

Jenna paused and pulled deeply on the cigarette that never seemed to grow any shorter. When she spoke again her syllables were punctuated with serpentine coils of smoke that rose to festoon her face with a silky white obscurity.

"It was very hot the night I met him, so I was sitting on the front stoop when Lazarus first came by astride a tall gray mare. I was not an expert in horseflesh but that was the most handsome animal I had ever seen. A black man riding a horse was something of a rarity in those times and unheard of in the tenement yard but there he was, looking as if he belonged on that horse.

He wore a cloak and a black felt top-hat even in the heat, but he did not sweat. He was accompanied by a man-servant, a short ugly man who walked ahead of him carrying a torch. There was something special about Lazarus, beyond the fact that he was a black man on a horse travelling

227

through what was at the time, one of the poorest and most violent communities in Trinidad. His uniqueness was a combination of little things, his unhurried movements, his aura of confidence, the way he spoke. He also rode as if he was born on the back of a galloping stallion. When he brought the horse to a stop the animal stood stock still, no pawing the ground, no nervous sidestepping, it did not even lower its head to crop the grass.

"Lazarus was a dark handsome man with narrow features. When he removed his hat I saw that his head was shaven and there was a small tattoo on the side of his scalp of a very lifelike eye. At first I thought he was looking for a whore, but then it occurred to me that a man who could afford a horse, a cloak, and a manservant could probably afford to go whoring in a better part of the country. He introduced himself as Lazarus and said he was looking for a live-in maid. I was skeptical. I told him that I had other friends who might be interested, but he replied that he came here for me specifically, that I had been recommended highly by someone for whom I had done some cleaning work.

"You might think that this would be a dream come true for a woman in my situation, eking out a life in the barrack-yard. To have a handsome man ride up asking for her by name to offer a steady job and maybe more.

"But no one ever remembers the name of a travelling cleaning lady. Besides none of the people I had ever worked for had cared to ask where I lived, nor would they advise another member of their circle to visit the barrack-yard at any time day, or worse yet, night. Lazarus was lying through his perfect white teeth. There was an air about him and his servant, something underneath the smile and the polished mannerisms. I struggled to put a finger on what it was about him that nagged me and then I realized that they put a feeling in my stomach. It was a feeling like how I felt about the large snakes that sunned themselves by the river while I did my washing, not an immediate fear but…perhaps an atavistic, instinctual dread."

Jenna's immortal cigarette had finally succumbed to her incessant puffing and she paused her story to roll a new one from a tin of tobacco she produced from somewhere on her person.

"Why don't you use a pipe?" Kat asked as the woman lit the end.

"When I was alive pipes were for rich men. And I have never been rich, neither in life nor in death." Jenna exhaled a billowing cloud and continued her tale.

"When I refused his offer, his eyes narrowed, but then he smiled and said he would be back in a couple days and that I should reconsider. His servant walked over to me and presented me with a heavy silver coin that was unlike any currency I had ever seen in Trinidad. Then they turned and left.

"The next night our apartment caught fire and burned to the ground. I managed to escape through a window but none of my friends were so lucky. The only item I could salvage, apart from the clothes on my back, was Lazarus' piece of silver. I had nowhere to go, no money, not even a change of small-clothes. The morning after the fire a horse-drawn buggy showed up driven by Lazarus' ugly servant. He said nothing as he came to a stop in front of the sooty stoop where I sat pondering my bleak future. What was I to do but get in?" Jenna looked into the distance as she said those last words perhaps pondering what would have happened had she made a different choice.

"I cried quietly the all the way to San Fernando. I had never been this far from Port-of-Spain. Cane fields everywhere as far as the eye could see, and the San Fernando Hill sticking out like a white ghost from the green forest. The man-servant took me to a large house within sight of the wharf. The grounds were immaculate, as was the interior. I asked the man-servant where Lazarus was. He did not respond then nor has he ever responded to any question I have posed. In fact I have never heard him speak. He just walked ahead and I followed him.

He opened the door to a room on the upper floor and closed the door after me when I entered leaving me alone with my worries. As it turned out Lazarus needed no maids. I never saw him at all. If he lived in the house he did an excellent job of staying out of sight. There was never any laundry to do, no ironing, dust never settled anywhere. In the beginning, the first few days I cooked and served three meals a day and left a man-sized portion at the head of the dining table. The food was never touched and so I gave up that practice. I saw the man-servant from time to time, rarely before sunrise, but after dark he roamed the halls, silent as a greased adder. I received my weekly salary, though for what, I did not know.

"I was not a prisoner. One day I left without telling anyone and spent three days in Port-of-Spain visiting some old acquaintances. I got somewhat drunk and was walking down Duke Street when three men grabbed me. They hauled me into an alley, punched me in the face and began tearing off my clothes. They smelled like shit and piss, mangy vagrants they were and I remember thinking they were going to have their way with me then cut my throat."

Jenna paused again, she had stopped sucking on her cigarette for a while and it had burned down to her fingers. She discarded it and rolled another.

"But Lazarus' man-servant appeared out of nowhere. He killed those three men so quickly with his bare hands, they didn't have time to scream. If I had any doubts about the type of people I was dealing with I knew now. I ran out of the alley and went home. By the time I got there the man-servant was already back and, of course, he never said anything, but now I knew I was a prisoner of sorts, that this man would not let me go far, that he was my shadow.

"One day Lazarus came to the house. He was the very embodiment of handsomeness and fine tailoring. He behaved as if he had not been absent for the last ten months. He told me I was pregnant with his child. This was a shocking bit of news seeing that I had not seen him since the night he first came to my apartment. I had not been touched by any man in that way since the day I came to the house. I laughed and told him he was crazy. But he looked at me and said that it would be a girl and she would be very special.

"I was afraid. The entire occurrence was deeply unsettling. Before Lazarus left he cautioned me to eat well. I missed my blood that month and I denied it. I missed my blood for another month and I denied it. Then certain smells began nauseating me. My face grew fuller, then my abdomen began to rise. I was pregnant. Immaculate conception or whatever you might call it. Seven months later there was a knock at the front door. By this time I was the size of a heifer. Lazarus' manservant ushered in a tiny woman. She could have easily fit five times into my maternity dress. She was a midwife, dispatched by Lazarus right on time, as all things with him are. At the sight of her I immediately went into labor.," Jenna said.

"The child was a girl, I picked the name D'mara and Lazarus approved, D'mara Lockhart. She is the reason I remain in this world, the reason I am helping you today.

"For what it's worth he was a loving father. After her birth he spent far more time at the house and for a while we were actually a family, strange as that might seem. Then one night when D'mara was four years old she awoke from a nightmare and calmly said that her father was coming to kill her.

"I tried to convince her that it was a bad dream, but there was no changing her mind. She said that we had to leave now and that she knew how to hide us from the ugly man. I had no idea where we would go and I felt silly for letting my four-year-old daughter convince me of such foolishness. But I asked myself how she knew she had to hide us from Lazarus' manservant. How did she know he could and would follow us? I had never told her about the night in the alley.

"I packed quickly, some clothing and money. But when I opened the bedroom door the silent manservant stood there, blocking the way. I ordered him to move and he simply grinned with teeth the color of urine-stained enamel. Then D'mara repeated the command in her little voice. At first nothing happened, then the man began to sweat. His smile faded, his knees began to tremble, and blood sprung from the corners of his eyes like tears. It was clear that some monumental struggle was taking place. He was fighting a command that the very fibers of his body were compelling him to follow. Finally, he fell to the ground and we stepped over him. D'mara commanded him not to follow and we hurried out into the night.

"I saddled Lazarus' gray mare and placed D'mara in front of me. At first the horse would not budge, and then D'mara commanded it and it broke into a gallop like a gazelle. There was a crash of glass above and behind us. The manservant had leapt through one of the upper storey windows and landed about one hundred feet behind us. He began running after the horse, he lurched a bit at first, overcoming D'mara's command by sheer force of will. But then he began to run and he was fast, faster than the galloping horse. The thoroughbred mare ran at full tilt but he was gaining. Then he dropped to all fours and started closing in even faster.

D'mara reached into the saddle bag and produced a silver revolver. She told me the horse would hold its course so I need not worry about controlling it but that I needed to shoot the man since she was not strong enough to pull the trigger herself. The gun was loaded and I turned around as far as I could and fired an awkward one-handed shot at our pursuer from the back of the sprinting mare. Luck was on our side, the bullet struck him in the face. He stumbled and fell in a cloud of dirt and dust and the horse widened the gap. I did not spare a glance back. D'mara whispered something into the horse's ear and it ran harder and faster into the night. Somewhere behind us I heard a terrible roaring howl, like an angry, wounded animal.

The horse galloped for hours, and then suddenly it collapsed, dead, throwing us both. We got up and checked ourselves for broken bones. I realized I could hear the sea.

"Beyond a low rocky cliff were wooden boats beached on the sand and a man preparing to leave on a dawn fishing run. We found a path down. I made up a story about an abusive husband and told the fisherman we needed to be taken to Venezuela. So he took us there, dropped us off on a lonely beach, and said he would check back at sunset to see if I had a change of heart.

"I knew we could not stay in Venezuela. Lazarus and his man would find us quickly. For the next eight months we travelled around South America, finally settling with an Amerindian tribe deep in the Guyanese rain forest. D'mara said that the tribe's magic combined with her own abilities would help protect us from the lackey's tracking skills. So we stayed. We learned to hunt, fish, and grow manioc. We learned how to grind cassava flour. The year we stayed with the tribe was the most peaceful time of my life.

"But then Lazarus' man found us. D'mara was out hunting agouti with a friend when they were attacked by a jaguar. Her friend was killed, but D'mara managed to kill the cat. She tore out its throat, the men who found them said. D'mara had been mauled badly and had lost a lot of blood. She was completely unconscious when they brought her back and remained in a coma for a week. Whatever she was doing to hide us appeared to require some degree of consciousness so the protection dissipated while she was comatose.

"Lazarus' man came for us in broad daylight. He simply walked out of the forest smiling his piss-colored smile. I gathered D'mara in my arms and ran. The villagers knew instinctively that he was something that needed killing. They feathered him with arrows and pin-cushioned him with poison darts. He ignored them and came after me, walking. He knew I could not get far carrying D'mara. Then the village elder blocked his way and spread his arms. Lazarus' lackey could not advance. They stood about a foot from each other smiling into each other's faces, one straining to move forward, the other straining to hold his ground. The air around them became so thick that it warped the view through the space between the opposed men.

"I slung D'mara over my shoulder. There was no gray mare this time but I did have the silver revolver. I handed it to a tribe's man, told him to empty it into the lackey's face, then I ran into the bush. The lackey caught us an hour later. His face was a red ruin of bullet holes, but his forearms were covered in blood and gore and I knew he had killed the tribe's folk.

"I put D'mara down and drew a knife, knowing I could not beat him. I rushed him and he toyed with me, dodging the knife centimeters before it would have struck. He moved like liquid and my arms were soon heavy. I made a desperate slash and he caught the knife blade between a thumb and forefinger as if it were a sitting butterfly. He yanked it out of my grasp and his hand flashed by my face in a blur. He walked past me and, when I tried to follow him my legs would not move. I looked down and my entire front was crimson.

"I fell never to rise again. The last thing my living eyes saw was him placing a small black box on the ground. The box grew to a cube about two-feet high. He picked up D'mara from where she lay, slung her over his shoulder, got on his knees, and crawled into the box. I followed him. I did not realize how at first, but when I glanced behind and made eye contact with my cooling corpse and I knew.

"I went after my daughter. I needed to protect her even thought I was dead and even though she is stronger than me. Lazarus or Lucien or whatever he is calling himself today knows I'm around. He may even know that we contacted you. As long as he holds D'mara I am bound to him.

"Rohan was not supposed to survive the attack in the forest, but Lucien did not care, after all Rohan was just one man. But then you survived the woman he sent to kill you, the rescue raid to retrieve Cassan was successful, and you killed the people he sent to kidnap Lisa. The captured spirits in the places we haunt are all whispering that he is taking you seriously now and will double his efforts to see you all dead and Stone blotted out."

Kat took a moment to soak it all in. She struggled to make sense of it all and to determine how this information would help them defeat Lucien. "So what do you advise."

Ghita spoke for the first time in hours or was it days. "He wants to open the Grey, it has been his obsession for years, but first he needs power, and lots of it. Lucien discovered a repository of power left over from the collapse of Amerindian civilization. When a civilization dies, that civilization's gods also die, and when those gods die they leave behind raw power, sort of like a collapsed star. This power can be tapped by those who know how. The repository is impure and unpredictable, but it is massive, more than enough to open a permanent hole to the Grey. To tap this power he needs a key, Lisa stole his key and so he needs it back.

"Aside from power he needs knowhow. The specific knowledge he needs is held by the person who opened the hole that triggered the Recompense, the Amerindian medicine man's apprentice Bitol. Lisa inadvertently stealing the key bought you some time. But he has dispatched his man Gershon to search for her and Gershon is a force of nature."

"Well, there are no problems then, even if he can get the key back from Lisa, that apprentice is hundreds of years dead," Kat said already suspecting how Ghita would respond.

"He isn't dead, not anymore," Ghita continued. "As Jenna said, Lucien is a powerful necromancer. His abilities are not limited to animating the dead, he has also learned how to awaken past incarnations of people who are still alive. A few years ago he awakened the apprentice. The result is that two incarnations, past and present, of the same person are now dwelling simultaneously in one body. Lucien has not found that person yet but it is inevitable. Lucien and Gershon are very good at finding what they want when they want it. My advice? Find and kill Lucien and do this before he gets to Lisa and the apprentice."

"How do we find and kill him?"

"It will not be easy. When he is injured or when one body gets old, or when he grows tired of it he simply takes possession of another. We do not know his original identity. However, the bottled spirits in the walls of the house in Laventille whisper a story of a young obeah man whose name has been lost in time. He believed that mankind's relative safety in the Absolute, a safety further enhanced by the protection of the Order, was an ill-conceived notion. He believed that the walls between the Absolute, Grey, and Ether should be broken down and that the most powerful beings should inherit the whole. The society of his obeah-man brethren did not like his idea. They tried to convince him otherwise, going as far as trapping him inside of a silk cotton tree, where they left him, unable to move, for a year. At the end of the year they took him out and again showing uncharacteristic patience, they asked him to reconsider. The young man was beyond convincing. The obeah men saw that there was nothing to be done but to execute him.

"Executing a real obeah man is not easy. It requires rituals and attention to detail to ensure a complete death. They buried the young man up to his neck in the earth, and inserted a long metal funnel down his throat. They then heated ten pounds of pure silver in an iron vat until it was molten and alive like mercury. While chanting the required words they poured the entire contents of the vat down the funnel and into the belly of the hardened young man. Then they cut the head off the body and burned both pieces at separate crossroads and scattered the ashes into separate bodies of running water.

"This young nameless obeah man was special, however. He evaded death. As the molten silver seared into the walls of his stomach he separated his spirit from his body and possessed the nearest living creature he could find, a crapaud. You must, of course, appreciate how difficult this was, he had to time the separation just right so that his body did not go limp too early, nor could he allow the body to completely die with his spirit still inside.

"Now there are several abiding rules of spirit travel and one of them is that you should never possess an animal lest you forget your manhood. But the young obeah man had no choice, he was not yet sufficiently strong in the power to oust the incumbent soul of one of his captors, animals however have no souls and thus possessing them is easy. He was inside the crapaud for several months before he remembered that he was indeed a man. And so, the young obeah man strengthened his craft of possession, he began going from body to body, like some sort of metaphysical hermit crab. The story does not say where he ended up. But I assume that this young obeah man grew in strength until he could take possession of a human body once more."

Katharine and Kariega exchanged shocked looks. Katherine was sure his thoughts mirrored hers. *The method of the execution, the stubborn arrogance of the young obeah man, could it be coincidence?* Katharine turned back to Ghita who had not noticed Katharine's reaction to her news.

"As for Lucien's servant, the man only seems to grow stronger with age. I have seen the lackey, stabbed, shot, run over by automobiles, beheaded, and burnt. He is implacable and ruthless and perhaps truly immortal."

"We will put his immortality to the test," Kat said with an air of finality.

"You must," Jenna replied. "I want my daughter safe from them. Lucien controls her in some way. Not completely, but he can call on her and he can inflict pain. He wants her to lead his army of maboya. Without a strong leader they are feral and she is the only one with the strength to do it. He raises other captains from time to time, but all his attempts at making another true leader have failed."

"I think your daughter grabbed Lisa and is helping her hide, I sent Clarence after her and they both went invisible to Lazarus.."

"Yes, she can do that, hide metaphysically, like she did in South America. She has gotten better at hiding but Gershon has also gotten better at tracking. Sending Clarence after them was a good idea, Clarence is not as strong as Gershon or D'mara for that matter, but maybe he will buy them critical moments they need to survive."

Kat nodded solemnly and turned to Ghita, about to ask her to share how she came to be trapped in Lucien's service when she felt a familiar metaphysical pull. Tarik was calling her back, this could only mean that something was urgently wrong.

She turned to Kariega. "Our son is calling me back. Something has happened in the Absolute. I must return.".

"Come then, we can show you the best way . There is a man in Cumana village, people call him Crayfish. Find him, tell him Jenna sent you, he can tell you some of the parts we have not had the time to share. Every detail counts. Also we cannot contact you again, Lucien has been preoccupied with his plans and this has allowed us greater latitude than we usually have, but opposing him is a risk."

The two women rose to their feet. Kat turned to Kariega. He wore a stoic look on his face but Kat could tell that it pained him to see her go.

"Do not wait for me any longer. You must go to the Ether, Kariega."

"Since when does Katharine tell Kariega what he must and must not do?" Kariega replied in exaggerated indignation. "How can I rest on my laurels with the ancestors while the Order rots?"

Katharine did not argue. She knew he would not cross until they could cross together and she loved him for his stubbornness. She hugged him fiercely and kissed him so hard her mouth felt bruised, "Until next time then, sir."

Ghita and Jenna began walking away and she turned to go after them. Shepherd rubbed his massive head against her as she moved past. When she glanced back to get one more glimpse of Kariega, he was gone. His absence mirrored an emptiness in her chest, which the lump in her throat was unable to fill.

Chapter 26

Lisa was famished and parched. She felt like she had not eaten in days, but that could not be right, the trip into the Grey had been instantaneous. One minute she had been holding D'mara's hand and touching the box, the next minute she was here, wherever here was. As far as she could tell 'here' was a massive sugarcane field that stretched towards the horizon in all directions as far as the eye could see.

She lay on her back atop a grassy knoll that she imagined was the very center of this world. D'mara was nowhere to be found. The sky above was a cloudless sea-green in lieu of the usual blue. It was as unnerving and alien as it was beautiful. A single black vulture wheeled in the green expanse. The air was clean, crisp and easy to breath absent of the stench of industry and mankind. Everything was silent except for the susurration of the sugarcane in the breeze.

Lisa considered her next steps. This was the Grey, the place that spawned the thing that broke the table at the Watchers' House. She should find shelter, but where could she go?

She rose and began to walk through the cane. She looked into the sky, trying to determine the sun's position to at least track her progress in some way. She noted that where before there was just one vulture, there was now a dozen. The birds formed a feathery vortex as they circled effortlessly in the air. The sun looked like what it should, perhaps a bit bigger and brighter than the one she was used to, but that might just be because of this smog-free air. Lisa recorded the sun's position and continued to walk.

After a while she glanced at the sky again. This time there was a cloud of vultures, hundreds of them and the foot of the vulture vortex seemed to be anchored directly above her position. Concern bloomed in her chest. The big black birds literally seemed to be pointing out her location, anything for miles that knew how to read the signs would know where she was.

She began to run as fast as the cane would let her, occasionally checking to see if her hypothesis about the vultures was correct.

The birds moved with her and more continued to join their number. She was like the Pied Piper of vultures. There were so many now that she could hear the sound of air as it sighed past their many wings. Then she heard something else, something behind her breathing heavily. She looked back and saw the cane stalks about two hundred meters behind her, bending and swaying as something large bulled its way through. Lisa ran and the birds seamlessly adjusted their synchronized flight to track her progress. The thing behind her began running as well, breaking through the cane stalks with a crashing rush.

She felt like now was a fine time to entertain a full panic, and so she panicked. *Where was she even running to?* she wondered. The cane field had no end and the vultures were pointing right at her. There was nowhere to hide. She decided that it was more horrible to wait to be pulled down from behind by the unseen pursuer than to stand and face it. Maybe it was something benign.

She stopped and turned to wait for her tail, but a moment later she wished she had kept on running. The beast that came through the cane stalks could best be described as a bear that was covered in bony spines rather than fur...a bearcupine? It had a long prehensile tail and stood almost ten feet high at the shoulder. Even from fifty feet away it stank as if it had rolled in a latrine. The spines covering its body shivered in excitement making a noise like a bag of bones being shook. A long tongue lolled out of its broad snout as it salivated, its dull red eyes focused on her exclusively. It took two deliberate steps toward her and then charged like a cape buffalo. She ran to her right as fast as she could. *Big animals were bad at rapid maneuvers,* she thought. But she knew it was futile. The thing had all day to chase her down and with no cover in sight she was doomed.

The crash of the creature's onrushing charge through the cane grew louder behind her, then there was silence and she knew it had pounced. She dropped flat to the ground and the beast sailed above and past her leaving a fetid wake. It landed and turned around with the agility of an animal half its size. She was still on her stomach atop a bed of battered cane stalks. It didn't even bother leaping. Instead, it shambled up to her.

From her prone position the spiny bear looked even more massive. She looked up at its ugly maw. "If Voss was here, he would make a rug of you," she said out loud. Voss did not come but someone else did. The man who speared the beast through the neck with a bamboo pole was tall, slender and boyishly pretty. He wore black skinny-jeans was in his mid-twenties and looked like he had just stepped out of a vintage record shop. He was entirely out of place here.

The pole went in one side of the creature's face and out the other in a spray of blackish blood. The spiny bear bellowed in rage and twisted around violently to meet its attacker. How the man kept hold of the spear was anyone's guess, it bent and broke leaving half its shaft in the beast's face and the other half in the man's grip. The bear charged him and he stepped to the side like a bull fighter, when the animal wheeled he shoved his broken bamboo stave into its left eye and simultaneously yanked the other half of the broken weapon from the creature's neck while dodging a swipe of its dinner-plate sized paws.

The brute was wounded but far from dead. It did not charge again but began circling looking for a weakness, acknowledging the stranger as an adversary rather than an easy meal. The newcomer looked very small battling the giant bear but he was very fast and very strong. Lisa did not want to move for fear that she would break his concentration. The bearlike beast charged again, and again the man stepped aside, but this time the charge had been a feint, at the last moment the creature's tail whipped forward and coiled around the man's ankles. He recovered his balance quickly but not quickly enough. The beast's clawed fist slammed into the man's face with a sickening crack.

The man fell to the ground in a heap and the bear moved in for the kill. Lisa shouted instinctively and it turned. Reminded of its first prize, it came for her.

D'mara Lockhart, erupted from the cane fields with the suddenness of a summer storm. The little girl held a twelve-foot bamboo spike in front of her like a pole-vaulter determined to clear the high beam. The spiny beast gathered itself for violence, but at the last moment the girl leapt high.

Lisa's eyes tried to follow her upward journey but D'mara had leapt into the light of the big bright sun. Lisa was momentarily blinded and so was the spiny bear. When Lisa's vision cleared D'mara had driven the wooden spike down the mouth of the beast so powerfully that it had run through the entire length of the bear and into the ground. The spiny beast was dead, but the impaling stake prevented it from falling over, so it sat upright looking ridiculous and undignified with three feet of bamboo protruding from its open mouth. D'mara ignored the fallen man and walked over to Lisa, her brown face looking like a hurricane sky.

"You have lost your mind," the girl said, not as a question but as a statement of fact. "We get here, you are thirsty, you need water, but you refuse to walk with me to find the water because you are, as you put it, 'about to turn into a raisin and die.' I hide you and tell you stay where you are in the grass. The moment I turn my back to get the water that you asked for you wander off for a nature walk. Do you have any idea what lurks in the Grey? This isn't West Moorings or even Belmont. You think that was bad? There is far worse out here. Were you bitten or scratched?"

Lisa had no recollection of any of the conversation about the water. "No I was not bitten, I…I don't remember any of that conversation." Lisa's mouth was not producing any saliva and she suddenly felt light headed.

D'mara stooped next to where she lay and placed a hand on Lisa's forehead. "You're burning up. Here sit up, drink this and eat this." The girl gave her a skin of liquid that Lisa hoped was water and a weird fruit that was perfectly spherical and covered with a waxy, deep-blue rind. Lisa drank from the skin.

It was not water. It was unlike anything she had ever had before. It had the consistency of water, but it tasted like…life, if all the best flavors in life could be distilled into a liquid she though. The first sip refreshed her from her toes to the ends of her hair. The best description for its taste was sweetness but to describe it as sweet would not do the drink justice. It was cold, crisp, and wild. It was, in all honesty, the best thing she had ever tasted. "We should take some of this home," Lisa said.

She bit into the fruit, it was not as good as the 'water' but it was still amazing. She felt completely better. D'mara walked over to the prostrate man and toed him with a slippered foot. "Clarence Jeremy, you can either get up or get left for the buzzards and I assure you, they are gathering." The man groaned and rolled over, the right side of his face was covered in blood, but under the blood the flesh looked whole.

"Fifty-seven, I was almost decapitated." Clarence said as he sat up.

"Yes I saw. You need to be sharper if you are going to be of any help here. Get your shit together, Clarence."

The pretty man looked genuinely hurt, "Hey, if it wasn't for me she would have been dead when you got here," he said.

"Fair enough, but when you are attacked in the future go for the heart and don't get tripped up by a silly tail trick again. Did Kat send you?"

"Yes, she said I needed to find and protect Lisa, she gave me a whistle to blow when I found her." He pulled a thong out of his shirt and stared at the crushed bit of bone attached to the end of it. The whistle had been smashed in the fight.

"Well, that's not going to help us much now. It does not matter, Lisa knows the way back, and we won't be returning until Lucien is dead."

"I do? Don't you have another of those black travel boxes?"

"Nope, fresh out, but you know the way, when it's time to go we will be able to go. For now, welcome to the Grey. We need to get moving, the birds will give away our position as long as we remain in view."

"Why are the birds following us?" Lisa asked.

"Because outsiders are always soon to die in the Grey?" Clarence ventured.

"Well yes, that's part of it. But all the creatures here share a low-grade psychic connection. The vultures signal the predators both visually and mentally. The predators come and do the killing then the vultures benefit by getting to eat the scraps. It's symbiosis on a grand scale. If Lisa had stayed on the grassy knoll, where it smelled of maboya she would not have been hunted."

D'mara sniffed the air, "Clarence, you are better at this, help me."

242

Clarence also lifted his head and tested the air. "It's faint, but it's there, east?"

"Yes I agree, east. Let's go Lisa, we have miles to walk and this probably won't be the last time we have to kill something big and nasty. By the way, this young man is Clarence Jeremy. He led a team of kidnappers to Stone, where they intended to kill your friends and bring you back to Lucien. Don't worry, he's a nice guy, had a bit of a hard life but you can trust him. We can trust you right, Clarence?"

Clarence's head was bowed in what Lisa thought was shame. "Yes, you can trust me."

"Good, we are all sorted now, single file. Clarence you lead with that amazing nose, Lisa take the middle, and I will bring up the rear. Oh, wait, one last thing…"

The one last thing was utterly disgusting. D'mara tore open the corpse of the spiny-bear and smeared them with its blood, guts and feces. Lisa gagged at the stench.

"We stink of the Absolute, and out here, that is a dinner bell. So we will trade that smell for a different stink."

They set off heading east, accompanied by the maelstrom of black vultures and a retinue of fat golden flies.

Chapter 27

Rohan Le Clerc was uneasy. Kat had been under the dirt for six days and seven nights now and he was becoming a bit concerned. Even though Tarik had shared the tale of how long he had waited for Kat to return the last time she had slept, Rohan still could not shake his worry. Voss was on guard duty at the grave site and Rohan monitored the camera feeds in the security room. He knew he should be sleeping in preparation for his shift, but he couldn't tonight. There was a weird feeling in the air, an expectant feeling.

Awaiting Kat's resurrection was boring and stressful work and he was on edge. Before Kat's burial it had been years since Rohan had spent seven consecutive nights at Stone and his self-imposed house arrest was starting to generate cabin fever. While Kamara and Tarik were bound to the grave neither he nor Voss could do much else other than perform their security shifts. Yes, he could retreat inside Stone between his watches, but he was not confident enough to leave the premises even with Voss on guard.

At least I can leave the graveside, he thought. Tarik and Kamara had been bound to the same one hundred square feet of space for the last week. They seemed to be coping with the situation better than he was though. Kamara did Yoga daily and practiced with her sword. Rohan had been able to bring it to her after getting her to explicitly say that he could touch it. Tarik ate, slept, and read.

The weird feeling in his gut would not dissipate. Something about the night was odd. A suspenseful mood held sway. Rohan went downstairs and out onto the wide marble porch where he listened. It was quiet, no jumbie birds or crickets sounded. The air was still, no breezes stirred. Twice Rohan started towards the grave site but swallowed his uneasiness and sat on the steps of the porch to wait for Voss to call him for his shift.

There were not many trees on the grounds immediately around Stone House. Beyond the walls there were many ancient trees and Rohan knew them all. That night there were three strange new trees beyond the wall. When one of the trees leapt over Stone's walls in a single stride the odd feeling in Rohan's stomach coalesced into something tangibly familiar, alarm.

***

Voss' watch was almost over and he knew Rohan would be impatiently waiting to relieve him. The Orderman had become stir-crazy recently, unable to sleep, keen for Kat's return, and concerned that Kamara's and Tarik's attachment to the grave made them all vulnerable. His concerns had merit. Being out in the open with two people metaphysically tied to a small square of earth made them an easy target.

Lucien knew where they were and to be honest he was a bit surprised that no other monsters had been deployed to kill them. If he was Lucien he would strike now while the soucouyant-witch slept or rotted, while he and Rohan were the only ones guarding, and while no one could stray too far from this patch of dirt whether by compulsion or dedication. Given the circumstances, Voss was almost relieved when he saw the three giants sprinting towards them across Stone's lawn. An attack was to be expected and it had finally come. He had always been a better soldier than sentry.

The creatures approaching looked like men who had been stretched to a height of twenty-five feet. All sinew and bone, their massive, bare feet were surprisingly silent as they came. They were dressed in the garb of field slaves, ill-fitting, stained cotton trousers and tattered shirts that were left unbuttoned to flap in the wind as they sprinted forward. One was shirtless. In their matted hair they wore branches and leaves, Voss assumed for camouflage. Their faces were those of old negro men, sun-creased and lined, but their eyes burned silver like moonlight. Moongazers they were called because they drew their power from moonlight; rare creatures even in the stories. Nonetheless here they were, three of them, coming to kill him.

"Kamara, Tarik, we have a real problem here," Voss called out as he took a knee and opened fire with his assault rifle. The goliath hound that kept watch with him grew to its massive size and charged out to meet the intruders. Kamara emerged from her tent carrying a long-gun. She raised the weapon, sighted, and opened fire too. The giants were still about a quarter mile away but closing fast. Voss knew at least some of the bullets were on target but the giants seemed unfazed. Voss heard an engine roar as Rohan crested a rise at the wheel of a pickup truck in pursuit of the monsters. Voss could see Agrippa in the passenger seat and one of Cassan's dogs in the back. Rohan was firing a submachine gun through the window with one hand and steering with the other while keeping the accelerator floored. The creatures paid as much attention to Rohan's bullets as they did to his and Kamara's.

Tarik emerged from his tent armed with an AR-15 and began firing at the oncoming trio. The first of Cassan's dogs hit the lead Moongazer with an impact that sounded like a car collision. The monster and the huge hound fell to the ground entangled in a vicious battle. Rohan caught up with the remaining two and swerved to ram the truck into the shins of the nearest one, bringing it down in a heaped tangle of long limbs. He then set the dogs on it before the giant could regain its footing. Agrippa and Cassan's second dog lit into the fallen Moongazer as Rohan chased after the third one on foot, still firing his weapon. The giant easily outran him ignoring his gunfire. It was obviously focused on the people by the graveside, who were pegged to the spot like the bait-goat in a lion hunt.

"Kamara, its coming," Voss said.

"I guess it is," she replied displaying surprising calm.

The giant was now fifty feet away and Voss ran out to meet it. He aimed at its knees in an attempt to slow it down, but the bullets may as well have been a drizzling rain. Voss dropped the gun and called the beast that lived inside him. It had always been there, the beast, existing as a ferocious companion since his first memories of himself, always eagerly waiting to be released from the cage of his humanity. The beast flowed from within him, warm as a shot of alcohol. He did not allow a complete transformation, he just needed claws and fangs for this job. Talons erupted from under his finger nails and his fore-arms doubled in size and became covered in fur. The change used to be painful at a time, now it was routine.

He now had the tools he needed. With a bestial roar he leapt at the creature, clambered up its calf, and tore into its leg with tooth and nail.

The flesh tasted foul and the blood that ran from the wounds shone silver like moonlight. He got the reaction he needed, the giant bellowed in pain and stopped to swat him off. He dodged its blows clambering around the creature's thigh like a monkey on a tree trunk.

The delay caused by Voss allowed Rohan to catch up. Voss saw the man leap from the ground armed with two machetes, one in either hand. He plunged them into the giant's lower back clinging to the embedded blades some twelve feet off the ground. When the creature reached behind and tried to grab Rohan he slashed at the hand with one blade while clinging on to the other that was still buried in the giant's flesh. The blow removed one of the giant's fingers and it fell to the ground like a branch.

The Moongazer frantically tried to dislodge its two tormentors while Rohan and Voss tried to do as much damage as they could. Voss clambered higher onto the creature's thigh and began to root into its groin, while dodging the giant's crushing blows. Rohan hacked into its spine, hoping to land a disabling strike.

Another of the Moongazers ran past them. Voss glanced behind and saw one of Cassan's dogs lying on its side, dead or unconscious, Agrippa was nowhere to be seen and the other goliath hound was still locked in mortal combat with the first Moongazer. Voss hoped Jonah had heard the commotion and would soon arrive with the third oversized dog.

There was only one choice to make, Voss sprang onto the back of the passing Moongazer.

***

Rohan was now in a spot on the Moongazer's back that it could not reach no matter how it contorted. Soaked in silver blood, he hacked repeatedly into the giant's back. The blood was as cold as ice water and tasted bitter when it inevitably got into his mouth. Rohan persisted, thinking he was making progress but then the tormented giant began growing, stretching skyward like the mythical beanstalk in the children's story.

In seconds it doubled in height. Its arms grew too, longer, it could reach him now and it did. He was in its grasp before he could react. Its massive hands were calloused and strong. It could easily crush him, but instead, the Moongazer hurled Rohan as hard as it could, launching him upward and away. He tumbled end over end like a chicken carcass in a rotisserie grill as he ascended skyward, powerless to stop his flight. He reached the zenith of his trajectory then began to fall.

His decent terminated abruptly when he slammed through the foliage of a mango tree, hitting what he imagined, was every single branch on the way down. Miraculously he landed on his feet. An ordinary man would have died. Rohan Le Clerc managed to escape only with a broken right arm, two broken fingers on his left hand and a broken left shin. His body began to knit itself, not as fast as a lycan and not as fast as it would with one of Kat's potions but far faster than any other human being. He could not afford to be out of the battle. He picked up one of the larger branches that his body had broken as he fell through the foliage and used it as a crutch as he hobbled back towards the fight.

***

Voss saw Rohan sailing through the night air like a Frisbee. He heard the man's body crash into the trees in the distance and hoped he had not broken his neck. Either way Rohan was out of the fight for now. The Moongazer that had flung Rohan now stretched twice as tall as the one that Voss was currently attempting to disembowel. He had to find a way to put the first creature out of commission so he could focus on the other. Kamara and Tarik were still firing ineffectually and the tallest Moongazer began walking toward them.

Voss clawed his way up his giant's body, dodging its powerful attempts to swat him off. He clambered around to the creature's back and dug into its flesh, trying to reach the heart from the same inaccessible spot that Rohan had attacked earlier. He burrowed into the bitter flesh head first, worming his way forward like a man-sized parasite. The freezing, glowing blood got into his eyes and filled his mouth as he advanced deeper into the body of the Moongazer searching for a heart. He crooked his neck forward to his chest creating a few inches of space to breathe. Forward advancement became difficult then it became impossible, the flesh of the creature was congealing into a cold implacable jelly.

He tried to back out, only to find he could not do that either. He was trapped in the body of the Moongazer in a cavity that was closing in on him. He was going to drown in the ice-cold silvery innards of a giant man from folklore.

***

Kamara was terrified. Rohan had been thrown so hard that he had vanished beyond the treetops. Now it appeared that the flesh of the second creature had healed with Voss inside. The third giant was dead. Its open eyes no longer glowed, Cassan's dog had prevailed. The giant dog however was badly hurt. Three of its legs were broken, but it still crawled in pursuit of the remaining enemies and Kamara appreciated its tenacity.

The remaining giants sauntered towards her, all their pursuers apparently vanquished for the moment. Neither she nor Tarik fired, but only because they were out of bullets. The taller giant, the one that had flung Rohan reached down toward them. Then several things happened at once. A massive hound erupted from the undergrowth, with Rohan clinging to its back. One of his arms was dangling and obviously broken.

The dog leapt and bit into the throat of the shorter giant. The dog's muscular weight dragged the giant to the ground. Rohan leapt off the back of the animal while the dog pinned the giant to the ground and began wildly stabbing the felled giant with a big branch.

Tarik's body lit into a soucouyant nimbus, but instead of attacking the taller giant, he dove into the mound of dirt that covered Kat. He did not burrow or dig into the dirt, he simply melted into the ground like a ghost, disturbing not a clod in his passing.

He did not abandon me, Kamara thought. *He must have gone to summon Kat.*

Someone fired a rocket propelled grenade from the bushes. It hit the last giant in the face and exploded, wreathing its visage in fire and oily smoke. That did not stop it from reaching for Kamara. She grabbed her sword and began running towards the boundary of her invisible confinement. She did not make it far before the giants grasp, pinned her arms to her body preventing her from drawing the weapon.

The Moongazer lifted her heavenward, until they were eye to eye. Its face was a scene from a nightmare, the grenade had completely burned away the hair on one side of its head and had charred the skin black. Where the wound had not been cauterized it oozed glowing, silver ichor.

The eye on the side of the grenade's impact had imploded into a pool of silvery gum. The giant's mouth opened wide, a foul humid wind escaped. Then the unthinkable happened, the giant ate her.

***

The Moongazer ate Kamara and ran off into the night. For a moment, Rohan wondered why Kamara's compulsion to remain in the area around Kat's grave did not apply when she was consumed by the giant. With a roar Rohan plunged the mango-limb club into the eye of the prone giant as it struggled against the mass of the largest of Cassan's hounds. He leapt to the ground, landing on his one good leg, and hobbled after the escaping giant.

Where the hell is Voss? he wondered, assuming the worst.

Jonah drove up to his side astride an ATV, a grenade launcher slung across his back. Without a word Rohan mounted the bike behind Jonah and they sped off after the fleeing giant. The dog dispatched the fallen giant with a crushing bite to the head and bounded after them in pursuit.

***

Thankfully, the Moongazer swallowed her whole. Her sword was gone, lost somewhere in the giant's cavernous mouth. She managed briefly to cling to the back of the thing's throat before the muscles in its esophagus clenched around her and dragged her down. It was dark and airless. She gasped for breath but, instead of air she got a mouthful of the cold liquid that coated the alien creature's gullet.

She coughed and gasped again only to choke on more of the frigid slime. She was drowning in a fetid soup of icy foulness.

Need. She frantically clawed upward, but the flesh around her was like the embrace of a constrictor. She was headed down. Desperately she reached upward again and her fingers closed around something hard.

Sword. But it had come down the wrong way, scabbard-first, there was no way she could flip it around in these tight quarters.

Air. She felt as if someone was pulling a black hood over her eyes. Even in the pitch darkness she could discern the deeper black of waxing unconsciousness. She was falling asleep never to wake again.

Wake. She was awake, but wakefulness was an airless place. She did not want to be awake. Her chest would not burn if she was unconscious. The oblivion of insensibility was enticing. She willed herself to cling to wakefulness, to quell her panic and think clearly.

Her efforts were rewarded. Somehow the sword worked its way downward and it was now pressed next to her. Her fingers closed around the hilt. Kamara executed a cutting draw, marshalling all the power she could. The Nights of Need burned on the back of her hand as if the tattoo had caught fire. Air.

***

Jonah drove the ATV like a man possessed. Rohan hadn't known that the old man had it in him. The four wheeled bike leapt over mounds of dirt, powered up inclines and crashed through bush and shallow streams in hot pursuit of the last Moongazer. Rohan ignored the pain in his leg every time the bike jolted.

They crossed an open field, gaining on the running giant. They were about forty feet behind when Rohan unclipped the grenade launcher from around Jonah's back and began trying to center a shot on the back of the creature's knees. Maybe if he brought it down they could cut her out before she suffocated or was digested. But if it had chewed her? He was about to pull the trigger on the grenade launcher when the torso of the giant, split horizontally in a heavy torrent of silvery blood.

The Moongazer tried to hold its ruined body together but the damage was too great. It fell forward like an oak tree with worm-eaten roots in a gale. Rohan and Jonah sped over to the dead creature and began rooting through the ice-cold entrails looking for Kamara. When they found her, she was soaked in glowing blood and fluids, unconscious but breathing and gripping the hilt of the sword so tightly that she had crushed the hardwood of the handle and driven the splinters into her palm.

***

Voss had never beheld a better sight than Kat's lovely face looking down on him as she and Tarik cut him free of the Moongazer's flesh. Only Kat could die and return looking better than she had when she left.

251

Chapter 28

Agrippa was missing and one of the giant hounds appeared close to death. Another had three broken limbs and several missing teeth. If Agrippa had been thrown like Rohan had been, there was no telling where he had landed or if he had survived. Kamara had regained consciousness but was shivering uncontrollably, chilled to the bone by her silvery bath. Voss too was cold. The blood was strange, it felt ice cold regardless of how long it remained out of the Moongazer's body, and it clung to them, making them wet and cold and uncomfortable. Kat saw to the wounded while Tarik went to look for Agrippa. The boy returned about thirty minutes later at a run and carrying a large black form cradled against his chest like a child. Blood had soaked the front of his shirt. The dog he carried was unmoving.

"I did what I could, but the medicines do not work on animals as well as they work on men. He needs to be stitched." Tarik said. Rohan noted that he was not breathing hard even though he had arrived at a dead run.

"That dog must live." Kat responded, urging everyone towards Stone. "The two big ones will be fine, even that one that is barely breathing. Those beasts won't die easy."

The group bruised and battered, with the exception of Kat, headed back to Stone. She looked like she had just returned from a relaxing trip to the Grenadines. She even had a tan. She set Agrippa on the dining-room table and set to work. The dog was bleeding badly from a big gash in its side. Rohan could see the slick white of ribs through the tear in the dog's flesh. Kat began to shave the dog's side with an electric razor, to better access the wound. As the hair fell away Rohan's heart began to pound. The dog was covered in tattoos, Orderman's tattoos, Kimani's tattoos.

"Kat, is this a joke? Because if it is a joke it is not funny," Rohan managed to croak.

"This is no joke I would play, Rohan," Kat replied, barely audibly.

Kamara took Rohan's arm. "What does it mean?" he asked.

"Your brother has been reincarnated as our Agrippa. I suspected it earlier." Kat said as she cleaned the wound with salves. Agrippa whimpered.

Rohan moved next to Kat and looked at her as she worked on the ugly jagged gash. "Will he live?"

"This is bad, Rohan. He's lost a lot of blood, but he's a young dog and he has the marks."

"He is a young man," Rohan said angrily.

"Kimani is gone, Rohan. Agrippa has no memory of the man. Only his warrior spirit remains."

Rohan felt like he had lost his brother for a second time. "You must save him," Rohan said, a fullness welling up in the back of his throat.

"I promise I will do my best. You should go scrape that stuff off. You all look like ghosts."

Imelda began making dinner or breakfast or lunch or whatever giant-slayers eat at indeterminate hours of the day. Rohan could neither eat nor leave Agrippa's side. He watched as Kat did her work. When the wound was clean she packed it with a yellow powder the consistency of cornmeal. Then she stitched the wound closed around the packing. It was a nasty jagged gash. In some places there was not enough skin left to pull the sides of the wound together.

Where the flesh could not be stitched Kat simply packed the wound with the yellow dust and left it open to the air. Jonah brought IV bags and a stand and they carefully moved Agrippa to the white leather couch where they set up a mini hospital bed. When it was clear that there was nothing else to be done but wait, Rohan sat next to the couch to keep watch over the dog.

"Rohan, I will keep watch tonight. You and Kamara get some rest." Kat said. "We have a lot to do tomorrow."

Kat had to repeat the offer twice before he left reluctantly. Kamara was waiting for him.

"How did you do what you did earlier, cutting the giant in half?" He asked her before she could ask him how he felt about Agrippa. He was not ready to address those emotions.

"I'm not sure. It has to be the marks. It all just comes to me."

"The marks enhance physical abilities they don't teach you new sword techniques or how to apply them. Also, I don't think either me or Voss could slice our way through a giant, marks or no. What you did was impossible."

"I don't know. The need to survive took over, in the moment I know what to do and the marks grant the power to do it. There is something about this sword too. I feel like it is part of my arm."

Rohan looked thoughtful for a moment before he spoke again, "When I saw you get swallowed…"

"Are you crying Ro?" Kamara asked.

"No, of course not, some of this silver shit got into my eye." Rohan replied with mock gruffness. "Kam, I don't know what I would do without you," Rohan said kissing her forehead.

"Well you won't have to do without me if you behave yourself," she said. "Did you notice Kat is back," Kamara said changing the subject before they got too sentimental.

"That she is. Is it just me or is there a glow about her, she looks… rested."

"Well we did lay her to rest, and she did get to see her lover."

"He's been dead for hundreds of years I'm surprised he still has that effect on her."

"What are you saying Rohan? When I die you'll stop loving me? Hmm?" Kamara got in Rohan's face and punched him playfully in the arm. Kat appeared before Rohan could place his foot any further into his mouth.

"Rohan, Cassan is here."

At this hour, what could it possibly be? Rohan and Kamara followed Kat back into the living room where Agrippa lay attached to an IV bag, breathing slowly, but breathing.

Cassan was well-dressed as usual. The left sleeve of his smoke grey jacket was folded and held in place with a large gold pin. *Leave it to Cassan to turn an amputation into a fashion statement,* Rohan thought. Cassan's face was somber. Standing off to the corners of the room were two lean men who made no attempts to hide the fact that they were hired muscle.

"To what do we owe the honor Cassan?" Rohan asked.

Cassan spoke without preamble. "Uriah's family has been killed, everyone, down to the poodle. He flew back to London yesterday after making sure I was back on my feet. When he got to his flat it was surrounded by police. They were wheeling out the bodies."

"Jesus Christ." Was all Rohan could manage.

"What happened?" Kat asked, her eyes narrowing to slits, her brow furrowing.

"Official report, break-in, home invasion, murder, but of course I dug deeper. It was a werewolf, a European werewolf. It broke through the skylight, slaughtered them all. My only family."

"I'm so sorry, Cassan." Katharine said.

"How is Uriah doing?" Rohan asked.

"He is doing precisely as he should be, bloody fucking poorly. He is sedated, on suicide watch and has been unavailable for comment since the incident. I would go to him, but I suspect that the man responsible for sending the wolf is here in Trinidad. Lucien must be paid in full."

"Why do you think it was Lucien?" Kamara asked.

"Because the wolf wrote a note in blood, that pretty much congratulated us for escaping the house, but reminded us that good fortune has its price. Lucien needs to be found and killed."

"We couldn't agree with you more. We have some new clues in the search, I was told to seek out a man called Crayfish," Kat said.

When Cassan heard the name, he hawked as if to spit, then remembered that he was indoors. "That lying, cheating, liar."

"You've met him?" Rohan asked.

"Yep, he moves around a lot, sailing between the islands but I have heard that he is in Cumana now."

"That is what we were told," Kat replied.

And with that there was nothing more to be said. "We are very, very sorry for your loss." Rohan said somberly.

"Lucien must die painfully then we can mourn our losses. You folks appear to have had an exciting night. There's a dead giant man on the lawn. What are you planning on doing with it?"

"There are two more of them in the back. I was thinking a bulldozer, a backhoe, and a big hole in the woods," Rohan said.

"Oh three, nice. I can take them, I know a great taxidermist and I think they would look awesome in the King's bar doing the see-no-evil, hear-no-evil, speak-no-evil monkey bit."

"That's pretty damn disturbing, but if you want them they are yours. They've been mauled, shot, and hacked to shit though."

"Like I said, great taxidermist, I will be back in the morning to pick them up." With that Cassan headed toward the door. But before he left he added, "Rohan, he is enjoying the sport. He doesn't think we're lethal. We must show him differently."

After Cassan left, Kat sat on the couch next to Agrippa, opened a large ancient book, and began reading. Rohan did not know what the book was about and did not have the energy to ask. He followed Kamara upstairs where they got into the shower together and helped each other scrape off the remnants of the silver blood. Then they lay in the tub. Kamara began to kiss Rohan hungrily and Rohan responded with equal passion, but suddenly she went heavy on his chest. She had fallen asleep mid-kiss.

Rohan stood cradling her to his body. He dried her off as best as he could then lay her on the bed upon a towel. He tucked the sword in with her, placing her right hand on the splintered hilt. Then he got behind and spooned her. Rohan Le Clerc fell asleep almost instantaneously; tomorrow they would try to get truths from a liar.

Chapter 29

The Grey was breathtakingly beautiful. Virgin wilderness extended in all directions. There were forests, marshes, mountains and cliffs of such spectacular majesty and of such a grand scale that the vistas stretched comprehension and overwhelmed the eye.

Lisa however never found herself spellbound. The Grey's fauna was simply too lethal. The omnipresent potential of sudden death completely negated any appreciation of the unspoilt landscape.

Earlier they had had to outrun a pack of large beasts that looked like some unholy cross between overgrown hyenas and greyhounds. The creatures had spotted coats and were sleek with heavy shoulders and mouths filled with stout teeth. D'mara and Clarence could run forever. Lisa, on the other hand, quickly came to terms with the realization that she was not a gazelle. To escape the pack Clarence had slung her over his shoulder in a fireman's carry and had continued running at the same pace without even breaking stride, how embarrassing.

Later that same day they were crossing a sunlit, grassy clearing when Lisa suddenly found herself twenty feet off the ground and rapidly rising. Daring to glance upward she realized that she had been plucked away by some sort of colossal raptor, a bird so large that it carried her easily in the taloned grip of one claw.

From far below either D'mara or Clarence hurled a wooden stave that speared the thunderbird through its neck. The wounded monstrosity kept a death grip on her but fell from the sky in a dizzying, crippled spiral. A stand of giant pines broke her fall and broke the birds grip on her body. She crashed through the branches and Clarence caught her before she hit the ground. The pretty man was proving very useful. D'mara butchered the bird and they feasted on its flesh. It tasted a lot like turkey.

The episode earned her a dislocated shoulder and enough bumps and scrapes to last a lifetime. She surmised that any of the injuries she sustained was infinitely better than being torn apart by a giant bird or falling onto a rocky outcrop and shattering every bone and so she was thankful even as Clarence set her shoulder back in place with a painful pop.

Clarence and D'mara knew where they were heading. Clarence led, tracking the smell. Whatever spoor he was following was beyond her discernment and so she followed, trying hard not to look like a moving meal.

"It's not far now. We should get there by sundown," Clarence said. Lisa regarded the sun's position and concluded that sunset was an hour or so away. *It was shocking the skills you develop when living in the wilderness*, she thought.

"You guys never said where we were heading," Lisa said, breaking the self-imposed vow of silence she had adopted since Clarence had put her shoulder back into its socket.

"A safe place, well, at least safer than this nature walk we've been doing. We can wait there until the time is right to go back to the Absolute."

They walked on in single file, the two maboya keeping vigilant watch. The sun was sinking ever lower in the emerald sky, slowly painting it violet. Through the trees Lisa saw several plumes of smoke rising above the forest canopy. *Cooking fires?* she wondered.

"We're almost there now. Couple more miles."

"Is that a village? People live here?"

"The souls of people who have been killed by greyborn sometimes end up here. A long time ago my mother and I were helped by a village of Amerindians, they hid us from Lucien. When Lucien's man found us he slaughtered the villagers, they are here now and we are going to them."

"They will shelter you again? Doesn't seem like it worked out so well for them the last time."

Clarence shushed them, "Do you hear that, do you smell it?"

Lisa strained her ears but could hear nothing. "Is it the pack again?"

"Yes, it is a pack, but of a different sort, lagahoo. We cannot outrun them." Clarence said, even as he picked up Lisa and began sprinting towards the plumes of smoke. She had never felt so thoroughly useless. D'mara matched strides with Clarence as they plunged onward at an inhuman pace."

A hungry, blood chilling howl pierced the air. The first howl was answered by several others. Lisa glanced over Clarence's shoulder. Behind them, about a dozen lagahoo flowed around the trees like a torrent of sinew and teeth. They would be overtaken before they reached the village.

One of the red-eyed beasts broke off from the pack and flanked right. On its path and at its pace it would cut them off within five hundred meters. The fastest of the lagahoo had closed the gap to twenty feet. Clarence and D'mara were running so swiftly that they barely seemed to be touching the ground. Their legs moved with cartoon-like speed but the dog-men gained on them anyway.

In desperation Lisa began searching within herself for the metaphysical key to the power that she stole. She had told Rohan and the Guild that she had lost it, but in truth she had not. She was not entirely sure why she had withheld that information, it just seemed like she should wait until everyone had proven themselves to be trustworthy. The key gave access to a lake of raw power left after the Amerindian gods had died from a lack of veneration. She understood this by merely having possession of it. She took hold of the key. That part was easy. If she closed her eyes she could see it floating in her mind's eye like a golden hoop. Drawing power through the hoop was another matter. She reached out through the hoop but found nothing, no repository of magic. She pulled harder, straining toward some unseen psychic goal.

After what seemed like an eternity she saw a spark beyond the hoop. She stretched her metaphysical hands towards it willing the power to come, stretching even as the spark danced just beyond reach like an elusive firefly. Pulling power through the hoop was like drinking a thick milkshake through a small straw. She had to overcome some sort of psychic inertia that prevented the initial contact. Behind them the lead lagahoo leapt, fangs agape. Lisa squeezed her eyes shut and reached one more time.

Her mind's eye was assaulted by visions of blood and smoke. Shrieks and screams and the stench of burning flesh overwhelmed her metaphysical senses. Some distant voice was shouting for her to stop. She opened her eyes. All around her for a twenty-foot radius the forest had been leveled as if an asteroid had struck. Clarence lay in a heap just outside the blasted area. Most of his clothing had been burned off and the exposed parts of his body smoldered. Charred red flesh was visible along his chest and his arms had been burned black to the elbow. D'mara, was clutching her shoulders in an iron grip and shaking her violently while shouting for her to stop. The girl was not as badly burned as Clarence but she had lost all her hair, even her eyebrows. As for the lagahoo, there remained not a trace, save for a few errant tufts of fur floating in the breeze.

The world slowly came back to her, starting with the pain of the recently dislocated shoulder that D'mara was treating with such an utter lack of tenderness.

"You'll kill us all woman." Were the first words she truly heard, "Stop now, or the villagers will never let us in."

She released the psychic connection to the lake of power. The power retreated through the hoop and she released the hoop to float in her psyche once again.

Lisa looked towards where Clarence lay. "Oh God, Clarence, he's…"

"Resilient." The man finished as he rolled into a sitting position, hacking and coughing up ash and soot. "God, I hurt so bad right now," he groaned.

"You'll heal," D'mara said without mercy. "Let's get to the village before more come."

"Hey, we got the power," Clarence retorted, turkeying his neck in a parody of a saucy school girl. "Do you think more will dare to come?"

"Lucien's power is unpredictable and seductive. She should not call on it again." D'mara eyed Lisa, making it clear that her words were not a mere suggestion.

The village was visible about two hilltops away. Clarence rose to his feet. His arms were already beginning to look burnt-meat-red rather than charcoal black. He led the small party towards the village. After about twenty more minutes of walking, they broke through the forest again and into a large circular clearing in which not even a single blade of grass had been allowed to grow.

The village itself sat in the center of the clearing ringed by a twenty-foot tall boma of wickedly thorny branches. Every branch was as thick as a man's arm and the thorns, each about three inches in length, covered the branches densely. The branches were woven in such a manner that a wren could not safely fly between any space in the wall without becoming impaled.

There was a gap in the thorn-wall wide enough for two or perhaps three men to enter shoulder to shoulder. The gap was guarded by one large man and a woman who was just as tall as the man but more slender. Both leveled their long spears as the trio approached.

"Follow my lead. Do not look anyone in the eye, do not speak and if I say run just run." D'mara spoke in a breathy whisper. As soon as her feet hit the red, hard-packed dirt of the clearing she dropped to one knee, lowered her head and held her hands out parallel to the earth palms facing upward. Lisa and Clarence adopted the same posture.

"We would speak to the First," D'mara said loudly.

A moment passed. Lisa did not dare look up for fear that a spear would take her in the eye. She kept her gaze downcast as the first drops of a light drizzle hit the nape of her neck. Like a child seeking comfort in an old blanket, she looked inward for the key. There is was, twinkling just beyond metaphysical reach but she instinctively knew that she could take hold of it and draw power through it more easily a second time, perhaps she could draw enough to burn the village to cinders if they were attacked.

"The last time I gave you refuge a demon slaughtered our entire village. Now we are here in the Grey." The voice was speaking about two feet away from them.

Lisa strained her eyes upward as far as she dared, but all she could see were a set of toes, tattooed black.

"Stand and let me get a look at you three."

Lisa looked up slowly. A very short, very old man stood before them. The skin of his face was lined like the hide of an elephant, but when he smiled he displayed a mouthful of white teeth and his eyes twinkled with vitality. His hands and feet were tattooed in black but unlike the sentries who now flanked him, his face was not tattooed and his head was unshaven.

He inspected each of them in turn then stopped before Lisa and took both her hands in his leathery ones. He closed his eyes. For a moment she thought this was some manner of greeting, but then she could sense that he was looking within her the same way she had delved within herself for the power. When she felt him reach for the key she slammed a metaphysical shield between his search and the source then slapped him across the face.

The guards were shocked that she had struck the elder, but that shock only lasted a second before they leveled their spears again. The old man chuckled. "That is the prescribed response," he said. Then, more to himself than to any audience, he continued, "A lot of potential in this one."

The guards relaxed as the old man continued to speak. "Sicarii," he said addressing D'mara with the Amerindian name for an assassin. "The last time I saw you, I was alive in the Absolute. You and your mother came to us for shelter and we were all killed. Here you are again begging safe harbor. Why should I allow you into my village?"

"Because we can deliver the one responsible for sending you to the Grey. We can deliver him, bound and powerless for you to treat as you wish, but we can't do that if we die out there." D'mara inclined her head in the direction of the forest from which they had come.

"Sicarii...Sicarii," the old man said clucking his tongue and shaking his head. "You could not kill him before. What makes you think you can capture him now?"

"I was younger then, besides I never said I would deliver him, I said we, specifically her. She has something he needs and the strength to stop him." D'mara cocked her head toward Lisa.

"Me? No, nooo. Aren't we supposed to just wait here until they kill Lucien? Then I can go back to doing what I was doing before all this mess."

The old man smiled, his bright eyes almost vanishing into the wrinkled tissue of his weathered face. "Life can never be the same. Now that you have touched the power you are linked to it forever. That link will change you in ways you do not yet know. Even if Lucien dies, there will always be some other evil, power-hungry devil who will seek you out. You are the keeper of one of the keys now." He turned his attention back to D'mara. "Sicarii let me think about your offer. You and your companions may enjoy the hospitality of my hut tonight. Let us get indoors before the rain comes."

No sooner had the elder spoken than peals of thunder heralded a torrent the likes of which Lisa had never seen. She was almost instantly soaked. The sun set as they crossed the perimeter of the wall of thorns. Lisa glanced over her shoulder and saw the gap in the fence shrink as the living thorn-wall grew to leave a seamless palisade of sharp organic pikes.

***

Kat and Voss sat across from Crayfish under a cocoa tree in an abandoned cocoa grove in Anglaise Road, Cumana. Cassan had characterized him as a thief, a pirate, and sometimes a murderer, who had offended so many people he could not spend significant time in any one place but sailed up and down the Caribbean, hiding in the country where the memory of his crimes had gathered the most dust.

Kat did not think he looked like a notorious criminal. He was lean and sinewy like someone who had always had only just enough to eat. His hair was an unkempt afro of grey and black knots and spikes, the tips of which were bleached brown by the sun. His skin was sun-darkened and weathered by the salt. His eyes twinkled, and he spoke like a man who regretted nothing.

Crayfish had not been all that hard to find, considering he was a fugitive, but then again, the people of Cumana village were notoriously attuned to the goings and comings of strangers. They had found Crayfish asleep in the derelict cocoa house. Kat and Voss had introduced themselves, spent some time convincing him that they were not there to capture him, and now they sat outside.

"We were told that you may be able to help us find Lucien Sardis. But I am also interested in learning how you came to have the information we hope you will share with us." As she spoke Kat noticed Voss frowning.

"I've sailed around the Caribbean for years and years, you hear things." Crayfish replied as he blew a thick cloud of bluish smoke from the large blunt he was smoking, towards them. The smoke did not smell like any marijuana she had ever smelled, it was warm and rich, lacking the semi sharp occasionally unpleasant punch that one would expect. A twinge of discomfort stirred in her chest, but she forced herself to focus on Crayfish as he launched into his story.

"This is the story of Lucien Sardis as I heard it along the way. The tale is of fairly recent vintage, less than three or four decades old, from back when Lucien Sardis was a young man. He left Syria and came to Trinidad looking for a better life. He had no money, but he had willpower, he had discipline, he had a work ethic. One day he was walking through San Fernando looking for work when he saw an Indian girl, the most beautiful girl he had ever seen."

"I don't trust this guy an his 'nancy stories," Voss growled, his voice low as if struggling to reach Kat's ears through the smoke from Crayfish's blunt. Crayfish's voice was clear.

"One thing led to another and they fell in love and married. Lucien worked three jobs and his wife worked just as hard to set aside money to start a business. But within a year Lucien's wife fell suddenly and terribly ill.

"Lucien spent all of their savings on medicine and doctors but to no avail. The love of his life grew more and more ill. When the money ran out Lucien prayed to every god he knew, and one night when she was very low, barely breathing, Lucien whispered a prayer to the devil.

"Some time after, I'm not sure how long, there was a knock at the door. Lucien ignored it but the person knocked again. He went to the door and in the apartment hallway stood two men, one short and as ugly as sin, the other tall and handsome. They told him they would save his wife with one caveat. 'Your wife is pregnant. The child is a girl, she will be called Ghita and when she is twelve years old, I will come for her,' the tall man is reported to have said.

"Lucien rejected the man's offer but as the man turned to leave, Lucien's wife began coughing and hacking up blood, and even that she did weakly. As Lucien looked on, his wife stopped coughing, a rattling wheeze escaped her lips and her chest stopped rising and falling.

"Lucien turned and ran after the man who had just begun descending the steps of the building that led to the street with his ugly assistant in tow.

"'I accept the terms,' Lucien shouted. The tall man looked at him and nodded. When Lucien returned to the room his wife was sitting up in the cot. Her eyes were bright and she had no memory of her illness.

"Months went by, Lucien's daughter was born. He let his wife choose a name and she chose Ghita, after her grandmother, she said. Lucien tried to veto the choice but his wife was adamant, bursting into uncharacteristic tears when Lucien pressed the issue.

"The months became years. Lucien and his wife built a textile business that bloomed to prosperity beyond their wildest dreams. Their family also grew with the addition of two more children.

"Then Ghita's twelfth birthday came. Her mother dressed her in a red and gold Sari. They say that a niggling discomfort must have arisen in the back of Lucien's mind, but he suppressed it and as the day wore on, felt more and more at ease. He went to his office before the guests began to arrive and behind his desk sat the tall handsome man from so many years ago. He had not aged a single day.

"'Lucien Sardis, the years have treated you well,' the man said, smiling.

"Lucien closed the door. 'What are you doing here?' he asked.

"'What do you mean?' the visitor said. 'I am here for Ghita, you have had her for twelve years as we agreed and now she is to come with me. Honor your promise or suffer.'

"Lucien's hands shook. He believed the man's threat, but there was no way he could give Ghita to this stranger. She was made of all the best parts of him and his wife, sweet, beautiful, and wise beyond her years.

"When Lucien refused, the man sighed deeply and left closing the door behind him. Lucien knew his family was in grave danger. The man who had healed his wife had abilities beyond anything he understood. He picked up the desk phone to place a call to a travel agent, but, according to the people who told me this story, instead of a dial tone, there was a strange sibilant static. At first Lucien thought it was just white noise but then something about the sound made him listen closer. The harder he listened the more he could pick individual words out of the noise, dozens of whispering voices and the things they were saying were hellishly obscene. Lucien slammed the receiver into the cradle.

"He opened his desk drawer, retrieved the handgun he kept there, and sprinted for the door. Just as he was about to turn the knob, the door swung open, his wife and his three children were shepherded into the room by the man who had accompanied the tall stranger. The man's proximity to his family sickened Lucien. He leveled the gun at the man's chest. The man moved quickly and the next thing Lucien knew, he was staring at the ceiling through blurry eyes, the taste of blood in his mouth and a gap where his front teeth used to be. The gun lay on the carpet just out of reach.

"The man lined Lucien's family against the wall where Lucien could look at them. He then picked up the phone on the desk and brought it toward Lucien where he lay. About half-way to Lucien the telephone cord came up short and the little man simply yanked it out of the wall. He placed the receiver in Lucien's hand. The voices on the other end of the line did not seem to care that the phone had been ripped out of the socket. They were as incessant as ever. One voice, male, rose above the others. He was hungriest, neediest, and most likely the spirit that took physical form. A white liquid the consistency of melted latex erupted through the perforations in the receiver. Lucien's wife shrieked and the children buried their faces in their mother's bosom. The liquid continued to flow, coalescing into a creature with limbs jointed as if it was some unholy cross between a man and an insect.

"It sat astride Lucien's chest. The thing grabbed Lucien's arm and bit into it. The ugly little man looked on with glee, his cracked yellow teeth displayed in a rictus grin. Suddenly an explosion erupted in the room then another and another. Ghita had grabbed the fallen gun and had shot the ugly little man in the back while he was distracted.

"Lucien could clearly see his daughter through the hole in the ugly man's chest. The man roared in rage and surprise. He spun around and was on Ghita before she could shoot again. He hit her and she fell to the floor in a heap. Lucien struggled to rise but he had lost so much blood he was losing consciousness. The thing on his chest continued to savor the flesh of his arm.

"The ugly little man produced small black box from his pocket and set it on the floor. The box grew until it was a cube about waist-high. The man then picked up Ghita and leaped into the box, piercing through the side as if it was a curtain of viscous tar. The thing on Lucien's chest stood, grabbed a handful of his hair and dragged him into the box as well. That was the last that was seen of Lucien Sardis. Crick crack monkey break he back for a piece of pomerac."

The clouds of smoke Crayfish exhaled while he spoke hung about them like a mist. The man's voice sounded as if he was speaking directly between her ears. His every word blossomed in her mind to paint an image as vivid as if she had been there. She struggled to make sense of his story. "So Ghita died?"

"Yes she died," Crayfish replied.

"And Lucien was taken? Does the story say what happened to him?"

"No, he was taken into the box. That's all the story says. However, the original bargain was for a living girl, and that, I assume, is an important fact. Instead of a living girl, the obeah man got a dead girl and an almost dead Lucien Sardis. I would think that this had to affect his plans."

"Why did he want Ghita in the first place?"

"Me? I don't know but there are stories about special children whose births are very rare. These children can channel power from the Ether."

"So Lucien Sardis is Ghita's father and was kidnapped by the obeah man. If he has her father that explains why she works for him and it also explains why she is resisting him. Voss, we must go. I'm fairly certain I know who we are dealing with." Kat made to stand but found her legs unusable. She could not move them and they definitely would not support her weight. She looked over at Voss and he was unmoving, his eyes had rolled back and he sat in a trance-like state, a line of spittle wetting his chin.

"What have you done to him?"

"I'm tired of being a nomad Katharine, tired being chased and hunted. I was offered peace in return for delivering you," Crayfish said as he blew another cloud of smoke into her face.

"When this is over, I will come for you." Kat promised as a small ugly man stepped out of the shadows cast by the cocoa house. He stood projecting silent malice looking down at the paralyzed Kat. Kat returned his stare and smiled. "I know who your master is."

The short man, unimpressed walked over to Kat and kicked her violently across the jaw. Her head swam, she could not even lift an arm to defend herself, but she did not fall unconscious. The man ignored Voss. He slung Kat over his shoulder then produced a little black box. He set it on the ground allowed it to grow. It took six more vicious kicks before she finally blacked out.

***

It was several hours before Voss' body shook off the effects of the smoke. When he came to, he had a piercing headache and there was trace of neither Kat nor Crayfish, but there was blood in the leaf litter and one of those infernal boxes sat on the floor. Voss placed a call to Stone then leapt into the box.

***

Voss' words on the phone had been brief. He believed that someone had taken Kat through one of the boxes and he was going after her. Rohan relayed the message to Kamara. They had to hope that wherever the box led, that Voss could place a call when he arrived and let them know where to lead the cavalry. After hanging up the phone, Rohan and Kamara went to check on Agrippa. The dog was doing a lot better and was now able to sit up and eat. The pair stood observing the dog as it ate from a bowl when a low growl started deep in the beast's chest and eventually erupted into a snarl. Rohan tried to calm the animal but the dog would not be mollified.

Agrippa was focused at something beyond the window and had he been healthy enough to run Rohan had no doubt he would have charged out to meet whatever it was. Rohan and Kamara shared a look. Kamara picked up her sword from where it lay propped against Agrippa's couch. Rohan shouldered a semi-automatic that was always close at hand of late. They waited, staring out the window following Agrippa's gaze. Dusk had descended. Tarik was with Jonah and Imelda which left just Rohan and Kamara in Stone. When the target of Agrippa's rage finally appeared outside the window in the red glow of the fading sun, Rohan was filled

268

with disgust and sadness so deep that his weapon fell from his hands. A gut-wrenching pain tore through him.

He heard Kat whisper. "Rohan, be strong, they are not who you remember them to be."

Beyond the window, wearing the same clothes in which they had been buried, their pale faces smeared with grave dirt, stood Dorian and Isa. Dorian was armed with gleaming axes and Isa with a short sword. Their eyes were empty as they met Rohan's gaze through the reinforced glass of the window. They did not attempt to force their way in and there was no need. Rohan was honor bound to put the reanimated corpses to rest. He instinctively knew that guns would not work on them, only dismemberment and fire. From a cabinet in that same room he took his weapons of choice, two machetes one twice the length of the other. " Kamara, this is something I have to do alone, I owe it to them."

Kamara nodded.

Rohan unlocked the door and stepped outside.

Chapter 30

Sam felt like he had reached a truce with the voice in his head. They were friends, almost and strangely he felt a sort of kinship with it. Sam was teaching the voice about the modern world and in turn the voice told him stories about the time when it had been alive. Sam now knew that the voice in his head had been named Bitol when he was alive in the fifteenth century. He was surprised at how comfortable he had grown sharing his mental space.

Sam did odd jobs for money by day and slept in underground car parks and empty lots at night. Maybe at some point he would feel stable enough to go back home. Or maybe he never needed to go back home. He felt self-sufficient out here on the streets. He was not hungry, he could earn whatever money he needed and most importantly out here he was not placing his family in danger.

That day had been a good one. He had done some heavy lifting for a lunch cafeteria in Port-of-Spain and in return they had given him fifty dollars and as much food as would fill one of the Styrofoam lunch containers. That night he took shelter in one of the multistory car parks on Frederick Street. He had snuck past the lot guards and settled down in a secluded corner behind an SUV that he hoped would remain parked there until morning. He was eating his dinner and chatting with Bitol when he heard the hum of an engine followed by the hydraulic whine of brakes as a vehicle pulled to a stop close by.

Something about the voices of the people who had exited the vehicle caused Sam to pay closer attention. There was something familiar about the voices, not the actual voices themselves but the tones. Then a dreadful thought dawned on him. The voices conveyed the same ugliness as the maboya that had killed the people in the Tamarind Square. Sam was suddenly mortified. Bitol spoke to him.

It's them, Sam. You cannot run. They are sure to see you.

What am I supposed to do let them eat me?

They will not eat you, they want me.

Oh, and that makes it better. You and I are sort of inseparable. I'm going to run.

Please don't run.

I'm running. Sam got to his knees, preparing to make a dash for it.

Remember our deal, you promised to listen to me and I promised not to try to wrest control of your body.

Those words gave Sam pause. He had promised that in times of supernatural danger he would listen to Bitol's instructions.

Yes, I remember the deal.

Good, give me control, not partial control, I need all of it. It is the only way we will survive this.

What?! No way. I'm going to run.

Sam no...

Sam bolted out of his hiding place not even bothering to look for possible pursuers. Before he had gone twenty steps someone grabbed him from behind and clapped a hand over his mouth. The person lifted him from the ground and began taking him back to the car as if he weighed no more than a small bundle of linen. Sam struggled but the arm was like a steel cable around his body.

Let me take control Sam.

No! just tell me what to do.

There is no time to teach you all that needs to be done, just let me control.

Sam craned his eyes upward and glimpsed the faces of the car's other occupants. They seemed ordinary but liquefied evil might as well have been oozing from their pores for all the fear those ordinary faces inspired.

Will you ever let me back into the driver's seat? Sam asked through the silent mental connection he shared with Bitol.

You have my word...if we survive.

Sam wrestled with the decision. He had been struggling so long fighting to survive, fighting to maintain even a shred of human dignity on the streets of the Capital. It would be nice for another person to take over for a little while. The stress of surviving had frayed him, he needed a break.

So Sam relinquished control of his own body. As soon as he did he knew he had made the right decision.

Letting go was easier than he thought it would be. He felt his own consciousness recede like a falling tide. It was like his consciousness was a power cord plugged into the sockets of his muscles and he had unplugged all those sockets. He felt disembodied, as if the events were unfolding without his participation. As his consciousness receded, his body began to dangle loosely in his captor's arms. But then he sensed another sentience sweep past like the wake of displaced air left by a large truck speeding past on the freeway. He was the observer now. He watched as his hand rose to touch his kidnapper's arm. Where his hand made contact, the arm of the kidnapper turned to a finely powdered ash. Sam's body fell to the floor. Sam looked on as his body landed on hands and toes with catlike grace, rolled to the left, and was up and running in a dead sprint.

A little spell from my days of witchcraft.

Nice. Was all Sam could reply.

The Other, now in control of Sam's body, leapt through one of the open ventilation gaps in the parking garage's walls. It was a three storey drop to the pavement but Bitol aimed for the branches of one of the ornamental sidewalk trees and quickly clambered down to the pavement. Sam wondered at Bitol's ability to marshal his body into such an easily graceful economy of motion.

I lived in a place and time where we had to hunt to survive. The Other responded to Sam's silent musing.

That was the problem with a shared consciousness, no privacy, Sam thought.

Bitol chuckled.

They were now running down Frederick Street. The maboya were nowhere to be seen. Sam began to feel relief. Maybe this had just been a dinner hunt and they had moved on to easier prey. Then something slammed into them. The force lifted his body clear off the sidewalk. Sam was glad that in his current state of physical detachment he could not feel the impact of the landing. As it was, Sam's body under the control of the Other landed hard but nimbly.

They started to run again but this time they tripped on something. Bitol struggled to get Sam's body back on its feet but a shadow, like a small swarm comprised of billions of black midges, danced around his legs and prevented him from moving.

Do you have a spell for this? Sam asked through their mental channel.

No, no I don't, I was only an apprentice when I died.

Oh, now he claims limited capacity.

This really isn't the time to point fingers, Sam.

They were caught. A tall man sauntered out of a dim alley. The street-light seemed unable to illuminate his face.

"Hello Sam." The man spoke in a cultured, unaccented voice.

Neither Sam nor Bitol replied. The man stooped in front of them, his proximity was not at all welcome. His face remained indiscernible.

"I have been looking for you, Bitol. I need your help with a very important task."

Bitol allowed Sam to speak.

"My name is not Bitol."

The man's shoulders heaved in a genuine chuckle. "Hmm, so you haven't been communicating with a voice inside your head?"

"I have no idea what voices you are talking about sir."

The man's smile vanished. "Oh Sam, you know exactly what I'm talking about. Stop lying to me, Sam. I saw what you did to my assistant's arm. I know that he is controlling your body now, cleverly allowing you to speak so that he does not give himself away. It is in your best interest to cooperate."

The man never raised his voice in anger, in fact he maintained the same pleasant, radio announcer baritone the entire time. Sam however, was under no illusion that the man was anything but deadly serious.

There seemed to be no point in stalling any further and potentially angering the man. He obviously knew everything. Sam allowed Bitol to control the conversation.

"When I triggered the Recompense it was purely by mistake. I was actually trying to call spirits from the Ether, assistance from the gods to beat back the Spanish. I have no idea how to repeat the trick."

"Ah, but you must try. Besides, I have ways of resurrecting those memories, tapping into your skill."

"I do not have the power to do it. My gods all died when there was no one left to venerate them. The only power I have is that which I can channel using the strength of my vessels life force."

"Don't worry about power. There will soon be sufficient power to tear the veil ten times over. Your gods may have died, but some of that raw power remained for anyone who has a key."

"And if I refuse to assist you in this foolish plan?"

"Then you will suffer. Maybe I will send another four or five spirits to join you two in that body, nasty spirits. Maybe they will make you a passenger while they slit your father's throat and stab your mother in her belly." The man mimed a stabbing motion.

Sam shuddered and gagged at the thought of being forced to kill his parents. Bitol replied, "Well it does not seem like there is much of a choice."

"No, no there isn't. So what is your answer?"

"We'll come. But I ask that you allow Sam to go free, provide me another body to take possession of."

"Bitol, you are not merely a summoned spirit, Sam is you, your latest incarnation. You two are inseparable. Whatever harm comes to Sam because of a choice that you make will be self-harm."

Sam realized that the memories he had experienced in his fugue state, the actions he had taken, they were not merely the actions and memories of a usurper, they were his own memories from a past life. To some degree this made his situation easier to bear. Bitol was not a stranger.

A panel van pulled to a stop next to Sam. Inside were the three kidnappers from the garage. The shadows binding Sam's body dissipated but Bitol made no move to run again.

The tall man spoke to the driver. The two passengers got out. One of them was missing an arm. Bitol smiled up at the man.

"I hope you can wipe your backside with the one you have left," Bitol sniggered.

The man responded by punching Sam in the nose, breaking it. The tall man walked up behind the one-armed man and placed his hand on the crown of his head. The one-armed man's body burst into a cloud of fine ash which floated away. Within moments there was no trace that a man had even stood there, even his clothing was gone.

"See, I know a few of the old tricks too," the man said looking toward Sam, while Sam thought, *Hold your breath Bitol, do not breathe that man-dust in.*

Then the man spoke to the remaining two. "Sam is to be taken back, placed in a cell, and guarded. Not a hair on his head should be made to be out of place. If anything is amiss when I return, you will all be set to float in the breeze like Daniel."

The survivors nodded and hauled Sam into the back of the panel van. Once they had loaded him into the van, they pulled a black hood over Sam's head, and bound his hands and feet as the van pulled away from the curb.

Sam, be strong. It is going to be a long night, Bitol said.

Sam was surprised he was not more perturbed about his current circumstances. Perhaps after months of living on the edge of society in the company of his own old incarnation, he had developed a higher tolerance for the strange.

We'll be alright, Bitol, he replied.

Chapter 31

The morning after arriving at the village Clarence, D'mara and Lisa were allowed to wash in a nearby stream under the watchful gaze of the two sentries from the gate. Lisa felt strangely comfortable even in this strange place.

Clarence swam in a deep pool, naked as a newborn babe. After they were done and air dried they were each given skirts of blue feathers and the females were given a multitude of necklaces with which to cover their breasts. The clothes they had arrived in, tatters now more than garments, had been discarded.

Lisa wondered how D'mara felt about their nakedness. She was old enough to be Lisa's great-grandmother, but still bore the outward appearance of a child. The necklaces covered her pubescent chest. Did she harbor adult sensitivities about nudity? Then again, after more than a century of life, did anyone still harbor sensitivities about something as trivial as nudity?

After breakfast, the First announced he would meet with the guests one by one. The individual evaluations were to be held in a log cabin at the center of the village. Lisa was called first and Clarence and D'mara were left sitting cross-legged on the hard-packed dirt outside the hut guarded by the two sentries.

The interior of the log house was filled with incense smoke and the furthest corners were obscured in shadows. The First stooped close to a smoldering fire with a long-stemmed pipe clenched in his teeth.

"Please sit."

Lisa sat and the First spoke. "If you had to choose between a powerful enemy who threatened certain death, and an unproven ally who offered the dubious possibility of revenge. Which would you pick?"

The First's voice sounded defeated. Lisa responded, "That's a difficult question to answer. Certain death may be better than choosing the wrong side."

"But if that death is multiplied across your entire people. Could you choose the moral high ground then? Morality over the lives of dozens?"

"This seems like something you should discuss with your people. What decision would they make if asked? Perhaps they would prefer not to side with evil."

"As leader, the decision is mine."

Lisa did not like where this was going and as her eyes adjusted to the gloom she noticed that they were not alone in the hut. Someone sat in the shadowed corner to the back. Feeling very uncomfortable, she rose to leave, the First made no move to stop her and there was no need. Just as the thorn wall had grown closed after they entered the village, the entrance to the hut had vanished leaving an unbroken log wall all the way around.

"I cannot risk the villagers' lives by betting against one who is even stronger now than when he slaughtered us so long ago. He wants you in return for my people's safety and it is the only sensible choice I can accept."

Lisa reached for the key and its power. She would turn this village into a smoldering crater if she had to D'mara's admonitions or not. But the moment she reached inward, a massive wave of nausea overcame her and she fell to the floor, her knees as weak as a newly-born foal's. She reached again and this time the nausea was so powerful she retched.

"Stop trying. The smoke of the incense contains a narcotic to prevent you from burning us all to cinders."

Lisa barely managed a response. "Don't...please."

"I'm sorry, but I cannot risk my people again. That girl who brought you leaves only death and grief in her wake."

A short, ugly man emerged from the shadowy murk of a corner and came forward. He was carrying a woman over his shoulder."

Kat? "What have you done to her?" Lisa's anger cleared her head for a moment. The newcomer only sneered. As he approached, Lisa scooted backward until the cabin wall prevented further retreat.

"D'mara! Clarence!" she shouted in desperation. The little man kicked her in the stomach with the toe of his boot.

The force of the blow combined with the sickness brought on by the incense left her choking on her own bile. The man dumped Kat on the floor, then signaled the First over. The First held Lisa's shoulders against the log wall while the ugly little man forced her head back, crushed her mouth open, and tilted a vial of bitter liquid down her throat. He pinched her nose and covered her mouth so she could neither spit nor breathe until she swallowed.

Lisa had thought herself weakened by the smoke but whatever was in the vial completely sapped any strength she had left. Keeping her eyes open became a monumental task and every lungful of air required her to marshal all her strength. Through the drug induced fog she noticed that Kat's eyes were open but unblinking. How was it possible to drug Katharine?

Lisa dipped in and out of consciousness but she saw the little man fish one of the black boxes out of a satchel he carried and toss the box to the ground. When it grew to the appropriate size he grabbed Lisa and Kat by the ankles and stepped into the box dragging them after him. As they entered, Lisa went completely unconscious.

***

Outside Clarence and D'mara's keen ears picked up the sound of Lisa's cries through the thick, wooden, doorless walls. When they rose the two guards pressed the points of their spears against their chests forcing them back to the ground.

"What is this?" D'mara growled, prepared to fight.

There was a commotion; an intruder had entered the village. Clarence recognized the sullen looking man being pursued by three village sentries. The guard standing over Clarence hurled his spear at the newcomer. He ducked and it sailed past. Clarence and D'mara took advantage of the distraction and attacked their guards, dispatching them swiftly. Then the trio then fell upon the remaining guards. The scuffle was brief, violent, and one-sided.

"Where is she?"

"Lisa? She's inside there." Clarence pointed to the log house. "But she was screaming."

"Yes, Lisa and maybe Katharine. The man who took her came this way. I've been tracking him through this cursed wilderness."

"We saw no other man."

Voss immediately feared the worst. "We need to leave before more people come. Let's get Lisa."

"The hut has no entrance. We'll have to dig under the walls," D'mara said.

So they dug. The three of them made short work of the task even with their bare hands. The scene on the other side of the log wall told a grim story. The First lay dead, his throat crushed by a powerful blow. An empty vial lay on the dirt floor and one of the travel boxes beckoned them to some unknown destination.

"The man who took Kat was here. Kat as well," Voss declared sniffing the air.

"We must assume they went via the box," D'mara said.

"Then we go as well."

Clarence sighed. "I wish just one time, that something good would come of these boxes."

The three passed through the wall of the box which very well might be leading them to an awful death.

Chapter 32

A cooling slab of pale flesh
A writhing amalgam of pale worms
A brittle pile of pale bones
The inevitable end to even the most noble human endeavor
                    - An Immortal's Musings by an unidentified soucouyant

The dead men stood stock still, their blades gleaming in the light of the setting sun. An errant draft ruffled their matted locks. The reach of Lucien's necromancy disgusted Rohan but he was loathe to be the aggressor against his mentor and brother, even in these, most unnatural circumstances. Rohan's blades were naked in his hands, long blade in his right hand and shorter blade in his left. Rohan halted his approach about fifteen feet from the men.

"Isa, can you hear me? Dorian? Brother? Grandfather?"

"We hear you just fine. We came to welcome you and your bitch to the joys of servitude to Lucien." Only Isa's lips moved as he spoke. His eyes appeared to look through Rohan rather than at him. The only other movement was the fluttering of his grave-soiled garments in the nervous evening breeze.

Isa's words chilled Rohan to the marrow. In life, the elder of Stone would never speak in such crude terms.

"So you have come to kill us?"

"Yes, but you must suffer first." This came from Dorian's corpse. "Are you ready to die, Rohan? Perhaps Lucien will make us a gift of your woman if your suffering is sufficiently great."

These were not the men he knew. These were empty carapaces like those abandoned by molted cicada. They had to be slain. Rohan readied himself and the dead men charged.

The elder was the epitome of cerebral grace and speed while Dorian was brute force, rage and instinct. Rohan forced himself to relax and let his muscle memory take over. Too much thinking and he would die. Against multiple foes there was only time for reaction.

He stepped backward, moving to prevent them from circling around him or boxing him in, using his footwork to force them to attack in a queue instead of in unison.

Dorian rushed forward crowding Isa to the side. His axes lacked the range and versatility of the machete. The arc of Dorian's attack was swift but predictable. Rohan dodged and sliced through Dorian's throat leaving a thin bloodless slit. Keeping Dorian between his body and Isa's, he struck downward in an overhead strike with the second machete gripping the handle as low as possible maximizing its range and force. The blow cleaved Dorian through one shoulder down to the groin. The wound released the stench of decay as Rohan yanked his weapons free and leapt back to put some room between him and Isa.

The body of Dorian Le Clerc did not fall but neither did it move anymore, it just stood, stock still, dead eyes clouded with a bluish cataract, mouth hanging open in the shock of a second death.

"You killed your own Chapterman, Rohan? How shameful," Isa said in mock surprise. "Don't worry, I will make you repent."

Isa was not Dorian. The older man was anything but predictable. He circled Rohan, twirling the blade between his hands in a confusing blur.

"You couldn't save us in the forest, you let us die. You even killed poor Dorian a second time. You are a disgrace." Isa struck suddenly, Rohan parried but the darting blade still nicked him above his right eye.

"Not bad for an old dead man, yes?" Isa feinted as if he would strike the same place again but this time went low. Again Rohan parried but the blade managed to cut him across the thigh.

Rohan growled. If he let Isa set the terms of the fight, he would be slowly sliced to death. So, he did something Isa would not expect. He rushed him, like Dorian would have. The bullrush had the desired effect, but that was not the whole plan. Rohan stopped short and Isa took the bait. The older man overextended himself thrusting where Rohan should have been. Rohan stepped aside and, employing both blades, sliced off the dead man's sword arm and head. Like Dorian's body, Isa's did not fall but neither did it move anymore. It stood rooted to the spot, frozen in a grim parody of a headless Greek ruin.

Within the stump of Isa Le Clerc's neck, and from the gash in Dorian Le Clerc's torso Rohan spied movement. Fat grubs with black beady heads crawled out of the wounds and fell to the earth. Hundreds of them flowed out hitting the ground with a pitter-patter like rain on leaves. The grubs began growing, rapidly increasing in size. Rohan took a step back but could not tear his eyes away from the macabre spectacle. The first of the grubs grew to the size of an infant child. Then it began sprouting weirdly jointed arms and legs, assuming a shape that Rohan knew only too well. It was the twisted phenotype of feral maboya. The other grubs began a similar transformation.

Rohan turned and ran for the house.

"They will have to squeeze under the doors one by one right. We can hold them off." Kamara suggested as he slammed the door behind him and engaged the lock.

"No, in their completely degenerated form they can liquefy and flow beneath the doors in a torrent. We have a moment while they grow. Grab Agrippa and get through the service tunnel. Tarik can burn them like he did in Laventille."

The first of many demonic shrieks ripped through the air of dusk as a marauding horde of pale monstrosities descended on Stone.

Chapter 33

Lisa awoke from a black stupor disoriented, achy, hungry, and badly needing to go to the bathroom. The memories of the moments before she went unconscious slowly began to assemble themselves like a jigsaw puzzle pieced together by a toddler. *Where am I now?*

"Hello." A quiet voice jolted her fully awake. She sat up and looked around. A young man sat on a cot in the far corner of the clean, minimally furnished room. The man did not seem immediately threatening but Lisa was quickly learning that an unassuming appearance meant very little in her new reality. The man stood.

"Don't come any closer, or I'll…I'll." She realized that there was very little she could do to establish a convincing threat. There was a lamp on the bedside table, so she grabbed that and held it at the ready. The man sat back on the cot.

"Hold on, I won't hurt you. My name is Sam, we, umm, I was taken and we, I mean, well… I'm here against my will, like you."

Rather than being put at ease, the young man's difficulties selecting the appropriate pronoun made Lisa more uncomfortable. "If you were taken then you've got some sort of power, something he needs."

The man nodded and muttered something inaudible, as if he was having a conversation with someone she could not see. Lisa raised the lamp a little higher.

"Oh, I'm sorry, I know how strange this might seem, my situation is complicated. I don't have power, but I have knowledge."

"What sort of knowledge."

"I know how to open a permanent hole to the Grey."

"Shit, I have the key to the power needed to open that hole."

"And we are both here together. That is probably not good."

Their conversation was cut short when a girl in a red and gold sari materialized through the closed door. Lisa instinctively reached for the power of the key and was once again hit by a wave of nausea and a pounding headache. She tried to push through the pain, but the agony swelled and swelled ruining the focus needed to touch the source. When she finally gave up, she found herself doubled over. Sam and the newcomer were staring at her, with worried expressions.

The girl broke the silence first. "You will kill yourself if you continue doing that."

"I know you," Lisa managed, gritting her teeth as she waited for her stomach to stop roiling. "You're the girl who tried to grab me in that awful house."

"I'm Ghita, Lucien's gatekeeper. It is very rare that people come to that house willingly. I just wanted to talk to you."

"What are you? Some sort of ghost?"

"You could say that. But that is unimportant now. I must take you to Lucien. He is ready to begin."

"Why are you helping him? He's evil."

"I have no choice, he has power over me. You will soon see how hard it is to resist him. I tried to help by warning Katharine, but I see she too has been captured."

"Is she ok?"

"She's alive for now, but she is still unconscious."

"Can't you just let us go?"

"No, Lisa. Once he gives me a direct order, I am compelled to carry it out. I barely survived the punishment after Lucien found out I had spoken to Katharine."

"Lisa, it's up to us then. We can't help him, no matter the cost," Sam said.

"Come now, Lucien is getting impatient."

"And if we choose not to come?" Sam asked.

"Then I will be punished, and he will send someone far more unpleasant to drag you to him."

Lisa decided to comply at least for the moment. She and Sam followed the little girl out of the room and through hallways hung with finely detailed and exquisitely colorful paintings from Hindu mythology. It was a beautiful place. The garden threw off the scents of many flowers, most prominently frangipani. The sounds of bullfrogs and crickets blew in from the surrounding countryside. The place seemed surreal, Eden-like.

"Where are we?" Lisa asked.

Ghita did not respond immediately, as if she was gathering her thoughts to provide a satisfactory answer. "Time, I have learned, is a strange concept, even stranger when you compare the difference between how time is perceived amongst the three realities. Only in the Absolute do we have rigid temporal structures for the past, the present and the future. In the Grey, time is far less rigid and, in the Ether, past, present and future may all occur simultaneously, or not at all, or in any sequence.

"To support the rigid temporal structure of the Absolute, every moment of the so-called past is immediately erased as the future is written. The past thus only exists in the memories of those who have experienced or learned about it.

"Because of this, every moment in the Absolute is unique, non-recurring, and fleeting. Human beings, generally, cannot travel backward or forward in time because there is no backward or forward destination, there is only the here and now. But sometimes, when a moment in time has been particularly tragic or significant, that moment cannot be completely erased. The heightened emotions and memories of those who have experienced it prevent that moment from being removed from the web of time. That moment becomes frozen outside the passage of time forever.

"It may be easier for you to conceptualize the occurrence as similar the circumstances under which ghosts are created. Ghosts linger because of some tragedy or deeply unpleasant emotions which assume energy of their own and linger after death.

"However, whereas ghosts are emotional wrinkles in the fabric, places like this one are physical wrinkles. I guess you can call them inanimate structural ghosts. This of course is an oversimplification, no one fully understands how or why these places exist. As you can imagine there are countless wrinkles and those who know where and what to look for can find them and travel to them. Back to your original question, we are in one such wrinkle now. This is the house I grew up in, the home of the Sardis family, my family."

Lisa heard Sam mutter something like "I told you so," but she ignored him. He was obviously wrestling with some personal strangeness.

"So, Lucien Sardis, the man waiting for us, is your relative?" Lisa said, recalling what Clarence had told her of the details discussed at Stone the day she and D'mara fled to the Gray.

"No, my father died a very long time ago. Whatever now occupies my father's body is a stranger. I should have told Katherine this when she came to us in the sleep, but it is not an easy thing to speak about and we ran out of time." Ghita paused thoughtfully then continued. "Lucien, the stranger, has several of these locations. Sometimes it's an entire house like this one, sometimes one room in a building. He uses them as staging areas. They are the perfect prison. Only the dead can enter and leave freely. The living can only leave via certain pathways which are very hard to find. The paths are the seams where the wrinkle is attached to the temporal web. Otherwise you can only leave and enter through one of the boxes, like you did."

"The house in Laventille, where Cassan was kept, it's a wrinkle isn't it?"

"Not quite. Remember, your friends were able to get there physically and that the house takes up actual space in the visible world. Wrinkles do not take up physical space, they are outside of the three realities. The demonic ambiance that place possesses exists because Lucien trapped a multitude of angry, evil, malicious spirits in the very mortar and bricks of that house. Your friends are lucky to have escaped."

"So, I've heard."

They were still walking, passing from hallway to hallway each marked by an ornate arch. "He is in there, you must go in," Ghita said stopping in front a nondescript door.

Sam touched the door handle, about to open it when Ghita spoke.

"One more thing, nothing is as it seems. Remember that and you may survive what is about to happen."

"Is that all you can give us."

"I have already given you too much." With that the girl faded to translucency and then altogether leaving behind the scent of frangipani.

Sam took the lead and pushed the door open. Lisa swallowed her pride and took his hand as they entered together.

Chapter 34

Evil is a seed that must be planted in the filth of indecency, watered in the blood of the innocent, and denied all illumination so that it may best fester to maturity.

All workers of iniquity must become intimately familiar with the dark, both the dark without and the dark within. – Undated excerpt from one of the last surviving pages of Onyeka's five manuals on Necromancy

Voss could hear the heartbeats of Clarence and the girl. Clarence's was elevated, pounding like the a tassa drum. The girl's was as calm as if she was lounging on the sands of Pigeon Point. He could smell them, they were on either side of him, but he could see nothing. The darkness of the place to which they had arrived was complete.

The three of them remained stock still and silent, listening, sniffing the air, and willing their eyes to see. It was easy to imagine that they were standing on a tall round spire and a footstep to either side was all that stood between them a freefall to Hades.

Voss risked a hoarse whisper. "Do either of you know where we are?"

"I remember this place, the smell at least," Clarence said. "This is where Lucien creates maboya and other things. Fifty-seven would have been here longer, I think."

"D'mara," she corrected, but did not offer any further information.

"Do you know your way about?" Voss asked.

"Not really, but I know we can't stay here. There are bad things down here." Even at a whisper, Voss heard fear in Clarence's voice. "We're probably in a holding cell. There should be a hallway outside this door, and stairs leading up to the main house."

"Clarence is right. We can't stay here," D'mara whispered. "Every expert in obeah was once a novice. Lucien keeps some of his earlier failures in places like this. Unstable creatures."

Somewhere in the dungeon something wailed in a scream that sounded like many voices but started and stopped all at once as if made by a single tortured being.

"The monsters know we are here," D'mara whispered.

Voss had not been frightened in decades so the unfamiliar gnawing in his stomach annoyed him. Now however, was not the time to lose himself to panic. Panic would get them all devoured in this dark and hellish place. He steeled himself, "Kat has been here. Her smell is faint, but she has been here. We will leave this room and kill whatever comes after us or die in the attempt. There are monsters out there, but we too are monstrous."

With those words, Voss allowed his beast to come forth. His body morphed and grew, and he became covered in tawny fur. Fangs and claws replaced teeth and nails. In the end he stood in the form of a lion-man like Narisimha, the avatar of Vishnu. Now he had eyes that could pierce the darkness and he almost wished that he could not see.

They were in a large cell just as Clarence had said. But they were not alone. Twisted things clung to the walls and the ceiling like a living carpet, things that looked like they used to be people or animals, now they were both and neither. They adhered to the walls and ceiling like spiders, apparently in some sort of stasis or slumber. Every now and again one would twitch nervously as if dreaming.

Voss whispered, "Take my arms and tread very lightly. We are not alone in here."

He reached out to them in the dark, they must have sensed the change because neither seemed surprised by the thick fur now covering his arms. They moved towards the wooden door, inching their way painfully, afraid even to breathe. Voss thought it a miracle worthy of virgin sacrifice that the door was unlocked. When he opened it however, he realized that the fates were being cruel. The hallway was just as dark as the room, and the perverse results of Lucien's early forays into spellcraft and necromancy lined the hallway.

Twisted beings filled the corridor. They were all in some sort of dormant state, but Voss knew they were alive. Some looked almost human, but it was obvious that Lucien had been trying to create his own versions of the Grey's lycans through obeah. Here there was a large dog's head on a man's body, there a woman in petticoats with one dainty slippered foot matched with the cloven hoof and thick leg of an ox. Before them was a living maze of horror through which they must tread.

Voss hated suspense, if he had to choose between having a gun merely pointed at him and having a gun fired at him, he would always choose the latter. A pointed gun was deeply worrisome, a firing gun had declared its intent. Thus, picking his way through the static bodies of Lucien's creations was one of the most unpleasant things he had ever had to do.

The being ahead of him, a clumsy amalgamation between a woman and a massive snake, suddenly wailed but its eyes remained closed and once the wailing ceased it moved no further, Clarence almost leapt out of his skin. He led Clarence and D'mara gingerly through the garden of horrors to the staircase that Clarence had described as leading up and out of the hallway.

But the staircase was occupied, crowded with Lucien's failed creations. They lay and stood and stooped, twitching in their alien slumber, there was no way around them.

"We will have to move them." Voss whispered.

"They may wake up." Clarence replied.

Yes, they might, Voss thought but did not voice. Competing solutions blossomed in his mind; How hard would the monsters be to kill while they slept? Should they try to move the things gently or should they just bolt for the door, bulling their way forward, in the hope that they could escape through the door before being overwhelmed? As he approached the nearest monstrosity intent on testing the depth of its slumber, its four eyes blinked open, glowing green in the blackness. This set of a chain reaction in the hallway, one by one, green points of light came to life around them as the monsters woke up. The trio was quickly surrounded by a sea of eyes. With a roar Voss sprang at the first foe. They were going to die down here.

A shaft of light pierced through the murk as violently as light from heaven would penetrate the shadows of hell. Several of the monsters squealed in agony at the sudden unwanted intrusion. Voss had to squint.

Silhouetted in the doorway atop the stairwell was an Indian girl in a gold and red sari. She spoke down into the pit with authority.

"You will all go back to your cells. I'm the keeper."

The subterranean monstrosities rushed to comply streaming past Voss Clarence and D'mara as they returned to the deeper cells.

"You three, come with me. Your friends need you."

Clarence perked up. "Ghita, how nice to see you again."

D'mara simply inclined her head at the girl. The three stepped into the light with Ghita and she closed the door which, once closed became indistinguishable from the wall.

"The door does not open unless I want it open," Ghita said noticing Voss' examination. "But we must hurry. Follow me."

The trio did not argue. They followed her through the large airy house, as the eyes of Hindu deities monitored their progress from paintings on the walls and statuettes in alcoves.

Chapter 35

Kamara and Rohan ran through the underground tunnel that connected Stone to Jonah and Imelda's cottage. They had closed and locked the thick steel door on Stone's side of the tunnel, but they knew it would not hold back the tide of pale demons for long. Rohan cradled Agrippa to his chest as he ran. He imagined the dog wore an expression of minimal tolerance and offended pride at having to be carried. Kamara ran, sword in hand. They climbed the metal ladder which led to Jonah's cottage. The hatch at the cottage side of the tunnel was locked from the other side and Kamara pounded on the steel door with the butt of her sword to be let in. When the door opened, and they climbed out of the hatch they found themselves staring down the barrels of the old couple's guns.

"Is it really you?" Jonah asked, gun pointed steadily.

"No one told me the password, so I don't really know what to say," Rohan replied. He would have raised his arms, but he was still cradling the big dog.

"Come on now, climb out and close the hatch," Jonah said motioning them through.

"Where is Tarik?" Rohan asked.

"I'm right here."

"Can you burn the maboya, like you did in the safe-house?"

"No, there are too many and I'm lending my mother strength now."

"Lending her strength? Do you know where she is?"

"No, I do not, but wherever she is she needs all the power she can get. She has been drawing on me heavily. Blood related soucouyant can share power and the most powerful relative need not wait for the weaker ones to volunteer their power, they can simply tap it."

"Well we damn sure can't stay here. They will overrun this house very soon. We can take the old truck. Where we should go?" Jonah asked.

"One of the other Houses. We can return in force and kill these things."

"I don't think that's a good idea, Rohan. You asked them for help, and they have yet to send a single man. Stone is alone."

Rohan weighed Jonah's words. He took out his phone and called Richard. Richard answered on the first ring his voice was breathless over the roar of an engine. "Rohan, you're alive."

"Yes, you sound like you expected otherwise. Richard we are being overrun by maboya. We need every Orderman at Stone."

"I was already on my way to you to share some disturbing news. Lucien has corrupted all the other Houses as well as the Watchers. They were all promised a place of power when he opens the Grey. No one will aid Stone. In fact, the other elders knew that you would be attacked tonight. They knew of all the other attacks beforehand. Isa was the only elder who was not turned by Lucien. His stubbornness is why the Watchers sent you to the forest telling you that there was one Lagahoo to be slain but instead you found a pack waiting to kill you."

"How do you know all this?"

"Three of them came to convince me to join them. I had to kill them and run. I killed my own brothers, Rohan. The corruption is complete. Stone stands alone. Tonight, is supposed to be the night that Lucien changes the world by opening the Grey. I'll be at Stone in about five minutes."

"Don't bother coming here. We'll meet you on the road."

Rohan ended the call. The conversation had left more questions than answers. If Isa had been approached why hadn't he warned the rest of the men of Stone? Had Isa suspected that the other houses had been approached as well? The thought that the entire Order had been corrupted by a promise of power was terrifying to say the least.

"Let's get the truck and get out of here," Rohan said.

They left the cottage, constantly scanning for the pale, predatory pursuers as they made their way to where the Toyota 4x4 was parked. There were no maboya to be seen as they piled into the vehicle with Imelda at the wheel. Rohan did not want to risk attracting the beasts with the noise of the engine, so he pushed the van forward. He intended to coast silently to the front gate, which was possible because the driveway sloped downhill all the way to the exit. As the van picked up speed he jumped into the front seat. Kamara and Jonah acted as gunners at the rear windows. They hoped all the maboya were inside Stone or working their way through the tunnel.

That hope was short-lived. As they rounded a bend in the driveway dozens of pale maboya stood on the blacktop sniffing the air. Their eyeless gaze fell upon the truck as it rounded the curve. Imelda turned the ignition and pushed the accelerator pedal to the van's floor. Several of the creatures leapt vertically clear of the truck, but several more were mowed down. Kamara and Jonah opened fire as the van sped past. The pack of maboya gave chase, running with superhuman speed and agility, some on all fours, others upright, and still others bounding in disturbingly alien ways.

Imelda handled the truck like a professional getaway driver who had six kilos of cocaine in the boot and the Trinidad Police on her rear bumper. Rohan fired out the front passenger-side window as maboya rushed in from the darkness of the surrounding grounds like pale phantoms. Jonah and Kamara pumped a steady stream of lead out the rear windows. The gate was up ahead. They triggered a remote switch and the entry-way slowly opened. At this speed of approach, the gap would be just wide enough to admit the van, if Imelda held it steady.

The 4x4 barely fit past the gap between the slowly opening steel lip of the gate and the concrete gatepost and lost both side mirrors as it lurched onto the roadway. By some violation of the laws of physics, Imelda managed to hold the van on the road without letting up on the speed. Suddenly bright headlights from an oncoming vehicle blinded the van's occupants. Rohan had the briefest moment in which he noted that the oncoming vehicle was in their lane before the scream of the collision.

Untethered by a seatbelt, Rohan was ejected from the jeep face first through the windshield. The passenger-side airbags deployed but did not stay his passage through the membranous, gummy glass. He was momentarily airborne before the blacktop rose up and caught him. His body bounced along the pavement like a pebble skillfully skipped across the surface of a lake. When he came to rest fifty feet from the van he had to cling to consciousness by sheer force of will. As his vision dimmed, he heard a dog barking, someone shouting, someone shooting, then a warm red silence descended. Kamara.

Chapter 36

Lisa and Sam entered the large airy room hand in hand. There were three people inside. Lisa recognized the man who took her in the Grey, standing off to one side, malicious in his appearance. Kat was present as well, lying on a waist-high, flat-topped slab of stone in the center of the room. She appeared to be peacefully asleep.

The third person Lisa did not know, but she assumed this was the man they were here to meet. He was a tall good-looking man, with square, well-defined features, intelligent eyes, and a head of dark hair beginning to silver at the temples and at the nape of his neck.

When he spoke, it was with a pleasant voice that Lisa did not expect to hear from a maniacal obeah man.

"Welcome, I'm sorry that you got mixed up in all this."

"I'm sorry about that too," Lisa replied. "How is Kat?"

"She is alive for now. Sedated, of course. You have to agree that she would be a lot less compliant otherwise."

Sam appeared to have nothing to say so Lisa continued talking. "Why are we here? None of this makes sense."

"You know why you are here, Lisa. You have something I need. When you saw me on the astral plane, you did something in error that many people with centuries more experience could not do by design. You separated me from my power and took it for yourself. You even used it to heal Rohan, allowing him to defeat the master lagahoo. Quite impressive. Silent Sam over there." Lucien gestured with the wave of a hand. "Well, he's an entirely different matter. You see, I performed a ceremony to call forth a spirit with the knowledge to open the Grey. That spirit is Sam's previous incarnation. Both past and present Sam are sharing that one body. And your soucouyant friend her, Kat? I have hated her from the moment I first saw her. But that's another story."

"Why are you doing this, opening the Grey? I've been to the Grey, it is not safe."

"Ah, let me answer by asking you a question. What did you think about obeah before you got caught up in all this? What did you think about the lagahoo, the soucouyant, Duens, the moongazer, or any of a number of things with which you are now intimately familiar? Answer honestly."

"I thought they were all Anansi's stories, folktales."

"And what do you think now?"

Lisa thought she knew where this was going. "Obviously they are real, tragically and terrifyingly real, but you want to destroy the world to prove that the monsters exist?"

"Oh no, you misunderstand my goal. I do not want to prove anything. I intend to elevate the obeah man to his true place of power. When the Grey was first opened, the Absolute was only tainted with a trickle of the true horrors that place conceals. But even that trickle was enough to turn the night into a time of terror. People vanished without a trace, bodies turned up drained of blood, men and women were dragged from their hovels and their mansions and bitten and clawed and disemboweled. Things came through locked windows, through keyholes, under doors. Things waited under the silk cotton tree for the lone traveler. Children were called from their yards by the lure of the Duen-song. Bullets and blades could only do so much and when men realized this, they turned to the obeah men and the sorcerers. They turned to magik."

"So, you want to bring back the good old days."

"Not the good old days," Lucien shook his head with impatience. "I want the Absolute and the Grey to be one. When the relentless flora of the Grey starts to take root, man will be unable to cut the trees or burn the grasses fast enough. The lesser grey-beasts will kill the creatures man relies on for food. Man will fight. He will shoot at the leviathan and be swallowed. His aircraft will be brought down by the thunderbirds. Man's armies will march against hordes of lagahoo, but every man bitten will spring up and fight under the thrall of the master. The night sky will be filled with soucouyant, burning bright, thirsty. The Grey is vast, easily a thousand times the size of this realm. Man will be outnumbered, choked-out, and slain. Eventually, as the remnants of humanity cling to a bestial and hunted existence, they will venerate the magiks again, it will be a golden age of obeah. With his spellcraft, the obeah man will carve out toehold for man. We will beat back the darkness, stave off death. The trappings of modernity cannot survive the ruthlessness of the Grey. Man will have to adopt an existence that is more harmonious with his surroundings. You saw it yourself Lisa, you saw how the villagers in the Grey lived and were sustained by it. Obeah will never again be a ridiculous old wives' tale."

Lisa was horrified. "Millions will die before anyone even knew what was going on. I went to the Grey with two very powerful people who were fully aware of the peril and quite capable of defending themselves, yet we spent every moment a mere misstep away from death. How can you even guarantee your own safety when those things start coming through?"

"If I cannot protect myself then I'm unworthy to be part of obeah's renaissance."

It suddenly dawned on Lisa exactly whom she was dealing with, Lazarus, Lucien, whatever or whoever he called himself, was insane. "You are mad. And we cannot willingly help you in this."

The man smiled. "Do you think I would let the success of this plan hinge on your willingness to participate?"

When he said those words, Lisa glanced at Kat, thinking that Lucien meant to hurt the prone woman in order to wring compliance from them.

Lucien noticed the look. "Oh no, I have special plans for her so don't worry. For you, I have something else."

Lucien began mumbling something inaudible. Sam, who had held his tongue up until then, whispered to Lisa. "We have to go now. We should not have come."

But it was too late. Lucien pointed to them both and from his hand's sprung whips of a shadowy substance. The tendrils of shadow snapped toward them before they could move and pierced Lisa in the chest and Sam in the head. The wounds were bloodless and did not seem to even be physical at all, but the pain was so intense that Lisa could not even scream. She was paralyzed by the agony.

Then she felt the smoky tendrils delving her. She knew what they were searching for, the key. She marshaled her strength and threw up a shield made of pure willpower between the shadow and the key. The shadows slashed through the shield as if it were made of rags. She threw up another, gritting her teeth. Again, the shadow broke through. This continued until she had no more strength to give. She sank to her knees as the shadow accessed the source and Lucien was reunited with his power.

Sam also seemed to be locked in a metaphysical battle, one which he was losing. Tears streamed down his face. Lisa knew the moment he gave up because a small uneven hole appeared in the air behind Lucien, at first the hole was black, but then Lisa spied a landscape through the hole that she recognized only too well. Beyond the hole she saw the green lushness of the Grey. A breeze now came through the hole, bringing with it the crisp cool scent of the Grey and the howls of an approaching pack of lagahoo.

Chapter 37

Rohan came to slowly. His eyes felt gummy and he sensed a thousand tiny shards of glass and bits of pavement embedded in his face and hands. The marks had saved his life, but he would be a long time in healing.

"Kamara."

"She ran off through the woods, Ro, she and that dog with the boy and the old man."

It took Rohan a moment to realize that it was Richard speaking to him. He was sitting on a chair an arm's length away from Rohan.

"Richard? What? Where?"

"We are back in Stone."

"But the maboya…" A nasty feeling took root in Rohan's gut. He tried to raise his hand but realized he was bound to the bedposts with plastic cuffs.

"Richard, what is this?"

"You know, Lucien might be insane, but he has a point. The Order needs the greyborn."

Rohan's stomach sank. "Richard, what are you doing?"

Richard continued, "The entire Order is not corrupt, neither is the entire Guild. Just a few of us who can see reason and logic have sided with Lucien. Can't you see it, Rohan? The Order's strength has waned steadily over the centuries. We did our jobs too well. The greybeasts we haven't killed have been tamed. Shapeshifters are now so well-integrated with society they consider their power a disease, fucking lycanthropy they call it. They hide when the moon is full, Rohan. They stockpile meat from dead livestock in their fridges for when the hunger overcomes them. Soucouyant are rare and those that exist feed mostly on animals. Obeah is dying, Rohan. The magiks have been reduced to parlor tricks occasionally employed to enchant a lover or make a business competitor shit his pants in public. Humanity has been allowed to prance around and indulge in frivolous pursuits. When Lucien opens the Grey, it will be a revival. Power will again vest where it belongs, with the strong and the cunning."

"Richard, millions upon millions will die. The Grey is separated from the Absolute for good reason."

"Rohan, there are seven billion people in the world, seven billion. Many are lazy, insane, morally bankrupt, and self-centered. The greybeasts will cull humanity of these weaklings. The Grey's invasive and resilient plant life will destroy the trappings of civilization. The strongest will survive and the Order will be restored to its rightful place."

With sadness Rohan realized that he was talking to a converted man. This was not the Richard he had grown up with. "How long have you been on his side? How many of you are there?"

"Just a few Rohan, just a few. I met Lucien by accident or maybe it was by design. Someone at the Watchers house fed us a report about an obeah man who was doing human sacrifices. I went to the location by myself, the same house we raided in Laventille. I got inside easily enough but no one was there and when I tried to leave I could not. The house was alive, and it tortured me for a very long time. Then a man appeared offered me a bargain. He would show me the path out. He said it would not be easy and my escape would not be guaranteed, but if I survived, I had to meet him for lunch at a specific place. I escaped, and out of curiosity I met the man. He explained to me that the power of necromancy and obeah allowed him to create the house that trapped me. He told me that the Order was atrophying because of a lack of employment, that we had become an anachronism."

"But that's a good thing, Richard. It means people are safe."

"People don't need to be safe, Rohan. Humanity needs a predator. When the sun rises tomorrow, the world will be a different place, a more brutal place, the type of place in which the Order will flourish again."

Rohan was trying to slip his hands out of the cuffs, but they had been tied tightly. "Why have you kept me alive?"

"We will need every Orderman to face what's coming Rohan. It will be the ultimate test of our mettle."

Rohan felt helpless. He was not getting through to Richard with reason and he cast around for another avenue of attack. As he thought, he realized that Richard mentioned that Kat had run off with the men and the dogs. "Where is Imelda?"

"I left her for the maboya, or more accurately, your woman left her. Even Jonah ran off. See how cowardly humanity is." Richard laced his fingers together and smiled.

Rohan could not fault them for fleeing. Part of him was happy Kamara ran. Fleeing meant she had a chance. A small part of him, however, was disappointed that she had not stayed to fight beside him. Between having to cross swords with the re-animated corpses of Isa and Dorian and now Richard's betrayal, his faith in the people he knew was taking a beating. He shook his head. He could not allow himself to go down the treacherous path Lucian had led Richard. Isa and Dorian had been remarkable men, and Kamara? He had to trust she had made the best decision she could. He had to maintain his trust in humankind in order to fight the horrors that were surely coming.

Rohan had nothing else to say to Richard. As he was about to turn his head away from the man, a maboya entered the room. It was tall and its skin was milky white marbled with greenish blue veins. Richard turned and spoke to it. "I thought I told you all to stay out on the grounds. Clear the house immediately."

The creature did not budge. Richard stared at it and slowly rose to his feet. The he went for a gun at the small of his back and at the same moment the creature rushed forward. Richard managed to fire twice, one went through the creature's left eye socket the other through its chest. Neither had much of an effect. The creature bore down on Richard and tore into him with its mouth of needle-like teeth. Richard wrestled with the creature. The pair rolled beyond Rohan's line of sight. Soon the only sound was a wet chewing as the maboya fed on Richard's body. Rohan lay very still. Bound and weak, he could only hope that this one would leave when it was done with Richard and that no others came through the door.

Then another form filled the doorway. It was Kamara. Agrippa was at her heel and behind her Tarik and Jonah supported a battered Imelda.

Kamara spoke to the maboya. "Take the body and share it with the others. Then wait for me."

The grotesque creature left the room dragging Richard's remains by the ankle. Kamara rushed to Rohan's bedside and cut his bonds with the edge of her katana.

"Jesus you are badly hurt. Tarik, he needs healing."

Rohan was baffled. "How?" was all he could manage.

In reply she held up her hand. Showing him the Nights of Need. The tattoo had taken on the form of a maboya in chains.

"I can control them, because I need to."

Chapter 38

Lucien sucked the power he needed from Lisa and Sam through black umbilical cords of magik. They were so young, so fresh, and though they considered themselves adults they were still children really. He would remind them of the true power of obeah. They would come begging for him to use his knowledge in the fight against the things from the Grey.

By now Richard should have descended on Stone with a horde of maboya and killed everyone in that place. He smiled at the thought of Stone's violation. He had a special hatred for Stone, inhabited as it was by Kariega's descendants. The other houses would either stand or fall in the days to come, but Stone had to be blotted out of existence.

Isa had been stubborn and had passed his stubbornness to the younger members of his house. Rohan, his woman, Voss the betrayer, Katharine the soucouyant, they would always fight for humanity's cause. The only pity was that he had not been able to kill them all sooner. They were resilient, he would give them credit for that.

He glanced over at Katharine. In the centuries that had passed she had aged not one day. Lying, still as she was, you could almost forget the lethal danger she posed. She was the worst of the lot, a greyborn who sided with humanity. He would deal with her as soon as the doorway reached the critical state where it no longer needed his influence to continue opening. That state was close, and when the time arrived the doorway would continue to widen until the Absolute and the Grey were one.

Lisa and Sam, tethered to him by ropes of black magic, looked as if they were near to death. Sam knelt, staring ahead sightlessly and muttering incoherently. Lisa lay on her side, with her back to him, occasionally convulsing. They were not likely to survive the process. He held no specific malice towards them, beyond the fact that they were blind and weak. Their demise was simply collateral damage of his necessary and noble quest. Many more would die as obeah was returned to its rightful place.

When the wall of fire slammed into him, burning the clothes off his back, and causing his skin to crackle and bubble in places, Lucien Sardis had to admit he was taken by surprise. He turned around and there she stood, a nimbus of soucouyant fire burning blue about her body, white flames dancing in her eyes.

"Onyeka, you should have stayed dead," she said as she strode towards him. He tried to gather the power to do something, but the pain, as roasted flesh sloughed off his arms, made concentration difficult. He teetered as if about to fall but she caught him digging her nails into his shoulder. She leaned close to his ear

"That was a strong drug in Crayfish's smoke. You should have given me more." With that she tore out his throat with a clawed hand.

Lucien Sardis fell to his knees dying, finally free of Onyeka's controlling influence.

***

Kat looked at the doorway to the Grey expecting it to grow smaller and smaller and eventually vanish without Onyeka's magic. Instead of growing smaller the gateway still steadily grew larger. Lisa should have begun recovering but she still lay on her side, shivering as if in the grips of a fever. Something was wrong. Kat stood over Lucien's fallen body. Was he still alive? She tore open the cadaver's chest and destroyed its heart for good measure.

She was sure that Onyeka's spirit had not fled the flesh before the flesh had died. Yet the portal now spanned from floor to ceiling and was about three men wide. Kat prepared a spell to slow the opening while she figured out why the porthole had not failed the moment she had torn out the man's throat. A massive form appeared in front of the rift. It was a lagahoo all teeth and muscle. It paused momentarily at the threshold before stepping into the Absolute, howling to alert the rest of its pack.

"Go back or die here," Kat said, meeting the beast's amber eyes.

It grinned, drool falling from its lower jaw and replied telepathically, You are a traitor, soucouyant, you will be the first to be devoured.

The lagahoo rushed her and she killed it, tearing off its lower jaw and wrenching its neck around. It fell to the floor while another leapt through followed by three more. She was a hurricane of fire and brute force. But she could not maintain the defense indefinitely. More creatures came through the hole and she began to sustain injuries, a claw ripped through her face, fangs opened her thigh. She killed six, seven, twelve but she was being taxed now. They were fast, claws raked her back opening her from shoulder blade to waist. She fell to the floor on her hands and knees and they were all around her.

A hail of arrows flew through the porthole and feathered the lagahoo closest to her. Beyond the porthole she saw men and women with tattooed heads and loincloths of long blue feathers loosing arrow after arrow from beyond the hole. The press of lagahoo broke. Some rushed back into the Grey while others scattered about the room. Kat rose and killed the first two she could get her hands on. The men and women who had loosed the arrows were now forced into close combat with the lagahoo that had retreated through the gateway. The men wielded spears, the lagahoo tooth and claw. The ones that remained in the room closed on her again.

Four people entered the room, momentarily surprising everyone; it was a lion-man who Kat somehow knew was Voss, Clarence, Ghita who she had met in limbo and another girl she suspected was the one that had taken Lisa to the Grey. Clarence, Voss, and the girl spared no time attacking the lagahoo in the room. Ghita closed the door behind her to confine the conflict, at least temporarily.

"We must hold the gateway," Kat shouted over the snarls and shouts. "Whatever comes out must die in this room."

Something was definitely wrong; the hole was not closing and Lisa was not recovering.

"Ghita." Kat shouted over the howls of dying lagahoo as Clarence, Voss, and the girl tore into the pack savagely, killing some and forcing others to flee through the hole. For a moment the room was quiet. Ghita vanished and reappeared close to Kat.

"Yes?"

"When your father was taken by Lazarus, where did it happen?"

"In his office, in this very house, do you want to go there?"

"Yes, that might be a good place to start looking."

"Looking for what?" The girl held out a hand.

"Onyeka, the man who killed your father," Kat said as she took the small hand in hers. "Voss, you must hold the porthole. They will come again, more lagahoo and other things. The Grey knows that the hole is open. They will come."

Voss nodded solemnly.

Ghita squeezed Kat's hand and the next minute she was standing in a carpeted hallway in front of a tall door in dark wood. Though the door was closed she knew that beyond the door someone was doing something with obeah. The cool dark winds of magic forced the hair on the nape of her neck to stand on end. A thousand restless spirits whispered in her ears, some warning her to flee, others encouraging her to advance. Ghita was gone.

***

Hold the porthole, Kat had commanded before vanishing into thin air with Ghita. The soucouyant obviously had a good deal of misplaced confidence in them. They were battered, bruised, and thoroughly exhausted. Their superior flesh was healing with almost mortal sloth. They needed rest. Clarence and D'mara looked gaunt as their bodies self-cannibalized to heal the fresh wounds they sustained beating the lagahoo back through the hole. Voss knew he looked similarly frail.

The porthole was open to a clearing in a forest of gigantic trees. The sun kissed the horizon and in the gloom cast by the unfamiliar woods, dark silhouettes congregated, their eyes aglow. The people who had shot the arrows had either been killed or had retreated to the village. Voss, Clarence and D'mara were alone to face whatever was coming.

A cool breeze came through from the Grey, smelling and tasting like no breeze that had blown on earth for millennia. Something about the wind called to Voss. It tugged at the fibers of his being. He felt a desire to cross the threshold, not as an aggressor but as a brother. He wanted to join the shared consciousness of the greyborn.

"Do you feel that?" Clarence asked.

"Yes. The Grey is calling to us. We have more in common with them than with man."

More dark shapes appeared, eye shine glittering in the twilight murk. Suddenly Voss realized what was going on, they were being given a chance to join the greyborn or die defending the hole. A voice called to them, speaking directly into their minds asking; Why do you stand in their defense?

Voss pondered that question. Why should he stand with humanity, die for them in this bespelled room? So many human beings were liars and cheats and worse. But he remembered that long ago, a poor rice farmer and his wife had adopted him as their seventh child and raised him as one of their own. That spirit of kindness was worth defending.

When the trio made no move to cross the threshold the psychic voice spoke again. You have made your choice to die.

Creatures began stepping out of the gloomy forest and across the threshold, lagahoo, soucouyant, Duen, trolls, blue devils, faeries and other creatures that Voss did not even recognize. They were the strongest of the greyborn and thus the first able to cross. Soon the lesser greyborn would follow, the leviathan, the thunderbird, the coursing grey-dogs of the fields and forests. Mankind would be overwhelmed.

Voss roared at the oncoming masses, knowing that there was no way they could stem this tide. He felt a liquid rush around his ankles. Glancing down and back he saw that from beneath the door white liquid seeped into the room. The liquid coalesced into a pale twisted humanoid form that Voss knew only too well. Dozens of maboya rose all around them. Voss moved to strike the closest one, but a woman's voice shouted, "Stop! They are under my control."

Kamara entered the room accompanied by Ghita who held the door open. Maboya poured in. Voss, Clarence, and D'mara fell back and allowed the milk-white denizens to meet the onrushing tide of greyborn.

***

The big double door opened slowly moved by an unseen hand. A cold, dry wind escaped as if from a subterranean crypt that had been sealed for a century. Light from the hallway halted at the threshold in a sharp umbral line. The restless little spirits stirred. Their frail voices spoke at her ear, cold breaths whispered down the nape of her neck saying Come. Go. Stay. Flee...

Though Kat could not see into the room, she felt the power. In the unseen depths of the room someone was weaving a rotted tapestry of magik. It was not just the magic necessary to keep the porthole expanding but other things, black things, grave magic, necromancy, the sorcery of the Loa. It a dangerous cocktail of witchcraft and obeah much of which should never be done at all, let alone simultaneously.

Kat allowed the soucouyant fire to well up from within her. It sprang to life shrouding her in molten blue halo like a low gas flame. White flames like candle light burned in her eyes giving her a second sight that penetrated the ossified gloom.

The room was thick with familiar spirits. They crawled the walls, they hovered in the air, they thrashed violently between the ceiling and the floor. Now that she could see them she could also hear them. They wailed, they cried, they laughed, they cackled. The room was like some low outpost of hell, forgotten by gods and devils alike, a repository for all the worthless souls undeserving of paradise yet insufficiently significant to warrant proper punishment.

The ghosts were so numerous that their dark essence absorbed the light from the hallway, leaving the entrance to the room a solid wall of black to those without the third eye. To Kat the interior of the room was a restless maelstrom of tormented beings. Kat had never seen anything like it in her centuries of existence. She had never felt power like that which was being woven in the room. It was not just the quantity of power but its malevolence. This type of power could raise a thousand dead and make them dance.

It had been many decades since Kat had prayed. She had become so self-sufficient that she believed that any prayer she uttered would only clutter the celestial airwaves with its non-essential nature. But now prayer seemed appropriate and she felt no shame in it. She prayed to the ancestors, to the Christian god, to the good spirits of the Loa, to Krishna and Allah and a hundred other deities long forgotten. Then she drew power from her son. He would expect that. She drew power and stoked her fire. When she had drawn her fill, she stepped into the room cautious but without fear, bolstered by her hatred for Onyeka and her resolve to kill him.

The sensation of entering the room was like being lowered into a cold bath of congealed blood. The air was thick, cloying and foul. Phantoms brushed across her skin like smoke from a mosquito coil. It was hard to breathe, and the fog of ghosts limited her visibility to a few feet. She peered into the obscurity looking for Onyeka. Obeah swelled in the room. The walls creaked as the black magic tested their strength.

"You came for me again, Katharine, just like when I was a boy." The voice came from everywhere, the spirits spoke in Onyeka's voice. It was powerful display of the reach of his necromancy. The delivery was disjointed, sometimes spoken by one ghost, sometimes spoken by several.

"Yes, I came for you, but this time I'm not here to do you a kindness, Onyeka."

"Brave words from a tigress that has blundered into a trap." The word 'trap' echoed and faded.

"How did you escape death when your guild executed you?" Kat said, hoping to buy time before the attack that she knew would come.

"Wouldn't you like to know?"

"Yes, I would."

A multitude of unclean spirits chuckled.

"You are not as smart as you think you are, Kat. Maybe I was unaware you would burn through the drug or maybe I knew and predicted you would play along to find me. Maybe I wanted you right here right now. After all I also fooled you into thinking that I was in the body of Lucien Sardis as opposed to simply enslaving his soul and forcing him to do my bidding. Perhaps I'm not even in this room."

"You are here, Onyeka. This is too much power to control remotely."

"You want to know how I escaped dying. I took possession of one of my executioners. Just before my body died I jumped out of my unfortunate corpse and into his. It took everything I had to accomplish that and afterward I was weak for a long time. He did not even know I was there. I was a fly on the wall as he went around accepting sexual favors from women and men in exchange for silly potions. I was there when he manipulated some small village's council members and while he performed sham ceremonies for money. His behavior is part of the reason for obeah's decline. The practitioners lost respect for the craft. When I regained my strength I forced him out of his own body and bottled his soul. He's flying around here somewhere in the room, along with Lucien, Lazarus and a thousand other souls I have captured and enslaved."

"Crayfish told me it was a frog you possessed not a man," Kat sneered.

"There is little difference between the two, so the story was not entirely inaccurate."

"Do you even know what you are doing? There is too much power here. What do you hope to achieve?"

"Why did you come for me in Africa? You, a small light-skinned woman, fair enough to pass for white, out in the bush, searching for the son of an exiled witch-doctor? That was dangerous, even for one with your gifts. Was it out of a sense of duty to my father?"

"I have told you the story many times, Onyeka, it has not changed. I love your father fiercely, and I caused his death. So yes, once I found out he had a son, I felt honor-bound to find you, to bring you back, protect you and teach you his craft. To raise you as if you were my own son."

"My father. Kariega was possibly the most powerful sorcerer in Africa, yet he was sold into slavery. You Katharine are easily ten times stronger than any human being, you grow neither old nor ill, yet you abide by their laws, you even protect them. They should bow to our kind."

"Your father respected the law and was aware of his limits. Out of his exile and enslavement came the Order. I know that after Kariega was exiled your life was not ideal, I know the people of your village treated you with scorn, but you bring shame to your father."

"Scorn? Scorn would have been an improvement Katharine. My mother and I were treated like living latrines, spat upon and abused until she died from the shame. All the while Kariega was playing at being a slave master with his foreigner lover. My father made the choice that led to his death. In the new world only the fittest shall rule."

"You are a fool. The Grey will swallow the Absolute. Most human beings will die and the rest will be turned to greyborn. There will be nothing left to lord over. No one will remain to witness obeah's renaissance. Can you visualize Sally saleswoman or Andy the accountant facing down the spiny-bear or the thunderbird? By the time the human armies mobilize it will already be too late."

"Not if they come to me in time."

"They don't know who you are, Onyeka. Will presidents look you up in the yellow pages. Are you listed under 'lagahoo exterminators'? Besides, you will need an army of your own greyborn to defeat the onslaught."

"I have an army at my disposal."

Kat continued to move through the poltergeist soup. She wondered what he meant when he said he had an army. Then it began to dawn on her, an explanation of why he was using so much grave-magic.

"You're going to raise the dead to fight?"

"Now you are starting to think. And you're close but not completely correct. Packs of lagahoo would roll through animated dead like a buzz saw through canvas. Maboya would be great, they are strong and savage but difficult to control in large numbers. The problem of how to beat back the greyborn once the porthole was open troubled me for years. I discovered the solution purely by accident. When Gershon accidentally killed Ghita, her soul didn't cross to the Ether instead it retained some of its life and tried to go to the Grey. I caught her before she could do so. She was something different, not quite alive but not quite dead. Even ordinary humans can sometimes see her. She can touch things when she wishes. She is literally on the cusp of being alive. Moreover, I discovered that while in the Absolute she is stronger than any greyborn. When the greyborn begin to kill I intend to capture the souls as they try to cross to the Grey and press them to service by turning them onto the very creatures that so shortly slayed them."

"You cannot juggle all those balls simultaneously Onyeka. Too many moving parts. Some part of this plan will fail."

"If it fails it fails. We have been chatting too long, now you must join my friends Lucien and Lazarus."

A massive form broke through the fog of ghosts and charged toward her. It was a large hairy beast with a white scar along the side of its head. She recognized the yellow eyes. It was Onyeka's servant, Gershon. Apart from his eyes nothing else was recognizable as human. The beast was broad-chested and thickly-muscled with a snout filled with tusks and fangs. Kat hurled fire at it. She expected the fire to cling to it like liquid and burn until she willed it to stop, but the balls of fire hit the beast and extinguished almost immediately. She dodged the shape-sifter as it charged and leapt upon its back like a lioness upon a buffalo. The animal immediately sprang upward slamming her between its back and the ceiling. Kat held on. She bit into the beast's throat until she broke a major vessel. She hadn't needed to drink blood ever since Kariega had freed her. But blood drinking was still her birthright, and shapeshifter blood, filled with power, was like a peppered steak of some exotic meat.

The beast clawed at her trying to yank her off its back, but a soucouyant's bite severely and immediately weakens the victim. She drank and the beast's form shrank to that of a man, a small ugly man. When she had drunk the corpse dry, she yanked at its head violently snapping the man's neck then dropping him to the floor."

"Katharine. Gershon was the closest thing to a friend that I ever had."

Kat turned around and there was Onyeka like a younger more severe version of his father. He hovered above the ground, a specter.

"Well, like I always say, don't leave your best friends lying in the driveway if you don't want them to get run over when dad backs the car out." Kat wiped blood from her chin with the back of her hand and licked it off in one long stroke, she knew she was being cruel, she did not care. "I tried to be your friend, Onyeka. But you could not overcome your childish anger, you never even tried. So here we are centuries later and you are still the same petulant, arrogant child I smuggled out of Africa and tried to raise as my own."

"I have always liked your body, Katharine, so strong, so powerful. Maybe I will use it for a couple centuries while I torture your soul."

"Try me, boy. You are not half the man your father was and he gifted me all his power when he died."

Onyeka flew at her so fast she could not move out of the way in time. He speared into her body. He was inside her, under her skin like some massive wriggling invertebrate. He was trying to possess her, to force her out of her own body. He was strong. He had done this to a thousand other men and women, all of whom were now hovering in the room in a maelstrom of ectoplasm. She felt him expanding inside her, filling her, she was losing control.

She knew what needed to be done. There was no one to perform the proper ceremonies, no grave, no one to keep watch. But she was full of powerful blood and she was connected to her son so perhaps that connection would bring her back. She embraced Onyeka's spirit as tightly as possible, weaving her own essence around him. Then she fumbled in her pockets for the leviathan tooth blade Kariega had given her. Before Onyeka realized what was happening she plunged the knife into her own heart and slammed it home with the heel of her palm. Too late he realized what was happening. He tried to escape her flesh, but her essence clung to his and they were both dragged down into the soucouyant sleep, into Limbo.

***

The maboya were all but impossible to control, each one rebelled against her, attempting to break free of her influence. Kamara felt like a small child trying to wield a knight's broadsword to herd a bunch of rabid cats. The maboya could be pointed and unleashed but that was about it. She stood on the outskirts of the fight. Voss, Clarence, and D'mara formed a ring around her and she concentrated on maintaining some modicum of control over the pale monsters.

Lisa and a young man lay at her feet unconscious. Rohan sat near her, whispering encouragement even though he was himself in dire need of medical attention. The fight was brutal and it was impossible to tell who was winning, but the relatively narrow width of the opening to the Grey helped them staunch the tide of greyborn. Then the porthole winked out of existence with a blinding flash and a sound like a thunderclap. Many maboya were trapped in the Grey when the hole closed and many greybeasts were trapped on their side of hole. The sudden closing of the porthole broke Kamara's concentration and she lost control over the maboya.

312

"We have to go. I don't have them anymore," she said as one of the creatures turned on Voss. He snatched it by the throat and broke its spine, but it began healing even as he tossed it to the floor.

Most of the maboya were still engaged in the fight against the creatures from the Grey, but Kamara knew that sooner or later they would all become more interested in human flesh.

Voss and Clarence punched a hole through the press of bodies as they rushed towards the door. D'mara grabbed Lisa and the unconscious man by their shirt collars and dragged them after the vanguard. Kamara brought up the rear supporting a limping Rohan and holding her sword.

They made it through the double doors and shut it behind them.

"I cannot believe we escaped that," Clarence said doubled over, hands on his knees, breathing hard.

"Yes, let them kill each other in there. We can clear out the survivors when it's over," Voss said.

Ghita materialized from thin air wearing a concerned look. "All of you come with me. The soucouyant has done something very reckless."

"Are we going to do something with the door so that the maboya don't slip out?" Clarence asked.

"Clarence and D'mara, stay here and guard the door." Ghita said. "But do not risk your lives needlessly. Nothing can leave this place unless shown the way out."

Lisa bolted upright screaming as if in the grip of a night terror. Kamara knelt next to her holding her and trying to calm her. The other man remained unconscious.

Ghita led those who could follow, to another part of the house.

***

This time there was no peaceful awakening. Katharine's arrival in limbo was abrupt and painful. She bolted upright on the beach sands in the midst of a violent hurricane. The waters of the glassy sea churned and heaved in massive green swells capped with white. Desperately angry winds drove sand and sea blast to sting her naked skin and from above, rain fell in blinding sheets that forced a chorus from the leaves of the jungle canopy.

Onyeka was not with her. Had she really managed to entwine his spirit with her own as she fell into limbo? Had he broken free? Spirit travel was by no means an exact science, and she had transgressed every rule regarding the sleep. Could a strong spirit like Onyeka be dragged into limbo at all?

The last two times she entered the sleep Kariega had been there when she awoke. He had been in limbo so long that he knew all the rules. It would be prudent to wait for him but there was no time to waste. She had felt Onyeka's power and he was potentially strong enough to jettison himself from limbo and return to the Absolute.

She sniffed the air but scented only the rain and sea. She looked to the ground for signs of a man's passage. Finding none she fashioned a crude spear, closed her eyes and allowed her mind to wander. Then, following her intuition, she picked a direction and set off, loping along at a quick pace.

She left the sands and entered the jungle where the trees shielded her from the worst of the wind and rain. She stalked through the undergrowth, low and quick. Her bare feet made almost no sound. Katharine had always been an avid hunter, and Kariega had honed her skills.

She hunted, constantly searching for some sign of Onyeka's passage, wondering if he was also stalking her. A massive withered poui tree drew her attention, its bark had been blackened and its sparse leaves were covered in a mealy white blight. Kat had never seen dead vegetation in limbo but Kariega had once told her that the passage of an evil soul could cause things to die here.

A trail of dead and dying vegetation led from the tree. She followed its path, stalking from one patch of cover to the next silent as the wing beats of a jumbie bird. Then she saw him. He moved confidently, not bothering to slink or stalk. She was about fifty paces behind and from this range she could take him in the back with her spear. Killing him here would force his soul out of limbo and into the Ether, effectively ending him. She rose slowly and took aim, but at that moment he turned around and looked her directly in the eyes. He had known she was there.

"Clever dragging me here, Katharine," Onyeka said through a sneer. "Very clever."

Kat tensed to launch her make-shift spear at Onyeka. She would put his reflexes to the test, but before she could release the weapon, a wooden pike erupted through her chest as someone impaled her from behind. A second stake pierced her just below the first. She felt no pain which she thought was a bad sign. No pain meant she was not injured but dying.

Katharine fell to the leaf litter, her legs suddenly incapable of bearing her weight. With a massive effort she rolled over to look at her attacker. Fat, warm drops of canopy filtered rain spattered wetly onto her upturned face. Staring down at her were the yellowed eyes of Onyeka's man-servant Gershon. He grinned at her with his tobacco-colored teeth. Faithful even in death his soul had somehow followed his master into limbo.

The forest around her began to take on a translucent nature and beyond the translucence she saw what she imagined was the Ether. Mostly it was just a bright expanse from which voices called her name. She had been mortally wounded while in limbo and now she had to cross to be with the ancestors.

She tried to focus on staying where she was, on not crossing over, but it was growing harder.

Onyeka approached her and stooped low. "Die knowing that it was all for naught, I cannot be trapped here. I'm going to go right back and take control of that pretty little body of yours. I will walk right up to your son and rip his arms off."

Katharine tried to say something sharply sarcastic and cunningly insulting, but she could not come up with anything good. She managed to spit a wad of bloody phlegm into Onyeka's face, cursing him darkly as jagged fingers of pain finally began to radiate from the site of the wounds.

"Katharine, the ancestors would have problems embracing you with that dirty mouth." The words were from a familiar voice, a voice she loved. She turned her head to see a massive lion stepping out of the undergrowth and behind it, her beloved Kariega.

"You know that you should wait for me when you come here," he said with a disproving tone, ignoring the two other men.

"I could not," Katharine managed.

"Don't worry everything will be alright. Hang on, think about our son and focus on being here."

Katharine clung to a vision of Tarik like a drowning woman clinging to branch as a torrent swirled around her.

Kariega turned his attention to Onyeka and his lackey. "Son, step away from her."

"You have the gall to command me? You passed your power and knowledge of witchcraft to this woman and here she lies in defeat, yet you dare command me?"

Kariega leaned on his spear and spoke. "You shame me and you shame the ancestors."

"What? I have surpassed you in power, I have singlehandedly elevated obeah to its place of supremacy. I have mastered the arts of necromancy. I could drag your soul back to the Absolute and enslave you. How exactly is that shameful?"

"Shameful because you forgot that the first and most important lesson of obeah is to know the exact end result of every action."

"What are you talking about?"

Kariega sighed. "You still don't get it. You should not have killed Katharine here. If either of us had attempted to kill you and failed you could have simply reincarnated yourself, as you have done before. But now, that will be impossible."

"You are mad."

"And you have mortally wounded one of the two last surviving gets of Bazil's line, the other being Tarik, your half-brother. In case you did not know Bazil was the first and most powerful soucouyant to ever enter the absolute."

"What?" Genuine confusion blossomed on Onyeka's face.

"Katharine's mother was a direct get of Bazil herself, and one of the first soucouyant he made when he came to the Absolute, so in some way Bazil considers Katharine a grand-daughter. He will not be happy with how you have handled her. Also, the souls of all soucouyant return to Bazil in the end. He makes a point to collect them personally."

A thunderclap sounded and a shadowy figure descended to the earth like lightning. The shadow was about the size and shape of a man, but Katharine could feel power rolling off it.

The being then spoke in a language that Katharine had never heard before but for some reason she understood. "Onyeka, I have watched you from across the boundary as you played at being a god and eluded the Ether with your necromancy. I watched as you leapt from body to body, infesting impressionable minds with your nonsense and filth. Your plan to bore a hole in the barrier reveals a fundamental disrespect for the order established by Moko, and a false assumption that we of the Grey want your help to enter the Absolute. I was not forced back into the Grey, I chose to return, and I choose to remain."

In response Onyeka gestured to cast a spell and his servant rushed the shadowy figure, they both caught fire. For a full minute the only sounds that could be heard were the screams of Onyeka and his servant. Yet while the fire blazed upon their flesh their flesh remained whole. If Katharine had to guess she would bet that they could burn like this indefinitely. Just as suddenly as it began the fire went out. "That was but a taste of what I have in store for you, Onyeka. Now stay put until I am done talking," Bazil said.

"Katharine, you are mine now, all soucouyant return to Bazil in the end you know that," Bazil said.

Kariega cleared his throat. "I freed her from that fate Bazil. She is not yours."

"You insulted me by breaking the tie in the first place now you add injury by questioning me here, Kariega?"

"You know it's true otherwise, you would have taken her years ago."

"Yes, but she was all the way in the Absolute. Now she is here in the Sleep, in the Sleep for which she has not properly performed any of the rituals and has also managed to get herself staked…twice. What is to stop me from simply taking her?"

"Well for one, she will probably usurp your place in the Loa. You've monitored her entire life. You know she is nothing but trouble. In addition,

I have a bargain to make. Send her back to the Absolute and instead of going to the ancestors I will serve you for a hundred years."

"Kariega, no, no," Katharine managed. "Do not do this."

"What is a hundred years to one who has already been dead for several times that?"

"Tying yourself to Bazil makes you no better than I was before you freed me."

"Katharine, you must live. Rohan needs you. The girl you marked needs you. Lisa needs you and our son needs you." He turned to the shadowy form. "Do we have a deal? I know my way around limbo, I can enter and leave the Grey, and I know the magiks. You could use a messenger like me."

The dark form exuded pensiveness for a short while, but then spoke. "You are right, I have kept an eye on her and she is nothing but trouble. We have a deal, but Katharine, you are not allowed into the sleep again. The next time you come, it will be to join me." And with another thunderclap the being vanished taking Onyeka and his servant with him. The weird translucence dissipated. The surrounding forest solidified and Kariega and Katharine were enshrouded in the white noise of rainfall.

The stakes had vanished from Katharine's chest leaving two puckered scars.

"Now you have scars like mine," Kariega said touching the place on his chest where he had been speared through so long ago.

"What have you done Kariega?"

"Saved your life. You always tell me to cross over, now I'm going to do so."

"I told you to cross over to be with the ancestors, not to serve the Loa."

"It is only for a century." Kariega grinned. "You must go now, and I must go too."

Katharine realized that tears were falling from her eyes. "If I die before your service is done I will wait for you here, I don't care what Bazil thinks."

"Hush. Focus on living." With that Kariega handed her one of the black travel boxes. "We will meet again, Katharine. Our destinies are entwined forever."

She closed her eyes and Kariega kissed her forehead. When she opened them, he was gone.

She placed the box on the ground and allowed it to grow. Then she took a final look around and entered.

Chapter 39

They sat in a loose circle around Kat's body. No one knew what to do. When they found her she was laying on her back with some sort of bone knife protruding from her chest. She was breathing but very shallowly. They debated over whether they should remove the knife and finally they decided not to, but Voss cut his palm and allowed blood to run down the handle of the knife and into the wound, the rest of them did the same even Lisa and Sam who were slowly regaining their faculties following the closing of the gateway.

The room where Kat lay had been empty but for one other corpse, that of the ugly little man. All they could do was wait, they were afraid to move the soucouyant or do anything that might exacerbate her condition. They kept vigil for about an hour when Voss noticed tears running from the corner of Kat's eyes. Moments later she shot upright and began sobbing. The group first reacted with shock and then Lisa and Kamara hugged Kat and she clung to them. The women seemed to intuit that Kat had suffered some loss. Voss was just glad she was alive.

Kat, removed the knife and looked at the wound in her chest, crimson with the blood they had each donated. Though she only nodded and said nothing Voss sensed she felt gratitude. She looked tired and frayed, but then again they all looked similarly exhausted.

"Ghita, show us the way out," Kat said when she had collected her composure.

"What about the things in the basement and the greyborn that escaped into the room and the maboya." Lisa asked.

"This place is not easy to escape, and we are in no condition to enter more battles today. We will deal with those problems another time. For now we leave them to their own devices."

Voss agreed. Even if the creatures escaped, humanity and the Order had been dealing with the odd rampaging greyborn for years. The far more serious threat of a constant stream of greyborn was averted and the problem could wait. As Ghita led them out of the room Kat caught Voss' arm and whispered in his ear as the rest of the party moved on.

"I know what you are Voss." Voss halted as Kat continued speaking. "Onyeka called you the betrayer and I know what that means."

"What does it mean?" Voss replied.

"Coyness does not become you Voss. Onyeka called you the betrayer because you switched sides on him. You were supposed to kill Rohan when the opportunity presented itself. Weren't you?"

"Seeing as lying is useless with you…yes I was supposed to kill him. Planned to do it the first day I saw him, while he was on his run." Voss' voice was cool.

"Why didn't you?"

"I'm not sure. I was convinced that our position, Onyeka's position, was right. Right in that the Order had weakened humanity by protecting them from the greyborn. But then I wondered why Rohan should be cut down for it, didn't quite seem fair. If our position in the debate was so strong then it should be able to stand on its own merit. Regardless of who opposed it, the proof would be in the pudding and one more death or one less death would not turn the tide either way."

"What do you believe now?"

"I believe that we should leave this place."

"You know that is not what I meant Voss. If you change your mind again, if you make an attempt on the boy's life I will kill you. It would be hard for me, but you should take me very seriously when I tell you I will do it."

"I understand, and I believe you."

As Voss turned to leave Kat spoke again, "One more thing, Voss. You'll have to help me eliminate the rotten apples in the Watcher's Guild and in the houses."

"Why should they die when I live? We are all guilty of the same betrayal."

"That may be true but that burden is yours to bear. I'm sure you understand my position. The Order is Kariega's legacy, as much as Tarik is. We need to cleanse the houses and the Guild of anyone who sided with Onyeka."

"Yes, that is fair, but by now those people know what happened, they know I did not assassinate Rohan. If they have any sense they will be long gone."

"Perhaps they are gone or perhaps they are waiting to see if you return. In any case those who have fled must be brought to ground. Those who remain must also be executed."

"They are powerful people."

"As was Onyeka, and he is somewhere in the Ether or the Grey entertaining a master soucouyant."

There was an uncomfortable silence between the two each waiting to see if the other had something to add. It was Kat who broke the discomfort at the end. "Lisa fancies you."

"Does she?"

"Coyness does not become you. She will need a guard in the days to come, she still has Onyeka's key and that will attract evil men and women."

"I could think of more unpleasant situations."

"Good, it's settled. Let us be away from this place."

"I know something happened with Kariega while you were in the Sleep. I'm sorry for whatever loss you have had to bear."

"I appreciate that sentiment, Voss," was all the soucouyant could manage.

Chapter 40

The primal beats of soca music invoked a thousand lively spirits which congregated to saturate the cool, pre-dawn air. During the mystical hours before the sun climbed above the horizon and while the dew still clung to the weeds at the roadside, J'ouvert masqueraders inhaled these spirits and became possessed.

They were compelled to dance. They were enchanted. They were rendered incapable of resisting the music's call. Katharine was no different and like a cobra captivated by a snake charmer she swayed to the rhythms and rode them to euphoria. J'ouvert was very special to her, after all she had been there for the very first one and she understood the significance. Her preternatural ears could hear the sweet song chanted by the ghosts of emancipated slaves as they sang in remembrance.

It was not all for fun, the greyborn loved to mingle with the costumed masqueraders sometimes for nefarious purpose. Her senses were sharply attuned to their presence.

That they had survived was a miracle. But they had survived. Rohan was recovering and was almost back to being his sarcastic self. Voss was acting as Lisa's bodyguard while hunting down the faction of the Watcher's Guild and the Order that had sided with Onyeka. Clarence, D'mara and Ghita had moved into Stone. Kamara had returned to classes and was trying to salvage her grades. Kat suspected that she had leaned on the Nights of Need to help her stay awake for six consecutive days to prepare for exams.

Tarik was also now living at Stone and would likely become an apprentice Orderman. Apart from the tattoos, Agrippa displayed no indicators that he was Kimani's reincarnation, by all appearances he was a regular dog. After Lisa had moved back into her home, the dog had vanished from Stone and turned up in Belmont a few days later. Rohan conceded that Agrippa preferred Lisa's company over his. Uriah had abandoned his practice in London and was now staying with Cassan. Kat surmised that after the loss of his family, staying close to his brother was therapeutic for him.

Stone, formerly a fraternity, had become a far more diverse and eclectic place virtually overnight. Rohan would have to rise to the challenge of being the head of Stone, he was young. In fact he was the youngest Chapter head to ever assume the role and it would not be easy for him.

Kat's own path was also uncertain. She had devoted so much of her life to helping the Order survive this one specific challenge that she was at a loss about what she should do next.

As she danced amidst the early morning revelers, she spied a woman leading a man into an alley. Something about the woman drew her eye, the way she moved, the way the man seemed enthralled, the way the woman favored one leg. Her Victorian era costume was too authentic, her aura was too ancient. Kat separated herself from the crush of revelers and followed the pair.